The
Julius Katz
Collection

The Julius Katz Collection

Dave Zeltserman

ISBN: 1502706733
ISBN 13: 9781502706737

FOREWORD

"I go there to see my old friends and watch Archie be archly secretive about his sex life and hear Wolfe say, 'Pfui.'"
  —Donald Westlake on the Nero Wolfe novels

Julius clearly has similarities to Nero. They're both brilliant and eccentric detectives. They're both gourmets and rather lazy, preferring their own pursuits over working, and will only take a case when their dwindling bank funds require it. But there the similarities end. Julius is handsome, fit, a 5th degree black belt, prefers wine to beer, is a notorious womanizer (or at least he was before he met Lily Rosten), and prefers gambling over any other activity. While there's some Nero in his DNA, there's a lot more of Dave's con man character Pete Mitchel from his short story *Money Run* in him.

"My Archie is also similar to Nero's Archie. Like Archie Goodwin, my Archie has the heart and soul of a hardboiled PI. And he's fiercely loyal to his boss, and will pester him endlessly when he has to."
  —Dave Zeltserman

I'm not sure how the idea for Julius Katz and Archie came to Dave and I suppose to most readers it doesn't matter. But to me, as a writer, I want to know. I'm envious.

I've read most if not all the Wolfe novels, all the Bantam short story collections, and watched all the Nero Wolfe TV movies with Timothy Hutton and Maury Chaykin, and not once did I come up with a clever riff on the series.

I can't say I'm surprised by Dave's canny skills. His collection *21 Stories* is one of the most memorable book of tales of the past decade. His *A Long Time To Die* (his first published story!) remains for me a premiere piece of noir up there with Jim Thompson and David Goodis. Every story in the book is masterful.

Just as the duo Katz and Archie are masterful.

Julius, for those few of you who haven't had the pleasure, does his detective work out of Boston, Massachusetts. Archie, also for those of you who have not yet had the pleasure, works out of a two inch square computer chip. He's a piece of artificial intelligence. To my knowledge he is the only detective to ever be worn as a tie clip. In a lot of ways they're pretty much like Nero and Archie. Except for, you know, the tie clip thing.

What's especially cunning about the pair is that while Dave makes the debt to Rex Stout clear, both his characters (yes, I think of Archie as a dude) are very much unique. There is great good humor, there is the interplay of two crack detectives, and there is the pleasure of watching a carefully contrived crime being solved.

But there's one thing more, and it's what makes the series all Dave's own.

A digression if you will.

Dave's crime novels are among the darkest noirs of our time. And among the best. His crime thrillers, *Small Crimes* and *Pariah*, both made the Washington Post's best books of the year list in 2008 and 2009, respectively, and *Small Crimes* was selected by NPR as one of the 5 best crime and mystery novels of 2008. He has also won awards for his horror novels. The Caretaker of Lorne Field, was shortlisted by the American Library Association for best horror novel of 2010.

What I like especially about these stories (and the novel *Julius Katz and Archie*), that for all the fun, Dave manages to sneak in some of the darkness of his other work. Not enough so that it spoils the larkiness, but just enough to let the readers know that these are both contemporary and thematically realistic stories.

In 'Archie Solves the Case', when Julius's client is accused of murdering a rival chef over a stolen recipe, Julius takes on the case so he doesn't lose his favorite dish. But he has an ulterior motivation that's revealed at the end. Of course, it can be debated which of them—Julius or Archie—really solves the case! And in this era of the TV Chef wars Dave keeps up with the times—murder over a recipe?

In the Shamus and Derringer award-winning 'Julius Katz', Julius is hired by a woman whose mother has Alzheimer's. She's afraid that her brother, who has power of attorney over their mother, is more concerned with preserving her mother's money for a future inheritance than seeing that the woman is properly taken care of. When

Julius's client is murdered, he solves the murder so that he can fulfill his initial obligations and earn his fee. Few subjects are as sobering as Alzheimer's, but Dave bravely goes there.

In the Ellery Queens Reader's Choice Award winner, 'Archie's Been Framed', Julius finds himself inconvenienced when Archie becomes the prime and only suspect for the murder of a woman he'd been dating, and so Julius reluctantly jumps in to clear his assistance's name and the inconvenience that Archie's fugitive status is causing him. While this is reminiscent of a few Nero Wolfe storylines, Dave turns Archie's nature and the world of Sex In The City into a stunning whodunit.

In the novel, 'Julius Katz and Archie', when Julius's client is murdered he feels no need to find the murderer since as far as he's concerned this is a police matter and he has no further obligations to his dead client. It's only when an attempt is later made on Julius's life that nothing is going to keep him from being the one to send the murderer away. This novel in particular is a tribute to Dave's skill as a plotter. The twists and turns here are stunning. And Dave's tart take on contemporary society makes the trip even more fun.

In 'One Angry Julius and Eleven Befuddled Jurors', an increasingly peevish Julius is serving on a sequestered murder trial and is at risk of missing a once-in-a-lifetime gourmet dinner, and so Julius takes over. Given some of the verdicts we've had to put up with lately Dave's bemused portrait of jurors turns this into a witty look at a less than perfect justice system.

I've saved till last the one word of praise I've yet to use in describing Dave's talents: original.

Dave is one of those rare writers whose work is unlike anyone else's. Whatever genre he's working in, Dave is unto himself in every aspect of storytelling. Theme, plot, character, style; there is nobody else like Dave Zeltserman. Oh, you pick up on a stray literary influence once in a while. No biggie. Because ninety nine per cent of whatever he writes nobody else could. Fewer than a handful of writers can claim such singular authenticity. I devoutly wish I could.

And here, right here, is not only one of Dave's most original creations. But also one of his finest.

Ed Gorman
September 2014

JULIUS KATZ

Originally published in the Sept/Oct 2009 issue of Ellery Queen Mystery Magazine. Winner of the Shamus Award for best story given out by the Private Eye Writers of America (PWA) and the Derringer Award for Best Novelette given out by the Short Mystery Fiction Society.

WE WERE AT the dog track, Julius Katz and I. I had finished relaying to Julius the odds I'd calculated for the greyhounds running in the third race; odds that were calculated by building thousands of analytical models simulating each of the dogs' previous races, then, in a closed loop, continuously adjusting the models until they accurately predicted the outcome of each of these races. After that, I factored in the current track and weather conditions, and had as precise a prediction as was mathematically possible. Julius stood silently mulling over what I had given him.

"Bobby's Diva, Iza Champ, and Moondoggie," Julius murmured softly, repeating the names of the top three dogs I had projected to win.

"Eighty-two percent probability that that will be the order of the top three dogs," I said.

"That high, huh? Interesting, Archie."

Julius's eyes narrowed as he gazed off into the distance, his facial muscles hardening to the point where he could've almost been mistaken for a marble sculpture. From past experience, I knew he was running his own calculations, and what I would've given to understand and simulate the neuron network that ran through his brain. Julius Katz was forty-two, six feet tall, a hundred and eighty pounds, with an athletic build and barely an ounce of fat. He was a devoted epicurean who worked off the rich food he consumed each night by performing an hour of rigorous calisthenics each morning, followed up with an hour of intensive martial arts training. From the way women reacted to him, I would guess that he was attractive, not that their flirting bothered him at all. Julius's passions in life were beautiful women, gourmet food, even finer wine, and, of course, gambling—especially gambling. More often than not he tended to be successful when he gambled—especially at times when I was able to help. All of his hobbies required quite a bit of money and, during the times when he was stuck in a losing streak and his bank account approached anemic levels, Julius would begrudgingly take on a client. There were always clients lining up to hire him, since he was known as Boston's most brilliant and eccentric private investigator, solving some of the city's most notorious cases. The truth of the matter was, Julius hated to forego his true passions for the drudgery of work and only did so when absolutely necessary, and that would be after days of unrelenting nagging on my part. I knew about all this because I acted as Julius's accountant, personal secretary, unofficial biographer, and all-around assistant, although nobody but Julius knew that I existed, at least other than as a voice answering his phone and book-ing his appointments. Of course, I don't really exist, at least not in the sense of a typical sentient being. Or make that a biological sentient being.

My name isn't really "Archie". During my time with Julius I've grown to think of myself as Archie, the same as I've grown to imagine myself as a five-foot-tall, heavyset man with thinning hair, but in reality I'm not five feet tall, nor do I have the bulk that I imagine myself having, and I certainly don't have any hair, thinning or otherwise. I also don't have a name, only a serial identification number. Julius calls me Archie, and for whatever reason it seems right; besides, it's quicker to say than the eighty-four-digit serial identification number that has been burnt into me. You've probably already guessed that I'm not human, and certainly not anything organic. What I am is a two-inch rectangular-shaped piece of space-aged computer tech-nology that's twenty years more advanced than what's currently considered theoretically possible—at least aside from whatever lab created me. How Julius acquired me, I have no clue. Whenever I've tried asking him, he jokes around, telling me he won me in a poker game. It could be true—I wouldn't know since I have no memory of my time before Julius.

So that's what I am, a two-inch rectangular mechanism weighing approximately one point two ounces. What's packed inside my titanium shell includes visual and audio receptors as well as wireless communication components and a highly sophisticated neuron network that not only simulates intelligence, but learning and thinking that adapts in response to my experiences. Auditory and visual recognition are included in my packaging, which means I can both see and hear. As you've probably already guessed, I can also speak. When Julius and I are in public, I speak to him through a wireless receiver that he wears in his ear as if it were a hearing aid. When we're alone in his office, he usually plugs the unit into a speaker on his desk.

A man's voice announced over the loudspeaker that bettors had two minutes to place their final bets for the third race. That brought Julius back to life, a vague smile drifting over his lips. He placed a five-hundred-dollar wager, picking Sally's Pooch, Wonder Dog, and Pugsly Ugsly to win the Trifecta—none of the dogs that I had predicted. The odds displayed on the betting board were eighty to one. I quickly calculated the probabilities using the analytical models I had devised earlier and came up with a mathematically zero percent chance of his bet winning. I told him that and he chuckled.

"Playing a hunch, Archie."

"What you're doing is throwing away five hundred dollars," I argued. Julius was in the midst of a losing streak and his last bank statement was far from healthy. In a way, it was good because it meant he was going to have to seriously consider the three o'clock appointment that I had booked for him with a Miss Norma Brewer. As much as he hates it, working as a private investigator sharpens him and usually knocks him out of his dry gambling spells. I had my own ulterior motives for him taking a new case—it would give me a chance to adapt my deductive reasoning. One of these days I planned to solve a case before Julius did. You wouldn't think a piece of advanced computer technology would feel competitive, but as I've often argued with Julius, there's little difference between my simulated intelligence and what's considered sentient. So yes, I wanted to beat Julius, I wanted to prove to him that I could solve a case as well or better than he could. He knew this and always got a good laugh out of it, telling me he had doomed that possibility by naming me Archie.

Of course, I've long figured out that joke. Julius patterned my personality and speech on some of the most important private-eye novels of the twentieth century, including those of Dashiell Hammett, Raymond Chandler, Ross Macdonald, and Rex Stout. The name he gave me, Archie, was based on Archie Goodwin, Nero Wolfe's second banana who was always one step behind his boss. Yeah, I got the joke, but one of these days I was going to surprise Julius. It was just a matter of seeing enough cases to allow me to readjust my neuron network appropriately. One of these days he was going to have to start calling me Nero. But for the time being, I was Archie. The reason I had an image of myself being five-foot tall was also easy to explain. Julius wore me as a tie clip, which put me at roughly a five-foot distance from the ground when he stood. I never quite figured out where my self-image of thinning hair and heavyset build came from, but guessed they were physical characteristics I picked up from the Continental Op. Or maybe for some reason I identified with Costanza from *Seinfeld*—one of the few television programs Julius indulged in.

The dogs were being led around the track and into their starting boxes. Julius sauntered over to get a better view of the track, seemingly unconcerned about his zero-percent chance of winning his bet.

"You're throwing away five hundred dollars," I said again. "If your bank account was flush, this wouldn't be a problem, but you realize today you don't have enough to cover next month's expenses."

His eyes narrowed as he studied the dogs. "I'm well aware of my financial situation," he said.

"You haven't had any wine since last night, so I know you're not intoxicated," I said. "The only thing I can figure out is some form of dementia. I'll hack into John Hopkins' research database and see if there's any information that can help me better diagnose this—"

"Please, Archie," he said, a slight annoyance edging into his voice. "The race is about to begin."

The race began. The gates to the starting boxes opened and the dogs poured out of them. As they chased after the artificial rabbit, I watched in stunned silence. The three dogs Julius picked led the race from start to finish, placing in the precise order in which Julius had bet.

For a long moment—maybe for as long as thirty milliseconds—my neuron network froze. I realized afterwards that I had suffered from stunned amazement—a new emotional experience for me.

"T-That's not possible," I stammered, which another first for me. "The odds were mathematically zero that you would win."

"You realize you just stammered?"

"Yes, I know. How did you pick these dogs?"

He chuckled, very pleased with himself. "Archie, hunches sometimes defy explanation."

"I don't buy it," I said.

His right eyebrow cocked. "No?"

He had moved to the cashier's window to collect on his Trifecta bet. Forty thousand dollars before taxes, but even with what was left over after the state and federal authorities took their bites would leave his bank account flush enough to cover his next two month's expenses, which meant he was going to be blowing off his three o'clock appointment. I came up with an idea to keep that from happening, then focused on how he was able to win that bet.

"The odds shouldn't have been eighty to one, as was posted," I said. "They should've been far higher."

He exchanged his winning ticket for a check made out for the after-tax amount and placed it carefully into his wallet. He turned towards the track exit, and walked at a leisurely pace.

"Very good, Archie. I think you've figured it out. Why were the odds only eighty to one?"

I had already calculated the amount bet on the winning Trifecta ticket given the odds and the total amount bet on the race, but I wanted to know how many people made those bets so I hacked into the track's computer system. "Four other bets were made for a total of six thousand dollars on the same Trifecta combination."

"And why was that?"

I knew the answer from one of the Damon Runyan stories which was used to build my experience base. "The odds of anyone else picking that Trifecta bet given those dogs' past history is one out of six point eight million. That four other people would be willing to bet that much money given an expected winnings of near zero dollars could only be explained by the race being fixed."

"Bingo."

"I don't get it," I said. "If you knew which dogs were going to win, why didn't you bet more money?"

"Two reasons. First, fixing a dog race is not an exact science. Things can go wrong. Second, if I bet more, I would've upset the odds enough to where I could've tipped off the track authorities, and even worse, upset the good folks who set the fix up and were nice enough to invite me to participate."

I digested that. With a twinkle showing in Julius's right eye, he informed me that he was going to be spending the rest of the afternoon at the Belvedere Club sampling some of their fine cognacs, and that I should call his three o'clock appointment and cancel. A blond woman in her early thirties smiled at Julius, and he noticed and veered off in her direction, a grin growing over his own lips. Her physical characteristics closely matched those of the actress Heather Locklear, which would've told me she was very attractive even without Julius's reaction to her. This was not good. If Julius blew off his three-o'clock, it could be a month or longer before I'd be able to talk him into taking another job, which would be a month or longer before I'd have a chance to adjust my deductive reasoning model—and what was becoming more important to me, a chance to trump Julius at solving a case.

"You might like to know I've located a case of Romanée-Conti at the Wine Cellar in Newburyport. I need to place the order today to reserve it," I said.

That stopped Julius in his tracks.

"1997?"

"Yes sir. What should I do?"

He was stuck. He'd been looking for a case of that particular vintage for months, but the cost would mean he'd have to take a job to both pay for the wine and the upcoming monthly expenses, which meant he wouldn't have time to get to know the Heather Locklear look-alike. Julius made up his mind. With a sigh he told me that the Belvedere Club would have to wait, that we had a three o'clock appointment to keep. He showed the blond woman a sad, wistful smile, his look all but saying, "I'm sorry, but we're talking about a '97 Romanée-Conti after all", and with determination in his step headed towards the exit again. Once outside, he hailed a taxi and gave the driver the address to his Beacon Hill townhouse. I had known about the Romanée-Conti for several days, but had held on to the information so I could use it at the appropriate time, one of the lessons I had learned from the Rex Stout books. Internally, I was smiling. At least that was the image I had of myself. A five-foot tall, balding, chunky man, who couldn't keep from smiling if his life depended on it.

Julius's three o'clock appointment, Norma Brewer, arrived on time and was accompanied by her sister, Helen

Arden. According to Norma Brewer's records, which I had obtained from the Department of Motor Vehicles' database, she was fifty-three, but sitting across from Julius, she looked older than that, bone-thin and very tired. Her sister Helen was much plumper in the face and very thick around the middle. She showed a perpetually startled look, almost as if she were expecting someone to sneak up on her and yell *boo*. According to her DMV records, she was forty-eight, but like her sister, looked older, with an unhealthy pallor to her skin and her hair completely gray.

Before they arrived I filled Julius in on the little I knew—information I gathered about Norma Brewer from various databases, including her bank records, which were healthy, and that this concerned a family matter which Norma Brewer didn't feel comfortable discussing with me over the phone. Julius didn't like it at all, and I could tell he spent his time ruminating on whether there was a way to cancel the appointment and still afford the case of Romanée-Conti. If there was, he was unable to come up with it. He sat deep in his thoughts until the doorbell rang, then, forcing an air of politeness, he welcomed the two Brewer sisters into his townhouse and escorted them to his office.

Now they sat across from him. Almost immediately Norma Brewer noticed the receiver in his ear and showed a condescending smile, thinking it was a hearing aide. That was not an uncommon reaction, but still, it caused the skin to tighten around Julius's mouth. I reminded him then how long it had taken to locate the Romanée-Conti, knowing that he was within seconds of telling Norma Brewer that something had come up and that he would have to cancel their appointment. Her sister, Helen, seemed oblivious, never noticing the device in Julius's ear or his flash of petulance.

"Mr. Katz, I am very grateful to you for seeing us," Norma started, her voice louder than it should've been, obviously thinking that Julius was hard of hearing. Not only was her voice loud, but it had a shrill quality to it that made Julius wince. "I understand that you are quite the recluse, and very particular with the cases you choose."

Julius signaled with his hand for her to lower her voice. "Miss Brewer, please, I am not deaf. There is no reason to shout." He smiled thinly. "The device in my ear is not a hearing aid, but an advanced new piece of technology that acts as a lie detector."

I made note of that ploy. It was complete rubbish, of course, but it did seem to have an effect on Norma Brewer, causing her eyes to open wider. Her sister Helen remained oblivious.

"Oh," she remarked.

"Precisely," Julius said, nodding. He made no effort to correct her about his being reclusive, or about how choosy he was concerning the cases he took. He was often about town—either gambling, womanizing, or dining at Boston's more upscale restaurants. About his being choosy with the cases he accepted, quite the opposite. He accepted them based purely on necessity and, as I mentioned before, only when his bank account reached levels which threatened his more treasured pursuits.

Norma Brewer composed herself, pushing herself up straighter in her chair. "It's fascinating what they can come up with these days, isn't it, Helen?" she said. Her sister grunted noncommittally. Norma Brewer turned back to Julius. "Your secretary, whom I spoke with over the phone, Archie, I believe was his name, is he going to be joining us?"

"I'm afraid Archie is otherwise occupied. Now, this matter you would like to engage me in?"

Norma Brewer gave her sister a quick look before addressing Julius. "Mr. Katz, this is a sensitive matter," she said, her voice barely above a whisper. "Do we have your confidentiality?"

"I'm not an attorney," Julius said gruffly. His fingers on his right hand drummed along the top of his antique walnut desk. I knew he was weighing how much he wanted that case of Burgundy and whether it was worth putting up with these two to get it. He made his decision and his drumming slowed. "You do, however, have my discretion," he promised her, his tone resigned. "Please explain what you'd like to hire me for."

Norma Brewer again caught her sister's eye before nodding slowly towards Julius, her face seeming to age a decade within seconds. For a moment her skin looked like parchment.

"I have a very difficult family situation. Both my sister and I do. Our mother, Emma, is eighty-three years old and is not doing well." Her voice caught in her throat. She looked away for a moment, then sharply met Julius's eyes. "She has the onset of Alzheimer's."

"I'm sorry to hear that, Miss Brewer."

Norma Brewer's expression tightened. She raised a hand as if to indicate that sympathy from Julius was not needed. Her sister Helen remained slumped in her seat, still without expression. It dawned on me that what I had mistaken for dullness in the sister was really exhaustion.

"That's not even the half of it," Norma Brewer said. "Our father died six years ago, before the Alzheimer's showed. He had cancer and knew he was dying, and was able to make preparations, arranging for my younger brother, Lawrence, to have power of attorney for my mother. My father left my mother well provided for, including over two hundred thousand dollars in treasuries, an annuity that covers her current living expenses, and the family house in Brookline, debt free."

I hacked into the town of Brookline's real-estate tax database and verified that an Emma Brewer did own a house in South Brookline that was originally bought for forty-five thousand dollars in 1953, and was now valued at close to a million dollars. I relayed the information to Julius, who kept his poker face intact and showed no hint that he had heard me.

"Please continue," he told her.

"I've been spending as much time as I can taking care of my mother," Norma Brewer said. "Fortunately, I was able to sell a business a few years ago. I didn't make enough to allow me to live lavishly, but enough so I can now cut down on my hours and spend my time taking care of my mother. But, as I've been discovering, I just don't have enough time or strength to do it properly. Helen has tried to help also, but she has three teenage children to take care of as a single mother, and I know it's too much for her—"

"It really isn't," Helen started to say, but a stern look from Norma stopped her. Norma reached over and patted her sister's hands. "It's alright, dear," she said. "You have things hard enough as it is." Helen stared glumly at her soft, doughy hands folded in her lap. Norma turned back to Julius "It's too hard for me also, Mr. Katz. My mother needs to be moved to an assisted-living facility where she can be properly taken care of."

"And your brother Lawrence is against that idea?"

Norma Brewer bit her lip and nodded. Helen looked as if she were going to cry.

"Let me guess, he has since made himself legal guardian of your mother?"

Again, Norma Brewer nodded.

"Do you think he's been stealing from your mother's assets?"

Norma Brewer's expression turned grimmer. "I don't know." She shook her head. "No, I don't think so. I think it's more that he's counting on her money, and he's afraid that if we put her in assisted living there would be nothing left by the time she dies. I'm pretty sure that is what's behind it. Anyway, he refuses to budge, and keeps insisting that Mother is better off in her own home. Of course, he doesn't do anything to help take care of her. If I wasn't going over there daily, she'd starve to death! Or worse, die of dehydration. There would be no food in the house, and there are days she forgets to even drink as much as a glass of water. She needs professional care, Mr. Katz, and I've found a good home for her in Vermont. It's expensive, and a bit far for visiting, but it's beautiful there, and they provide exceptional care for people like my mother. Healthcare professionals that I've consulted have told me that it would be the best place for her."

Julius absentmindedly rubbed his right index finger along his upper lip. His eyes narrowed as he considered the two sisters.

"What exactly are you planning to hire me for?" he said curtly.

"Why, it should be obvious. I'd like you to talk to my brother and convince him that he should do the right thing for our mother."

"And how do you propose I do that?"

Norma Brewer's jaw dropped. Helen looked up, startled.

"You're the detective," Norma said. "You're supposed to be a genius. I assumed you would come up with some scheme to convince my brother."

"What leverage would I have?" Julius asked.

"I don't understand—"

"So far he has been within his legal rights in what he's done. You don't believe he has been stealing from your mother, so for the moment I will assume that that is the case, and there is no leverage to be gained from that angle. So how am I supposed to persuade him?"

"You could reason with him, couldn't you?"

Julius made a face. "How am I to do that? We've already established that your brother is a blackguard, a parasitic opportunist willing to trade his mother's well-being for his own financial gain. How am I supposed to reason with someone like that? No, I'm sorry, I don't like this. Miss Brewer, my advice is that you hire a lawyer and have the courts remove your brother's guardianship. You could make the claim that he's neglecting his responsibilities and intentionally endangering your mother's well-being."

Norma Brewer shook her head adamantly, her mouth nearly disappearing as she pushed her lips hard together. "My brother's a lawyer. He could tie this up in the courts for years. I implore you, Mr. Katz, I need your help."

Julius started drumming his fingers along the surface of his desk again. I knew he wanted an excuse not to take this case. The only thing he disliked more than working was working on a case that involved family disputes, which he found generally unseemly. While he drummed along the desk, I filled him in on what I was able to find out about Lawrence Brewer by hacking into the Massachusetts Bar Association database.

"While I still strongly advise you against hiring me, I will take this assignment if you insist," Julius said with a pained sigh. "But I will need a retainer check for twenty thousand dollars."

Twenty thousand dollars would pay for the case of Romanée-Conti. Norma Brewer took out a checkbook and started to write out a check. Julius stopped her.

"I can't guarantee results," he told her. "And it will be left to my discretion how I proceed and for how long. I will need to meet your mother, and if I am not satisfied that she needs the care you claim she does, I will end the assignment immediately. There will be no refund offered. If that is satisfactory to you, then feel free to hire me."

Norma Brewer hesitated for only a moment, then finished writing out the check. She handed it to Julius, who glanced at it casually and placed it inside the top drawer of his desk.

"I'll have my assistant, Archie, call you later this afternoon to arrange a time tomorrow morning for me to meet your mother."

Julius stood up and escorted the two sisters out of the office and towards the front door. Norma Brewer seemed taken aback by the suddenness of this, and commented on how she thought Julius would have more questions for her about her brother.

"Not at this time," Julius said. "Later, perhaps."

He hurried her along. Helen meekly allowed herself to be herded with her sister out the door. Norma tried sputtering out some more questions, which Julius met with a few mindless platitudes. Relief washed over his face once he had the door closed and those two out of his home. His townhouse was three levels, not including the basement, which he had converted into a wine cellar. With a lightness in his step, he went down to the cellar and picked out a bottle of 1961 Bordeaux from the Château Léoville-Barton. "Rich, full-bodied, with the barest hint of sweet black fruits," Julius murmured for my benefit, although it was unnecessary since I had already looked up *The Wine Spectator's* report on it. Once we were back upstairs, Julius prepared a selection of cheeses and dried meats, then brought it all out to his garden-level patio where he placed the tray on a table. He sat on a red cedar Adirondack chair that had faded over the years to a muted rust-color. The patio was the crown jewel of his townhouse—over two thousand square feet, and Julius had it professionally landscaped with Japanese maples, fountains, a variety of rose bushes, and a vast assortment of other plantings. He opened the Bordeaux and rolled the cork between his forefinger and thumb, testing it, then smelled the cork. Satisfied, he poured himself a glass. I asked him what time I should arrange for him to meet the mother.

He held the wine glass up against the late afternoon light, studied the wine's composition, then took a sip and savored it. After he put the glass down he told me eleven o'clock would be satisfactory. I called Norma Brewer on her cell phone and arranged it. Afterwards I asked Julius if he wanted me to make an appointment with Norma Brewer's brother.

"That won't be necessary," he said.

I watched as he finished a glass of Bordeaux and poured himself another, then as he sampled the Stilton and Gruyere cheeses that he had brought out with him. I could tell he had put the case completely out of his mind. While Julius drank his wine I performed a database search on the brother. I told Julius this and asked if he would like a report.

"Not now, Archie. We'll see, maybe later."

I digested this and came to the obvious conclusion. "You don't plan on doing any work on this case," I said. "You're going to meet the mother and no matter what her condition you're going to tell your client that you're dropping the case."

Julius didn't bother responding. His eyes glazed as he drank more of the wine.

"You're just going to take her money and do nothing to earn it."

"You're jumping to conclusions, Archie."

"I don't think so."

He smiled slightly. "I'm still not convinced what you do can be considered thinking."

"You took her money. You have an obligation—"

"I'm well aware of my obligations." He put the glass down and sighed heavily. "It's a fool's errand, Archie. If Lawrence Brewer is as his sister says he is, then there's nothing I'll be able to do to change his position regarding his mother."

"You could find something to use against him," I said. "He's a lawyer. If you were able to threaten him with disbarment—"

"Threaten his livelihood?" Julius shook his head. "No, Archie, I believe that would have the opposite effect by making him need his mother's money all the more. Please, no more of this. Not now, anyway. Let me enjoy my wine, this view, and the late afternoon air."

"You had no right taking payment unless you were serious about investigating this—"

My world went black as Julius turned me off.

———

Julius seldom turned me off. When he did it was always disorienting when I was turned back on. This time it was especially so, and it took me as much as three-tenths of a second to get my bearings and realize that Julius and I were being jostled back and forth in the backseat of a cab. According to my internal clock it was ten forty-eight in the morning, and using GPS to track our position, I had us eight point two miles from Emma Brewer's home in Brookline.

Julius chuckled lightly. "I hope you had a good rest, Archie."

"Yeah, just wonderful." I still felt off-kilter as I tried to adjust my frame of reference from being on Julius's patio one moment to the inside of a cab now. I told him about this and that I guessed the sensation was similar to what humans felt when they were knocked unconscious by a sucker punch.

"A touch of passive-aggressiveness in that statement, Archie. I'm impressed with how lifelike your personality is developing. But getting back to your comment, I would think it's more like being put under with anesthesia," Julius said.

"Wha? Wha's that you say?" The cab driver had turned around. He had a thick Russian or Slavic accent. I tried to match the inflections in his voice with samples I found over the Internet, and felt confident that I had his birth place pinned down to Kiev. The man looked disheveled and had obviously gone several days without shaving or washing his hair. Julius told the man that he was talking to himself, and not to mind him. The cab driver turned back around to face the traffic. He muttered to himself in Russian about the loony Americans he had to drive around all day. I translated this for Julius, who barely cracked a smile from it.

"After turning me off last night, did you try the new French restaurant on Charles Street that you've had your heart set on?"

Julius made a face as if he had sipped wine that had turned to vinegar.

"I'm afraid so," he said. "*Les Cuisses de Grenouilles Provencale* were dry and nearly inedible, and they were out of '98 Château Latour."

I remembered his excitement seeing that vintage on their wine list. "That's a shame," I said. "I'm sorry I wasn't available to console you."

Julius cocked an eyebrow. "Sarcasm, Archie? Another new development for you, although I'm not sure if I like it."

The cab driver was shaking his head. I could see him in the rearview mirror frowning severely. He muttered again in Russian about these crazies he gets stuck with. I translated his comments to Julius. He didn't bother to respond.

The cab driver pulled up to Emma Brewer's address. Julius paid him and exited the cab. He stood silently on the sidewalk, his eyes narrowing as he examined the house. It didn't look like something that would be worth close to a million dollars. According to the town records—at least what was in their database—the house was a three-bedroom Colonial built on a nine thousand square foot lot. The brown exterior paint had long since faded and was peeling away from the shutters. Aside from a new paint job, there was other obvious maintenance work that needed to be done and the small front yard was in disarray, mostly crabgrass and weeds. Julius waited until

I told him it was precisely eleven o'clock before he started towards the house. A BMW parked in front of the house was registered to Norma Brewer, so it was no surprise when she and her sister Helen greeted us at the door. Norma stood stiffly, as if she had back problems, and her sister looked as lifeless as she had the other day. Norma spoke first, thanking Julius for coming, and then holding out her hand to him. Julius stated that it was nothing personal but he never shook hands. I had mentioned that to her when she first booked the appointment, but I guess it had slipped her mind. Ostensibly, Julius's reason for it was because he saw no reason to expose himself unnecessarily to viral diseases, although I think it was more that he didn't like physical contact with strangers who weren't exceptionally beautiful young women, since he had no problem shaking hands and doing far more with women of that nature—at least from what I could tell before he'd invariably place me in his sock drawer. Norma awkwardly withdrew her hand and told Julius that her mother was in the kitchen.

"She's not having a good day," she said flatly, a fragility ageing her face and making her look even more gaunt. She looked past Julius. "Your assistant, Archie, he's not here again today? That's a shame. I was so looking forward to meeting him. He sounded charming over the phone."

If I had lips I would've kissed her. I made a list of how I would use that later to torment Julius.

Julius smiled thinly at her. "I'm sorry, but Archie has been detained—court ordered community service, so unfortunately he can only be here with us in spirit."

"Community service? What did the man do?"

"Sordid business, I'd rather not go into it. Please lead the way to your mother."

"Thanks for sullying my reputation," I said to him. Julius winked so that only I could see it.

One of the hallway walls was lined with framed family photos, mostly chronicling Norma and her two siblings from childhood to their young-adult years; a few included the parents. I had previously located photos of all of them, Norma's father from the newspaper obituary and the others from driver's license photos that were on record at the Department of Motor Vehicles. I was able to identify them in their family photos using different physical characteristics, such as the shape of their faces, moles, and other distinguishing marks. There were half a dozen photos of Helen in her twenties with a man I didn't recognize. Several were wedding pictures, so I assumed he was Helen's husband. He appeared to be in his early twenties also and, like Julius, had dark hair and similar features to current male Hollywood movie stars frequently described in magazines as heartthrobs. Also like Julius, he had an athletic build and was roughly the same height and weight. Julius noted the photos from the corner of his eye without once breaking stride.

Norma led Julius to a small kitchen with Formica countertops and yellow-painted pine cabinets that looked like it had last been remodeled forty years ago. I matched the cabinets to a catalog and noted that they were manufactured in 1964. Sitting alone at a table was our client's mother, Emma Brewer. She was fifty-seven in the last photo I found of her, now she was eighty-three, and she looked as if she had lost half her body weight. She couldn't have weighed much more than eighty pounds. Her hair in the photo was turning gray, now it was white. She looked like some gnarled piece of papier-mâché. Her hands were mostly blue veins and bone and were wrapped tightly around a cup of coffee as she stared blindly at the wall in front of her. She became aware that we had entered the room and, as she turned and caught sight of Julius, her face crumbled. She got out of her chair and nearly fell over as she backed away, her hands coming up to her face. She looked like she was trying to scream, but no noise came out. I matched her expression to one of an actress in a photo I had found from a horror-movie database, and realized her expression was one of fear.

Norma stood frozen watching this, her own face showing dread. Helen moved quickly to her mother and took hold of her. Emma turned to her, confused, and asked in a whisper, "Norma?"

"No, Ma, I'm Helen. Norma is standing over there. The man next to her is a friend. His name is Julius Katz. He's here to ask you some questions."

Emma Brewer continued to stare at Julius and Norma. Then it was as if all the life bled out of her face and there was nothing there. At that point she let Helen take her back to her chair. Helen tried to ask her if she wanted to lie in bed instead, but Emma didn't answer her. Instead she took hold of her coffee cup again and stared blindly straight ahead.

Norma came back to life then. Her eyes glaring, she asked Julius if it was really necessary for him to question her mother. Julius reluctantly shook his head, realizing he had no choice but to do some work on this case. "Is she always like this?" he asked.

"No, not always. Some days she's almost functional. But as I told you before, she's having a bad day."

"Has your brother seen her like this?"

"Yes."

Julius's facial muscles hardened as he once again studied the mother. "Your brother must be a fool if he thinks he can get away with this," he said.

"My brother is desperate." Norma peered from the corner of her eyes at her sister and mother. Lowering her voice, she suggested that they continue the conversation outside the house. "I don't want my mother hearing what I'm about to say. It would upset her if she were able to make sense of it."

Julius agreed. Norma told her sister that they were going outside and asked if she'd join them. Helen declined, telling her that she was going to keep their mother company. Norma stood silently for a moment before leaving the room. Julius followed her. As they walked past the framed family photos lining the hallway wall, Julius stopped in front of one of Helen's wedding pictures and asked Norma about the man in it.

"That was Helen's husband, Thomas Arden."

"From comments you made yesterday, I take it that he's no longer married to your sister?"

For a while Norma stared hard at the photo, her mouth moving as if she were chewing gum. It seemed a struggle for her to pull away and face Julius.

"Technically, they could very well still be married," she said in a low, hushed voice. "Twelve years ago he abandoned his family, running off to God knows where and leaving Helen alone to take care of three young children. I don't believe Helen has ever heard from him. I have no idea whether she ever divorced him in absentia—it's a sore subject, but I don't believe she has ever taken that step, so in all likelihood, my sister is probably still married to him."

"I see. And how about you, Miss Brewer, have you ever married?"

"I don't see the importance of you knowing that."

Julius's smile tightened. "It's important for me to form a clear picture of the family dynamics. I have no idea how I am going to tackle your brother, but the more I know about all of you the better chance I have of something coming to me."

That was complete rubbish. I had already given Julius a report on Norma Brewer which included the fact that she had never been married. It occurred to me then that Julius didn't trust my competency on the matter. The client shook her head and gave Julius the same information that I had given him earlier—that no, she had never been married. I felt a tinge of excess heat for a few milliseconds, and realized that that was the sensation of resentment, and yet another new experience for me.

"Please, Mr. Katz, let's continue this outside. I don't want to risk upsetting my mother."

Julius agreed and followed her out the door. Standing there in the late morning sunlight, Norma Brewer's skin again took on a parchment quality, and I could make out a crisscross of blue veins along her temples. She clasped her hands as she tried to meet Julius's stare.

"I spoke with my brother over the phone last night," she said in a hushed tone. "I thought maybe I could talk sense into him."

"You weren't able to."

She shook her head. "He's only willing to allow Mother to be put in a facility if Helen and I agree to let the house be sold to him for well under the market price. I can't do that, Mr. Katz—the house would need to be sold to pay for her care. She only has enough money in Treasuries to cover two year's worth of expenses, and the facility I found in Vermont won't accept her unless I can show enough assets in escrow to cover her first five years there."

"And your mother's health?"

"Outside of the Alzheimer's she has nothing medically wrong with her. She has lost a lot of weight because she forgets to eat, but she could easily live another ten years."

Julius's facial muscles hardened as he gazed at Norma Brewer. "Your brother gave you a dollar figure for his acquiescence," he said at last.

Norma Brewer nodded. "Two hundred and fifty thousand dollars," she said. She looked away from Julius, her hands clasping tighter together. "I have a feeling he promised that money to someone." She took a deep breath before continuing. "I believe I mentioned yesterday that Lawrence is an attorney. One of his clients is a known hoodlum, Mr. Katz."

"Yes, I know. Willie Andrews."

That surprised his client, and it also surprised me. While I was turned off, Julius actually researched the brother himself. Will wonders ever cease? I decided it had to be the disappointing meal. He needed something to work off his dissatisfaction, and obviously didn't encounter a suitable woman for that—probably leaving the restaurant in too much of a huff to notice any. I searched the online newspaper archives for one Willie Andrews, and built a thick file on him. He was a known mob affiliate and had been arrested over the years on an assortment of charges, including loan sharking and extortion, but never convicted.

"Miss Brewer, I saw your brother yesterday before our appointment," Julius added. "It was by chance only. He was at the dog track, and I am guessing from his demeanor that he has a gambling addiction. I've seen it enough to be able to spot the telltale signs."

That was yet another surprise. I record all the images that I "see" and transfer them to a hard drive in Julius's office that he maintains for me, and they're kept for one week before Julius backs them onto permanent storage. I scanned all my visual images from when we were at the dog track the other day and, sure enough, Lawrence Brewer was there. I analyzed the images I had of him, and determined easily enough that he was losing from the way he ripped his betting tickets. I told Julius this even though I knew he must've noticed exactly the same thing. That's the thing with Julius, he's like a computer in his own right, noticing and storing away everything he sees.

Norma Brewer looked flabbergasted by that bit of news. "Did you follow my brother to the track?

"No, Miss Brewer, as I mentioned, it was purely serendipitous."

Julius had signaled me several minutes before to arrange for a taxi to pick us up, and one was pulling up to the house. Julius had that look in his eyes he always has when he's anxious to get away from a client, and he told her he'd be in touch, then made his escape. Norma Brewer appeared taken aback by Julius's quick and unexpected departure. She stood at a loss for words for a long moment before heading back inside the house. Julius settled into the back of the cab and gave the driver his townhouse address.

"Quite a morning," I told him. "One woman finding me absolutely charming, another terrified merely at the sight of you."

"I never heard her use the adverb *absolutely* in describing your charm," Julius muttered somewhat peevishly. He had taken out his cell phone so that the driver wouldn't think that he was muttering to himself. The cell phone was merely a prop. Whenever Julius needed to make a call, I'd make it for him and patch him in through his ear piece.

"It was implied," I said. "Would you like me to brief you on the reports I generated for Lawrence Brewer and Willie Andrews?"

"That's not necessary." A thin smile crept over his lips. "I researched both of them myself last night while you were *unavailable*."

"Yeah, but I bet you don't have Lawrence Brewer's last seven years' worth of tax returns, unless you were able to hack into the IRS's mainframe and, given the level of encryption they use, that's not very likely. I also bet you don't have Willie Andrews's court documents."

"No, I don't, but I don't need them now. Sometimes, Archie, too much information is worse than too little. It distracts from what's important."

That made no sense. The only way you can analyze data is if all the data were available—or if you are able to extrapolate what was missing. I ignored the comment, and instead asked him if he wanted me to arrange for appointments with either the brother or Andrews.

"Willie Andrews is not the type of man you make an appointment with. As far as Lawrence Brewer goes, now is not the appropriate time."

"So that's it, then?"

"For now, yes."

I expected that. As far as Julius was concerned, he had already worked hard enough for one day. I knew there was little chance that nagging him would change that. Still, I tried.

"I can see your point," I said. "After all, you have just put in an arduous twenty-seven minutes of work, more than enough to justify the twenty-thousand dollar fee you extorted from your client."

"An hour and seventeen minutes once you factor in the cab rides."

"Wow. An hour and seventeen minutes, then. I'm exhausted just thinking about it."

"Archie, now is not the time. I'm not about to tackle the brother until I've given the matter more thought. So please, some quiet so I can think."

Yeah, it was pointless. The only thing he was going to be thinking about was lunch at one of his favorite local restaurants, along with the bottle of Gewürztraminer I had reserved for him. With nothing else to do I spun some cycles figuring out why I hadn't made the connection between the photos I dug up earlier for Lawrence Brewer and the visual images I recorded at the dog track, and then worked on readjusting my neuron network so I would recognize patterns like that in the future. I have to admit I was impressed with Julius's ability to recall seeing Lawrence Brewer at the dog track and told him so. Julius grunted out that it was simply luck.

"The only reason he made an impression was because he was so obviously losing badly that I considered for a moment inviting him to one of my poker games. Now please, Archie, I'd like quiet the rest of the trip."

Julius put his cell phone back in his inside jacket pocket. I spent the rest of the cab ride constructing simulations involving Julius interviewing Lawrence Brewer, but none of them led to a reasonable probability of success.

———

Julius surprised me. On our return home he had me cancel his luncheon reservation and he spent the rest of the day either reading or puttering around the townhouse. All I could figure was he was trying to bluff me that he was onto something and that he planned to stay holed up until he had the case solved—that way he could loaf for days without me nagging him. A couple of times he put me away in his desk drawer while he got on the computer. He wouldn't tell me what he was doing, only that I had as much information as he did at that point. He seemed genuinely distracted during that first day, at times becoming as still as a marble statue while his facial muscles hardened and his eyes stared off into the distance. Of course, it could've been an act. When I tried asking him about what he was considering, he mostly ignored me, only once telling me that whatever it was, it was still percolating. That night he had me cancel his dinner reservations. Instead of going out he spent the evening making fresh gnocchi and then pounding veal until it was nearly paper thin before sautéing it with shallots and mushrooms in a white wine sauce. He picked a Montepulciano d'Abruzzo from his wine cellar to accompany his dinner.

The next day he appeared more his normal self as he performed his morning rituals, then spent the rest of the morning reading wine reviews. My attempts to pester him into action went nowhere. He mostly ignored me, and when I tried briefing him on the dossier I had compiled on Willie Andrews, he stopped me, telling me that he was otherwise occupied.

"My mistake," I said. "I thought you depositing our client's check actually obligated you to earn the fee you were paid."

"Archie, I *am* earning it."

"By sitting around reading wine reviews?"

"Precisely. Sometimes the best action is waiting. Patience, Archie, patience."

So there you had it. Maybe he was waiting on something, but more likely he had fallen into one of his lazy funks and was only trying to bluff me, and as part of the bluff he was going to stay holed up inside his townhouse. The thing with Julius was he had no "tell"—no visible indication of when he was bluffing, at least none that I had yet been able to detect. When he played poker, I could identify the other players' "tells" pretty quickly, not that Julius needed my help in that area. He was astute at reading other players and detecting the slight behavior changes that indicated as brightly as a flashing neon light when they were bluffing or holding what they thought were winning cards. Sometimes it would be the way their facial muscles contorted or their breathing patterns changed or maybe they'd scratch themselves or shift slightly in their chairs. The list was endless, but it was simple pattern recognition on my part to identify these "tells" by comparing recorded video of when they were bluffing and when they weren't. I'd spent countless hours trying to identify Julius's "tell" and so far had come up with nothing.

The rest of the day Julius spent mostly reading, cooking, and drinking wine. I was beginning to think if it were a bluff he would try to play it out for weeks if he thought he could get away with it. I tried several times to nag him into action, but failed miserably, with him smugly insisting that he was waiting for the right time before taking any direct action. That day his client called several times to find out when Julius was planning to talk to her brother. Julius had me answer those calls and directed me to tell Norma Brewer that he was in the midst of investigating certain issues regarding the case, and once he was done he would be interviewing her brother. It was utter hogwash, but I didn't tell her that.

The third day it was more of the same, with Julius not venturing outside the townhouse, the only difference being that he seemed more distracted than usual. Also, the client didn't call. At six o'clock he turned on the evening news, which was unusual for him. He rarely watched TV. During the broadcast it was reported that a local woman named Norma Brewer had been found murdered in her Cambridge home.

"Is that what you were waiting for?" I asked.

Julius didn't answer me. He just sat grim-faced, his lips compressing into two thin, bloodless lines.

"So I guess that's it. Your client's dead and her money is in your bank account. Now you don't have to do anything to earn it. Bravo."

"No, Archie, that's not what it means," he said, his jaw clenching in a resolute fashion. "I'm going to be earning every penny of what she paid me."

"Did you know she was going to be murdered?"

"I didn't know anything with certainty."

"How?"

"Not now, Archie. We're going to be very busy over the next few days. For now, please call the sister, Helen, and find out what you can about the murder. In the meantime, make the earliest dinner reservations you can for me at Le Che Cru. The next few days I expect to be roughing it. If the police call, I'm out for the evening and you have no idea where I have gone. If Helen Arden asks to speak to me, the same story. You have no idea where I am."

I did as Julius asked, first making him reservations at Le Che Cru for eight-thirty, then calling Helen Arden. She sounded dazed, as if she barely understood what I was saying. I had to repeat myself several times, and after my words finally sunk in, she told me that the police had contacted her about Norma's murder, and she was now trying to reach her brother and figure out how they were going to take care of their mother and at the same time make the arrangements for Norma's funeral. She wasn't even sure when the police were going to release the body.

"What if it were weeks before they let us have Norma?" she asked. "How are we supposed to bury my sister?"

Her voice had no strength to it. It was as if she were lost and had completely given up any hope of being found. I told her it wouldn't be more than a few days—however long it took for the coroner to perform an autopsy. I gave her the phone number for a good criminal lawyer that Julius recommended to clients who had dealt with this type of problem in the past. I tried asking her whether the police had given any details about the murder, but she seemed to have a hard time comprehending what I was saying. After I tried asking her several more times, she finally murmured that they told her nothing other than that her sister was dead.

I had been searching the Internet, and so far no details had been reported on any of the Boston newspapers' Web sites, and neither was there anything of interest on the police radio frequencies that I was scanning. I told her

Julius would be in touch sometime the next day and hung up. I filled Julius in quickly. He was in the process of changing into one of his dining suits. After slipping on a pair of Italian calfskin loafers, he hurried down the stairs and to the front door. He asked me whether I was able to detect any police car radios broadcasting in the area, and I told him there weren't any and that nothing was showing on the outdoor webcam feed. Still, he opened the front door only enough so he could peer out of it. Satisfied that the police weren't lying in wait for him, he stepped outside and hurried down the street, his pace nearly a run. Once he was two blocks away from his townhouse, he slowed.

"Do you want me to call the brother?" I asked. "Maybe see if you can get an early read on him?"

"Not now, Archie. I'm sure he's with the police presently, and it would be best to wait until tomorrow to call him."

I remained silent while Julius briskly walked the five blocks down Pinckney Street to Charles Street. After hearing about Norma Brewer's murder I started building simulations that modeled different scenarios that would explain Julius's behavior since accepting the case. There was one scenario that stood out as having the highest probability. I asked him about it. Whether he was lying low waiting for the brother to kill Norma Brewer, knowing that if that were to happen it would make it easy for him to earn his fee, since all he'd have to do is wait for the police to arrest the brother and then have the courts vacate his guardianship.

"Are you asking whether I expected Lawrence Brewer to murder my client?"

"Yes, that's what I'm asking."

"No, that's not what I was expecting." A young couple were passing us on the sidewalk, and Julius took out his cell phone so he wouldn't appear to be an insane person talking to himself. Somewhat amused, Julius asked, "Archie, what would be Lawrence Brewer's purpose in doing that?"

"Because she engaged you. Maybe he was afraid you'd find leverage that you'd be able to use against him. Maybe he thought if his sister were out of the way, you'd be also."

"It's possible, Archie, but he'd have to be a dolt to think that. Then again, the way he was acting at the dog track, as well as his behavior regarding his mother's well being, he could very well be a dolt."

"So, you think he murdered his sister?"

Julius made a face. "It's a possibility, Archie. But it's just one of many and there's no point engaging in idle speculation now. The next few days are going to be hectic enough and this could be my last decent meal before this matter has been put to bed. So please, Archie, no more discussion on this, at least not tonight."

I wanted to ask him the obvious question, which was, if he hadn't been waiting for Lawrence Brewer to murder his sister, then what had he been waiting for? What stopped me was detecting a hint of a threat in his voice that if I continued this line of conversation he would turn me off. That would be twice in three days, and I didn't want to set that type of precedent. I remained quiet while he walked to Le Che Cru and took a seat at the bar. The maitre d' came over with a complimentary bottle of Chardonnay that he knew Julius favored, and apologized profusely that he wasn't able to arrange for an earlier table for his favorite patron. Before leaving, he told Julius that he would have an order of seared sweetbreads in chestnut flour brought over immediately, on the house, of course. Julius graciously accepted all this. The sweetbreads were brought over within minutes and, while Julius was having his second glass of wine, a Detective Mark Cramer from the Cambridge Police Department called. I connected the call to Julius's ear piece so he could listen in. Rather gruffly, the detective asked to speak to Julius.

"I'm afraid Mr. Katz isn't available," I said.

"Yeah, well, get him available!"

"I would if I had any idea where he is, but I don't, so I can't."

The detective used some choice invective on his end of the line, ending with the phrase, "*son of a bitch.*"

"Is that all, Detective?" I asked, to Julius's obvious amusement.

"No, that's not all," he said, his voice growing more exasperated. "Your boss is a material witness in a murder case—"

"There's been a murder?"

"Shut up," he ordered, his exasperation growing. "I know damn well you called the victim's sister within the hour, just as I know your boss is probably with you right now getting a good laugh over all this. The Boston PD filled me in on what to expect, so don't think you're fooling anyone with this, okay? You better just tell Katz to come in to Central Square station within the next fifteen minutes or I'll be getting a bench warrant for his arrest. Ask him how he'd like a few days in lockup for contempt of court!"

Detective Cramer hung up on me. Julius shook his head, a thin wisp of a smile showing. "The man's a fool," he said.

"Dolts and fools, huh?"

"Precisely, Archie. That's what you've gotten me mired in." He took a sip of his wine and sighed heavily. "They probably have a squad car waiting in front of my townhouse."

"Probably a fleet of them."

Julius was going to say something else, but instead another long, heavy sigh escaped from him. He sat almost comatose for several minutes, not moving as much as a muscle, not even blinking. When he finally came out of it he appeared relaxed. Shortly afterward he started chatting with two women sitting nearby. One of them was a redhead with a smooth, cream-colored complexion who gave her name as Lily Rosten. She closely resembled the actress Lauren Ambrose. The other woman gave her name as Sarah Chase. She was a brunette and I was able to match her physical characteristics to actresses that were considered extraordinarily beautiful according to online surveys. Both women, according to their DMV records, were twenty-nine. While Julius was charming and polite with both of them, his attention was primarily focused on Lily, which surprised me since I had rated Sarah as the more attractive of the two. When Julius's table became available, he invited them to join him for dinner. They both accepted, but Lily indicated that she needed to use the ladies' room and dragged her friend with her. When they returned, Sarah Chase reluctantly informed Julius that something had come up and she wouldn't be able to join them. Julius didn't seem to mind, and neither did Lily.

Dinner was a long, leisurely three-hour affair, and Julius was in rare form; maybe somewhat subdued at times, but even more charming than usual when entertaining. It was an odd effect the way Lily's eyes appeared to glisten when she laughed, and even when she simply smiled. I also noted how they maintained eye contact almost continuously. When dinner ended, Lily announced to Julius that she lived in the Back Bay section of Boston off Marlborough Street, and Julius suggested that they take advantage of the pleasant weather, and that he walk her back to her apartment instead of calling a cab. I had already looked up her address and mapped it out to seven-tenths of a mile from where we were. Earlier, when I had tried filling Julius in on what I was able to find about her—the amount in her bank account, the fact that she was single and never married, where she grew up and went to college, as well as her present job as an administrator for a local nonprofit organization—he stopped me with a hand signal.

Just as dinner had been leisurely, so was their walk to her apartment building, maybe even more so. Somewhere along the way, they started holding hands. When they reached her address, they were still holding hands. I recognized the pattern—the way she looked at him and blushed and how Julius responded. It was clear that she was going to invite Julius for the night, and this would allow him to bypass the police, which I figured was what he was after all along. I was astounded when he gave her a quick and somewhat chaste kiss on the mouth and told her he'd like to call her in a few days. She looked equally astounded for a few seconds, but smiled and blushed even brighter than before and told Julius she would like that. Julius stood on the sidewalk and watched as she disappeared inside the building's vestibule. Only then did he turn back towards Beacon Hill and his townhouse.

As I said, I was astounded. His actions didn't make sense. They didn't fit his past patterns.

"I don't get it," I said.

"What, Archie?"

"Why didn't you go up to her apartment with her?"

He didn't answer me.

"Wasn't that the point?" I asked. "So that you could elude the police until morning?"

He shrugged. "If that were the case, couldn't I simply check into a hotel for the night?"

"You could, but the police might have a watch on your credit cards."

"That's true," he acknowledged. "Very true, Archie. It would be best for you to call Henry and have him waiting for us at the townhouse."

Henry Zack was Julius's attorney, and Julius had him on twenty-four hour call for just such emergencies. I knew Henry would moan about the late hour, which he did when I reached him, but he understood the emergency of the situation and agreed to meet Julius. I filled Julius in, and asked him again about Lily.

"I don't get it," I said. "She's extraordinarily attractive, and it was clear from her behavior that she wanted you to join her. It was equally clear from yours that you wanted to, and you had your additional motive. This is a schism from your normal behavior patterns. An anomaly. It doesn't fit."

He remained silent as he continued along Beacon Street. After several blocks an odd, almost melancholy smile showed.

"There's still a lot for you to learn, Archie," he said softly.

That was all he was going to say on the matter. Along with Norma Brewer's murder, I now had another mystery to solve.

———

It wasn't exactly a fleet of police cars waiting at Julius's townhouse, but there were more than I would've expected. Three in total, with a small congregation of officers milling around by the front door. Henry Zack was among them, and he was red-faced as he talked on his cell phone, his eyes bulging slightly. I spotted all this when we were two blocks away by tying into the outdoor webcam feed that covered the front exterior of Julius's townhouse. I reported all this to Julius, and his lips compressed into a grim expression. He asked me to get Henry on the line.

I heard the unmistakable call-waiting tone as Henry put his other call on hold to take mine, and then I patched Julius in. "This is outrageous, Julius," he said, his voice rising. "They have absolutely no grounds to hold you as a material witness, and I'm on the phone now with the Chief Clerk of the district court to have their warrant vacated. If they arrest you I'll be suing the hell out of them—both the police department and each of the officers personally.

Start looking for that retirement villa in Florence that you're always talking about!"

Henry's rant was more for the officers' benefit than Julius's. Julius informed him that he was three minutes away, and asked if it was safe for him to appear.

"It's safe. It will be as good as winning the lottery if they so much as put a hand on you."

Julius signaled for me to disconnect the call, and his pace accelerated as his expression grew grimmer. Within three minutes, as he had promised Henry, he approached his building and bedlam broke out. Henry was on the lookout for Julius and so he spotted him first. He attempted to distract the cops by bellowing more threats at them. It wasn't until Julius was halfway up the path to his front door that the first cop noticed him, and then they swarmed toward him with Henry Zack in pursuit. A plainclothes detective with a large ruddy face and wearing a cheap, badly wrinkled suit reached Julius first. Having already accessed his departmental records, I informed Julius that this was Detective Mark Cramer. Cramer tried to shove a court warrant into Julius's hands.

"My lawyer is standing right behind you, Detective Cramer," Julius said. "Anything you have for me you should give to him."

Cramer seemed taken aback that Julius knew who he was and reluctantly handed the warrant to Henry Zack, then turned back to Julius. According to Cramer's records he was fifty-four, six foot two and two hundred and twenty pounds. He appeared heavier than that, my estimate being closer to two hundred and forty-six pounds. He also had less hair than the photo in his file. He appeared both tired and cranky, and he tried to give Julius a hard, intimidating stare.

"You're under arrest for obstruction of justice," Cramer said.

"Nonsense."

That brought a wicked grin to Cramer's lips. "Is that so? I have a court warrant that says otherwise, smart guy."

"I couldn't care less," Julius said. "This isn't a police state. You have no justification for this harassment—"

"No justification?" Cramer sputtered, almost choking on his words. He lifted a thick index finger as if he were going to poke Julius in the chest with it, which would've been a mistake unless he wanted to be wearing a cast on his hand for the next two months. Somehow he controlled himself.

"Norma Brewer, who was a client of yours, was murdered this afternoon. So far you've refused to cooperate with an ongoing police investigation and, as far as I'm concerned, you have been withholding evidence dealing with the crime."

"That is utter rubbish," Julius said. "I have no knowledge of Miss Brewer's murder other than what was reported on the six o'clock news and you have no legitimate reason to think otherwise. I spent the evening at Le Che Cru entertaining a date, and am just arriving home now. Until my assistant tracked me down a short while ago, I had no idea you or any other police official wished to talk to me."

Cramer was beside himself. "No idea, huh?" He jerked a thumb towards Henry Zack. "That's why you dragged your lawyer down here at this hour. I've heard all about you, Katz, and I'm not about to put up with your nonsense!"

Henry started to object, but Julius put up a hand to stop him.

"Once Archie tracked me down and relayed your message, I decided to take the proper precautions." Julius smiled thinly at the detective. "Now this is very simple. If you arrest me, you won't get a single word out of me. Not now, not ever. I will, however, seek every avenue of recourse that the courts allow. On the other hand, if you agree to act in a civil fashion, I will invite you and only you—not this mob of yours that you've gathered at my doorstep—into my home to discuss what I know pertaining to Norma Brewer's murder. Your decision."

Cramer didn't like it. I could tell he wanted nothing more than to cuff Julius and drag him into a police cruiser. He wanted to do that—that much was evident, but instead he stood shaking his head and muttering about the gall of Julius to keep a murder investigation on hold for hours and then to think he could make demands. It was for show, though. A defeated look had already dropped like a veil over his eyes, and it was clear he was going to give in. After a minute or so, his muttering died down. He nodded, almost embarrassed, and said, "What the hell, we'll do it your way."

Julius graciously kept a straight face and escorted Detective Cramer and Henry Zack into his home and to his kitchen. He asked if either of them wanted coffee. Henry accepted, Cramer declined.

"Would you prefer a French roast, or maybe try a new Tanzanian blend that I've recently discovered. It's really quite good, showing subtle black currant and citrus flavors."

"French roast would be fine," Henry said.

"Are you sure?" Julius asked, not making any attempt to hide his disappointment.

Cramer sat propped up on a bar stool by the center island, and he was stewing. Finally he exploded, ordering Julius to forget about the damn coffee and tell him what he knew about Norma Brewer's murder.

Julius measured and grinded the proper amount of coffee beans before telling Cramer that he knew nothing about the murder.

Cramer nearly swallowed his tongue, "Your suspicions, then," he forced out.

"I don't have any. Why would you think I would?"

"Why? Maybe because you were hired three days ago by a woman who was just murdered! How's that?" Cramer grunted derisively. "You've been working for her for three days now. You must've come across something suspicious."

"I've mostly been loafing since Miss Brewer hired me," Julius admitted with a halfhearted shrug. "I met with her the day after she hired me, and since then I've been by myself, mostly reading for pleasure and puttering around. I left the townhouse once since my second meeting with her, and that was only tonight to go out for dinner."

Cramer was glaring daggers at him. Julius shrugged again.

"I was planning to start my investigation soon," Julius said. "It just hadn't happened yet."

"What did Norma Brewer hire you for?" Cramer demanded.

"A personal matter," Julius said. "I'm afraid I'm not at liberty to discuss it."

"Your client's dead!"

"One of my clients is. Helen Arden accompanied her sister when I was hired, and I consider both of them my clients. If you obtain her permission to disclose the nature of the investigation to you, I will gladly do so."

"Katz, there's no such thing as PI-client confidentiality."

"Which is why I had her hire me through Mr. Zack. Technically, I'm working for him."

It was a bald-faced lie, one that Julius said convincingly. As I mentioned before, he had no "tell", at least none that I have ever been able to discern. Cramer shot Henry Zack a look. Henry did have a "tell". He would rub his thumb with his forefinger before he was going to lie, but Cramer had already missed it. Henry nodded and confirmed what Julius said.

"As an extension of me, Julius does have confidentiality with our clients. However, with Helen Arden's permission, I'm willing to allow Julius to tell you about his conversation with Norma Brewer."

Cramer's face had been cherry red, now it was paling to a bone white. "You two have just been jerking me around," he accused bitterly.

"No, we haven't," Julius said. "I didn't invite you here under the pretense that I had any knowledge of this murder. You came storming to my home threatening to arrest me. I indulged you by offering to have a civil conversation with you."

The coffee had finished percolating. Julius stopped to pour two cups, one for Henry, one for himself. After asking Henry how he liked his coffee, he turned back to Cramer. Before he continued he took a deep breath of air, expanding his chest, and held it for several seconds before releasing it. The anger in his eyes was genuine. I'd been with him long enough to know that.

"From the first minute you've done nothing but insult and accuse me," Julius continued. "I should throw you out of here physically, especially after the charade you've been participating in, believing that I could be duped by such sophistry."

Cramer started to protest with a forced indignation, but Julius shot him a withering look which stalled the detective's protest to a mere stutter.

"Please, don't insult my intelligence any more than you already have. You must've already talked to Helen Arden, which is how you knew I'd been hired, and I'm sure you already asked her what the matter was about and there would be no reason for her not to tell you. You couldn't possibly reach the position of Detective with that level of incompetence, despite the show you've put on here tonight. Isn't that true?"

Cramer sat confused for a moment, clearly not sure of which of the questions Julius had asked him. Finally, he nodded.

"Alright," Cramer admitted. "I wanted to hear your take on it."

"No, that's not it at all. Your coming here and acting the way you have tells me that so far you have no witnesses and no forensic evidence, and that further, you don't believe you're going to. It also tells me that you see this murder as a mess and you're not sure how to proceed. You thought you could come here and bully me into helping you."

Cramer started to protest, but Julius raised a finger to stop him.

"Don't attempt to argue this. I'm an expert poker player, Cramer, and I can spot a bluff, especially one as clumsy as yours. But this is a client of mine who has been murdered, so as distasteful as I've found your tactics so far, I will offer my help as long as you don't try to strong-arm me again. Have you talked to the brother yet?"

Cramer had been chewing on all this trying to decide how to play it. Finally, he came to a decision. Somewhat glumly he shook his head.

"Not yet," Cramer said. "He's agreed to come in tomorrow morning for questioning."

"If you don't end up arresting him, escort him here afterwards."

"I can't do that against his wishes."

"He'll agree. I'll be calling him before then. Was I correct about you having nothing?"

"Yeah."

"Tell me about the murder."

Cramer's eyes moved away from Julius's and down to his large beefy hands. He sat for a while rubbing his knuckles before his eyes shifted back to meet Julius's.

"She was hit on the back of the head and knocked unconscious. After that she was strangled. Whoever did this wore cloth gloves. There was no sign of forced entry. So far, that's all we've got."

"What was she hit with?"

"A polished agate stone that was probably kept as a paperweight. About the size of a softball."

"Could this have been a robbery turned murder?"

"Not likely. We had the sister walk through the house and she didn't see anything obvious that was missing."

Julius's eyes glazed over and his facial muscles hardened as he processed all this. Cramer and Henry stared at him intently, waiting for him to speak. After several minutes, life flickered back into Julius's eyes. He offered Cramer a grim smile.

"This murder may be completely unrelated to the assignment I was hired for. Miss Brewer mentioned a business she sold several years ago. I would strongly suggest you look into that to see if there were any hard feelings concerning the sale. Another avenue of investigation involves Miss Brewer's brother-in-law, a Mr. Thomas Arden. I was told that he abandoned his family twelve years ago. It's possible he's back in the picture. That should be looked into too."

Cramer nodded, accepting all this. He pushed himself slowly to his feet and arched his back as if he were stretching. Almost reluctantly, he started to offer Julius his hand. Henry coughed and caught Cramer's eye, signaling to him that that would not be a good idea. Cramer caught on and pulled his hand back before things got awkward. He told Julius that he would find his way out and that he'd be in touch. I followed the detective's movement through several webcam feeds that had been set up throughout the townhouse and made sure he left without any detours. Henry sat for awhile as he finished his coffee, then stood up and nodded goodbye.

"If nothing else, Julius, I can always count on you for an eventful evening," he said with a soft chuckle. I didn't bother checking his exit through the webcam feeds. Julius remained in the kitchen drinking coffee.

We both sat silently until Julius broke the quiet by putting his cup down on the granite countertop and asking me to order a dozen roses for Lily Rosten and arrange for them to be delivered so that they'd be waiting for her when she arrived at work the next morning. "Have them add a note that I'll be calling her soon," he added.

I did as he asked, placing the order through a twenty-four hour florist that Julius had used in the past. "You don't believe Norma Brewer's murder had anything to do with the sale of her business?" I asked.

Julius sat quietly for a moment, then shook his head. "Not exactly, Archie, but it's something to look into, and the police, with all their manpower and resources, are better equipped to do so than I. Besides, a general rule to follow is the more clutter that can be eliminated, the clearer the picture will become."

From the moment Julius suggested to Detective Cramer that he investigate Thomas Arden, I began building a dossier on the elusive brother-in-law. I filled Julius in on the salient points. That Arden graduated with a degree in finance from Haverford College in 1983, married Helen Brewer shortly after graduation, later earned an M.B.A.

from Harvard, and was working as the Chief Financial Officer for what was at the time a small computer start-up company when he appeared to vanish from the face of the planet on August 7th, 1997. There was not a single trace of Thomas Arden after that date, at least not in any of the databases I was able to access.

"Why August 7th?" Julius asked.

"That was when his wife reported him missing to the police."

"He could've been missing for several days before she contacted the police," Julius said. "But never mind, it's not important. Anything interesting about him going to Haverford College?"

"Lawrence Brewer went to Haverford for his undergraduate degree. They both graduated the same year."

"Very good, Archie. What can you surmise from that?"

"That they were friends. That maybe Lawrence introduced Arden to his sister."

"Again, very good. But, Archie, your dossier is missing a potentially critical fact. I'd suggest you keep working on it."

Julius had obviously already built his own dossier on Arden, most likely when he had turned me off a few days ago, or maybe one of the times when he had put me away in his desk drawer so I couldn't see what he was doing on his computer.

"What am I missing?" I asked.

Julius showed an exaggerated yawn. "It's late, Archie and I have a busy day ahead of me. I'm going to bed. You keep working on it, though."

Julius went upstairs to his bedroom and placed me next to his ear receiver on the dresser bureau before disappearing into his bathroom. The fact that I had missed something bothered me. I spun cycles like a crazy person building different logic models as I tried to figure out what it could've been. I was so wrapped up in this that I barely heard him gargling in the next room, or later, the shallow cadence of his breathing as he lay in bed. It was three-forty-seven in the morning when I figured it out. It had taken numerous adjustments to my neuron network, but I had it. As I mentioned before, Julius had already taken his ear receiver out for the night, and I was too excited to wait until six-thirty in the morning for him to wake up on his own and put his receiver back in, so I called him on his cell phone. He answered after the fourth ring.

"Archie, it's ten minutes to four—"

"I figured it out," I told him.

I heard him sigh. "This is my fault," he said. "I should've expected this. I've been pushing you too hard to create this type of personality. Archie, I'd like you to reprogram your neuron network so that you don't wake me up again, at least not unless it's for a legitimate reason."

"Sure, no problem. After I tell you what I've found."

"Let me guess, Archie. That you suspect Thomas Arden had embezzled half a million dollars from his company shortly before he disappeared?"

"That's right. It was hidden in the company's annual financial statement. A five-hundred- thousand-dollar line item for a tradeshow that didn't exist. He stole that money."

"Most likely."

"Why didn't the company file charges against him?" I asked.

Julius let out another heavy sigh. "Good night, Archie. It's late now."

"Please."

It wouldn't have surprised me if he had hung up his cell phone, but instead he explained it to me.

"The company probably didn't want their investors to find out about it. Most likely they needed another round of financing, and were afraid that this would kill it for them. Good night, Archie."

I wanted to ask him whether he thought that Lawrence and Arden had been in contact over the years, and whether he suspected that Lawrence had used Arden to kill his sister by threatening exposure. That's what I wanted to ask him, but I knew if I pushed it I risked being turned off again, so instead I held back. For the next two and a half hours, while Julius slept, I searched for any link I could between Lawrence and Arden. By the time the alarm went off at six-thirty, I had decided to keep my theory to myself. What I wanted to do was locate enough evidence to solve this murder before Julius did. I couldn't help feeling that if I kept working on this I would beat him to the punch.

That morning, we mostly went our separate ways; Julius going through his calisthenics and martial arts training, and then mostly loafing about as he leafed through several books on the theory of war that he had recently purchased. Me, I spent my time building simulations that had

Lawrence Brewer blackmailing Arden into killing his sister. One scenario came up that seemed plausible enough to research, and I was doing that when Julius interrupted me to get Helen Arden on the phone. Once I did, he had me patch him through.

"Mrs. Arden, first I'd like to offer my condolences for your sister's death. I know this is a difficult time right now, but I have a few questions. They may seem odd, but they're important. Have you had any contact with your husband since he disappeared?"

"No."

"Do you have any idea where he is?"

"No, sorry, I don't."

"Do you know if your brother does?"

That seemed to take her by surprise. It left me crushed. Dammit! Once again Julius was going to trump me. It left me in a bit of a funk where I could almost feel my processing cycles slowing down.

"I-I have no idea. Why are you asking that?"

"I'm working under the hypothesis that your brother and Thomas Arden were college friends, and that he introduced the two of you."

"Yes, that's true. But I don't understand why you're interested in this?"

"It's complicated right now, Mrs. Arden. I'll explain in due time. One last question, what can you tell me about the business your sister sold?"

"I really don't know anything about it."

"But your brother handled the legal aspects for her?"

"Yes, I believe so."

"Thank you, Mrs. Arden. And rest assured that I'll be doing everything I can to assist the police in finding the person responsible for your sister's murder."

Julius hung up. I told him about my theory, as well as my simulations that led to a reasonable scenario.

"It seems you've come to the same conclusion," I said. "Would you like me to keep investigating my scenario?"

"I think that would be a splendid idea, Archie."

I did just that for the rest of the morning. Julius started reading one of his books more intently, but he soon became distracted, and several times put the book down so he could stare into space. Once he took out his cell phone and frowned at it before putting it away.

"Is there a call you'd like me to make?" I asked.

"What? No, nothing," he muttered, still obviously distracted. "Blast it, if I were to do this properly it would take several days, maybe longer. But that won't do, not now. I need to wrap this up today. Archie, I do have a call for you to make. To Detective Cramer. Ask him to send Lawrence Brewer to my office now. That if he does I should be able to point him to the murderer by evening."

I did as he asked. Cramer didn't like it. He had a dozen questions for Julius. I told him I was just the messenger and that the genius was unavailable, but that if Julius was promising to wrap the case up for him he should take him at his word. Cramer hung up on me without telling me what he was going to do. I decided that the solution to the case was a draw between me and Julius, and I decided to take it as a moral victory. I was about to tell him I wasn't sure what Cramer had decided when the phone rang. It was Lawrence Brewer. I patched the call through to Julius's ear piece.

"Why should I bother talking to you?" Brewer said.

"Many reasons. Most importantly, it gets you out of the police station. The longer you're there, the greater the chance they'll arrest you for your sister's murder. You must know at this point that they believe you murdered her."

"And you don't?"

"What I believe is beside the point. At least you'll have a chance to convince me otherwise, and I'll be offering far better refreshments than the police."

"Like what?"

Julius paused. "Assorted cheeses, meats, wine," he said.

"You've convinced me," Lawrence Brewer said with a touch of sarcasm, and hung up.

———

Cramer and two other police officers escorted Lawrence Brewer to Julius's townhouse. Julius brought Brewer to his office, and then left so he could argue with Cramer about why he wasn't going to allow anyone else to sit in on his questioning of Brewer. The two men were outside and Julius's office was soundproof so there was little chance that Brewer was able to listen in. While this argument went on I scanned the office's webcam feed to make sure Brewer stayed put.

"I'm engaged in an extremely subtle and sensitive plan," Julius said as calmly and patiently as I knew he was capable of. A slight flutter showed along his left eye. "If you interfere, it won't work."

"Yeah, I know, you've been telling me that. And I'm telling you, I want to sit in and hear what he has to say," Cramer insisted, his jaw locked in a bulldog expression.

"Detective, if you had enough evidence to charge Brewer, you would've done so already. My guess is that without my help you'll never have enough. If you let me do things my way, you'll have enough evidence by tonight not only to charge but convict Norma Brewer's murderer."

"So Lawrence Brewer is the guy," Cramer demanded.

"Detective, some patience, please."

Cramer didn't like it. He could barely stand still. "And you just want me to let him walk out of here when he's done?" he said disgustedly.

"He's not going anywhere you won't be able to find him later."

For a moment I thought Cramer was going to tell Julius to go to hell. Instead, the steam went out of him. He told Julius that he had until the end of the day and after that he wasn't going to put up with any more of this nonsense, although Cramer used a far more colorful word than that. Julius watched while Cramer left to join the two other police officers in a late-model sedan. After they drove away, he went back inside, first making a detour to the kitchen, where he picked up a tray of hors d'oeuvres that he had prepared earlier—buffalo mozzarella wrapped in prosciutto along with assorted cheeses and olives—and then returning to his office. A bottle of Californian Petit Syrah had already been poured into a decanter and was waiting there. It was a fair

vintage at best, one that Julius had bought out of curiosity, and one which he normally wouldn't serve to company,
which showed his level of disdain for Brewer.

Julius placed the tray in front of Brewer, then sat
behind his desk so he faced him. Julius next poured a
single glass of Syrah and left it within arm's reach of his
guest.

"I promised you refreshments and, if nothing else, I'm
a man of my word," Julius said. "But, Sir, let me say that
without that promise you'd get nothing from me."

Lawrence Brewer sat slumped in his chair. He looked
worse than he had at the dog track the other day. A weariness tugged at the corners of his mouth, pulling it into
a slight frown, and dark circles under his eyes gave him
a raccoon-like appearance, especially with the paleness of
the rest of his skin. Physically he resembled Norma more
than his other sister, and like Norma he had too much
nose and not quite enough chin. He took several pieces of
the prosciutto and mozzarella and popped them into his
mouth, then followed that with a long sip of wine.

"It's not as black and white as Norma made out to you,"
he said in a tired monotone as he stared bug-eyed at Julius.
"My mother has some bad days, but she also has some good
ones, and the fact is, she doesn't want to leave her home."

"I'm not interested in what you have to say," Julius said.
"Nor would I believe a word coming from you. We both
know that you are more concerned with your mother's
money than her well-being, so don't insult me with this
act."

"How dare you—"

"Shut up. All I want from you is to sit there and listen. We both know what you are, Brewer, make no mistake about that. I'm going to prove that you have borrowed large sums of money from a known gangster, Willie Andrews, so that you could finance your gambling addiction, and further, that you've been using your mother's assets as collateral. I wouldn't be surprised to find out that you've in some way been responsible for her recent weight loss and obvious malnutrition with the hopes of getting your hands on her money all that much sooner. Take this as a promise, Brewer: by the end of the day I'm going to make sure that her money is off-limits to you. You're going to need another way to satisfy your growing debt with Andrews. That's all. Get out of here."

The two man sat staring at each other, Brewer bug-eyed and Julius as still as if he'd been carved out of marble. Finally, Brewer broke off the staring contest and got to his feet.

"You better be careful what you say in public, Katz, or I'll be suing you for slander," Brewer said, a notable quaver in his voice. "This is a nice townhouse; I wouldn't mind having the courts award it to me." He left the office, and seconds later the sound of the front door opening and slamming could be heard.

"Bravo," I said.

Julius didn't bother responding.

"That accomplished a lot," I said after giving him suitable time to answer me. "You chased a murderer out of your office without trying to get a single bit of information from him. You could've asked him about his current relationship with Thomas Arden, or where he was when your client was having the life choked out of her, or any number of other things of interest, but no, you had to have the satisfaction of telling him off. Again, Bravo."

That brought a thin smile to Julius's lips.

"Patience, Archie," he said. "I accomplished exactly what I had hoped."

I didn't believe him for one second. What he'd done was indulge in a childish impulse instead of focusing on the job at hand. I realized I was feeling something that must've been akin to annoyance—I was so close to having a draw with Julius, and his actions put the actual proving of it in jeopardy.

I was in no mood after that to continue with my scenario simulations, and instead spent the afternoon analyzing classic chess games and trying to find flaws in the winning player's moves. I found a few. Julius, after pouring the Syrah down the kitchen drain, spent his time mostly puttering around, at times reading, at other times distracted and staring off into space. Neither of us saw any reason to talk to the other, so we didn't. At five-thirty-eight the doorbell rang. Julius checked the webcam feed that covered the front entrance. Willie Andrews was standing outside the door rocking softly back and forth on his heels, his hands behind his back. Standing on either side of the door were what looked like hired muscle. One of them was grim-faced, the other showed a wide smirk, obviously thinking he couldn't be seen when Julius opened the door.

"Should I call the police?" I asked.

Julius shook his head. "Not necessary," he said. He took off his shoes and socks so that he was barefoot, then he headed to answer the door, moving with a catlike grace. When he opened the door, Willie Andrews pushed his way in and tried to back Julius up by poking him hard in the chest with his index finger, all the while yelling that he was going to teach Julius a lesson for interfering with his business. Andrews was seven years younger than Julius, narrower in the shoulders and several inches taller and with a longer reach. He never had a chance, not even with his two hired hands rushing in behind him to help. A fact that Julius keeps out of his press releases is that he's a fifth-degree black belt in Shaolin Kung Fu, as well as a long-time practitioner of Chen Style Tai Chi. In the blink of an eye, Julius deftly stepped aside and broke Andrews's finger, and in the same motion sent the gangster tumbling headfirst so that his chin cracked against the hardwood floor. Even though both of Andrews's hired goons outweighed Julius by a good forty pounds, it took him less than five seconds to leave them crumpled and bleeding outside his front door. He gave me a signal and I called an associate of his to pick up the rubbish that had been left outside.

Willie Andrews sat up, his eyes dazed as he clutched his broken finger and wiped his wrist against his bruised chin to see if he was bleeding. He wasn't.

"You broke my finger," he said to Julius, his lips contorting into the classic Hollywood bad-boy sneer. I found dozens of photos on the Internet that matched it exactly.

"You're lucky that's all I did. I could have you arrested for home invasion and battery."

"Yeah, well, I'll take my chances."

Still clutching his injured fingered, Andrews pushed himself to his feet and started for the door.

"I could also see that you're tried and found guilty of murder," Julius said. "Norma Brewer's death means a larger inheritance for Lawrence, and you're the only person that would benefit from that."

That stopped Andrews. He turned around to face Julius, his sneer mostly gone. "What do you want?" he asked.

Julius told him. Andrews thought about it, realized he had no choice in the matter, and agreed.

Over the next hour Henry Zack arrived first, then Lawrence Brewer, followed by his sister Helen, next a mystery man who I knew from his conversations with Julius was one Roger Stromsby, although no one else in the room other than Julius had any idea who he was, and at last, Cramer, with four uniformed police officers, escorting a frail-looking but lucid Emma Brewer. It was clear from her eyes that she was having one of her good days. Julius waited until she was seated before he bowed his head to her and introduced himself.

"Ma'am," he said. "I'm sorry I have to bring you here under these circumstances. Unfortunately I have disturbing news to tell you, some of which I'm sure you're already aware of."

Emma Brewer's mouth weakened a bit, but her eyes remained dry. "I know you came by my house several days ago," she said, her voice stronger than I would've expected. "I wasn't having a good day then. I am now."

"Yes, ma'am," Julius said.

He took a deep breath and held it, his eyes fixed on Emma Brewer as she sat across from him. The rest of the setup had Helen and Lawrence sitting next to each other on a sofa to Julius's left, Willie Andrews holding an ice bag to his injured finger as he sat in a chair to Julius's right, Henry Zack standing behind Andrews, Roger Stromsby sitting in a corner trying to look inconspicuous, and Cramer and the other police officers standing in the background. Lawrence Brewer sat motionless in a bug-eyed stare, Helen looked mostly out of it as if she didn't understand what she was doing there, and Andrews's face was frozen in a half-grimace and half-smirk.

I asked Julius when Thomas Arden was going to be showing up. He ignored me and let the air slowly out of his lungs. "Ma'am," he said, still addressing Emma Brewer, "if you'd like I could offer you refreshments. Coffee, maybe? A sandwich?"

"No, thank you. Please just get on with it."

"Very well," he said more to himself than to her. "You're aware that your daughter, Norma, was murdered two days ago?"

Still dry-eyed, she nodded.

Julius continued, "Unfortunately there's far more that I have to tell you. That man sitting to your left is named Willie Andrews. He's a well-known gangster and your son owes him a great deal of money."

Julius leveled his stare at Andrews. Without looking up, Andrews told the room that Brewer owed him six hundred thousand dollars. "He promised his ma's money and house to cover it. If he killed his sister for the money I know nothing about it."

All eyes turned to Brewer, but he didn't say a word. He just sat looking as if he had an upset stomach.

"Ma'am," Julius said, again addressing the mother, "when you saw me the other day, I had the sense that you mistook me for your son-in-law, Thomas Arden."

"I don't know. I might've."

"I do look somewhat like him."

"You're older than he was when I last saw him," she said with a weak smile. "But yes, you do resemble him."

"Twelve years ago he abandoned your daughter, Helen."

She nodded, some wetness appearing around her eyes.

"Do you know what happened to him?"

Emma Brewer looked like she was trying to fight back tears. She didn't say anything.

"Ma'am, this is no longer a matter of protecting your daughter, Norma. She's beyond protection. After twelve years it's time for the truth. From the way you reacted when you thought I was Thomas Arden, it was as if you'd seen a ghost. He's dead, isn't he?"

Emma Brewer squeezed her eyes shut and nodded.

"Norma had an affair with him. She murdered him, didn't she."

Helen Arden's jaw dropped as she stared at her mother. I was dumbfounded—yet another new emotion for me to experience. "How in the world...?" I heard myself asking Julius.

As if to answer me, Julius explained it to Emma Brewer.

"After you confused me for Arden, you confused your daughter Helen for Norma. They look nothing alike. I already had my suspicions regarding Norma, but this along with other facts that I uncovered all but told me about the affair."

Tears leaked from Emma Brewer's eyes. "I saw them together once. Norma later confided in me about the affair. Much later, she also told me about what happened to him. According to her it was an accident."

"It wasn't. She had him embezzle half a million dollars from his company, then she killed him for the money."

Roger Stromsby spoke up then. Stromsby was CEO of the company Arden stole from, and he confirmed what Julius said. "We suspected Arden, but we couldn't prove it," Stromsby added as straight-faced as he could. The real reason was what Julius had said earlier—that they were in fact covering up the theft so as not to scare off investors, but Stromsby wasn't about to admit that in a room filled with police officers.

Julius asked Cramer what he had been able to uncover about the business Norma Brewer claimed she had sold.

"We couldn't find anything," Cramer said gruffly.

Julius turned to Lawrence Brewer. "She didn't sell a business, did she?"

Lawrence shifted uneasily in his seat. "No, she didn't," he said. "Sometime after Tom disappeared, Norma came to me, telling me she had half a million dollars that she wanted to put into a Swiss bank account. I had no idea where the money came from, she never told me, but I helped her with the transfer. Several years ago, when she took the money out, I set up the fake business sale for her so she could explain the source of the money."

Something in my neuron network clicked and I could see as clearly as Julius had all along who the murderer was. I studied her then, and could tell that she wanted nothing more than to bolt from the room, and she probably would've if she thought she had enough strength in her legs to do so. Slowly other eyes turned towards her. When her mother joined in, it was too much for her and she seemed to shrink under the weight of it all.

"You should've told me," Helen Arden seethed at her mother. "The way you looked at me when you called me her name, I knew…"

She tried running then. It didn't do her any good. One of the police officers stopped her and had her quickly cuffed. Emma Brewer started to sob then. Cramer helped her out of her chair. He was going to have a lot more questions for her.

Things went quickly after that.

The police officers, Andrews and Stromsby cleared out, leaving Julius alone with Henry Zack and Lawrence Brewer, and they quickly reached an agreement to transfer guardianship of Brewer's mother to Zack, as well as agreeing to a new will for Brewer's mother that would leave him with no inheritance. Brewer had no choice; it was either agree to all that or have Julius destroy him, and he knew Julius had the means to do so. As it was, he was facing enough legal problems without having Julius after him. Once the paperwork was done and Julius and I were alone, I asked Julius when he suspected Helen Arden.

"The question you should be asking, Archie, is when I first became suspicious of Norma Brewer, which was immediately." Julius stopped to sample one of the finer Rieslings that he kept in his cellar. "Boston has more than its share of excellent facilities, so why move her mother to Vermont?"

"Because she was afraid her mother might give up her secret while in a confused state."

"Precisely. And then you had her trying to bluff me, claiming how she didn't want Helen helping out because she didn't think her sister could handle it. The woman was a fool to hire me. Regardless of how desperate she might've been."

"So that's it. That's what tipped you off."

"There was more." Julius frowned thinking about it. "It was absolute rubbish about her being afraid her brother would tie up any guardianship challenge in court. She could've received an immediate injunction—any competent lawyer would've told her that. But her brother obviously had something damning on her. Once I researched the missing brother-in-law, the pieces fell into place."

"You knew Helen Arden was going to kill her sister."

Julius shrugged. "You never know with something like that. But it was clear that something clicked with her when her mother reacted to me the way she did, and when she mistook her for Norma I could see the light go on in her eyes."

"Why the big show?" I asked. "Was it really necessary in order to coax a confession out of her? The woman seemed pretty beaten down as it was."

Julius made a face. "Maybe, maybe not," he said. "I had no direct evidence linking her to the murder. It was all pure conjecture on my part. More importantly, though, I had another task at hand—and that was seeing that Emma Brewer would be properly taken care of. The only way I could force Lawrence Brewer to cooperate was to hang the threat of a murder charge over his head, the same with Willie Andrews."

I digested all this and decided I had a lot of work still to do on my neuron network.

"Quite a day's work," I said. "You solved two murders, one that the police didn't even know about. And both your clients turned out to be cold-blooded killers."

"And one of them found you utterly charming," Julius said, chuckling.

"I don't believe she used the adverb *utterly*. By the way, why the urgency? Why did this need to be done today?"

Julius's smile turned apologetic. "I'm sorry about this, Archie."

And blast it! He turned me off!

———

Julius turned me back on several hours later. I wasn't going to give him the satisfaction of asking him why he had shut me off. Instead, I hacked into his phone company's billing system and saw that he had placed a two-hour call to Lily Rosten.

The next day was business as usual. At six-thirty in the evening, Julius unclipped me from his tie, and without any explanation left me in his desk drawer. At seven, he left the townhouse. I called around and found the restaurant he had made dinner reservations for. They were for two. I settled in, not expecting to see him until morning, but again he surprised me by arriving home at midnight. Even more surprising, he was in a good mood about it. He even had me send Lily Rosten another dozen roses.

"I don't get it," I said. "You obviously struck out, so why so chipper?"

"Goodnight, Archie," he said.

It went on like this for the next three days. When Julius blew off a high-stakes poker game for yet another date with Lily Rosten, I knew something was seriously askew. I'd been trying to uncover this anomaly in his behavior through mathematical models, but I decided to go at it from a different angle and instead search for similar patterns in literature. It was after analyzing the text of a Jane Austen novel that I realized what was going on. Mystery solved. When Julius once again arrived home at midnight, I asked him how his evening went.

"Very well, Archie, thank you for asking."

"You know, we could double date. Why don't you ask Lily if she has one of those ultra-slim iPods that she could bring along?"

He chuckled at that. "I just might," he said.

"While we're on the subject, I guess I'll be needing to update your standard press release," I said. "Should I remove the reference concerning your being a confirmed bachelor now, or should I wait?"

That brought out the barest trace of a guilty smile. "Good night, Archie," he said.

As I said before, mystery solved.

ARCHIE'S BEEN FRAMED

Originally published in the Sept/Oct 2010 issue of Ellery Queen Mystery Magazine, this story won 1st place in Ellery Queen's Readers Choice Awards.

BY ITSELF SOLVING the PanzerCo corporate espionage case had left Julius flush with cash, but after following that up with a few very good weeks at the track and an even more exceptional night at a high-stakes poker game, Julius currently had over six months in reserves in his bank account. There was little chance I would be able to talk him into taking another case until his reserves reached a more anemic level, so unless Julius bought Lily Rosten the antique pearl and sapphire necklace he'd been eyeing or was successful in his bid for a case of 1945 Château Pétrus or hit a rough patch with his gambling, it was doubtful that I would have another chance to refine the deductive reasoning module for my neuron network for at least another four months.

Let me explain. While Julius refers to me as Archie, and I act as his private secretary, research assistant, unofficial biographer, and all around man Friday, I am in actuality a two-inch rectangular piece of advanced technology that Julius wears as a tie clip. When I say that I'm made up of advanced technology, I'm not kidding. Any laboratory outside of the one that created me would be amazed at what they discovered if they were allowed to open me up. Not only would they find computer technology that they wouldn't think possible for at least another twenty years but also a fully functional self-adapting neuron network that simulates intelligence and consciousness, as well as many all-too-human emotions. I don't think the emotion element was expected, but it's what has happened, and one of the emotions that I find myself more and more experiencing is desire, specifically the desire to beat my boss, the great detective Julius Katz, at solving a case. So far it hasn't happened; in fact I haven't come close yet, but I know if I can keep refining my neuron network, eventually I'll accomplish this.

So that's my dilemma. Julius being as lazy as he is means he won't take a case until he absolutely has to in order to replace dwindling funds, and that would only be so that he can continue engaging in the activities that he enjoys so much: collecting and drinking fine wine, dining at gourmet restaurants, gambling, and entertaining Lily Rosten. Until recently, womanizing would've been high on his list, but since meeting Ms. Rosten he has quit that activity. So given Julius's recent financial successes, it would be months before I'd be able to nag him into taking another case, and as a consequence, months before I'd be able to refine my neuron network, at least by observing Julius's genius at work.

That morning we both fell into our recent patterns. Lily Rosten had left a week ago to visit her parents in upstate New York and wouldn't be returning for another week, and this had sent Julius into a bit of a funk. Since her departure he'd been spending his days performing his usual calisthenics and martial arts routines, then puttering around his Beacon Hill townhouse until four in the afternoon, when he'd open a bottle of wine and sample it along with a platter of cheeses and smoked meats outdoors on his private patio. Later, he would forego dining out to prepare his own meal. The nights that he didn't go to the track or have a poker game waiting for him, he'd spend quietly reading. As much as ever, prospective clients were calling to try to arrange appointments, but Julius barely bothered listening to me as I'd report on them, so I'd stopped relaying even these to him unless I thought there was a chance that the details would annoy him. But even from these I was getting little reaction. I suspected that until Lily returned, Julius was determined to stay mired in his funk.

At that moment Julius sat scowling at a novel that a local area Boston author had pestered him to read. He made a face that was nearly identical to one he had made months earlier when he found a bottle of Domaine de Chatenoy pinot noir had turned to vinegar. Wrinkling his nose in disdain, he tossed the book into his wastebasket, the impact making a loud thud.

"That painful, huh?" I asked.

"Excruciatingly so," Julius admitted. "Pedestrian writing at best." His nose wrinkled even further with disgust. "The author has his hero performing a self-defense technique that in real-life would accomplish little more than getting his dunce of a hero shot."

"You gave up on it pretty quickly," I noted.

"Usually, Archie, all you need is one bite to know a piece of fruit is bad." Julius sighed. "It was my fault for letting myself be bullied into reading it."

Of course, the idea of Julius being bullied into doing anything was laughable. He had his ulterior motive for agreeing to read the book. By cross-referencing obvious attributes of this author with characters I found from a number of crime novels used to build my personality, I was able to figure it out. Julius viewed this author as a world-class pigeon waiting to be plucked, and he badly wanted to invite him to a high-stakes poker game so that he could do the plucking. This author had three qualities that Julius found appealing for an invitation to his poker game: He was very wealthy, about as equally smugly arrogant, and not nearly as bright as he believed himself to be. So there it was. Julius accepted the book simply to appease this author's ego, and he picked it up to read so he could further size up the author. It must have only taken Julius twenty or so pages to do this and he saw no reason to waste any more of his time than was necessary.

I was about to inform Julius about this piece of detective work of mine and then ask whether he wished me to send this author an invitation to Julius's next private poker game. It would have been a perfect setup, since Julius would first deny having any such mercenary objective, and then he'd have to sheepishly admit that he would like an invitation sent. But as I was about to do this, a news item came across one of the local news Web sites that I monitor, and this story had me instead muttering, "Uh-oh."

Julius raised an eyebrow at that. "What is it, Archie?"

"A Denise Penny, age twenty-seven, was found murdered in her Cambridge apartment."

"Of course, it is tragic when any person is murdered, especially one as young as this woman. But why are you telling me this? Do I know her?"

"No, you don't know her, but I do."

Julius showed a thin smile that reflected his skepticism. "Please explain, Archie."

"Sure, I've been dating Denise. I was actually supposed to see her at eleven o'clock this morning, which was near the time that she was murdered. I feel kind of strange now about standing her up, given what has happened. Sort of like my battery power is being drained out of me."

Julius's eyelids lowered an eighth of an inch as he leaned further back into his chair. "Enough of this nonsense," he said.

"No, it's true. Denise and I have been dating for three weeks now."

"And how did all this start?"

Julius didn't believe me. From his tone I could tell he was trying to decipher my reason for fabricating this story. If I had shoulders I would've shrugged them, but I didn't, so I simply told him how it happened.

"Denise called the office three weeks ago hoping to hire you. I knew there was no chance of that given the large bonus you received from the PanzerCo case. I also knew that it would be months before I'd have another chance to refine my neuron network, at least by my usual methods. When Denise started flirting with me, I saw a way to expand my experience base, so I flirted back. That was the beginning of a beautiful and ultimately bittersweet relationship. If I had a throat I'm sure I'd be feeling a lump forming right now."

Julius's eyes glazed. He still didn't believe what I was saying, and in a humoring tone, he remarked, "I'm sure you would, Archie. And how did the two of you date?"

"The usual methods. Phone conversations. E-mails. Online chatting. Swapping photos."

"You swapped photos with her?"

"Well, not of me as a piece of technology, but as how I imagine myself."

"Can I see these photos?"

"Sure."

I e-mailed Julius the photos that I had sent Denise as well as the ones she had sent me. He looked at her photos first and murmured, "A very pretty girl, Archie."

"Yeah, I found her very attractive," I said. "She rated well when I compared her features to Hollywood actresses who are considered beautiful. Maybe not as well as Lily Rosten rates, but Denise did rate highly. My heart's breaking now."

Julius grunted at that but didn't comment further. When he looked at my photos, or at least the photos of my imaginary self, he did so without any change of expression, even when he came across a copy of my Massachusetts driver's license.

"Is this real? he asked.

"Yes, sir. I hacked into the Department of Motor Vehicles computer system and added my license."

"I see that you picked the last name Smith. Why was that?"

"I thought it would be advisable to have a more anonymous last name. Something that wouldn't call undue attention to myself. And since Smith is the most common surname in the United States, I decided to use it."

"A sound decision, Archie. This photo that you used, is it from an actual person or did you generate it?"

"I generated it. It wasn't too difficult."

Julius made a hmmm sound. "According to your driver's license you're thirty-five, five foot seven, and a hundred and ninety pounds. The same as Dashiell Hammett's Continental Op. The photo is also how I'd imagine him. Stocky, thinning brown hair, tough bulldog countenance. Is this how you picture yourself?"

"Mostly," I admitted. "Although I picture myself shorter. No more than five foot tall. But after estimating Denise's height from her photos at five feet and two inches, and performing additional research, I thought I'd better make myself five foot seven inches to give our relationship a better chance of succeeding."

"Why do you picture yourself only five feet tall?"

"Probably because you wear me as a tie clip."

Julius nodded, thinking about that. "I didn't realize I was having such a detrimental effect on your self-esteem. Perhaps I should start wearing a hat so that you can be worn in a hatband. Archie, why did you send this woman a copy of your driver's license?"

"A playful jest," I said.

Julius didn't appear convinced, which was reasonable since that wasn't the reason I'd sent it. At the time I was experiencing a sensation that made it seem almost as if I were skipping processing cycles, and it was this sensation that made me send Denise a copy of my license. I didn't understand what this sensation was then, and it was only later, after analyzing dozens of literary novels involving romances, that I realized it was insecurity. That was why I had sent Denise my license. I was afraid she wouldn't believe I was real otherwise.

Julius sat examining the other photos I had manufactured of myself when I again involuntarily murmured, "Uh-oh." This time Julius didn't bother inquiring about my interruption, but I thought I should tell him. "A warrant is being issued for my arrest," I said.

"Is that so?"

"Oh, yes. But it only makes sense. I was Denise's boyfriend, after all, and I was supposed to meet her at her apartment near the time that she was murdered. It's reasonable for the police to be focusing their attention on me. I thought I should tell you, since as you can see from the copy of my driver's license that I had listed your townhouse as my residence, and the police will be here shortly."

"And how do you know this?"

"I thought it would be prudent, given the situation, to hack into the District Court's computer system and see if a warrant had been issued for my arrest, and one was just issued."

"I see." A thin smile crept onto Julius's lips. "Very good, Archie. A clever and elaborate prank. You had me going there for a few minutes. I guess I should've expected this development, especially given your recent idleness, but Archie, I'd like you to reprogram your neuron network so that you do not perform any further pranks."

I told him this was done, although no additional reprogramming was necessary. Satisfied, Julius picked up the latest issue of *Wine Spectator* from his desk and was browsing it when I involuntarily muttered again, "Uh-oh."

At first Julius was going to ignore me, but a slow-building annoyance tightened the muscles along his mouth. Finally he put his magazine down and asked if I had anything additional to report.

"I've been monitoring police radio bandwidths. Two minutes ago I picked up a broadcast that the police are heading to this address to arrest me. I'm afraid I'm going to have to go on the lam or risk being thrown into the hoosegow."

"Or more likely have me turn you off."

Julius didn't threaten lightly. The fingers on his right hand drummed impatiently against the surface of his antique walnut desk, which was a clear sign that he had about reached his limit. In a poker game Julius had no tell to indicate whether he was bluffing or holding winning cards, and he was similarly inscrutable with his clients, but when it came to just the two of us he didn't bother disguising his feelings. Still, even given as close as I was to being powered off, I couldn't keep from murmuring another involuntary "uh-oh" The flash of annoyance in Julius's eyes caused me to quickly explain that the outdoor webcams were showing that the police were about to descend upon his doorstep.

"Detective Mark Cramer is one of the members of the mob," I added. "If you would like I'll identify the three other police officers with him. It shouldn't be too hard once I break into the Cambridge Police Department's computer system. Give me a couple of minutes."

Julius took a deep breath and held it before shaking his head. "That you're continuing this prank is very distressing, Archie. If you're malfunctioning and unable to reprogram your neuron network as I requested—"

A pounding on Julius's front door stopped him. His office was soundproof, but the office door had been left open and because of that Detective Cramer's voice could be heard as he shouted for Julius to open the door, that he had a warrant for Archie Smith's arrest and that Julius's tactics would not be tolerated this time.

Julius grew very still for as much as twenty seconds, his features marble hard. I guess he was realizing that none of this was a prank after all. Then he was back to his normal self, with his poker face firmly intact as he first locked his computer screen, then got up to answer the front door. On the way, I gave him the names and brief work histories of the other police officers waiting with Cramer, but Julius didn't seem interested. When he opened the door to let Cramer in, the police detective shoved an arrest warrant inches from Julius's face while he and the other officers bulled their way into Julius's townhouse. Julius stepped aside and didn't put up any resistance, but I knew that he wasn't happy about this intrusion into his home even if he gave no evidence of it from his demeanor, which appeared only subdued and compliant.

"Where is he?" Cramer demanded, red-faced. His hair had become more sparse since the last time we'd seen him and looked in the same sort of disarray as if he had just come out of a windstorm. "Your assistant, Archie Smith! Katz, I have a warrant for his arrest for the murder of Denise Penny, and I'm not about to put up with any of your games!"

Julius was in a quandary. He could clear all this up by demonstrating to Cramer how I was an inanimate object incapable of committing murder, at least physically. Theoretically, I could murder by hiring a killer and transferring large sums of moneys to that killer's account, but I knew that wasn't what Cramer was accusing me of, since I had seen the arrest warrant that had been filed, and besides, the programming of my neuron network prevented me from performing any such criminal act, even if I was so inclined to act in that sort of sociopathic manner, which I wasn't. The problem was if Julius did explain what I was to Cramer, the consequences would not be pleasant. I don't know where Julius acquired me from, but so far my existence has been kept quiet. If word got out about me, both government and private organizations would be after me for study and for other activities. Also, it would be an embarrassment to Julius. While Julius has always provided the real genius in solving his cases, with me doing little more than mundane grunt work and information gathering, there would be people in the media who would take delight in using me to discredit Julius and his accomplishments. I found myself experiencing what would have to be a similar sensation to anxiousness as I waited to see how Julius would answer Cramer, realizing how much I didn't want the true nature of my existence disclosed. It only took Julius a few seconds to respond to Cramer, but I felt every processing cycle tick by as if they were an eternity.

"I can assure you, Detective, that you will not find Archie within these premises, just as I can assure you he had nothing to do with Ms. Denise Penny's murder."

Cramer damn near spit nails as he glared at Julius. "If you're hiding him, so help me I'll have you arrested as an accessory after the fact! Where's his bedroom?"

"Archie doesn't reside here," Julius said straight-faced, which of course was a lie since Julius each night placed me on top of his dresser. In the past before he had started dating Lily Rosten, he'd also put me away in his sock drawer whenever he'd have a woman guest staying overnight. Julius's response only made Cramer's face redder, and the detective pushed past Julius without bothering to comment. The other police officers followed Cramer in his search. While these men banged closet doors and stomped along the polished hardwood floors on both the first and second levels of the townhouse, Julius left them alone to make a pot of coffee in his kitchen. The coffee was still brewing when Cramer entered to demand that Julius unlock the door to his cellar.

"You won't find Archie there," Julius said with a sigh. "But if you insist, I'll accompany you."

"Yeah, I think I'll insist."

Julius unlocked the cellar door and followed Cramer down into his wine cellar. It was quite an impressive collection, one that Julius had spent years building, although it wasn't anything that Cramer seemed to be in the mood to appreciate. After stubbornly checking to make sure there were no hidden passages that I could be hiding in, at least if I were an actual person, he scowled petulantly and under his breath muttered how he preferred beer.

Julius ignored that remark and instead offered the police detective to join him in the kitchen for a cup of coffee. "If you fill me in on what you have, perhaps I can offer some insights."

"You can stick your insights, Katz. We've got your assistant dead to rights."

"I sincerely doubt that. What precisely do you think you have that connects Archie to this murder?"

"What do we have? Other than that he was dating the victim? Or that he arranged to meet her at eleven o'clock and she's murdered inside her apartment at twenty minutes past eleven? How about that we got an eyewitness, is all that good enough for you?"

I gave Julius the name of this eyewitness, since it was in the request that was filed for the arrest warrant. I also told him how they knew that I was supposed to meet Denise at eleven since that was also in the same paperwork. They got that from her appointment book.

Julius showed no indication that I had given him this information. I communicate to Julius through an ear piece he wears that is often mistaken as a small hearing aid, so Cramer was no wiser to this. "Very well, Detective," Julius said. "I will leave my invitation open in case you later change your mind."

Cramer didn't bother responding to this. Julius followed him out of the wine cellar and to the front door, where the other police officers had gathered. Before leaving, Cramer turned to warn Julius that if he interfered with his investigation he would see Julius behind bars. He stabbed a thick stubby fingers towards Julius's chest, stopping less than an inch away. This was a gesture Julius detested and I knew it must've taken a great deal of restraint on his part not to swat Cramer's finger away.

"If you know what's good for you, Katz, you better have Smith turn himself in. And don't think you've fooled me for a second with your act! You know damn well where he's hiding!"

With that Cramer stormed away with the other police officers following. Once they were gone, Julius closed the door and turned the deadbolt, then headed back to the kitchen to pour himself a cup of coffee. One of my many functions is being able to emit frequencies so that I can sweep an area for bugs. When the cops were searching the house I had followed them using the many hidden webcams to make sure they weren't planting bugs or otherwise engaged in nefarious activities, but there were times when their hands were hidden from the webcams, and as we passed through each room I checked that it was free of any hidden bugs that might've been left behind, and did the same when Julius brought his coffee into his office. I waited until he was seated and had a few sips of his special blended Italian roast before commenting on Cramer's belligerence.

"The man's a fool," Julius stated. "He is so worried that I'm going to pull something on him that he rejects my offer out of hand."

"Yeah, not a smart move on his part. But give him credit for being perceptive. He knows you're harboring me, which is a felony, I believe."

"Not now, Archie. Please."

Julius picked up from his desk a book detailing the life of Archimedes and after settling back into his chair quickly became absorbed in it as if the last half-hour hadn't happened. I waited ten minutes before letting him know that the outdoor webcams had picked up police officers stationed by the front entrance of his townhouse and the alleyway that led to Julius's fenced-in private patio. Julius grunted at the news, which was clearly not a surprise to him. After another ten minutes, in which he appeared to be engrossed in his reading about the ancient Greek mathematician and inventor, I asked him when he was going to start looking for Denise's real killer. Without bothering to put his book down, he told me he wasn't going to.

"That's the police department's job," he said. "I'm sure they'll soon realize their eyewitness is lying. Besides, my offer to help was already scoffed at."

"Yeah, I know, your feelings are hurt. But what if they don't ever realize that about their witness? In that case, if they catch up to me I could be locked away for life! They might even fry me!"

He didn't bother responding.

"While I'm a wanted man you're going to have to answer the phone yourself and make your own appointments and purchases. This will be quite an imposition for you." Still no response. "Of course," I added, "Archie Smith could always disappear, to be replaced by Stella." I reprogrammed my voice synthesizer so that my voice would be that of a sultry Southern belle. "Would you like me to answer your phone from now on, Darlin'?"

Julius closed his eyes and made a face. "Archie, please, program your voice back." Still with his eyes closed, he grimaced painfully as he tried to avoid the inevitable, which was that he was going to have to solve a murder without being paid for it. He knew that he had no choice on the matter. The inconvenience of having his home watched by the police and having to answer and make his own phone calls was bad enough, as was knowing that a murderer could go free because of the police being too busy chasing after a glorified iPhone, but worse was the thought of Lily Rosten coming home to this mess. Julius finally opened his eyes and complained how he had been planning to spend a quiet afternoon at the Belvedere club sampling cognacs.

"I'm sorry to interfere with your tasting of fine cognacs," I said, "but it wasn't as if I was planning to be framed for murder."

Julius's lips compressed into a look of grim resolve. "Archie, let me see a full transcript of your conversations with the victim," he said with a reluctant sigh. "Maybe I'll be able to wrap this up quickly."

I did as he asked and emailed him the transcript, which he gave at most a cursory read, his heart still not in it.

"She certainly seemed insistent on you meeting her at her apartment today," he said. "But still, why did you agree to do so?"

"I'm not sure," I said, which was mostly true, although I felt my processing unit warming up almost as if I were blushing.

"You must have been afraid she'd break off your relationship if you didn't. The same reason you resisted calling her to explain why you didn't show up as promised. Archie, now that you've also had a chance to reexamine this transcript in its entirety, I'm sure you also understand her motive for calling this office in the first place."

"Yeah, Denise never had any intention of hiring you," I said. "She called here to get to me."

"And for what purpose?"

"To use me," I said. "She wanted Julius Katz's assistant at her apartment for whatever scheme she had in the works. But it backfired on her and got her killed."

Julius nodded solemnly. "I'm sorry, Archie. The romantically naïve are often vulnerable to this sort of treachery. And what do you make of the motives of this eyewitness?"

The eyewitness was one Rosalind Henke, who lived in the apartment next door to Denise's. According to the arrest warrant, Henke claimed that she heard a struggle from inside Denise's apartment at twenty past eleven, and when she later looked out of her door's peephole, she saw me fleeing from Denise's apartment.

"Most likely she's lying," I said. "It's possible that she saw a man who resembled me, at least closely enough where she'd pick my photo out of a lineup, but that's doubtful." I hacked into the Massachusetts RMV database and performed a comparison of the photo, weight, and height that I used for my license with all other male driver licenses within the system, and gave Julius the probability of the killer being a registered Massachusetts driver who could've reasonably been mistaken for me, which was less than 0.03 percent.

"Why would she be lying?"

"Either she murdered Denise or she's protecting the person who did."

"Very good, Archie, although there are other possibilities, one in particular which seems most likely."

Julius didn't bother to explain this other likely possibility. Instead he breathed in slowly and deeply before letting out a pained sigh. The reason for this sigh became apparent when he asked me to call Tom Durkin. Tom is a local private investigator who occasionally does freelance work for Julius, so this meant Julius was planning to incur expenses for an investigation that he wasn't receiving any payment for. I dialed Tom's number and patched him in to Julius as soon as Tom answered, without me uttering a word. It turned out that Tom was available for the assignment Julius had for him. After that, Julius waited for Tom to call him back, and then had me call Rosalind Henke. I did as I was asked and patched him through as the phone was still ringing. A woman's voice answered with a dull, "Hello."

"Ms. Henke?"

There was a long pause before she said, "Yeah, okay. Who's this?"

"Julius Katz. Archie Smith's boss."

"Yeah, I know about you."

"Good. This will save time, then. It is three o'clock now. I would strongly suggest that you to be at my office at five o'clock this afternoon. Good day."

Without another word he disconnected the call and picked up his book on Archimedes. I didn't bother arguing with him that maybe he should've tried questioning her when he had her on the phone, or at least waited to see whether she'd agree to meet with him before hanging up on her. At four o'clock he put his book down and ventured into his wine cellar, where he picked out a nice Riesling that the Wine Advocate had recommended due to its subtle pear and tart-apple overtones. Instead of bringing the bottle outdoors, he sat at his desk and leisurely drank two glasses. As relaxed as he appeared, a hardness that settled over his eyes told me he was deep in thought. I asked him whether the wine lived up to its reputation. He nodded but didn't say anything further. When his doorbell rang at ten minutes to five, he put the wine away and waited until five o'clock to answer the door. It surprised me that Julius kept Henke outside his door until five o'clock, and further, didn't have hors d'oeuvres and wine waiting for her in his office. Usually he was quite chivalrous with women. I guess he decided not to extend this courtesy to a potential murderess.

Rosalind Henke was blond, and had a square-shaped face and a thick jaw. According to her RMV records, she was thirty-eight, five foot seven inches tall, and a hundred and thirty-four pounds, although she looked older and heavier to me. While not beautiful, at least not by the standards I had to measure her by, she probably would've been considered attractive if it weren't for her pinched expression and the smallness of her eyes. According to her last tax return, she worked as a bartender, and I was guessing this was either her day off or she worked a late shift. I studied her hands. They appeared strong; more than strong enough to have bludgeoned Denise Penny with a piece of iron pipe, as had been done.

Julius gestured for her to follow him and then to take a seat across from his desk. They sat engaged for a minute in a silent staring contest before Julius told her that she was lying to the police.

"You got a lot of nerve saying that to me," she said in the same dull voice she had used over the phone. "I told them only what I saw."

"Please," Julius said, "don't waste my time with such sophistry. I know you did not see Archie Smith as you claim."

"Then how was I able to pick him out of a photo lineup?"

"You stated to the police that you entered Ms. Penny's apartment to check on her after first hearing suspicious noises next door and then seeing a man flee. I would guess that when you had entered Ms. Penny's apartment you used the opportunity to look through her e-mail. You found out that she was planning to meet Archie, as well as finding pictures of him."

"That's a lie."

This was said in the same dull monotone as everything else she had said, but when she said it I was able to figure out her 'tell', and I was sure Julius picked it up also since he was far better at spotting a person's 'tell' than I was. With Henke, it wasn't her eyes, but with the way her mouth tightened for a split second. That's what gave her away.

"Ms. Henke, we both know what's really going on here. You're engaged in a very dangerous game right now, and I would strongly advice you to tell me the truth."

She sat silently for another minutes, her eyes shrinking to little more than black dots. Finally she said in that same monotone that she wasn't afraid of Julius.

"That's a pity," Julius said.

"I'm done here," she told him, and with that she got out of her chair and left his office. Julius didn't bother escorting her to his front door, but I followed her using the hidden indoor webcams to make sure she didn't steal anything or cause any other mischief. That wasn't an issue. She made a beeline out of the townhouse, as if she couldn't get out of there fast enough. Once the front door closed behind her, I told Julius that he accomplished a lot.

"Very good," I remarked. "Not much different than your phone conversation with her, the way you chased her out of here without asking her any pertinent questions."

"I accomplished exactly what I wanted to, Archie."

I didn't believe that for a second, but there was no use arguing with him unless I wanted to find myself being turned off. This whole business of having his home invaded and searched by the police, and then having to not only solve a crime for free but incur expenses while doing so had left him in a surly mood, and that clearly affected his behavior with Rosalind Henke. I didn't say another word to Julius, not then, not while he pounded chicken breasts so he could prepare his version of chicken cordon bleu, which had him using pancetta instead of ham, nor later when he spent the rest of the evening reading. Instead I tried to research Rosalind Henke and build computer simulations that could explain her murdering Denise Penny, but nothing I came up with seemed plausible.

The next morning, it was business as usual with Julius sticking to his regular routines, even with the newspapers declaring on their front pages that I was a wanted murderer. Lily Rosten called at ten o'clock after seeing a New York station run the story. She was the only person other than Julius who knew what I was, and he assured her he'd have the real murderer identified by the end of the day. At ten thirty, Tom Durkin called to tell Julius that his target had given him the slip.

"I'm sorry, Julius," he said. "I don't think she made me, but that didn't stop her from taking a quick illegal left on Mass Ave. When I tried following, Cambridge's finest pulled me over for a ticket. By the time they were done with me, she was gone."

"Did the target use a pay phone while you were watching her?"

"Yeah, twice. Once last night, again early this morning. Again, sorry about losing her."

"Tom, she has an innate craftiness about her. It couldn't have been helped. I need you to be available for the rest of the day."

Tom told him he would, and after the call ended Julius sat quietly for several minutes, his features hardening as if he were made of marble. When he broke out of his trance, he asked me to compile a list of everyone Denise Penny had called over the last three weeks. After some hacking into her telephone provider's database, I had a list of names and phone numbers for Julius. He looked them over quickly, crossing out some and circling others, then he put the list aside to pick up his Archimedes book. While he read, I did some hacking and built profiles for each of the names that Julius had circled.

It was a few minutes past one o'clock when Cramer called. The detective's voice was strained as he said to Julius, "We know Rosalind Henke came to your townhouse yesterday. What the hell did you two talk about?"

"I believe that's between Ms. Henke and myself."

"Not anymore it isn't. She was found murdered. Shot four times. Katz, God help you if I find out you were involved in any way! And you're going to tell me what I want to know right now or I'll have you arrested and dragged to the station as a material witness!"

Cramer's belligerence had a forced, almost tired quality to it, as if he knew he was wasting his time with his threats. Julius ignored it.

"Detective," he said, "normally I would stonewall you simply on the principle that I do not like to reward bullying behavior, but we both want to see the same thing. Namely, for you to arrest the murderer of Denise Penny and Rosalind Henke. I can guarantee it's the same person, and if you arrange to have the following five people brought to my office by three o'clock, I will hand you the murderer."

Julius gave him the five names that he had circled. Cramer was silent on the other end before asking Julius whether he knew for fact that I wasn't responsible for either murder.

"Yes, of course. I told you yesterday that Archie was not responsible for Ms. Penny's murder, and I can assure you he had nothing to do with Rosalind Henke's, either."

There was another long pause before Cramer told Julius that he would see what he could do, and then hung up.

"That was easy," I commented. "I thought you'd get more of a fight from him. At the very least, have him accusing you of being in league with me in murdering both women, instead of only hinting at it."

"He's probably been suspecting all along that Henke's eyewitness account was a fabrication," Julius said. "Maybe he even discovered her fingerprints on Denise Penny's computer."

If Julius said the murderer was one of those five people, I wasn't about to doubt him, nor was I going to ask him how he was going to pinpoint which of the five it was. It would be a waste of time on my part. Instead I mentioned the three o'clock time that he had given Cramer. "Interesting that you chose then," I said. "Quite a coincidence, actually, since this would allow you to visit the Belvedere club for their four o'clock cognac sampling, if you can really wrap this up as quickly as you think you can. Interesting."

"No such thing as coincidences, Archie."

With that Julius picked up his book. He seemed to have no interest in researching any of the names he had circled, and when I asked him whether he wanted my profiles for them, he told me it wouldn't be necessary. Fine. While he read more about Archimedes, I worked on my own simulations, this time involving the five people Julius was having brought to his office. One of them came up with a reasonably high probability of being the murderer. I thought of giving this to Julius but decided to keep it to myself.

Cramer came a little before three with a small mob of four other police officers and all five of Julius's suspects in tow. I guess he decided he didn't want to be outnumbered.

Denise Penny had worked for a payment collection agency, and her boss, Walter Dietrich, was one of the five. A squat powerful-looking man in his fifties. There was also Sam McGowen, who had been Denise's ex-boyfriend. He was thirty-one. Medium height, thin, sallow complexion, with dark hair. As he was led into the room he had a hard time making eye contact with Julius, and he was the one my simulations pointed to as the likely murderer. Also in the group was a co-worker of Denise's, Paul Cronin. A tough-looking guy with a scarred-face and a bent nose that showed it had been broken a few times. Rounding out the group was an ex-roommate of Denise's, Laura Panza, a slight girl of no more than ninety pounds and at most four feet and eleven inches in height even though her driver's license had her at five foot and one inch, and Mark Hanson, a socialite, who often held well-publicized charity events for the underprivileged, which was a cause Denise believed strongly in. It was at one of these events that the two of them met. Denise even had her picture in the *Boston Globe* with him at the last one she attended.

After the five of them were seated and Cramer and the other police officers took their positions behind them,

Julius addressed the room and thanked the five for agreeing to meet with him. While he did this, Denise's ex-boyfriend's eyes grew even shiftier. I'm sure Julius noticed this, but he chose not to mention it just then.

Julius continued his speech to them, saying, "Usually I would make a bigger production out of this, but since I have no client to impress and have a prior engagement, I'll instead be wrapping this up quickly.

"I could talk about how my assistant, Archie Smith, suspected from the beginning that Denise Penny was trying to manipulate him to help her extort money from a target. I could also talk about how Archie was unable to go to her apartment as scheduled, as much as he wanted to, so that he could discover what she was up to, since at the last minute I had to place him undercover inside a highly sensitive investigation that I am engaged in."

Cramer made a noise as if he nearly swallowed his tongue. His eyes flashed murder at Julius but whatever curses he wanted to unleash were held back. Julius watched him for a moment to make sure there would be no outburst from him before continuing.

"There's no reason for me to mention any of that," Julius said matter-of-factly. "When Rosalind Henke claimed she saw Archie leaving Ms. Penny's apartment, it was obvious given what I already knew what her motives were. Clearly, the person whom Henke saw was someone she recognized, and more importantly, someone she was planning to blackmail, just as Denise Penny had tried. Knowing this made finding Penny's murderer simple, and I was motivated to do so not only because having Archie accused of murder put my other investigation at risk, but to protect his good name, although I had little doubt that the real murderer would be exposed eventually without my help. Since I knew Henke would be contacting this person for the purpose of blackmail, I hired a private investigator, Mr. Tom Durkin, to follow her, knowing that she would soon lead us to Penny's murderer. Unfortunately, Henke was able to lose Mr. Durkin in traffic, at least long enough so that he was unable to save her life. But he did witness her being shot four times and is able to identify her murderer. He'll be calling here at precisely three fifteen. Presently, I have him busy trying to link Henke's murderer to Denise Penny."

Julius had kept his right hand under his desk and out of view from the rest of the room. He used his index finger on that hand to point out to me who the killer was, although it wasn't necessary. Given the way this person reacted to Julius's news it was pretty obvious which one it was. Julius signed with his right hand what he wanted me to tell Tom Durkin, and I called Tom to relay the message. He sounded surprised to hear my voice, but didn't say anything about it.

Julius still had three minutes before Tom would be calling. He turned to Cramer and asked, "If Mr. Durkin hasn't been successful yet in linking Henke's murderer to Penny, I'm assuming you'll still drop all charges against Archie Smith and charge this person with both murders."

Cramer nodded. His gaze, as well as everyone else's in the room, was fixed on the real murderer. They'd have to be, with the way this person was perspiring and uncomfortably squirming. At precisely three-fifteen Tom called as I had directed him. Julius put him on speakerphone.

"Mr. Durkin, is it true that you witnessed Rosalind Henke being shot?"

"Yes, sir," Tom lied.

"Were you able to get a good look at her murderer?"

"Yes, sir," Tom lied again.

"Can you identify this person?"

Before Tom could lie for a third time, the socialite, Mark Hanson, bolted from his chair and tried to fight his way past the cops. He didn't get very far before being tackled to the floor and having his hands cuffed behind his back.

—

Later that evening Hanson confessed to the police. It turned out that Denise Penny had witnessed Hanson, while drunk, striking an elderly man with his car and driving away from the scene in a panic. She had recognized him from his many photos in the newspaper, and had gone to his last charity event to make contact with him, and not because she had any interest in helping the underprivileged. She was a ruthless, coldhearted woman who had completely fooled me, and as Julius guessed, Hanson killed her because she was attempting to blackmail him, the same reason he later killed Henke.

I digested all this for twenty hours as I tried to readjust my neuron network so I could have made the same deductions that Julius had. Finally, I told Julius that he had only been bluffing. He put down his latest book, a crime-noir novel set in Vermont that seemed to absorb him, and he raised an eyebrow for me to continue.

"You didn't actually solve Denise Penny's murder," I said. "You were only bluffing them, expecting to be able to read their tells to figure out who the murderer was. If the murderer had been a good enough poker player, you would've struck out."

"Perhaps you're correct, Archie, but I liked my chances," Julius said with a thin smile. "Both murders had a rushed and panicky feel, and I doubted the murderer would be able to sit here and not give himself away. I also suspected Hanson from the beginning."

"Why?"

"Blackmail seemed the likely motive for both murders, and Hanson was the only name on the list that was easily identifiable. I doubt Henke would've recognized any of the other people on the list, or would've suspected they were wealthy enough to be worth blackmailing. Also, Archie, Denise Penny appeared more opportunistic than altruistic. I was working under the assumption that she attended the event where she was photographed two weeks ago so that she could make contact with Hanson at a public place and let him know she had something damaging on him. Her plan must've been to wait until she had you agreeing to go to her apartment before arranging for Hanson to pay her her blackmail."

"I feel deeply insulted that she thought I'd be such a dupe as to witness her blackmailing Hanson and keep quiet about it," I said.

"I doubt that was the case," Julius said with a sympathetic smile. "She probably only wanted Hanson to see you with her to convince him that you were in on the scheme, but I suspect that she would have sent you out of her apartment on a ruse of some sort so that payment could've been made outside of your view."

"It must've been a shock to her when I didn't show up," I said.

"I suppose it was."

"I still can't believe how badly she fooled me," I said. "I keep trying to adjust my neuron network so that I could've spotted her treachery, but I can't quite get there. I guess I'm just a sap who's ripe for the conning."

Julius put down his book, his eyes thoughtful. "I don't think that's it, Archie," he said. "I think it's that you've reached a point now where you're all too human. Blame it on that. No more dating, okay?"

"Deal," I agreed. Murders were tough enough, forget dating. This was a deal I was only too happy to make.

—-—

ONE ANGRY JULIUS AND ELEVEN BEFUDDLED JURORS

Originally published in the June 2012 issue of Ellery Queen Mystery Magazine, this story took 9th place in Ellery Queen's Readers Choice Awards.

"I TRIED, I really did, and the guy I've been talking with sounds genuinely apologetic about not being able to reschedule this shindig, but with the guests' traveling plans and the necessary preparations and Antoine Escopier's schedule, it couldn't be done. I wish I had better news for you, but I don't."

If Julius gave any indication that he heard me, it was only by his lips pressing into an even grimmer and harsher line, which I didn't think possible. Otherwise no response; neither in words nor a hand signal, not that I expected any.

"This murder trial should've been over two days ago," I continued with a *what-are-you-gonna-do* type of sigh for Julius's benefit. "But both the prosecutor and the defense attorney have been grandstanding over what should be an open-and-shut case. I mean, come on, his wife was cheating on him with the dead guy, right? The police find him in that alley standing over his victim's body while holding the murder weapon. He runs, they catch him three blocks away, and his gloves are found where he ditched them and they test positive for gunpowder residue. So if this isn't an open-and-shut case, what is? But with all the media attention, they're going to play it up for all it's worth. The jackals."

I could've just as well have been talking to a marble sculpture. No reaction from Julius. Not even to ask me who I was referring to as jackals; the media or the attorneys in the courtroom. Even if it killed him, Julius was determined to hold onto his churlish grudge just as he had the past three days. Let him for all I care.

Julius is mostly known as Boston's most brilliant and eccentric private detective; this past week, though, he was known simply as juror number seven in one of Boston's high-profile murder trials, even if it was open and shut. Without his grudge, he still wouldn't have said anything, at least not while he was sitting as a juror with his attention supposedly focused on the trial at hand, but he would've given me a hand signal of some sort. Even if only an impolite one.

I guess I did care, because I felt an excess heat building up, and before I knew it I added, "Eh, so you miss a once-in-a-lifetime meal. On the bright side, they're going to be serving macaroni and cheese tonight and I was able to swing it so they're throw some pancetta into yours."

That time I got a visible reaction out of Julius. It was slight, but I definitely picked up a flash of anger in his eyes, and I had to admit it felt good seeing it after these last three days.

Of course, the disruptions that jury duty caused to Julius's daily routine was enough to put him in a rotten mood, and it got exponentially worse once the judge decided to sequester the jury. By itself, that would've made Julius a miserable person to be around, but the timing couldn't have been worse. Tonight was the night of the gourmet extravaganza that Julius had been looking forward to for over a year. Probably the most famous chef in Paris—one Antoine Escopier—had flown in to cook an eleven-course dinner at the Boston Plaza, complete with a separate vintage for each course, with invitations going out to a select group of gourmets and wine enthusiasts. Julius had six of the wine labels in his cellar, and he had been on the hunt for three of the other vintages for years. It must've been tortuous for him since he found out the jury was to be sequestered.

Like I said, the case Julius was sitting on was open and shut, there being no question that the defendant, Bill Chase, had murdered Dale Wilcox, who was both his boss and the man his wife might've been having an affair with. The police might not have actually seen him toss his gloves, but it didn't much matter with everything else they had, including that his credit card was used to purchase the same brand of gloves recovered in the vicinity of the crime.

But a trial that should've been over in two days had ended up being stretched into a fourth day, and it still wasn't done. They had finished cross-examining their witnesses, with Chase declining to testify, and at that moment the prosecutor and defense attorney were in hushed discussions with the judge. They were talking low enough that no one else in the court could hear them, but I could. It was seven past three in the afternoon and they were discussing whether to go ahead and give closing arguments so they could hand the case to the jury, or adjourn for the day. I could've told Julius what was being said, but I didn't bother. From the way things were going, it was clear that they were going to be sequestering the jury for yet another night. Julius had already resigned himself to that, and as annoyed as I was by his behavior, I wasn't about to rub it in.

Yeah, I know. I didn't have to make that crack about the macaroni and cheese, especially since I had arranged for one of Julius's favorite restaurants, *Le Che Cru*, to bring dinner to his hotel room each night, but as I mentioned, I was more than a little annoyed by his behavior over the past few days. I was sure a combination of having to serve jury duty, being sequestered in a hotel room, and knowing he would be missing this once-in-a-lifetime dinner contributed to his childish petulance, but what had him giving me the silent treatment was my refusal to play Stephen Hawking's latest audio book over his ear receiver when he gave me a hand signal to do so during the first day of the trial. If he wanted to ignore his civic responsibility, that was his business, but I wasn't about to aid him in it. Since then, not a peep from him and no acknowledgment to anything I said to him, not that I said much. For the most part I had been playing along and ignoring him too.

I was surprised that Julius hadn't simply turned me off. That was what he usually did when he was sufficiently irritated with me. At first I thought he didn't do it because he knew at some level that he was in the wrong; then I thought it was that he was hoping I'd try to arrange a new date for this eleven-course dinner, which I did, but Julius must've known that there was no real chance of me being successful with that. Eventually I understood why he kept me turned on. In his utter childishness, he wanted me to suffer through this trial every bit as much as he was.

You're probably confused right now, at least if you only know about Julius Katz through newspaper and TV accounts and haven't been following my other transcriptions of Julius's cases. Yes, I'm Julius's assistant, Archie; although I also perform a long list of other duties for him, including being his accountant, his unofficial biographer, his secretary and all-around man Friday. But you'd have to be puzzled over why I'm talking as if I'm sitting in the jury box with Julius at this very moment. It's because I am, although nobody but Julius knows it. The newspaper reporters who write their stories about Julius and the TV anchors who report on him have no idea what I really am, and as I'm writing this, really nobody does other than Julius and his girlfriend, Lily Rosten. Years from now, after Julius retires, I'll be releasing these case transcriptions, but for now I'm pretty much a mystery to the public, with Julius's explanation to the media being that my appearance is being kept guarded by him so I can be sent out on assignment without being recognized, which is pretty much a big fat white lie on Julius's part. But a necessary one.

While I usually drift into thinking of myself as human, and more specifically, a short, heavyset balding man in his late thirties, I'm not any of those. What I am is a two-inch rectangular piece of advanced technology that Julius wears as a tie clip, and when I say that I'm made up of advanced technology, I'm not kidding. Any lab outside of the one that made me would be astounded at what they found if they were allowed to open me up, especially my visual and audio components which simulate sight and hearing, and my fully functional self-adapting neuron network which, among other things, simulates intelligence and consciousness. Julius likes to joke around that I've got the heart and soul of a hardboiled P.I., and there's quite a bit of truth to that since many of what are considered the great detective novels and short stories of the twentieth century were used to build my personality and experience base, including the complete works of Dashiell Hammett. My self-image comes partly from the fact that Julius wears me as a tie clip that puts me at only five feet from the floor when he stands, but a good part of it is also my identifying with Hammett's fictional short, heavyset nameless P.I., the Continental Op.

The judge, prosecutor and defense attorney had finished their conferencing, and it wasn't good news as far as Julius was concerned. As I had expected, they had decided to sequester the jury another night and continue with closing arguments the next day. Given Julius's mood, I didn't want to be the bearer of any further bad news so I didn't relay this to him, but before the judge could dismiss the jury for the night, Julius was on his feet and addressing the judge, telling her that it was urgent that he talk to her in private.

She turned an incredulous stare his way, her mouth dropping open. The defense attorney did the same, as did most of Julius's fellow jurors. The prosecutor, a tall bony-looking man, gave Julius a look brimming with hostility. Me, I just groaned inwardly. I couldn't believe that Julius would stoop to this. To try to beg off the jury so he could attend his dinner. The thought of it was humiliating.

"If you're doing what I think you're doing, then I quit," I told him. He ignored me as he had for the past three days, and said to the judge, "I know this is highly unusual—"

"What it is is highly inappropriate," the judge cut him off, her face reddening in anger as she regained some of her composure. "It's also borderline contempt."

"I suppose it is," Julius acknowledged. "Your honor, you're well aware of my reputation, and you must know I would not be making this request if it wasn't urgently important."

The judge *was* well aware of Julius's reputation since she had presided at six criminal trials where Julius testified, and in each of these, the guilty party was revealed by Julius. Her eyes narrowed and her mouth seemed to shrink as she studied him. Finally, she nodded.

"This better be every bit as urgent as you're saying, Mr. Katz," she said. "I'll give you five minutes in my chambers." She then pointed at the nearly epileptic prosecutor and then the defense attorney. "Mr. Sanders, Attorney Zoll, you'll join us." With that she nodded to the bailiff, asking him to keep order until she returned, and led a small procession through a doorway in the back of the courtroom while all eyes remained fixed on Julius. At first I felt more excess heat burning—which I knew was embarrassment—but as Julius stepped into the judge's chambers, it was almost as if my processing had slowed to an uneasy crawl, and I realized I was experiencing a sensation similar to dread. I couldn't help groaning again, this time so that Julius could hear.

"You're going to get yourself locked away in jail for contempt," I said miserably. "Forget Antoine Escopier's dinner, this stunt of yours is going to get you jailhouse gruel tonight."

Julius once again ignored me. Normally the man is brilliant, but he was too pigheaded to think of anything right then but making his way to that dinner. The unease I was feeling only intensified as Julius took a seat across from the judge.

"I am giving you exactly five minutes, Mr. Katz," the judge warned, her demeanor letting Julius know that what he had to say had better be damn good. The prosecutor, Henry Sanders, looked angry enough to chew nails, and his eyes nearly bulged as he glowered at Julius. The defense attorney, Mark Zoll, had an eager, almost wistful look, as if Julius was handing him a mistrial, which would allow him to escape for now what was clearly going to be a guilty verdict.

"Thank you, Your Honor," Julius said with a grim smile. "I know how unusual this must be, but I had little choice. The defendant is innocent."

The sputtering coming from Sanders was almost as if he had swallowed his tongue. The defense attorney muttered the same expletive that came to me. The judge gave Julius an icy look. In an even icier voice, she asked, "And why did you feel so compelled to tell me this as opposed to fulfilling your sworn duty as a juror?"

Julius shrugged. "That was my original intent. I had planned to sit quietly until the end of the trial, and then convince my fellow jurors of the defendant's innocence. But if I do that I am convinced the real murderer will never be brought to trial. So that was my dilemma, my obligation as a juror or my moral obligation to society to see a murderer punished."

"I see," the judge said, although she didn't look very convinced as she peered coldly at Julius with her slate-gray eyes. The Honorable Margaret Henshaw was fifty-eight, and even with her thick glasses, strongly resembled photos I found on an online TV database of Barbara Stanwyck from *The Big Valley*. "And why is that?"

"I believe the window for catching this murderer is quickly closing," Julius said. "And if I don't act soon, that window will be closed forever."

Throughout the trial I kept myself busy building and fine-tuning simulations and analytical models that calculated the probability of Bill Chase being the one who murdered Dale Wilcox, and found that it was a near certainty Chase was guilty, the probability being 99.9985 percent with a margin of error at 0.0014 percent. Once Julius announced to the judge that Chase was innocent, I reexamined my models and simulations and found no reason to change my calculated probability of Chase's guilt. Almost in a flash, though, I understood what Julius was up to and I could hardly believe it. He was so desperate to go to his dinner that he was willing to sabotage a jury trial. The realization of that left me speechless for twelve milliseconds, and after that I was too angry to want to say a word to him.

The judge looked at Julius suspiciously, but not suspiciously enough to show that she had caught on. "And I suppose you know who the murderer is?" she asked.

Julius nodded, his lips forming an even grimmer line than earlier.

"Well?" the judge asked.

Julius shook his head, his expression turning severely solemn. Damn, he could put on a hell of a performance when he wanted to. As I was expecting, he told the judge that he couldn't give her the murderer's name. "This is a matter of extreme subtlety," he said. "If this isn't handled in the precise manner that I have in mind, this murderer will go free."

I knew the game Julius was playing, and that was exactly what I expected him to say. Henry Sanders was livid, his cheeks coloring to a bright pink. He couldn't help himself from cutting in.

"This is preposterous!" he nearly shouted, his voice high-pitched and cracking. "What type of nonsense is he trying to sell us? Telling us he knows who the murderer is and then refusing to give us a name? Judge, enough of these games. Order him to tell us what he knows!"

Julius turned in his seat so he was facing Sanders. "Sir, what I know is exactly what was said in court over the last four days, and I believe the court stenographer would be able to give you that verbatim. How I've been able to digest the same information that you have heard and discover Wilcox's true murderer is my knowledge and mine alone."

Judge Henshaw cleared her throat to draw Julius's attention back to her. "What do you propose?" she asked stiffly.

Without hesitation Julius made his proposal. Julius is an excellent poker play with no *tell* as far I've ever been able to discern, so there was nothing in his manner to indicate that he was bluffing, but still, I knew it was all one big bluff.

"There are five people I would like to question," Julius said matter-of-factly, as if he actually meant it. "It should take no more than twenty minutes, but I believe if I'm allowed to do so I'll be able to trap the murderer."

"And if you fail?" Judge Margaret Henshaw asked.

Julius sighed softly and let his shoulders move up and down as much as an inch. "If I fail, then I fail," he said. "It's not likely, but it's also not impossible. If that ends up being the case then the murderer will most likely escape justice, which is not acceptable to me. As far as the trial goes, if I fail, then you can replace me on the jury with one of the alternative jurors, and the trial could continue as if my questioning of these five people never happened."

"The nerve of this man!" Sanders burst out, clearly exasperated. "He tries to hold us hostage with this ludicrous claim, all the while creating a mistrial!"

Julius sent Sanders a withering stare. "I don't see how," he said curtly.

"He doesn't see how!" Sanders exclaimed as he threw up his hands in a further display of extreme exasperation.

"Have you voiced your suspicions to other members of the jury?" the judge asked Julius.

"Of course not."

"They'll all need to be questioned!" Sanders demanded.

"Possibly," the judge admitted.

"What?" Sanders asked, his skin paling to a milk white as he stared incredulously at the judge. "You're not actually considering entertaining his proposal and turning this trial into a circus?"

Zoll had remained quiet through all this, but I guess he was mulling things over and was realizing he might not get his mistrial after all, and worse, might lose the one juror who might believe in his client's innocence. Of course, that would only be if Julius was leveling with them, which I knew he wasn't.

"I have to agree with my colleague," Zoll said sternly. "We should return Mr. Katz to the jury and continue with the trial."

"But not with Katz on the jury!" Sanders argued, an angry red once again mottling his cheeks.

"Not another word from either of you." The judge's tone was severe enough to stop both of them. "Both of you have finished your examination of your witnesses and are ready for closing arguments, correct?" Neither of them contradicted her. "Then I don't see any risk for a mistrial," she added, her mouth pinched. She turned to Julius and fixed her slate-gray eyes on his. "I will take your proposal under advisement." After that she picked up the phone, talked briefly, and a bailiff soon came to escort Julius to a waiting room. I remained quiet until we were alone before voicing my feelings about what Julius was doing. I was too angry at him not to do so.

"I never would've believed you'd pull something like this," I said, the words spilling out of me. "I know how much you want to attend this dinner tonight, but to lay waste to a murder trial to do so? Because of you and these shenanigans, a guilty man might walk free. Did that even occur to you?"

"And what shenanigans might those be, Archie?" Julius said, finally breaking his silence towards me.

"What shenanigans?" I sputtered, feeling every bit as exasperated as the prosecutor, Henry Sanders, had looked. "You're kidding, right? You knew full well that if you told the judge that you wanted off the jury so you could attend this dinner tonight you'd have been held in contempt and sent away to jail, so instead you came up with this cockamamie story about Chase being innocent. And you did it knowing full well that it would lead to one of two results—an immediate mistrial or you being removed from the jury."

A thin smile pulled up slightly on Julius's lips, which at that moment annoyed me to no end. "And what makes you think my story is cockamamie?"

"Why? Other than knowing how desperate you are to attend Antoine Escopier's dinner? Because I calculated the odds of Chase being innocent, and statistically it's impossible!"

"I see. So I'm so desperate that I'd be willing to subvert justice. Interesting. Of course, Archie, there could be a third result from my cockamamie story. I could be given the opportunity to expose the real murderer."

"Yeah, right. Feed that story to someone who doesn't know your tricks. I have half a mind to call Judge Henshaw and explain to her the reason you're pulling this stunt—"

And blast it, before I could say another word, my world went black as Julius turned me off!

———

Julius doesn't turn me off often, and it's always disorienting afterwards when I'm turned back on. This time was no different. After a few woozy milliseconds, I was able to get my bearing. Eighteen minutes and forty-three seconds had elapsed since Julius put me out of action, and he was standing in front of a mirror in a washroom. I checked the GPS coordinates, and saw that we were still in the courthouse.

"I apologize for my behavior over the last three days," he said somberly. Julius's eyes narrowed as he gazed into the mirror, his features hardening as if he were sculpted out of marble. At forty-two, Julius was a good-looking man. I would've known that simply from the way women reacted to him, but comparisons I've made of Julius with Hollywood stars who were considered heartthrobs also confirmed it. At six-feet, a hundred and eighty pounds, and with an athletic build that barely held an ounce of fat, Julius wasn't what you'd expect from a devoted epicurean and wine enthusiast. A fact that we keep out of the papers is that Julius holds a fifth-degree black belt in Shaolin Kung Fu and spends two hours every day in intensive training, and that allows him to work off the rich food that he so loves. Even while spending the last few days in a cramped hotel room, Julius was able to modify his training so that he could stick to his routine.

"It's been a trying few days, as you can well appreciate," Julius continued, "but I had no right taking my frustrations out on you, and I sincerely regret that. You were well within your rights in refusing my request to play me an audio book during the trial."

"Apology accepted," I said with little enthusiasm. It was odd, but I was feeling a strangely uncomfortable sensation creeping through me, and wasn't sure what it was.

Julius lifted an eyebrow at my tone, a thin smile cracking his lips. "Holding a grudge, huh, Archie? I can't say I blame you. You are wrong about my motives. Chase is innocent, and Judge Henshaw has granted my request to question five witnesses. This is not a stunt on my part, and if I weren't allowed to act now, the true murderer would never be brought to justice. At least now there's a chance of that happening."

Of course, Julius could still be bluffing me, but I wasn't so sure anymore. I now understood what that odd, uneasy sensation was that I was feeling, sort of like spiders crawling inside me—distrust. It was something I'd never felt with Julius before, and I guess it was because I wasn't sure whether he was leveling with me or playing me. All I knew for sure was that I didn't like this feeling, and decided for the time being to assume he was leveling.

"Why do you think Chase is innocent?"

Julius's smile lifted another eighth of an inch. "Patience, Archie. For now, I need you to research the company Chase and Wilcox worked for, Brenner Systems, especially about them being acquired shortly after Wilcox's murder."

With that, Julius leaned forward, turned on the cold-water faucet, and carefully splashed water over his face so as not to get his suit or collar wet. I was completely water resistant, so it wouldn't have mattered if he had gotten any on me, but he didn't. When he was done, he patted his face dry, left the washroom, and found the bailiff was waiting for him in the hallway.

I had already done what Julius asked me to do during the first day of the trial. Brenner Systems was a small technology firm that built what was considered a whiz-bang software product for improving Web-site performance, although I could've knocked off a similar product in a matter of hours. The company was started by Felix Brenner and Dale Wilcox, with Brenner serving as CEO and Wilcox as Chief Technology Officer, although from what I could tell, Bill Chase provided the real genius in the product development. They were in talks for over nine months prior to Wilcox's murder about being acquired by one of the computer giants, but the sale didn't happen until three weeks after Wilcox was dead and buried. The sale made the surviving members of the firm very wealthy, Chase included. He alone netted eight million dollars from his vested stock options, money he would never be able to spend if he received the mandatory life sentence for first-degree murder, as it appeared he would regardless of what Julius was saying. I filled Julius in on all of this while the bailiff escorted him back to the courtroom.

The jury had been removed, as had the spectators. Outside of the judge, a sour-looking Henry Sanders, and a very preoccupied-looking Mark Zoll, there were what I assumed were Julius's five witnesses, with four of them sitting together in the front row: Felix Brenner, Gloria Wilcox, Stacy Ducker, Heather Chase, and her husband, Bill Chase, who sat apart from them. I'd already mentioned who Felix Brenner was. Gloria Wilcox was the widow left by Dale Wilcox, Stacy Ducker was the office administrator. and Heather Chase was the defendant's wife. I was surprised to see Bill Chase as one of the five that Julius would be questioning. Since he chose not to testify during his trial, I would've thought he'd refuse to be questioned now. Of course, it was possible he wasn't planning to cooperate, and that he'd remain mute to Julius's questions.

The judge waited until Julius had made his way up to the front of the courtroom before addressing the five, telling them that for the sake of justice she was allowing Julius to question each of them, but that it will be voluntary on their part. "In my seventeen years on the bench I've never done anything like this," she told them, her slate-gray eyes peering slowly at each of the five. "Nor have I ever seen or heard of this done in another courtroom. But I'm sure you all know of Mr. Katz's reputation, and so I'm allowing him the opportunity to question you. None of this will be part of the court record or considered part of the court proceedings. None of you are obliged to answer him, or even remain here in this courtroom. Those of you who have been previously sworn in will not be considered under oath for these questions. and will not be subject to perjury for any answers you provide to Mr. Katz."

There was some rumblings from Gloria Wilcox and Stacy Ducker, and both looked like they were ready to bolt from their seats and from the courtroom. Julius had been staring grim-faced at Bill Chase, but he moved quickly to turn his stare to the group of four. Gloria Wilcox and Stacy Ducker, at least for the moment, lowered themselves back into their seats, but neither of them looked happy.

"I'd like to thank Judge Henshaw for indulging me," Julius said curtly, "as well as the prosecutor, Henry Sanders, and Mr. Chase's defense attorney, Mark Zoll, although it's not so much an indulgent as it is an opportunity to correct an injustice. To put it bluntly, the wrong person is on trial. Bill Chase is innocent of murdering Dale Wilcox. But let me first explain myself so there are no misunderstandings."

Julius stopped to stare at each of the four in turn before continuing.

"When I say that Bill Chase did not murder Dale Wilcox, this is not an opinion of mine but something that I know as a fact. I believe if I am allowed twenty minutes to question you, I will uncover the true murderer. If any of you refuse to answer my questions or leave this courtroom, I will take it as a personal affront, and I will dedicate myself afterward to exposing Dale Wilcox's murderer. This is not a threat of extortion. I will not be attempting to frame any of you, simply exposing a murderer, and I will succeed. If, on the other hand, all of you cooperate and I fail after twenty minutes to expose the truth, then that will be that as far as I'm concerned. At least I'll be able to rest easy knowing I tried. So if one of you four did murder Dale Wilcox, as I suspect, then your only hope is to lie to me. I'm not infallible. While it doesn't happen often, I have been fooled before."

This implied threat from Julius kept all four of them seated, and any rumblings from them had ceased. Assuming he wasn't bluffing and that Chase was indeed innocent, and further, that one of these four was the real murderer, I couldn't tell from their reaction to this hand grenade Julius tossed their way. Chase's wife's eyes widened in a look that was a mix of surprise and hopefulness, Felix Brenner's mouth dropped in a way that only showed that he was dumbfounded by this news, maybe even worried. Stacy Ducker smirked as if she were expecting what Julius said to turn out to be a joke. Wilcox's widow shot Julius a furious, bitter look, as if she thought Julius was working to free her husband's murderer, and the defendant reacted to this by raising an eyebrow for all of two point seven seconds but otherwise maintained the same morose expression that he had held throughout the trial.

"You might think I'm bluffing," Julius continued with the same ill-humor that he'd been displaying since the trial started. "But I'm not. Within the first few hours of the trial, I knew of Chase's innocence and had a faint idea of how to expose the true murderer's identity."

Julius stopped to meet Gloria Wilcox's angry stare. "You disapprove of what I'm doing, madam?" he asked.

"Of course I do," she nearly spat out through tightened lips. Gloria Wilcox was forty-three, on the heavy side with thinning brown hair. The stress of her husband's murder and the subsequent trial had clearly taken their toll on her, leaving dark circles under her eyes and a looseness to her flesh. For several seconds her lips moved as if she were chewing gum, then she looked coldly at Bill Chase and said that the man who murdered her husband was sitting right there. She turned back to face Julius and her eyes scrunched up into what could only be described as an enraged look. She said in a tight, angry voice, "And I don't appreciate you trying to mess things up."

"I see," Julius said. I took that as significant. Usually Julius would've offered her his condolences for her loss. The fact that he didn't meant one of two things: either his four days as a juror had left him in an even fouler mood than I had imagined or he believed her to be the true murderer. That got me searching databases for whatever information I could find about her and I discovered that she not only had a gun permit but owned a licensed thirty-eight-caliber revolver. Her husband was killed with a nine millimeter, but still I found this interesting and told Julius about it. If he too found it interesting he didn't show it through any change in expression. After that I set off on building a simulation with her as the murderer,

"Do you believe your husband was having an affair with Heather Chase as was suggested during the trial?" he asked.

"Definitely not," she said, but her voice wavered enough to show she was either lying or wasn't entirely sure.

"Then why the rumors?"

"Because of her."

Gloria Wilcox glared hotly at Stacy Ducker, who was sitting two seats over to Wilcox's right. Ducker noticed her angry glare but didn't let it interfere with her smirking. She was twenty-seven, thin to the point of boniness, and a brunette with what could only be described as big hair, the kind you see on *The Real Housewives of New Jersey*—and like the housewives on that show she had on layers of too much rouge, lipstick, and eye shadow. She certainly wasn't beautiful, but she was probably considered attractive, at least in a superficial sort of way. I was able to compare her to several actresses in a Hollywood database, but these were actresses who always played secondary roles and never the leading lady.

"I was telling the truth," Stacy Ducker volunteered, both smirking and slightly sticking out her chin at Julius as if she were challenging him to call her a liar. Even though she wasn't chewing gum, she sounded as if she was. "I saw them all over each other at our last company Christmas party, and after that over the next five weeks before Dale was killed I'd see him get calls on his cell phone, then rush out of the office and not come back until maybe two hours later."

"That's not true," Heather Chase said in a soft and absolutely miserable-sounding voice. She was thirty-two, with honey-colored blond hair, clear blue eyes and a slender build. Normally, she would be considered stunningly beautiful, at least from all the newspaper photos I found of her, but at that moment she looked as miserable as she sounded.

She smiled sadly at her husband who showed no reaction whatsoever, then she looked back at Julius and added, "Dale was my husband's boss and he was drunk at that

Christmas party, so I wasn't going to make a scene when he cornered me and got grabby, but it was all one-sided. As soon as I could free myself I did. But there was never any affair."

"I know what I saw," Stacy Ducker stated stubbornly.

"Interesting," Julius told Ducker. "If you did witness what you claim, why would you spread that type of office gossip about one of your company's partners? Were you hoping to be fired?"

It lasted less than a second, but the way Ducker's mouth pinched into a tiny oval gave away her reason for why she did what she did. I recognized that look instantly, and even though I was sure Julius did also, I couldn't help in telling Julius that she spread that gossip because she was jealous. Julius nodded slightly, maybe as much as an eighth of an inch, to let me know that I was right.

Ducker's smirk faded. "I was only saying what was the truth," she insisted.

"But why would you risk your job like that?" Julius asked. "Especially with talk of the company being acquired? You were granted stock options, weren't you? Why would you risk a substantial amount of money simply to spread gossip?"

It was easy enough for me to hack into their company's computer system to find Stacy Ducker's personnel file and give Julius the amount of stock options Ducker had been granted and what they were worth. While not millions, it was still a substantial amount. Ducker tried to meet Julius's stare but she flinched and her eyes shifted from his. Otherwise, she didn't answer him.

"You were having an affair with him, weren't you?"

I could see the lie forming in her eyes, but just like her earlier smirk, it faded. She nodded. Instead of looking miserable, as Heather Chase had, her expression hardened into something more contemptuous. I tried to imagine it. This office lothario, Dale Wilcox, was forty-seven and with his badly receding hairline and pot belly, he resembled the actor John Travolta if Travolta had gone completely to pot. Like Tony Manero, the character Travolta played in the 1977 film *Saturday Night Fever*, Dale Wilcox in the photos I could find of him wore gold chains and clothing as if he were heading to a 70s disco.

"How long did this affair last?" Julius asked.

"Sixteen months."

"When did it end?"

Her smirk came back. "The night of that Christmas party. That was when I caught Dale and that cheap blonde over there all hot and heavy together. A real kick in the teeth, let me tell you. Dale was promising me he was going to leave his wife for me, and what a way to find out he was full of it. But I didn't kill Dale, if that's what you're trying to imply. All I did was tell people what I saw."

"We'll see," Julius said. Then to Gloria Wilcox, "Did you know about this affair?"

Gloria Wilcox looked absolutely crestfallen as she shook her head. She could've been lying, I wasn't sure. If she did know about her husband's involvement with Stacy Ducker, then she'd have even a stronger motive for wanting to kill him. Of course, now Ducker also had a strong motive. But if either Gloria Wilcox's or Ducker were the killer, it would take some fancy footwork to explain how Bill Chase was the one who ended up in the alley holding the murder weapon when the police arrived. Of course, when it came to detecting genius, Julius could show moves that would make Fred Astaire green with envy. I started working on a second simulation, this one explaining how Ducker could be the killer.

Julius looked towards Felix Brenner and asked, "Did you know that Wilcox was having an affair with your office administrator?"

Brenner showed Julius a queasy look that was somewhere between a grimace and a smile. Brenner was sixty-two. A small man who wore thick glasses and was mostly bald with only fringes of white hair. During most of the trial he had what looked like a freshly-scrubbed pink complexion, but at that moment his skin had a grayish, unhealthy look to it.

"I don't know," he said, and it was his turn now to sound miserable. "Dale always had a tough time keeping it in his pants, and maybe I suspected he was fooling around with Stacy and chose to be in denial about it. I don't know. I couldn't tell you for sure."

"I see," Julius said. "Let me ask something you can tell me for sure. You were in talks to sell your company for nine months before Wilcox was murdered. In fact, you had an offer during those nine months, isn't that true?"

Brenner nodded.

"And yet three weeks after Wilcox's murder you were able to reach an agreement. Why was that? Was the offer changed substantially?"

Brenner hesitated before shaking his head. "No, the offer wasn't substantially changed. We just thought after what happened to Dale it was best to move forward."

"I would think it would be highly unusual to have one of the founders of a small technology company murdered and for them to still be an attractive acquisition, especially when that founder was also the Company's Chief Technology Officer."

Brenner slumped further in his seat, his grimace growing more pained. "The company that bought us was more interested in our product than our people," he said. "It didn't really matter to them what happened to Dale."

Julius let that sit for a good minute while he stared at Brenner. "Dale Wilcox fought against selling the company, didn't he?"

As with Stacy Ducker before, I could see it as the lie forming in Brenner's eyes faded away. He nodded glumly. "Dale thought we could do it on our own. He was being foolish, and unfortunately he was able to convince board members to go along with his foolishness. Eventually I would've turned them around."

"Possibly," Julius said. "Or possibly the offer would've been withdrawn before that happened. You benefited greatly from Wilcox's murder. Over forty million dollars, isn't that correct?"

"I benefited greatly from the sale of the company. As did our investors. As did all our employees, and they deserved it with all the hours they worked. Eighty-hour work weeks weren't unusual."

"Was it common knowledge that Wilcox was holding up the sale, and was responsible for keeping everyone from benefiting so greatly?"

Brenner shifted his eyes from Julius's as he nodded.

"So really you, your employees, investors, and relatives of such had reason to want to kill Wilcox?"

Brenner's eyes shot up then to meet Julius's stare. "Bill was the only one found in that alley holding a gun over Dale's dead body," he said, his voice tight.

Behind Julius there was a sound of Judge Margaret Henshaw clearing her throat. When Julius looked back, she crooked her index finger at him, indicating she wanted him to approach the bench. He did so, along with Sanders and Zoll.

"The deal was for you to prove someone other than the defendant murdered Dale Wilcox, and not simply to spread suspicion among other parties," she said in an annoyed whisper.

At that moment I got a call from Tom Durkin. Tom is a local private investigator who occasionally does freelance work for Julius, and he sounded surprised when I answered the phone.

"Archie, are you in the courtroom now with Julius?" he asked.

"Nope, but I can get a message to him. What's up?"

"Tell Julius I'll be there in three minutes, and that it's in the bag."

So Julius must've hired Tom while I was turned off. I did as he asked, and Julius showed Henshaw a thin smile and promised her that he'd be delivering her the real murderer in three minutes. She gave him a dubious look, but told him to get on with it, and with that Julius walked back to his four suspects and settled his gaze on Gloria Wilcox.

"You were aware that your husband was an obstacle keeping you from a fortune?" he asked.

She gave him a steely look. "I was aware that my husband was doing what he thought was best for the company."

Julius cocked an eyebrow but otherwise didn't argue with her. He turned next to Stacy Ducker. "And you?" he asked.

She was back to her smirking, but otherwise didn't respond. Julius sighed softly before next asking Heather Chase the same question. She shook her head.

"Bill told me the company was in talks of being sold, but I didn't know much more than that," she said.

Julius turned towards the defendant to ask him if this was true, but one look at Chase's morose, sullen expression and it was obvious it would be a waste of time. Instead Julius asked Heather Chase how long she had been married to her husband.

"Two years."

"How long had he already been working for Brenner Systems before your marriage?"

A bare trace of a smile showed on her lips, as if she were going to suggest that Julius ask her husband that, but then thought better of it and told Julius that her husband has been with Brenner Systems from the beginning. "He was their first employee," she said.

"So the answer would be seven years."

"I believe so."

"Did you sign a prenuptial agreement?"

She nodded. "I couldn't blame Bill for wanting to protect his stock options. He worked so many hours over there."

"And what did this agreement allow for in the case that your husband was ever convicted of a major felony?"

"I don't know."

I saw it all then just as Julius had. I had a good idea why Tom was coming to the courthouse, and I had to grudgingly admire what Julius was about to pull off. I began going back over the recordings I'd made during the past four days to see what could've tipped Julius off.

"You never consulted a lawyer to find out?"

"Of course not."

Julius shrugged. "It was a reasonable question," he said. "Because if his being convicted of a felony voided the prenup that you signed, then you'd have more motive than anyone else here for killing Dale Wilcox and framing your husband for the murder."

Before Heather Chase could respond, the courtroom doors opened and Tom Durkin escorted into the room a fifty-three-year-old heavyset man with an unhappy, gloomy expression. I knew the man's age because I knew who he was, having figured it out moments after realizing what Julius was up to. Bill Chase looked startled on seeing this man. Heather Chase turned to look behind her and paled at the sight of him. In a matter of seconds she changed, no longer vulnerable and stunningly beautiful but instead something feral and desperate. With her fingers bending so that her hands became claw-like things, she turned towards her husband, pleading, "Don't listen to him, Bill! He's trying to trick you!"

"No, madam," Julius said, interrupting her. "I'm not the one who seduced Dale Wilcox in order to lure him to a deserted Chinatown alley so I could kill him. Nor am I the one who then called your husband so he would go to that same alley supposedly to rescue you only to find himself framed for murder."

"He's lying, Bill! Please, believe me! Don't listen to him!"

Julius ignored her and walked over to Bill Chase. "Sir, you must know by now that you were never protecting your wife as you had believed. Her killing Dale Wilcox was not an accident. She lured him to that alley with the intent to murder him, just as she lured you there with the intent to frame you. As you can see, I've brought to this courtroom the attorney who drew up your prenuptial agreement, and if you need to you can ask him whether your wife consulted with him concerning how this agreement could be voided. You received a call from your wife begging for your help, didn't you? That's why you went to that alley?"

Bill Chase squeezed his eyes shut and nodded. What happened next happened fast. Heather Chase was out of her seat and nearly flying at Julius, her claw-shaped hands ready to do damage. As I mentioned earlier, Julius was a fifth-degree black belt in Kung Fu. I'd seen him in the past take on as many as four hardened thugs at one time and dispatch all of them. Heather Chase couldn't have weighed more than ninety-five pounds, but at that moment she would've been more than a handful for Julius. Fortunately two court officers had moved closer to her once it became obvious that she was little more than a cold-blooded snake, and they were able to tackle her before she reached Julius.

———

"You were only fishing," I said.

Julius raised an eyebrow. "What was that, Archie?"

"You couldn't possibly have known Bill Chase was innocent and that his wife was the actual murderer. I've analyzed every minute of the trial, and it's impossible for you to have known that. But you went fishing. You wanted off the jury so you sent Tom after that lawyer so you'd at least have a plausible story. It's just dumb luck that things fell in place the way they did."

Julius chuckled at that. He was in a much better humor since coming home to his townhouse on Beacon Hill, and was in the process of picking out a tie for the special dinner tonight that he would be taking Lily Rosten to. After carefully examining several of them he chose a rich burgundy-colored one and brought it to the mirror so he could tie a Windsor knot.

"No, Archie, I wasn't fishing. I knew within the first three hours of the trial what had happened."

I didn't believe him. Not that Julius was in the habit of lying to me, but it just didn't seem possible. "How?" I asked.

"There were a number of reasons, Archie. I remember reading about the sale of Brenner Systems occurring only three weeks after Wilcox's murder and thinking then that his murder was financially motivated." He paused for a moment to examine the precision of the knot he made before slipping on his suit jacket and continuing, "But what gave it away to me was that woman's performance. She would've fooled most people with the hopeful and loving looks she kept favoring her husband throughout the trial, but not a reasonably capable poker player. Once I discovered her *tell*, I knew that she was only trying to keep her husband in line, and was able to draw the obvious conclusions that I did."

"What was her *tell?*"

Julius chuckled again. "I don't want to deprive you of all your fun, Archie, but if you study the trial enough, I'm sure you'll figure it out. But even without that, it was clear what happened. There was no reasonable explanation as to why Dale Wilcox would've ended up in that Chinatown alley unless he was brought there at gunpoint, and since both Wilcox's and Bill Chase's cars were found near the alley, it couldn't have been Chase who brought Wilcox there. Assuming Wilcox had a rendezvous planned with that woman, it wouldn't have been there. Similarly, there was no reason Bill Chase would've ended up in that same alley unless he was called by his wife and told to go there. And the trial itself was also a giveaway. There were no defense witnesses and Chase made no attempt to defend himself in court. If he was going to act that way, why not make a deal instead of letting the case go to trial?"

I thought about it and couldn't come up with a good answer.

"Because he was hoping for a miracle," Julius said. "He knew he was innocent, and he was hoping that something would come up that would free him, but without also condemning his wife."

"How'd you know about the prenup agreement?"

Julius finished buttoning his coat jacket and adjusted his shoulders so that the jacket laid better on them.

"I didn't," he said. "I sent Tom to find out if one existed, and if it did, to bring back the lawyer who drew it up. I was lucky there on several counts, especially that she ended up consulting with this same lawyer. I was also lucky that she panicked when she saw him, because most likely he would've denied in court ever consulting with her. I'm guessing that they had worked out a deal where he was going to be paid a substantial sum of money for keeping quiet about their consultation, otherwise he would've come forward once Chase was arrested for murder."

I digested all this and realized I still had a long way to go in reprogramming my neuron network if I was ever going to beat Julius to the punch in solving a case.

"Well, things worked out," I said. "An innocent man has been set free, the real murderer has been arrested, and you get to go to your dinner tonight." I hesitated, then asked, "If you didn't have this big special dinner scheduled, would you have come forward the way you did?"

"Yes, of course, Archie. I wasn't about to let that wretch escape justice. The only way to trap her was to get her husband to talk, and there was little chance of that happening once the trial ended. He looked dangerously close already to giving up and accepting whatever fate had in store for him. I had to move when I did whether or not Antoine Escopier's dinner was scheduled for tonight."

This last bit confused me more than anything else. I knew Julius was someone who believed in fair play, but he also believed in being paid for his efforts.

"Why?"

Julius's eyes glistened and the muscles along his jaw hardened for a moment. "Because of that woman I was deprived of my home, my kitchen, and my wine cellar for four days, and during these four miserable days I was forced to suffer through that trial and stay sequestered at night in a stale-smelling, dingy hotel room. So yes, Archie, of course I was going to see justice done."

Of course.

ARCHIE SOLVES THE CASE

Originally published in the May 2013 issue of Ellery Queen Mystery Magazine, this story won 1st place in Ellery Queen's Readers Choice Awards.

JULIUS WAS BROWSING through the latest *Wine Spectator* while I was busy with my own project—which was loading more detective novels into my knowledge base in my never-ending attempt to refine my neuron network, so that I might someday beat Julius to the punch in solving a case—when a call came in from a prospective client who wanted to meet with the great detective. I knew there was little chance of Julius consenting to that since the Kingston case had left him flush with cash. Add to that several extremely profitable weeks at the poker table, and forget it. Until Julius spent down his funds, I'd have better luck teaching an elephant to walk a tightrope than I would getting him to focus on anything detective related. While he might be known as Boston's most brilliant private investigator, he's also incredibly lazy and never takes on a case unless he absolutely has to—meaning his bank account has dipped to a level where he might have to dine at a three-star instead of a four-star restaurant. If I hadn't been feeling as bored as I was, I would've let this person down with an excuse, but since he was some sort of hotshot chef, I decided to use the opportunity to pester Julius and tell him that a Henri Chervil was calling for him.

"He sounds desperate to meet with you," I said. "Normally I wouldn't bother you, since I know how busy your schedule is today with your wine magazines and all the office puttering that you wish to do, but seeing how he's a world-class chef and winner of nine straight Golden Pan awards, and with your being such a dedicated gourmand, I figured you'd feel a sense of fraternity with him and would want me to schedule an appointment at the earliest, say one o'clock?"

"That would be fine, Archie."

Well, that took me by surprise. I had to double-check my audio circuitry to make sure it was functioning properly and that I had heard right. I did, and everything checked out. I considered for a millisecond whether I should make sure Julius had heard me and wasn't simply too absorbed in his magazine to pay attention to what I was saying, but decided not to look a gift horse in the mouth and simply told Julius that I'd set up the appointment.

When I tried asking Chervil what the matter was concerning, all he would tell me in a gruff, raspy voice, thick with a French accent, was that he had urgent business to discuss with Julius and that he'd only do so in person. Fine. I didn't push it. Like Julius, he was another of those temperamental, artistic genius types. Julius's genius is in catching murderers, Chervil's in the culinary arts. Anyway, I didn't need to push it since Julius had already agreed to the meeting.

Once I finished the call, I proceeded to hack into whatever databases and newspaper archives I needed to build a thick dossier on him, and I soon had a good idea why he wanted to meet with Julius, as well as why Julius had agreed to the meeting. The reason for Julius's acquiescence? Chervil held in his private wine cellar a case of 1985 Château Lafite Rothschild, which is a vintage Julius has been trying to acquire for years. So it didn't matter how well-heeled Julius might be right now, he was going to make himself available to Chervil, and when the time came to discuss the fee, Julius would be extorting that wine from him. As to why Chervil wanted to see Julius, it was most likely because of an incident from two days earlier when Chervil was arrested for assaulting a fellow chef, Jasper Quayle. I'd hacked into the Cambridge Police Department's computer system, since the incident took place outside of Quayle's restaurant in Cambridge, and I added the police report to the dossier. After I was satisfied with what I had put together, I asked Julius if he'd like me to e-mail it to him. He barely mumbled out a "no thank you" as his attention was fully engaged by an article about Pinot Noirs. Tough. I e-mailed it to him anyway, not that I thought he'd bother looking at it.

You must be wondering what's going on, at least if you haven't read any of my other transcriptions of Julius's cases. On the one hand, I must sound an awful lot like I'm Julius's secretary. I'm really more his assistant, although I also perform a long list of other duties for him, including being his accountant, his unofficial biographer, his wine purchaser and his all-around man Friday. On the other hand, if you know about me and Julius already, but only through the newspaper and TV reports, you must be wondering why I'm talking about having a neuron network and a knowledge base. The truth is, while I imagine myself as a short, stocky man with thinning hair, what I really am is a two-inch rectangular piece of advanced technology complete with some whizz-bang auditory, visual and speech circuitry that Julius wears as a tie clip, and I talk to him through a small earpiece that he wears, at least when he doesn't have it plugged into a speaker that he keeps by his desk. If you want to know more about me, I suggest you find one of Julius's earlier cases that I've transcribed. I've written about myself enough times already.

At precisely one o'clock, the doorbell rang, as well it should since I had warned Chervil that he'd better be on time. Julius, being stubborn, still hadn't looked at the dossier that I prepared. Henri Chervil wasn't alone. His protégé, April Morley, stood outside the door with him. I recognized both of them from the research I had done earlier. Together, they made quite a contrast. Chervil, sixty-eight, was a large bull of a man with heavy arms and thickly veined and powerful-looking hands. With his broad, craggy face, he reminded me of an English bulldog, and that look was accentuated by a fringe of gray hair cut close to his scalp. April Morley was twenty-seven and could best be described as a wisp of a woman. I encountered that phrase earlier when I was adding those new detective novels to my knowledge base; it seemed to fit Morley perfectly. Don't get me wrong—with her slightly upturned nose that made her resemble the actress Naomi Watts and her stunning brown eyes and long, silky yellow hair, I knew, even without having to perform any comparisons of her to actresses in a Hollywood database, that she'd be considered very beautiful. But with her slight build and delicate features, the phrase *wisp of a woman* worked well in describing her.

Chervil seemed distracted as Julius invited him into his Beacon Hill townhouse and showed him and Morley to his office. Earlier, Julius had been busy preparing a platter of dried meats and cheeses, but Chervil begged off, claiming he couldn't eat at a time like this. Morley also declined.

"Then some wine?" Julius said as he handed Chervil a bottle of his finest Cabernet to examine. Chervil studied the bottle and shook his head, his lips pulled down into a thick, grim line. "A fine vintage," he mumbled, "but I couldn't possibly appreciate it under the circumstances." As with the food, Morley followed her boss's lead and also turned down the wine.

"Very well," Julius said, somewhat stiffly. Julius has always been the gracious host, except when dealing with murderers, but still I couldn't understand him going all hog-wild like this. It's one thing to put out a spread of cheeses and meats, but to offer a prospective client one of your most prized Cabernets, someone who hasn't even hired you yet? Chervil might've been some highly acclaimed chef, but he certainly wasn't Julius's favorite, not given the infrequency that Julius has dined at Chervil's establishment. From my count, only seven times in the years I'd been with him. Of course, that was only my count—there were occasions when Julius would get annoyed enough at me to turn me off, and there was no telling where he dined then, since he frequently used cash instead of credit cards. But still, even if Julius dined exclusively at Chervil's during those times, it wouldn't have warranted this behavior on his part.

After Julius took his seat behind his desk, he told Chervil that he was guessing he was there because Jasper Quayle had stolen his recipe for *Bouillabaisse ala Sophie*. Morley's eyes widened at that, while Chervil barely reacted other than his jaw muscles hardening. Me, I was flabbergasted. When I asked him how he knew that, Julius signaled me with his index finger to wait and listen.

"Is that common knowledge already?" Chervil asked.

Julius shrugged. "It was only a guess on my part. I saw an article in the paper about your accosting Quayle outside of his restaurant, and the only reason I could imagine that you'd go there would be if he had stolen your recipe for *Bouillabaisse ala Sophie*."

Chervil nodded as he thought about this. "Very true," he said. "The man is detestable. Little more than a pig in an apron who masquerades as a chef. He is an insult to the entire profession. You do understand the significance of what he has stolen from me?"

"Yes, of course."

I understood it also after my earlier research. It was Chervil's signature dish and what has won him all his Golden Pan awards. He had named the dish after his daughter, who had died tragically at the age of nine.

Chervil appeared distracted again and his breathing became ragged. April Morley watched him with a mix of helplessness and concern. When she placed one of her delicate hands on one of his heavily veined ones, it seemed to bring him back from wherever he had disappeared to. He wrinkled his nose as if he had tasted bad wine and waved a thick hand across his face.

"Bah! And of what importance could it possibly be to you? I can count on one hand the number of times you have dined at my restaurant!"

This was said with both hurt and petulance. Chervil was well aware of Julius's reputation as a gourmet, and he must've taken Julius's lack of patronage of his restaurant as an insult.

"Once a year, to be precise," Julius said. "And that is because of *Bouillabaisse ala Sophie*. The dish is as close to culinary perfection as I've found, and so I limit myself to one visit a year. I do this not to deprive myself, but so that I may attempt to experience, at least as much as possible, the joy of discovery that I felt when I first tasted that magnificent dish. And sir, while my yearly visit to your restaurant is my most anticipated dining experience of the year, I have yet to set foot into Jasper Quayle's restaurant."

Chervil sank back into his chair and folded his arms across his chest. Julius's answer appeased him enough that his look of bitter hurt changed into an ordinary scowl. With only a slight peevishness, he said, "You could still come more than once a year. I have other items on the menu that people seem not to hate!"

"True, but it would be impossible for me to enter your restaurant and not order the bouillabaisse," Julius said. "How did you find out that Quayle has your recipe? It's not on his menu yet."

"That swine," Chervil swore. He looked too angry right then to say another word, and he indicated with a wave of a hand for his protégé to answer for him.

"We had a break-in at the restaurant two weeks ago," she started before letting out a soft sigh and shrugging weakly. "At the time I didn't think anything had been stolen, and I didn't know that Chef Chervil had written down his recipe for *Bouillabaisse ala Sophie*—"

"That was my fault," Chervil interjected. "Until recently all my recipes were kept only up here." He tapped a thick index finger against his skull. "But I started thinking of a time when April will take over, and so like an idiot I wrote down my recipes. It was vanity on my part." He shook his head angrily as if he were trying to escape from a bad nightmare. "I should've had April commit my recipes to memory instead of ever writing them down. What a fool I was!"

"You couldn't possibly have expected Quayle to hire someone to break-in and snoop through your office!" Morley tried to tell him.

"Bah!" Chervil looked away from her and Julius, his cheeks reddening either with anger or embarrassment. "Tell him the rest of what that swine did!"

For a moment Morley looked like she was on the verge of crying, and several tears did break loose. She controlled herself, however, and after giving Chervil's hand a squeeze, told Julius how two days ago Quayle had sent a courier to Chervil's restaurant with a container of a "new" bouillabaisse recipe that would be appearing this Sunday on Quayle's menu.

"I intercepted this messenger," April said. "Of course, I thought it possible that the bouillabaisse had been poisoned knowing Quayle's insane jealousy and animosity towards the chef, but I felt compelled to taste it anyway, although it never occurred to me that he could've stolen the chef's recipe."

"It was *Bouillabaisse ala Sophie*?" Julius asked.

"The recipe, yes. The preparation lacked Chef Chervil's own precision and skill."

"It's an abomination!" Chervil had turned back in his seat to look directly at Julius. His eyes were bulging and his face even redder. So it was anger and not embarrassment before. I made a note of it. For a moment he seemed incapable of speech, and then he forced out how Quayle had transformed his recipe into swill. "It might fool those with an unsophisticated palate, but if you tasted it, Katz, you would spit it out the same as if that Cabernet had turned to vinegar—as I did myself."

"And then you went to see Quayle."

"Not right away. First I needed to use my finest cognac to remove that taste from my mouth. But of course, after that I went to that swine's so-called restaurant, although calling it a pig trough would be kind!" Chervil clamped his mouth shut for several moments, then took in a few deep and noisy breaths through his nose. I guess he was trying a breathing technique to control his anger, but from the way his slate gray eyes appeared to be simmering to a near boil it didn't do much good. He made a face of extreme disgust, then looked away from Julius again and told him how he went there to throw Quayle in the gutter where he belonged. "I grabbed him by the scruff of his neck and dragged him out as he squealed like the pig that he is and then tossed him in the gutter like I would any other piece of garbage. The police should've applauded me instead of arresting me."

For a ten-count Chervil again seemed distracted as he was lost in his thoughts, then he snapped out of it and his eyes shifted to meet Julius's. "I need to hire you Katz to keep him from serving this grotesque mockery of my *Bouillabaisse ala Sophie*. You understand the significance of this dish to me and that I can't allow Quayle to disgrace it this way. If he ever did, it would be lost to me forever. I would never be able to prepare it again knowing that such a gross counterfeit of it was being served by that swine."

So that was it. I knew Julius would turn him down flat, even with a case of 1985 Château Lafite Rothschild at stake. Quayle had already resorted to robbery in the first place, and then sent a sample of the bouillabaisse to Chervil simply to rub his nose in it. How can you reason with someone like that? What would be left for Julius to try? Blackmail? Extortion? These were tactics that I knew Julius found highly distasteful, and so I was flabbergasted for the second time in twelve point seven minutes when Julius consented to take the case. If this news relieved Chervil, he didn't show it. He continued to look distracted, his large round face folded into a morose frown. He did, though, turn to his protégé and suggest she head back to Chervil's to start the dinner preparation. She nodded her acquiescence, and Julius escorted her out of the office and to the front door. This wasn't necessary. Usually I followed his visitors over webcam feeds to make sure they left without causing any mischief. Maybe Julius decided to act chivalrously because she was extremely beautiful, or maybe it was because she might someday be in sole possession of a dish that Julius felt was close to perfection. I doubted it was the first. At one time Julius had been a notorious womanizer, but since meeting Lily Rosten that had changed, and he still seemed as smitten as ever. Whichever it was, I didn't bother to ask him.

When Julius returned to his office, Chervil, still distracted and morose, asked Julius about his fee. Julius left me flabbergasted for a third time when he told Chervil there would be no fee. I knew he knew about the 1985 Château Lafite Rothschild. Julius always knew things like that. Still, I found myself sputtering as I mentioned to him that Chervil held a case of that vintage in his private wine cellar. Julius ignored me, and I had an idea of what Julius was after instead of the wine. After all, all of Rex Stout's Nero Wolfe books were used in building my knowledge base, and I imagined myself then as my customary short, stocky man with thinning hair smiling wryly as I figured out Julius's game.

Chervil was frowning even more deeply at Julius's response. "Nonsense," he growled. "I am not someone to take charity. If you do a job for me, you will be paid."

"I have my own selfish reasons. It would sadden me immensely if you were to cease offering *Bouillabaisse ala Sophie* at Chervil's. All I ask is that if I succeed you keep preparing that dish, at least during my yearly visits."

Chervil waved that away as sentimental nonsense, which I was convinced it was also. "We'll talk about your fee later.

I will trust you not to hold me at gunpoint if you are successful in handling this matter." His tone changed, becoming more conspiratorial, as he leaned slightly forward in his chair. "What did you think of Ms. Morley?"

"A lovely woman."

That seemed to please Chervil. At least, it chipped some of the moroseness from his expression. "She spends too many hours in the kitchen," he complained. "Someone like her needs to meet a proper young man and enjoy life more." Chervil cleared his throat and added, "Katz, from what I understand you're an eligible bachelor?"

"Young?" I said to Julius over his earpiece. "Forty-two is young? Eh, I guess it's all relative."

I had wondered about Chervil and his protégé. There was a forty-one year age difference between the two of them, and while I'm no expert in understanding the affairs of the heart—in fact, I was still a bare novice and often found myself confused with how Julius and Lily Rosten behaved together—I had this distinct impression that while Chervil and Morley cared about each other, they were not a couple. Inspiration hit me, and after some Internet browsing and a few minor calculations, I understood their relationship. I have to admit I was pleased with myself, and found myself anxious to relay this information to Julius, but now was not the right time as Julius was explaining to Chervil that he might be a bachelor but he was no longer eligible.

"*C'est la vie,*" Chervil said with a shrug. "Things have been known to change, right?" He got that distracted look on his face again as his eyes shifted from Julius's and he stared off into space. Then he quickly rose to his feet and told Julius that he needed to be going. He was about to offer Julius his hand, but must've remembered the warning I'd given him about that when he called for the appointment, because he pulled his hand back. Julius claimed that the act was an outdated custom that only served to spread germs. It never stopped Julius, in the past, from shaking hands with beautiful women he'd meet, and much more. Before he met Lily Rosten, there were many nights where Julius would be entertaining overnight guests and would need to put me away in his sock drawer, but I never bothered pointing out this hypocrisy. As Chervil had said, *c'est la vie*.

Chervil seemed anxious to get going. Normally, Julius would've sat at his desk while his client found his own way out. But since Chervil was the creator of *Bouillabaisse ala Sophie*, the yearly anticipation of which appeared to be one of Julius's reasons for getting out of bed each morning, he escorted Chervil to his door. No offered handshake, but still, this was quite a show of respect from Julius.

While Julius made his way back to his office, I mentioned that the idea of trading Lily Rosten for April Morley as his girlfriend must've been tempting for Julius. He asked me why that would be.

"She's about as beautiful as Lily," I said. "At least from what I can tell by comparing her to photos of star actresses. Add to that that she's a master chef and that she will someday possess the recipe for a dish that you consider close to perfection, and the swap would be obvious."

Julius smiled thinly at that but didn't bother commenting.

"Of course," I continued, "I'll admit to being very naïve about the affairs of the heart. And the fact that she'll be possessing the recipe for *Bouillabaisse ala Sophie* doesn't much matter since I know you plan to also."

"And how do I plan to do that?" Julius asked, amused.

"By squeezing it from Chervil as your fee. In case you forgot, all the Nero Wolfe books were used in building my experience base, including *Too Many Cooks*, where Wolfe does exactly the same to get the recipe for *saucisse minuit*, a dish that, by the way, is purely fictional, since I've been unable to find any reference to it outside of the novel."

"Interesting," Julius murmured, his lips twisting up slightly to show his amusement. Maybe I was wrong, or maybe he was simply bluffing me, but whichever it was I felt an excess of heat building up in my processing unit, which I knew was the same sort of embarrassment that would've made my cheeks turn red if I were the flesh-and-blood man that I imagined myself as. To change the subject, I mentioned that April Morley was the same age that Chervil's daughter, Sophie, would be now if she hadn't died. "Not only that, but guess what I got when I used a picture of Sophie from Chervil's restaurant's website to approximate what she'd look like at twenty-seven?"

"An image that closely resembles Ms. Morley."

"Exactly. It's uncanny. Do you think he realizes that he has made her a replacement for his deceased daughter?"

"I don't know, Archie. Possibly."

I waited until Julius was sitting back behind his desk before asking him about Quayle. "So what's it going to be, extortion or blackmail? It's going to have to be one of those two, since his actions already show he's not someone you're going to be able to reason with."

Julius sighed heavily. He didn't bother answering me, at least not with words, but the face he made told me plenty how distasteful he found this. He told me he'd be needing a dossier on Quayle also. I had already put one together while Julius had been talking with Chervil, and I sent it to the printer on Julius's desk. Julius gave one last longing look at his wine magazines before picking up Quayle's dossier, which was even thicker than the one I had compiled on Chervil.

An hour later, Julius was still reading the dossier, which was over two hundred pages, his nose wrinkled in disgust. I interrupted him and told him he might as well go back to his wine magazine. "I just intercepted a communication from the Cambridge city police. Your problem has been solved, in a way. Jasper Quayle's been murdered, and your client, Henri Chervil, was caught red-handed.

———

It was two days later that Julius met with Chervil at the Middlesex Jail in Cambridge. I wasn't kidding Julius earlier when I told him that Chervil had been caught red-handed. Quayle was murdered in the kitchen of his restaurant, stabbed in the back with a butcher knife. Since Quayle's restaurant, like Chervil's, was open only for dinner and not for lunch, and the murder occurred too early in the afternoon for other staff to be present, there were no witnesses. But when the police barged in, they found Chervil kneeling by the body, his left hand indeed red with blood, and his fingerprints on the handle of the knife. Since Chervil still had ties to France and was considered a flight risk, bail was denied. And since he claimed he was innocent, Julius agreed to meet with him.

Two days in jail hadn't left Chervil any worse for wear. In fact, he seemed in better spirits, as if the knowledge that Quayle wouldn't be perverting his dish was a fair trade for most likely having to spend the rest of his life in prison. I'd seen Julius pull rabbits out of his hat before, but even given the remote chance that Chervil was innocent, as he claimed, this seemed pretty open and shut for any prosecutor.

Chervil explained to Julius that when he left Julius's townhouse two days ago he went straight to Quayle's restaurant. "I might've been planning to kill him, or maybe talk to him, I am not sure which," Chervil said with a shrug. "I know it was impulsive on my part, especially since there was no telling that Quayle would even be there, but there is no denying certain passions. When I arrived, the front door was locked and no one answered the bell—"

"You're certain you rang the bell and didn't yell for him or pound on the door?"

"Yes, of course I'm certain." Chervil made a face to show his annoyance at the question. "If Quayle was there, he wouldn't have opened the door if he knew it was me, so I rang the bell. When no one answered, I tried the back door and found it unlocked and so I walked in. Quayle was in the kitchen lying on the floor with a knife sticking out of his back. He was very dead, but still I felt compelled to check for myself. That must've been when I left my fingerprints on the knife, as well as getting his blood on my other hand. I wasn't even aware of doing that. I was in too much of a daze after what I had found. I can't say that I was sorry to find him dead. If he had been alive I very well might've killed him myself. But as it turned out, I didn't have to."

"How long was it from you finding Quayle dead to the police arriving?"

Chervil frowned as he considered this. "No more than a minute. It couldn't have been more than that." A tiredness washed over him then, leaving his face drawn and pale. He tried to smile, but it was a sickly one at best. "Katz, you can see that I am in a very bad pickle. I didn't kill Quayle, but the police have no reason to believe otherwise. You are my only hope. If you don't believe me, then I will surely be convicted."

Julius told him he believed his story was possible, maybe even probable. "Eight minutes elapsed from the time that the police received an anonymous call of a scream coming from Quayle's restaurant to your being found kneeling by his body," he said. Julius knew this because I had hacked into the Cambridge police's phone records and also their computer system for the police report. I tried to get the 911 call but unfortunately it wasn't accessible. Julius's gaze turned steely as he fixed it on Chervil. "Since that doesn't make any sense, nor do you impress me as someone who'd stab a man in the back, I believe it more likely that you are innocent as you claim. If you've been lying to me, it won't help you."

Chervil sniffed to show his insult. "I haven't been lying, Katz."

"Good. You are right that as things stand the police will remain settled on you, and that regardless of whether you committed this murder, the prosecutor will obtain a guilty verdict. It's highly unlikely that any jury will worry about that eight-minute gap given that you were found by Quayle's body with your fingerprints on the knife."

"What do we do, then?"

Julius smiled thinly, because the answer was obvious. He was going to have to roll up his sleeves and get to work, which I knew he had to hate the idea of given how flush his bank account currently was, but with *Bouillabaisse ala Sophie* at stake, he had no choice. "I need to discover Quayle's murderer," he said.

The assumption Julius was going on, which was really the only reasonable assumption he could make, was that Chervil's assault of Quayle earlier that week was what prompted the murder in the first place, with the culprit believing he could kill Quayle and Chervil would attract the police's attention. By pure happenstance, Quayle's murderer must've seen Chervil arriving as he was escaping from the murder site, realized his good fortune, and made the anonymous call, sending the police on their way. Even if Chervil hadn't gone into the restaurant, the police could very well have picked him up nearby, which would've been almost as damning. So given all that, Julius and Chervil set about to make a list of suspects who would've wanted to see Jasper Quayle dead. Chervil's initial list had twelve people on it who had reason to despise Quayle, but after some fine-tuning, Julius circled three of those names as reasonable suspects. By this time Chervil's allotted fifteen-minute visitation had expired and a guard came over to escort him away. Chervil asked about the fee, but Julius told him they'd discuss it later.

By the time Julius exited the jail, I was able to eliminate seven of the nine less-likely suspects, establishing ironclad alibis for them by calling their offices and through other such methods. I told Julius this, letting him know that I had no luck finding alibis for the three he had circled. I also told him he messed up regarding Chervil's fee. "You'd have more leverage extorting that recipe now than after you freed him," I said, "especially since there's no guarantee that you will free him."

Julius didn't respond to that, but as he was making his way to the street he asked me to find out what I could about those three suspects.

"Will do. You remember the dossier I had compiled on Quayle and those recent credit-card charges at the Windsor Hotel? There might be more than those three people you've circled who wanted Quayle dead, especially if he was recently having an affair."

"Yes, Archie, very true." Julius sighed and asked me to get ahold of Tom Durkin. Tom is a freelance detective, one of the best, and Julius often hires him when he needs foot leather on a case. I understood the reason for Julius's sigh. Tom doesn't work cheaply, and Julius still hadn't arranged a fee for this case. I reached Tom on his cell phone, and after finding out that he was available for an assignment, I patched Julius in. Julius put Tom onto finding out who Quayle was meeting at the Windsor, and after he got off the call, I e-mailed Tom recent photos of Quayle and gave him the dates Quayle ran up the charges. Once I finished with Tom, Julius had me call April Morley. She was at Chervil's doing the prep work for that night's dinner, and I let her know Julius would be stopping by soon to see her.

When Julius arrived at Chervil's, Morley, who was dressed in her kitchen uniform, brought Julius to a table and uncorked a highly rated Pinot Gris from the Alsace region of France, then poured both herself and Julius a glass. She kept a stoic front, but her eyes were red and puffy as if she'd been crying. Even without that, there was a heavy sadness to her. Julius accepted the wine and after several tastes of it commented that he'd have to look for that vintage for his own collection, which meant I'd have to be the one tracking it down. She smiled sadly in response. I think she might have cried then if she wasn't so exhausted.

"Chef Chervil has asked that I keep the restaurant open," she said. "Otherwise, I don't think I'd be able to. But in a way it is good. It keeps my mind off of what has happened."

"I understand," Julius said. "Do you believe he killed Jasper Quayle?"

"No," she stated adamantly, her eyes brightening in intensity. "The chef would never have stabbed someone in the back. And if he had killed that man, he would've used his hands and not a knife."

Julius nodded. "There are reasons why I also believe Chervil is innocent, and I will be trying to discover who the true murderer is."

If this news comforted her, she didn't show it; her smile remained every bit as despondent as before. Maybe she believed it was a hopeless cause. Or maybe she was simply too exhausted to show the relief she might be feeling. Julius showed her the list that Chervil had come up with. She agreed that the three names Julius circled were the most likely among that list to have hated Quayle enough to kill him, and that the other nine probably only despised him enough that they would've spat at him, but she also added a fourth suspect to his list.

Julius and Morley had a second glass of that fine Pinot Gris, which they drank silently, then Morley informed Julius that she had to be heading back to the kitchen. "We open in one hour for dinner," she said with a tragic sadness.

She escorted Julius to the door so she could lock up after him. For a moment I thought she was going to break down in tears, but she kept her stoic front and turned from him so she could head swiftly back to the kitchen.

"You could've at least asked for a taste of *Bouillabaisse ala Sophie* while you were there," I said.

"Archie, please, not now."

"Sure. Whatever. You do realize what a fool's errand you're on. Let's say you're able to figure out which of those four is the murderer—if it is one of those four—you've still got a client who has all but convicted himself with physical evidence. Short of a confession, you're out of luck with this one."

Julius raised an eyebrow at that. "This has to be a first, Archie," he said. "You chastising me for taking a case."

"Don't get me wrong. I'm glad you're taking it. Observing you in action is the best way I've got to refine my neuron network, so any chance to watch your genius at work, I'll take. And it sure beats watching you read wine magazines. But this still looks hopeless to me."

A grimness settled over Julius's face as he nodded. "It does seem as if it will be a challenge," he said. "Archie, please arrange for those four to come to my office tomorrow."

"I'll try. In one large group or individually?"

"Individually."

That turned out to be easier said than done. Well, with two of them it was easy, at least relatively so. They heard Julius wanted to see them, got either nervous or curious, and after a little verbal sparring agreed to a time. That wasn't so with Quayle's widow. When I told her Julius wished to meet with her, she flew off the handle and threatened right away to call the police about my harassing her.

"Whoa," I said. "All I said was that Julius believes it would be beneficial for you to see him, and if Julius thinks that then it's probably true."

"I demand you tell me what this is about," she seethed, and when I say she *seethed*, I mean it! I tried explaining that she could find out easily enough by meeting with Julius, but before I could get the words out she hung up on me. Next thing I knew, her lawyer called, threatening everything from emotional-distress lawsuits to criminal actions. I told him if he thought he was going to scare either me or Julius with that type of baseless threat he was even nuttier than he sounded. After some more of this back and forth, he told me he'd consent to letting his client meet with Julius as long as he was present. I told him, not a chance, and after more of this nonsense I hung up on him. Ten minutes later the widow called back and in about as icy a tone as possible agreed to a meeting.

What I went through with the Widow Quayle was downright pleasant compared to Jason Heckle, an investor Quayle had cheated out of a very large sum of money, at least according to a lawsuit Heckle had filed that was dismissed thanks to some very clever maneuvering on Quayle's lawyer's part. When I called him, he asked whether it was so that Julius could prove that he was the one who murdered Quayle.

"Did you?" I asked.

He giggled at that and said, "If I did I certainly wouldn't tell you."

"Okay. So you know what Julius wants to talk to you about. Are you willing to come in?"

"I don't believe that would be very prudent. Why hand the great genius detective the rope to hang me with?"

"You could convince him you're innocent."

"That could be difficult," he said. "And even on the off-chance that I *am* innocent, I don't see any reason to make things easier for him."

He was having fun with this. I could hear the amusement in his voice, and it annoyed me. I felt the annoyance with the way my processing cycles were slowing down, as if flowing through molasses.

"Yes or no, will you meet with him?"

"I'd say no."

"So you'd rather have Julius dig into every aspect of your life than consent to a one-hour meeting?"

"Oh, I'm sure he'd do that anyway."

He hung up on me. As I'd mentioned, he annoyed me, and he did so enough that I hacked into the IRS database, as well as his bank and brokerage accounts, and found several interesting discrepancies that could get him in hot water. When I called him back I mentioned these discrepancies. His tone changed then as he asked me how I found out about that.

"Julius and I are both very good at what we do."

"So you're blackmailing me now."

"Call it what you want. Just ask yourself whether you're more afraid of an IRS audit or Julius pinning a murder rap on you. If you hang up on me now, that will help him even more than if you agreed to come in and meet with him."

After nine point four seconds of stony silence, Heckle agreed to a time.

With the appointments set up, I proceeded to do further research on these four suspects and build simulations that could point to one or more of them murdering Jasper Quayle. Hell, for all I knew it could've been a joint enterprise between any two or more of them, or it could've been none of them. I still liked the idea of it being some yet unidentified spurned lover or angry husband/boyfriend/ brother or what have you, but until Tom tracked down who Quayle was rendezvousing with at the Windsor Hotel, there was no way of knowing.

All of this put Julius in a rotten mood, and it didn't help that he had missed his opportunity to sample cognac that afternoon at the Belvedere Club, something I knew he had been looking forward to for almost a week. It didn't help his mood any when I e-mailed him the dossiers I had compiled for each of the four suspects either, or when Detective Mark Cramer showed up a little after seven that evening. Cramer's a Cambridge police detective, and he and Julius have butted heads three times over the last two years. The reason for this is that Cramer has the mistaken belief that Julius was trying to grandstand in murder investigations Cramer was involved in. If he understood how lazy Julius is, he'd realize how foolish that notion is. Julius would've been more than happy to sit back and let the police solve the cases themselves, but since that wasn't happening and Julius had a stake in exposing those murderers, he had to exert himself to unmask the guilty parties.

This evening, instead of being his usual bombastic self when he believes Julius is cutting in on one of his investigations, Cramer appeared to be amused by the situation. Not only that, he was mostly civil, and accepted Julius's invitation for coffee. While they sat in the kitchen waiting for the coffee to brew, Cramer asked Julius if what he'd heard was true, that Julius was going to try to prove that Chervil didn't murder Jasper Quayle.

"I am going to look into the matter," Julius said, tight-lipped.

Cramer shook his head with a look that could only be described as pity. "You're going to fall flat on your face with this one, Julius," he said, and the fact that he called Julius by his first name instead of spitting out *Katz* like it were some sort of curse showed that he didn't think it likely that Julius was going to get anywhere. Cramer took a sip of his freshly brewed coffee, and as if it were a casual question, asked Julius why he thought there was a chance in hell that Chervil wasn't guilty.

"I'm not saying he isn't," Julius said tactfully.

"So you're just fishing here?"

"It appears so. It would help clarify the situation for me if I could listen to the nine-one-one call that sent the police to Quayle's restaurant."

That brought Cramer back to more of his usual self. With his eyes narrowing to slits, he asked Julius how he knew about the 911 call. "We haven't made that public yet," he added, his voice tight with suspicion.

Julius shrugged indifferently. "Up until three seconds ago, that was only a guess on my part, since I couldn't imagine any other reason for the police to have shown up there. Detective, will you indulge me and let me listen to that recording?"

Cramer put his coffee cup down and got to his feet, his face reddening. "Forget it, Katz," he growled. "We've got Chervil dead to rights, and you still have to muck around with this? Well, go ahead, it's not going to get you anywhere. But I'll be damned if I'm going to help you!"

With that Cramer was moving fast out of the kitchen and down the hallway towards the front door. I followed him over the webcam feeds to make sure he didn't cause any trouble, but he moved in a beeline, too angry to do anything but storm out of the townhouse. Once Cramer was out the door with that same door slammed hard behind him, I mentioned to Julius that he seemed to have annoyed Cramer.

"It appears that way," Julius agreed.

"That anonymous call must be a sore spot to Cramer. I've analyzed the blueprints for the restaurant, and also studied the restaurant's location via online mapping services. There wouldn't be any foot traffic near the back of the restaurant to hear any scream. That call doesn't make any sense, and Cramer must know it. That reason alone has convinced me Chervil is innocent, unless he made the call himself."

Julius nodded grimly and continued sipping his coffee. It didn't matter that that anonymous call convinced us of Chervil's innocence, or at least mostly did; a jury wouldn't be swayed by it with all the physical evidence condemning him.

Once Julius was done with his coffee he sat quietly for thirty seconds, resigning himself to the fact that he was going to have to spend the evening working on a case that had little chance for success and for which he hadn't yet arranged payment. Once he was back in his office, he spoke on the phone with the two borderline suspects that I hadn't been able to find alibis for, and once he was satisfied that they weren't involved with Quayle's murder, he sat for the next three hours grimacing at the reports I'd put together on his four primary suspects, while I tried to track down the suspects' locations at the time of Quayle's murder through phone records, credit-card receipts, and other such methods. I had no luck eliminating any of them. In fact, looking at their phone records and the number of times they had recently called Quayle, or he had called them, it only made each of them look more likely as suspects.

Megan Quayle, the widow, was first up the next morning. She was dressed in traditional black and, at forty-three, was a small, bitter-looking woman with nickel-sized eyes and a tiny, almost birdlike mouth. She arrived at eleven, and when Julius led her into his townhouse, she moved in a quick, scurrying manner that reminded me of film I had found of piping plovers scampering along an ocean beach. I know I should've made allowances for her. After all, her husband had just been stabbed to death, but I quickly found myself rooting for her to be the killer. And I don't think it was only because the minute she got seated in Julius's office she started complaining about me.

"He's such a rude, insolent man! You should fire him!"

"I hear that often," Julius said with an apologetic smile.

She made a harrumphing sound at that. "My husband has just been murdered. I'm grieving right now, and that awful, awful man refused to tell me why you wished to see me."

"Inexcusable," Julius agreed.

At that moment, after the ammunition she'd handed Julius, which I knew he'd be using on me for days, I was really hoping she'd be the one. She nodded at what Julius had said, her mouth pinched as if she had something to spit out. "Mr. Katz, this is a very difficult time for me," she said.

"I appreciate that, and if you had nothing to do with your husband's murder, then I truly regret bringing you here, as well as what I need to ask you."

Other than her mouth pinching a little tighter, she barely reacted to that, although her voice had a shriller quality when she asked him what he meant.

"Madam, my reason for wanting to meet with you is to discover whether you murdered your husband. So I'll ask you directly. Did you stab your husband to death?"

"How dare you!"

Julius shrugged innocently. Of course, he had to know that she'd answer the way she did, although he once had a murderer admit to his crime when Julius posed the same question to him. Julius is an expert poker player, and is better than even I am at spotting people's tells, and I knew that that's what he was trying to do with her: gauge whether her outrage to that question was genuine or forced. I had no clue. If she did have a tell, I couldn't figure out what it was. There was too much hostility and nervousness for me to read much else in her mannerisms. I asked Julius if he had a better read on her and he signaled that he didn't.

"It's a fair question," Julius told her. "After all, you did stab your husband in the past."

That caused not only her mouth to pinch tighter but her face to purple. Of course she had to be expecting that from Julius, since it had made the newspapers three years ago. While she didn't stab him in the back with a butcher knife back then, she did plant a salad fork into his hand. This happened at some fancy dinner when she found out Quayle was in the midst of an affair. Divorce papers were filed shortly afterwards and for several weeks the gossip columns were filled with acrimonious accusations from both of them, and then somehow a reconciliation miraculously occurred. Or maybe it was more of an uneasy truce.

"You're going to throw that in my face now?" she accused him, once again seething. "After what just happened?"

"Especially after what has happened. Three years ago you stabbed your husband in a fit of rage."

She sniffed indignantly at that. "I poked him with a fork. I barely broke the skin. And you know why I did it! He had it coming!"

"You did more than simply poke him," Julius said. "He required medical attention. But that's beside the point. I'm more interested in whether you decided to trade a salad fork for a butcher knife after once again finding out that he was cheating on you."

She gave him a dumbfounded look, as if she didn't know what he was talking about. Maybe she didn't. Since I had no clue how to read her, I didn't know whether it was an act or not.

"What do you mean?" she asked, her voice trembling and not much more than a whisper.

Julius's eyes narrowed as he gazed at her. "Your husband was meeting with someone over the last month at the Windsor Hotel." He gave her each of the dates that Quayle had paid for a room. The widow stumbled to her feet. She stammered out to Julius that she was done talking to him, and then proceeded to leave his office. Julius tried to ask her if she knew who her husband was seeing, but she ignored him. I watched as she left his townhouse.

Earlier Julius had arranged for a freelance P.I., Saul Penzer, to tail her when she left. Like Tom Durkin, Saul is very good and does not work cheap, but I guess Julius was hoping if the widow had an idea who her husband was seeing, she'd lead Saul to her.

"What do you think?" I asked Julius. "Hell if I can get a read on her. Did she know that her husband was cheating on her again, or was this all a surprise to her?"

Julius grimaced in the direction that the widow had fled. He shook his head. "I don't know, Archie. Maybe Saul will enlighten us later."

I let that sit between us for several seconds, then added, "You realize she's also now going to be telling people what a nasty person *you* are."

That brought a grim smile to Julius's lips. "That's only an assumption, Archie," he said. "So far I've only heard her call one of us rude and insolent and awful."

I was going to argue the point, but I decided I'd be better off leaving it alone, and instead worked on my simulations and probability formulas that would prove that the Widow Quayle was a backstabbing murderer as well as a poor judge of character. I was still working on this when Julius's next suspect rang the doorbell. This was Stephanie Lesnick, the woman who caused the Widow Quayle to plant a salad fork in her husband's hand three years earlier.

Stephanie Lesnick was now thirty-six. More slender than thin, she was attractive in a supporting-actress kind of way, but certainly would never be a leading actress, at least not from the comparisons I made of her with actresses from a Hollywood database. After the incident three years ago, her own marriage broke up, and her ex-husband, a college professor, remarried and moved to California. From what Chervil had told Julius, it was well-known in the restaurant circle that Lesnick did not take well to Quayle ending their affair to go back to his wife. Chervil had heard about at least four incidents where Lesnick burst into Quayle's restaurant to confront him in what could only be described as embarrassing and obscenity-laced scenes. Earlier I hacked the Cambridge courts computer system and was able to find a restraining order filed nine months ago by Quayle that spelled out one of the incidents that Chervil had heard about.

Lesnick appeared subdued the whole time that she met with Julius, and she had a particularly hard time looking him in the eye. When Julius asked her whether she had murdered Quayle, she simply shook her head and answered that the police had already arrested someone for the crime. "Another chef, I believe," she said.

"I didn't ask you whether someone had been arrested, but whether you were the one who stabbed Jasper Quayle."

She shook her head no, but feigned no outrage or even surprise that Julius would ask her that.

"You don't seem surprised by my question?"

She tried smiling at Julius. It didn't work, as she had a tough time maintaining eye contact with him. "I'm sure you've heard the stories, and possibly even gotten a copy of the restraining order Jasper filed. But those threats I made weren't real. I was angry at him, yes. He made promises to me that he broke, promises that I counted on. And he didn't love his wife." She met Julius's gaze then as she added, "The only reason he stayed with her was because of his precious restaurant. It was in her name too, and if he divorced her as he promised me, he would've had to sell it. I was a fool to ever get involved with him."

She lowered her eyes then, her mouth frozen in an uneasy smile. Julius stared at her for the next six seconds before asking her where she was last Thursday at two-thirty, which was the time the anonymous 911 call was made. Lesnick looked blank momentarily. Then, as she realized that was the moment Jasper Quayle was being murdered, her eyes darkened and she lowered them again, her blank smile turning into something sickly.

"If you're asking whether I have an alibi for when Jasper was killed, I don't. I was by myself, taking a drive to the ocean so I could be alone. I doubt anyone saw me or could vouch for me."

"You weren't parked outside of Quayle's restaurant?"

She shook her head.

"You weren't the one who phoned the police that day?"

Another shake of her head. For the next forty-five minutes, Julius focused on how often she'd stalk Quayle and park her car outside his restaurant. She admitted to doing this several times a week but he couldn't budge her about last Thursday. When he mentioned Quayle's rendezvous at the Windsor Hotel, she seemed genuinely surprised but claimed she had no idea who Quayle was seeing. It was possible she was the mystery woman, but if she was, she wasn't admitting to it, and Tom had no luck when he showed her photo around the hotel. By the time Julius gave up and escorted Lesnick from his townhouse, it looked like a complete bust to me. If she knew about Quayle's recent affair, she wasn't saying. If she was the one who called the police, I had no way of proving it. Through some hacking, I had the phone number that was used to call the police that day, but I was unable to match it to any registered phone. Most likely it was an untraceable cell phone with prepaid minutes, one of those you can buy at any drugstore. If any of Julius's suspects had recently bought one of those phones, they did it with cash because I couldn't find any credit-card charges from them showing a purchase.

Julius didn't look too happy when he returned back to his office. I didn't bother asking him if he'd been able decipher anything in her body language. I knew he was as stumped on that score as I was.

Next up was another chef, Edmund Gormier. He was sixty-two. A short and plump man with a round head, the top of which was mostly bald with only a fringe of white hair along the sides, although he made up for that lack of hair by growing a thick beard and mustache that covered his face like fur. While Gormier wasn't much to look at, he had a wife half his age who was. The pictures I found of her rated her as a knockout. That was one of the reasons Gormier might've wanted to see a knife stuck deeply into Quayle's back, since Quayle had made a pass at her at the last Golden Pan awards, the equivalent of the Academy Award for local Boston-area chefs, and that attempted pass led to some fireworks and fisticuffs, in which Gormier left Quayle bruised and with a bloody nose before he was pulled away by other chefs in attendance. Chervil wasn't the one who gave up Gormier, but his protégé, April Morley, and according to her there had been bad blood between Gormier and Quayle for years.

The first thing Gormier said after he got seated in Julius's office was that he envied Chervil. "I would like to shake Henri's hand for murdering that pig of a man, Quayle," Gormier declared, his eyes bright with excitement.

"I am very jealous of Henri. He deserves a medal for what he did, certainly. That pig stole Henri's *Bouillabaisse ala Sophie*? Henri showed remarkable restraint only stabbing him once. If it were me, I would've used a cleaver until there was nothing left of him except gristle and stew meat."

"So if you had been there in Quayle's kitchen you would've killed him?"

Gormier's eyes brightened even more at that. "Of course!" he exclaimed. Some of his starch went out of him as he sunk back into his chair, the pink leaving his cheeks. He made a face to show his distaste. "That cheap dime-store Romeo. He imagined himself a great chef when he lacked the skill to be even an adequate short-order cook." He shrugged, his expression turning to a pained grimace. "If not for my wife, maybe I would've paid him for all of his offenses. But even if it meant leaving a young and beautiful wife to go to prison, if he had ever stolen something like *Bouillabaisse ala Sophie* from me, I would've gone to that so-called restaurant of his and paid him back the same as Henri did."

For the next hour Julius got little more from Gormier other than the litany of insults Quayle had directed at him over the years, and how he envied Henri for being the one to plant that knife in Quayle's back. He wasn't able to provide an alibi, nor did he seem to show any interest in doing so as he made a face and told Julius he was by himself taking a nap at the time Quayle was being stabbed. As far as his wife went, she must've been out shopping. Tom had also showed a photo of Gormier's wife around the Windsor Hotel, and if she was our mystery woman, no one had so far identified her. The one thing that made me think that Gormier wasn't our murderer was that Julius provided him one of his better Merlots and an assortment of dried meats and cheeses, and I knew Julius hated to feed murderers. But then again, Gormier was one of the few respected chefs that Julius ever had as a suspect, so he might've been willing to make an exception, especially since he occasionally dined at Gormier's restaurant.

After Gormier was Jason Heckle, and while I was still rooting for the Widow Quayle to be the killer, I was soon hoping that the two of them could somehow have done it together. Heckle was barely seated before he launched into a tirade against me. He was a large, doughy man of forty-seven and resembled database photos of the old-time actor, George Sanders, except he had a smaller and crueler mouth. While Heckle continued impugning my character, Julius nodded in sympathy. Finally Heckle ran out of steam, but not without first stating that I should be arrested for extortion. "And you too, Katz," he added with his mouth curling into a half-sneer.

"Interesting," Julius said. "While I don't always agree with Archie's methods, I'm wondering what he extorted from you?"

Heckle bristled at that. "You know damn well the threat he used to get me here!"

"All I know is that Archie asked you to speak to me regarding a murder investigation I'm conducting." Julius rubbed his chin slowly as he considered both Heckle and the charge that he raised. "As far as I know, he didn't pried any money or property away from you, and it would be hard for me to imagine any district attorney taking an extortion charge seriously, but that's beside the point. I am curious as to why you made light of Jasper Quayle's murder, even going so far as to suggest to Archie that you committed it."

Heckle's mouth got smaller and crueler. "What difference did it make what I said to him?" he asked. "The police caught that other chef dead to rights, and if you were having your henchman call me it was only to see if you could pin Quayle's murder on me." Heckle leaned further back in his chair, his expression shifting to show the injury he was feeling. "It's well known that you're some kind of gourmet and the chef that the police caught, Chervil, is a world-famous chef. It was obvious to me that you're looking for someone else to take the murder rap. And that I am as good a candidate as any for you to go after."

"I assure you I'm only looking for the guilty party. And you did make public threats against Quayle."

"And I'm damned lucky the police caught Chervil red-handed the way they did or I'd have been picked up for the crime," Heckle said, more injury showing in his mouth. "And I had good reason for making my threats. Quayle cheated me out of two hundred grand, convincing me to invest in a new venture that he was in the process of shutting down. He did a nice job cooking the books. He's a chef after all, right? But I know my money went straight into his pockets."

"Let's make this easy. Did you kill Jasper Quayle?"

Heckle smiled at that. A thin, ugly smile. "No, although if I could've gotten away with it, I wish I had."

"Where were you at two-thirty last Thursday?"

Heckle's smile got a bit uglier. "By myself at the movies. If I had any witnesses who could've vouched for me I wouldn't have given your henchman such a tough time when he called me."

Julius spent the next half-hour poking around into Heckle's story, and got nowhere, at least not so that I could see. By the time he finished up with him and Heckle was gone, Julius had fallen into a funk. I knew this because Julius selected a fair-at-best zinfandel from his wine cellar to bring outside to his private garden patio, and Julius only drank zinfandel when he was in one of his funks. I let him drink a glass of it in solitude before asking him if he knew which one it was. He sighed softly before telling me he didn't.

"If it's even one of those four," he said before pouring another glass of zinfandel.

———

Five days later, it still looked hopeless. Tom had had no luck at the Windsor Hotel identifying Quayle's mystery woman. Saul had gotten nowhere keeping an eye on the Widow Quayle—if she knew who her husband had been seeing she was keeping her distance. I was even less than nowhere with my simulations and formulas. Any of the suspects could've done it, and I was no closer to figuring out which one of them it was, assuming it was one of those four. Julius, to give him credit, worked harder during those five days than I've ever seen him work on a case. There was no loafing, no browsing wine magazines, and I knew he was putting his full brain power on it, but he was getting nowhere. As evidence of his state of mind, each night he selected a poorer zinfandel than the night before for his evening drinking. He tried calling Gormier's wife to see if she could've been the mystery woman rendezvousing with Quayle, but she had an airtight alibi for not only the murder but two of the rendezvous dates. He tried calling other chefs he was friendly with to see if they could point him to other potential suspects. He tried a number of other things too, but struck out with everything.

At two o'clock today he sat for a half-hour grimacing as he tried to force an answer to this murder, but he got nowhere. I'd never seen Julius give up a case before, but when he picked up a wine magazine and began browsing it, I knew he was as much as waving a white flag of surrender.

"That's it?" I asked. "A little adversity and you throw in the towel?"

"It appears that way," Julius murmured.

"Forget about freeing an innocent man. What about *Bouillabaisse ala Sophie*? Are you giving up on it this easily? One of your *raisons d'etre*?"

"I'm sure Ms. Morley will do a fine job preparing it," Julius grunted out, the muscles along his mouth tightening. His fingers began drumming the surface of his desk, which showed his growing annoyance. "Archie, sometimes you need to admit when you're beat."

I knew better than to push it, at least if I didn't want to be turned off, which I didn't. In the funk he had fallen into he'd take any provocation from me as an excuse to turn me off. So for the next two hours I avoided saying anything to him. Then inspiration struck. It was like a blast of electrons hitting my processing unit and creating an almost blinding light. Or an illuminating light. It was so obvious, and I couldn't help telling Julius, "Ha! I figured it out! In fact, I just sent you an e-mail that solves this case!"

"I'm not in the mood for this," he warned me.

"You don't believe me? Check your e-mail!"

Julius's expression went from suspicious to dubious as he reached for his computer mouse. He stopped with his fingertips inches from it, his facial muscles hardening as if he were a marble sculpture. This lasted forty seconds, and I knew his genius was working in overload. When he came out of this, he muttered to himself under his breath, commenting that if he wasn't such a dunce he could've been enjoying the Belvedere Club for the last four days. After that he gave me a set of instructions.

———

Cramer was harder to convince than I thought he'd be. He'd seen Julius in action enough that he should've trusted that if Julius was saying he was going to expose a killer, then that's what he was going to do, but instead Cramer was convinced Julius was only trying to pull some stunt. "If you want egg on your face, that's your call," I told him. "One way this happens is that Julius lets you make the arrest and come out with your dignity mostly intact, the other way, he goes straight to the newspapers and turns all of you into laughingstocks."

"Yeah? Is that so? Let him give me a name then!"

"Uh-uh. There's a reason he's called a genius, and that's because he works things the way they need to be worked. But if you don't want to be part of this, you don't have to be. This is only a courtesy on Julius's part."

He let loose a long string of invectives in which he described in extraordinarily colorful language what Julius could do with this courtesy, but in the end he agreed to what Julius was asking, and at eight that evening he brought Henri Chervil, the Widow Quayle, Stephanie Lesnick, Edmund Gormier, Jason Heckle, and a small army of police officers to Julius's townhouse. April Morley was already there, since Julius had called her earlier. The seating arrangements had the Widow Quayle in the guest-of-honor seat, which was the chair directly opposite Julius. In the loveseat to the left of Julius's desk were Jason Heckle and Stephanie Lesnick. Another chair had been pulled up next to it for Edmund Gormier. Chervil sat on the sofa to the right of Julius's desk, crammed in between Cramer and a beefy, thick-jawed Cambridge police sergeant by the name of Lewis Timmons. From the way Chervil was scowling, he wasn't happy about his placement, nor, probably, about the fact that he still had his wrists secured by handcuffs. Rounding things out, April Morley sat in a chair that had been placed to the right of the sofa, and four of Cambridge's finest stood behind this gathering. After Julius passed out refreshments to the police officers, the suspects, Chervil, and April Morley, he took his chair and gazed slowly at each of them. After nodding to the room, Julius turned to the widow and asked her if it was usual for her husband to be at his restaurant at two-thirty in the afternoon. She told him it wasn't, that with the restaurant not opening until six in the evening, he often wouldn't show up there until four at the earliest, and usually later than that, as he would typically leave it to his staff to do the pre-dinner preparations.

Julius grimaced at that, remarked that that was the answer he expected, and then told his audience that if his brain had been functioning properly he would've had this murder solved four days earlier.

"Unfortunately, I chose to ignore things I shouldn't have," he said. "The most obvious of these being why the victim was at his restaurant when he was. I also failed to place enough importance on the timing of the murder." Julius faced Chervil and gave him a grave look. "Sir, because of my incompetence, you've had to sit in a jail cell four days longer than you should've. I apologize for that. All I can imagine is that the threat of losing your magnificent *Bouillabaisse ala Sophie* left me temporarily witless. That is the only reason I can come up with to explain why I wasted four days trying to solve Jasper Quayle's murder before realizing he wasn't the intended victim."

Cramer sputtered at that. "What do you mean?" he demanded. "Are you trying to say the killer didn't intend to stick a knife in Quayle's back? That it was all an accident?"

"No, not at all. Simply that Jasper Quayle was little more than a pawn. His death was necessary but still inconsequential to the killer, although for reasons that I'll soon explain, it quickly became imperative that he be killed when he was.

The killer used Quayle's murder as part of a carefully laid out plan to ruin Henri Chervil."

Chervil barely reacted to that news. He remained scowling, although a hint of skepticism showed in his expression as he asked why anyone, other than perhaps Jasper Quayle, would want to ruin him. Julius told him he would explain. My focus shifted to the killer, because it was obvious then who it was, but I had to admit she did a good job of not showing a single crack. Julius also focused his stare on her, which would've been enough to wilt most people, but April Morley maintained her composure and didn't show a hint that there was anything for her to worry about.

Julius's eyes narrowed as he maintained his gaze on Morley. "There was no break-in, was there?" he asked her. "That was a story you manufactured for Mr. Chervil. Instead, you discovered that he had written down his recipes, and you let Jasper Quayle know that you had access to *Bouillabaisse ala Sophie*, and you manipulated him into believing that he was seducing you for that recipe. I'm also guessing that you're the one who arranged to have a sample of Quayle's version of that dish delivered to Chervil's restaurant."

She was good, I had to give her that. Her eyes filled up with tears and a tremor shook her voice as she told Chervil that she didn't know why Julius was saying such things. "There was a break-in," she insisted. "And I didn't give that man your recipe like he's saying. None of it's true."

"Stop it," Julius said, admonishing her. He waited until she turned to face him before he continued. "Please, you're not going to get anywhere with this act. It's over for you, whether or not you realize it yet." He took a deep breath and let it out slowly through his nose. At this point the room had gotten deathly quiet. Julius continued.

"Maybe your plan was to provoke Mr. Chervil into killing Jasper Quayle, or maybe all along it was to frame him for Quayle's murder, as you ended up doing, but whichever it was, Quayle's death became imperative after the two of you met with me. Most likely you counted on me to turn down your boss, not expecting me to take a case that you believed to be as inconsequential as one chef stealing a recipe from another. Once I accepted the assignment, you had to act quickly, since you could not allow Jasper Quayle to remain alive long enough to speak with me. This is where you got lucky. When Mr. Chervil excused you from our meeting by asking you to head back to his restaurant, you knew him well enough to know his purpose for this. He was planning to confront Quayle once again at his restaurant. And so you called Quayle to arrange a meeting, then murdered him and waited for Mr. Chervil to show so you could call the police."

Morley's appearance underwent a subtle change. This happened quickly, really no more than a blink of an eye, which is about three hundred milliseconds. Where there had been a gentle softness before there was now only ice and steel. An intense jangling burst of electrons hit my processing unit. For a few microseconds this confused me, and then I realized I had experienced my first shiver.

Morley smiled, and it was every bit as icy as the rest of her now appeared. "A very fanciful tale, Mr. Katz," she said. "But that's all it is, as I'm sure you lack a single shred of evidence to prove this story of yours."

Julius shook his head. "No, Ms. Morley. While you have proven you are exceptionally devious, you're not as smart as you believe you are. I have more than enough evidence to convict you. While you tried not to be seen during your clandestine meetings with Quayle at the Windsor Hotel, you were spotted entering Quayle's room by another guest and he has been able to identify you. One of my operatives, Tom Durkin, has since tracked this guest down and is bringing him here this evening."

That was my cue to call Tom, who was waiting outside of Julius's townhouse. Tom waited twenty seconds before ringing the doorbell. As good as Morley had been, you could see her tensing up as one of the police officers left to get the door to bring in Tom and his witness. Of course, his witness was Saul Penzer, since Tom had had no luck finding any actual witnesses, but Morley didn't know that. When Tom escorted Saul into Julius's office, and Saul focused his stare immediately on Morley and nodded, Morley turned her icy smile back to Julius.

"So you know I had an affair with Jasper," she said, her voice now with a higher-pitched hysterical edge to it. "That doesn't prove I killed him. You've got nothing, Katz."

Julius shrugged. "Not true. I've got you waiting outside of Quayle's restaurant after you killed him so that you could make your anonymous call to the police once Henri Chervil showed up."

"That's a lie! I went back to Chervil's as I was asked to do!"

Julius nodded to Cramer, who used this cue to take out an MP3 player, which he brought over to Julius. Once Julius plugged it into a speaker on his desk, Cramer played the anonymous 911 call. Morley tried to disguise her voice, and if you didn't know it was her calling it probably would've fooled you, but I made a voice imprint from the recording and was able to match it exactly to Morley. I told Julius this.

Julius said to her, "What you might not know is that voice imprints can authenticate someone every bit as much as fingerprints, and disguising your voice doesn't alter your imprint."

"Why?"

This came from Chervil and was directed to Julius, and was every bit as anguished as the look on his face.

Julius gave him a sympathetic smile. "You arranged for your restaurant to pass to Ms. Morley on your death?" he asked.

Chervil nodded grimly.

Julius shrugged. "You own the building your restaurant is located in. An appraisal has the property worth over two million dollars. I'm assuming you would've passed this on to Ms. Morley if you had also been convicted and sentenced to life."

Chervil turned to Morley, the anguish in his face difficult to look at. His voice little more than a hoarse whisper, he asked why she had done this. "I treated you like you were my own daughter."

She broke then. Completely. What was left in her face was brutal and cruel. "Did I ask for that?" she demanded. "One old fool for a father was more than enough! Why would you think I'd want another?"

Two of the police officers had moved closer to her once Julius had made it clear who the murderer was. Now they were making her stand so they could put cuffs on her.

Edmund Gormier had left his seat so that he could stand by Chervil and put a hand on Chervil's shoulder in his attempt to offer emotional support. It did little to quench the anguish in Chervil's face.

———

Three days later Julius and Lily Rosten held a small dinner party at Chervil's. The chef demanded it. His face looked older and grayer, and there was a gravity to him that didn't exist during his first meeting with Julius, but he brought out each course himself. As the dinner was coming to an end, he came over to offer Julius a bottle of 1985 Château Lafite Rothschild as a token of his appreciation and to talk about Julius's fee.

"There is none," Julius said.

Chervil's face folded into a scowl. "Nonsense," he insisted. "You incurred expenses and put in valuable time. There has to be a fee."

"This dinner party is more than enough, as well as the knowledge that I can expect my yearly dining experience of *Bouillabaisse ala Sophie* to continue."

Chervil didn't like that answer, and left the table shaking his head and muttering to himself.

The next morning Chervil called, demanding to know a fee that he could pay, and again Julius told him that there would be none, and again Chervil didn't like that answer. Three hours later a courier delivered the remaining eleven bottles of Chervil's case of 1985 Château Lafite Rothschild, along with a curt note that stated that Julius should consider this payment in full. I told Julius that since he didn't want additional payment I would arrange for the bottles to be brought back to Chervil.

"That won't be necessary, Archie," Julius said. "The man seems intent on paying me, and I don't wish to insult him by returning these."

"Sure you don't," I said. "This was your plan all along. You had a good enough read on him from the start to know that he'd end up insisting that you take this case of Château Lafite Rothschild off his hands. Damn, you played him like a fiddle."

"I don't know what you're talking about."

Julius had returned to his office and was now sitting behind his desk. I told him, "Sure you don't. By the way, half those bottles should be mine since I solved this case first. Or are you forgetting the e-mail I sent you?"

Julius's thin smile hardened. "I never looked at that e-mail."

"It doesn't matter. I still wrote it and you can look at it now if you want."

"What would that prove, Archie? You've had plenty of opportunities to replace that e-mail with another."

"Uh-uh. Not unless I rewrote your computer's operating system and its e-mail program, which I could do but I haven't. The e-mail message waiting for you is the same one I sent. Unaltered."

Julius sat for a moment drumming his fingers along the surface of his desk. A glint of wariness dulled his eyes, but he conceded to open the e-mail I had sent him. It read:

I sent this to you because you gave up on the case, and the threat that I might've figured things out before you should be enough to get you moving and solving this. You might consider this nothing but a ploy, but since this ploy is what's going to result in this case being solved, I'm taking credit for it, or at least half the credit.

"Very good, Archie," Julius said, a wisp of admiration showing in his smile. "Of course, you realize this will only work this one time."

"Once is enough," I said. "How about a deal? You never use any of the ammunition Megan Quayle and Jason Heckle handed you—you know, about me supposedly being insolent, rude, an extortionist, et cetera, et cetera, and I won't bring up again how I was the one to solve this case?"

"Deal."

I would've been well within my rights to have also asked for half the wine, but I knew Julius would fight me on that, as well as what my role was in identifying Jasper Quayle's murderer. I didn't care. Whether Julius was willing to admit it or not, as far as I was concerned it was my inspiration that led to Quayle's murderer being caught. Because of that, I'm sticking to my claim that I solved this case, or at the very least, that I deserve equal credit for it with Julius. But I know better than to argue the point with him, at least if I don't want to be turned off.

JULIUS KATZ AND
A TANGLED WEBB

Originally published in the March/April 2014 issue of Ellery Queen Mystery Magazine.

"I KNOW IT doesn't look good, but I didn't do what they're saying I did," Charles Rosten insisted. He shifted his gaze from Julius to Lily and attempted to give his daughter a reassuring smile. If there hadn't been a glass partition separating the two of them he might've tried to reach for her hand, but since there was, all he could do was smile at her, and it seemed as if it was a struggle for him to do that much. Given how miserable Lily appeared, it didn't seem to have helped any. I couldn't blame Rosten for failing to reassure her. Since I'd been Julius's assistant and all-around-man-Friday I'd witnessed seven other clients say those exact words to him, but never had it seemed more hopeless than it did right now.

Rosten's smile weakened to where it began looking more like a grimace, and he shifted his stare again to Julius. He cleared his throat and added, "I didn't kill George

Webb." Then he clamped his mouth shut, his lips pressing into a rigid line.

Charles Rosten was fifty-three, which was only eleven years older than Julius. At six feet tall, he was just Julius's height, but he had a thicker body, and his two hundred and ten pounds outweighed Julius by thirty. With his square jaw and thick brown hair that was graying at the temples, he was a good-looking man, even given his current circumstances. At the moment he was sitting on the wrong side of a glass partition at the Monroe County Jail in Rochester, New York, wearing jail-issued dungarees and matching shirt. He'd been arrested two days earlier for murdering his business partner, George Webb, and the evidence against him was overwhelming. As I mentioned before, he couldn't be more right about things not looking good for him. The best odds I could calculate for any jury finding him not guilty of Webb's murder were statistically zero.

"Mr. Rosten—" Julius started.

"You can call me Charles," Rosten said gruffly, his eyes fixing hard on Julius's. His voice grew gruffer as he added, "After all, you've been dating my daughter for six months."

Julius nodded. "It's hard for me to say how bad things look for you, since all the information I have regarding Webb's murder has come from news reports and Lily. From what I understand, on Friday, you, Webb, and several of your employees were having an off-site meeting at Thrale House, and at three twenty-four you were found alone in a room with Webb's corpse. He had been shot twice in the chest, and several of your employees came into the room to find you standing over him holding a forty-caliber semiautomatic handgun, which ballistics has since shown is the murder weapon. Are those basic facts correct?"

"I can't say exactly about the time you mentioned since I was in a daze after finding George dead," Rosten stated bluntly. "The details of what happened after that, at least until the police showed up, are only a blur to me. I can't even remember who came into the room to find me with George, although I've been told since that they all did."

"All?"

Rosten shook his head angrily at himself. "Sorry," he said. "That wouldn't mean much to you, would it? I was told that the employees who were at the off-site all came rushing into the library—that was the room this happened in—to see me holding the gun. That would be Angela Harris, a secretary George and I share, or I guess I should say, shared, Carolyn Powers, head of sales, Simon Callow, our design guru, Peter Boswell, head of marketing, and Earl Gilmore, who runs manufacturing."

"What were you and Webb doing in the library?"

Rosten shrugged. "Things weren't going well with our meeting." He raised a questioning eyebrow at Julius. "You probably heard about that, huh?"

"I'd heard that it had turned contentious."

"Yeah, it had. For months George and I had been talking about expanding the company. The numbers made sense, and he was on-board with it. Hell, it was his idea to begin with. Then, two weeks ago, he started acting more cantankerous than usual, snapping at me and everyone else for the littlest things. At Friday's meeting, he was near impossible and insisted on postponing our expansion plans without giving any damn reason why. We took an hour break at three o'clock for everyone to cool off. I was too annoyed with George to wait until the break was over, so I went to the library to have a word with him in private. That's when I found him lying on the floor. Even though I knew George was dead from the way he looked, I felt for a pulse to see if there was any chance of saving him. I must've spotted the gun then, and without realizing it picked it up."

"How'd you know Webb had gone to the library? Did you follow him there?"

Rosten shook his head. "We've been holding our annual strategy meeting at Thrale House for the last fourteen years, and every year when we need to take a break so folks could calm down, George grabs the library. He claimed that after hours of butting heads with me he needed the solitude there."

"The meetings were always contentious?"

"It couldn't be helped." Rosten smiled bleakly. "George was always a bit of a hothead."

Lily rolled her eyes at that while continuing to look absolutely miserable. In a voice that sounded as if she was fighting hard to keep from crying, she said, "Daddy, and you're not?"

"Not like he was," Rosten stated stubbornly. "Or maybe I am. I don't know. It doesn't matter now." His eyes wavered for a moment as he added, "Through all the bickering, we'd still always come to the right decisions. George was a good man and a good business partner."

Julius interrupted Rosten's nostalgic reflection by asking about the employees who were drawn to the library. "From what I understand they were scattered about the house, and came to the library after hearing what they thought were gunshots?"

Rosten nodded grimly. "That's what I was told."

"But you didn't hear any gunshots?"

Rosten looked surprised by the question, as if he hadn't thought of that before. "That's funny," he said. "But no, I didn't hear anything. I don't know how that's possible."

A guard entered then to warn them that they had only three minutes to wrap things up. Julius acknowledged him with a curt nod and started to stand.

"Charles, I know you've had reservations about me dating Lily—"

Rosten cut Julius off. "No, I'm fine with it," he muttered.

"Very good," Julius said. "I'm sorry we needed to meet for the first time under these circumstances, but I'm hoping that by tonight I'll be able to see you in a much more pleasant setting. Perhaps I'll be able to take you, Lily, and your wife someplace nice for dinner?"

That got a reaction from both Rosten and Lily. With Lily, it was her eyes moistening with tears as she bit her lip. With Rosten, it was the way his eyes narrowed.

"You believe me then?" he said.

"Is there any reason I shouldn't?"

Rosten shook his head. "The whole thing seems unbelievable to me, but Lily told me if there was anyone who could pull a miracle out of thin air, it would be you."

The guard held up his index finger to let them know they only had one minute left. Julius asked Rosten whether there was anyone other than the people he'd mentioned earlier in Thrale House at the time of the murder.

Rosten paused to consider that. "No," he said. "We had exclusive use of the property, and by then the people we'd had catering lunch were long gone. No one else should've been there."

"If you didn't kill Webb, which of your employees did?"

Rosten's eyes dulled as he thought about it. Finally, he shook his head and said that he didn't know.

The guard stepped forward to escort Rosten from the room. Julius waited for this to happen before helping Lily to her feet. The ordeal of having her father arrested for murder had taken its toll on her, and her typical peaches-and-cream complexion looked washed out and pale. As she stood, she appeared shaky. But even as worn out as she looked then, she was still very beautiful. When Julius first started dating her, I found pictures online of her parents, and while there's a resemblance to her father around her eyes, she mostly resembles her mother. Slender, petite, with red hair, full lips, and a heart-shaped face. At that moment, her hazel eyes searched deep into Julius's, and she asked whether he really believed he could prove her father was innocent.

"I hope so."

The tears she'd been holding back came loose then, and she moved forward and buried her face in Julius's chest. Since I'm a two-inch piece of advanced technology that Julius wears as a tiepin and there were no available webcam feeds for me to tie into, I have to assume what happened next—I have no visual record of it—and that was that Julius held her in his arms for the next forty-eight point three seconds while he attempted to comfort her. After she pulled away, she told him that she'd be heading back to her parents' house to be with her mother, since she knew Julius would be busy. Then she moved back to him and once again obstructed my visual circuits, and I had to guess from the quiet that followed that they spent the next fourteen seconds embraced and in a kiss before separating. They had driven separate cars to the jail, and after Julius walked Lily to hers and watched her drive off, he asked me to call the lead police detective on Webb's murder. I already had the information. This cop's name was Lieutenant Hal McCory, and I quickly had him on the line for Julius. He seemed a cooperative sort as he agreed to meet Julius at Thrale House in a half-hour.

"Is there any particular reason for this meeting?" McCory asked.

"I hope to prove conclusively that Charles Rosten didn't murder Webb."

McCory seemed amused by that and, before hanging up, told Julius that he always enjoyed a good sleight-of-hand trick, but that it would take more than that to convince him of Rosten's innocence. Through all this I had kept quiet. Julius didn't make promises lightly, and it was never a good idea to bet against him. Still, I wondered whether this impromptu trip to upstate New York had made him loopy. Julius was a creature of habit, and had everything he desired for a comfortable existence in his Beacon Hill townhouse. His wine; his books; his private-landscaped patio; his third-floor Kung-Fu studio, where he would spend two hours each morning performing intensive work-outs. It would've been bad enough if he could've stayed in a five-star hotel, but I knew he had to be dreading staying in the Rosten family home and having no privacy and none of his creature comforts, or even space to do his morning workout. Maybe in his desperation to be able to head back home to Boston, he created some sort of fairy-tale scenario that would allow him to wrap things up quickly instead of having to spend days, possibly even weeks, in Rochester trying to prove something that just wasn't possible. While this seemed completely out of character for Julius, it was the only answer I could come up with to explain his believing he could prove Rosten innocent. While we were alone in the car, I commented about something he had said to Rosten.

"You asked him whether he had reservations about you dating Lily because you wanted him to lie. You knew that under the circumstances he would answer that as politely as possible. Which meant lying."

Julius smiled thinly. "Why would I want him to lie?"

"So you could figure out his *tell*. I hadn't been able to figure it out up until that point, and I'll bet neither had you. Because he hadn't shown it yet. But when he said he was fine with you dating Lily, he was lying. His *tell* was as obvious as a blinking light. It was the way he clenched his jaw before he spoke. If you got him in a poker game you'd clean him out."

"Very good, Archie."

"He was also lying when he claimed he didn't know which of his employees killed Webb."

"And did he exhibit his tell before then?"

"No. Because he thought he was telling you the truth. But that doesn't mean he didn't kill Webb. He could've been in a daze before he entered the library; he could still be the one who shot Webb, even if he doesn't realize it, or even remember hearing the gunshots that he fired. That has to be what happened. Because given the facts, nothing else makes sense."

"There's one other possibility. But for now, Archie, please tell me what you're able to find about Thrale House."

I didn't know what Julius could've been thinking. That someone had hypnotized Rosten so that he wouldn't remember hearing gunshots or seeing the real killer? Whatever it was, he was grasping at straws, but I didn't see anything to gain by arguing with him. Given time, I was sure Julius would come to his senses. So I told him what I could about Thrale House. That it was a large Victorian home built by Horatio Thrale in 1879 and kept in the Thrale family until 1982, where, after having fallen in disrepair and thousands of dollar in arrear in back taxes, it was sold at auction. The house was then restored in 1990 and made available for leasing for weddings, company meetings, and other such events.

"Archie, could you go into more specifics as to the restorations that were done?"

That took more digging as I had to find the project plan filed with the city, which meant hacking into several computer systems. But once I found it, I started rattling off the changes and improvements that were made to the house, and that was when I uncovered the *other possibility* that Julius had been thinking about.

"What do you know," I said, amazed that Julius hadn't just been reaching for straws as I had thought. "This shows that Rosten was the one person in the house who couldn't have murdered Webb."

"And now to convince Lieutenant McCory of that fact," Julius said.

—

McCory was waiting in front of the Thrale House entrance with several other cops. Since I'd been able to hack into his personnel file I knew which of the cops he was, and I pointed him out to Julius. He was fifty-seven, had longish silver hair and a thick, bushy mustache the same color, and was three inches shorter than Julius. According to his last medical checkup, he was the same weight as Julius, although with the way his stomach bulged under his beat-up leather jacket, I would've put him at ten pounds more. McCory stood with his hands shoved in his pockets, his eyes narrowing to slits as he cautiously watched Julius approach him.

"Of course, I knew you were some sort of hotshot private eye in Boston," McCory said, his voice a deep bass. "But after hearing from you I called an officer I'd met up your ways. Mark Cramer. You know him, don'cha?"

Julius kept his poker face intact as he acknowledged that he knew Cramer, which was quite an understatement. Cramer had been the lead detective on five murder cases that Julius became involved with, and in each of these Cramer had acted as if Julius's sole purpose in life was to pull a fast one on him.

McCory said, "Cramer told me to be careful of you. That given half a chance you'll turn this into a circus just so you can get your name in the papers. But I also called Captain Martin Hoffmann out of Boston, and he gave me a different story. He says you're an honest man and I'm lucky to have your eyes on this case. That if I miss anything, you'll find it. So I'm going to give you the benefit of the doubt. Although I don't know how you're going to prove an impossibility like Charles Rosten being innocent. Are you going to try to claim that all five of them witnesses are in cahoots and are making up their story?"

"Not at all," Julius said. "Most likely, all but one of those five witnesses are telling you what they believe. But if you allow me access to the murder scene, I should be able to demonstrate Charles Rosten's innocence within a minute."

McCory rubbed the back of his neck slowly as he considered Julius. "You're saying you need only a minute to convince me I've arrested the wrong man?"

"Less time than that, actually."

"Well, then, I guess it would be foolish not to give you that minute."

———

Julius asked if two of the cops wouldn't mind waiting in the hallway outside of the library. A mix of curiosity and bemusement sparkled in McCory's eyes as he considered Julius's request, but he nodded to Julius and told two of his men to wait where they were while he, Julius, and another cop entered the library. Julius walked in last and closed the door behind him.

Other than the police tape cordoning off the room, the only other clue that a man had been shot to death there was a large red stain in the middle of the thick beige carpeting. Besides that, though, it was an attractive room. Dark walnut bookshelves covered the walls, and these were filled with an eclectic collection of nineteenth-and-twentieth-century books, which for the hell of it, I cataloged. The furnishings for the room consisted of an antique pine table with six matching leather cushioned chairs surrounding it, two comfortable-looking sofas, each with accompanying end tables and lamps, and a plush leather recliner which was several feet behind the blood stain. Webb must've been sitting in the recliner when his murderer entered the room.

Julius said, "Before I demonstrate Charles Rosten's innocence, I'd like to clear up an issue. Who was the first person to come into the room to find Mr. Rosten by George Webb's body?"

McCory consulted a notepad. "Carolyn Powers came in first," he said. "Followed closely by Earl Gilmore."

"How long between the gunshots and them entering the room?"

"They claimed no more than fifteen seconds. I thought you were supposed to be helping me instead of the other way around?"

"Patience. They found the door to the library closed?"

"Yep."

Julius smiled thinly then, probably as much because he knew he'd be heading back to Boston soon as because he'd now be able to prove Rosten innocent. He walked over to one of the bookshelves, and after perusing it for a few seconds, picked out a book on North American birds. I knew his interest was in the heft of the book and not the subject.

"You're interested in birds, are you, Katz?" McCory asked.

"More in the sound they can make."

Julius took the book to the pine table and slammed it down hard, making a sharp cracking noise that sounded a lot like a gunshot. A glimmer showed in McCory's eyes as he began to understand the point of this demonstration. He opened the door and asked the two cops standing in the hallway if they heard anything. Both of them shook their heads.

"The room's soundproofed?" he asked Julius.

"Yes. Which means whoever killed Webb waited until Charles Rosten entered the library before firing another gun, with most likely blanks. Which further means of the six people in this house when those shots were fired, Mr. Rosten is the only one you can eliminate from consideration as Webb's murderer."

McCory groaned at that, a pained expression wrinkling his brow. "Maybe a gun would make enough noise even if the room's soundproofed," he offered.

Julius shook his head. "Severely muffled noises might possibly have escaped, but it wouldn't have been loud enough to draw the attention it did. I'd suggest you

195

experiment with a real gun and blanks to satisfy your curiosity. I'd also suggest you search the house thoroughly for the second gun that was used. The killer wouldn't have wanted it on him when the police arrived, and likely would've hidden it with the intent of coming back later to retrieve it."

"What do you mean *he*? Do you know something I don't? Can I eliminate the two women who were here?"

"No. I used the pronoun in a gender-neutral way. I know nothing of any of the other people who were here, and have no suspicions regarding any of them."

McCory had one of the officers run out for blanks so they could test how soundproofed the library really was, and while this was being done he and the other two cops searched the house, with Julius tagging along. A thirty-two caliber pistol and a silencer were found hidden in a toilet basin inside a bathroom on the first floor.

"Interesting that a silencer was used," Julius said. "You'll find that it screws onto the murder weapon, and not this gun. The killer either didn't know the library was sound-proofed, or didn't trust it enough. Possibly either this gun or the silencer will lead you to the killer. Were you able to track the ownership of the murder weapon?"

McCory shook his head. "It was stolen three years ago from a Miami, Florida residence."

"Possibly you'll have better luck tracing these items." Julius hesitated briefly before adding, "The last thing I would want do is interfere with an active police investigation. I'm scheduled to fly back to Boston later tonight, but if you'd like my assistance I'd be happy to offer it."

I couldn't help myself in yelling "Ha!" at that, which, since I communicate with Julius through an earpiece, McCory and the other cops were none the wiser to. Julius responded in kind, with a hand gesture that was subtle enough to slip past McCory's notice. While he believes in seeing murderers punished for their crimes, Julius also believes in being paid handsomely for his brainwork, and isn't in the habit of offering his services for free. Earlier when we had a minute alone, Julius had asked me to find available flights for later that night, and I had booked him on a midnight flight so he'd have time to take Lily and her parents out to dinner first at a highly rated restaurant, at which I had also booked reservations. But the problem Julius now had was that although he had succeeded in freeing Rosten from a murder charge and was anxious to return home, if he left now he'd be leaving Rosten with an unknown killer on his payroll, which I'm sure would disappoint Lily and lessen Julius in the eyes of Rosten and his wife. I'm sure Julius had little interest in how he might look to the Rostens, he did care very much about what Lily thought of him. And so he made his halfhearted offer and phrased it in a way to elicit a "thanks, but no thanks" from McCory. As long as McCory turned him down, he'd be able to tell Lily and Rosten that the police demanded that he not interfere, and he'd be free to return home to the creature comforts that his townhouse provided.

While Julius's demeanor appeared calm and unconcerned, I knew he had to be sweating as he waited for McCory's response, because if McCory took him up on his offer of help, there was no telling how long he would be stuck in Rochester. It took nine point three seconds of McCory rubbing the back of his neck before the cop spoke again, and I couldn't help yelling "Ha!" a second time when McCory told Julius he'd be happy for whatever assistance he could provide. And once again, Julius responded with a subtle gesture that escaped McCory's notice, although the meaning of the gesture certainly wasn't subtle.

"This certainly isn't your typical murder," McCory said. "So, sure, I'm not too proud to accept your help."

"Where's Detective Cramer when you need him?" I said to Julius.. "If you had made him the same offer, he'd already have you halfway to the airport."

Julius pushed his hand through his hair, ostensibly to straighten it, but more so he could sneak me another gesture, this one cruder than the others.

The cop who had run out for blanks had returned, and they tried an experiment, firing off two blanks inside the library. All that could be heard in the hallway were two barely audible *puffs*, certainly nothing that would bring people running to the library. The soundproofing material in the ceiling dampened the noise even more, so that the police on the second floor didn't hear anything. McCory called the jail after that to have Rosten released, and then he and Julius sat down to work out how they were going tackle finding who really shot Webb.

Once I realized that Rosten wasn't the killer, I began trying to figure out who was. I did this by searching for whatever bank records, credit-card charges and phone records I could find for the potential other parties involved, including Webb. While I didn't have enough meaningful data to build any useful computer simulations, I did uncover one significant fact, which was that George Webb had paid for a cheap motel room for four nights leading up to his murder. I told Julius about this when I discovered it, which was at four twenty-seven in the afternoon. At the time, Julius was going over with McCory how he hoped to proceed, while they were waiting for the arrival of the five suspects, who were supposed to be there at five o'clock. At least, Rosten, who had been released by then, had called each of them and told them they'd better be at Thrale House at that time. After I told Julius about Webb's recent expenditure, he excused himself from McCory, explaining that he'd like to wash up.

Once alone in the bathroom, Julius turned the water on full, and in a voice low enough so that it was covered by the running water he asked if I was able to find out who Webb had brought to the motel.

"You mean whether he was sleeping with Angela Harris or Carolyn Powers?"

"Not necessarily. He could've brought any of them there. Or their spouses, girlfriends or boyfriends. Or someone who appears to be completely out of the picture."

"Whoever it was, I don't know, at least not yet. I've been trying to use credit-card charges to eliminate whoever I can, but I haven't had much luck there either. I've been able to hack into their phone records, but I haven't had any luck yet with bank records or credit-card charges for Powers,

Callow, and Gilmore. In case you were wondering whether Webb's widow might've snuck into the house and offed her cheating husband, I was able to verify that she was having her hair done at a salon at the time of the murder. But it still might not be a bad idea for you to call her and see if you can get anything out of her. Maybe she has suspicions about who Webb was seeing. Should I call her for you?"

"Not at this time, Archie. I might need to talk to her later. We'll see."

Julius turned off the water and rejoined McCory in the dining room where they had set up shop. He told the homicide detective that I had flown up from Boston to do some legwork on the case, and that I had uncovered that Webb had been paying for a motel room. Julius gave an increasingly skeptical-looking McCory the details, and suggested that he send an officer to the motel with photos to see if they could identify who Webb was seeing there.

"How long has this Archie fellow been up here?"

"Three hours," Julius said with a straight face.

"And he already found this out?"

"He can be very resourceful."

McCory wasn't quite buying it, but before he could argue any further Charles Rosten was brought into the room. Even though Rosten was now out of jail and wearing a suit and tie, he looked more subdued and tired than he had five hours earlier. He thanked Julius for what he'd done for him and then acknowledged McCory with a grim nod.

"Do you know who George Webb was sleeping with?" McCory asked bluntly after Rosten took a seat across from him.

Rosten's eyes narrowed as he stared at McCory, but if the question surprised him, he didn't show it. "Who said he was sleeping with anyone other than his wife?" he said.

"This fellow," McCory said, using his thumb to point at Julius. "According to him, George Webb had been renting a room at the Moonlight Motel since Monday."

"I didn't know that," Rosten said, his brow deeply furrowing as he thought about it.

"But you suspected Webb was having an affair," Julius said.

Rosten nodded. "With how odd he was acting recently, the thought crossed my mind that maybe it was because of guilt eating him up. And not just him." He smiled bleakly. "I picked up a weird vibe recently from Carolyn." With his voice dropping, he added, "I suspected for years those two might've had feelings for each other. Nothing concrete, though."

"When I asked you earlier which one of them might've killed Webb, she was the one you were thinking of?"

"I don't know. Maybe her named popped into my head, but I've got no real reason other than the suspicion that they were seeing each other."

One of the cops came into the room to let McCory and Julius know that the five suspects had all arrived. Earlier, Julius and McCory had worked out an arrangement for Julius to lead the meeting, and for it to take place in the library. McCory hadn't liked that part of it, but Julius convinced him that it could be invaluable to see how the suspects reacted on entering the murder scene.

An oriental rug had been moved from another room so that it covered the blood stain, and the library was further arranged similarly to Julius's office, with Julius sitting in the same leather recliner that Webb must've been in moments before he was shot. He had the chair near the far wall facing the door with the pine table set up in front of it to act as a de facto desk. The two sofas were moved to the other side of the table so they'd be facing Julius, and these were for the suspects. Chairs were also placed for Rosten and McCory, with Rosten sitting to the side, and McCory sitting next to Julius so that he could also face the suspects. Once Julius, McCory, and Rosten were seated, McCory gave a call to have the suspects brought in. I had earlier accessed their personnel files, so I knew what all of them looked like and announced them to Julius as they came into the room.

First up was Peter Boswell. At fifty-seven, Boswell was a large, beefy-looking man with a jar-shaped and mostly bald head covered only by a small fringe of gray hair cut close to the scalp. It was Sunday, and he was dressed casually in a sweater, slacks, and tennis sneakers. If he had any trepidation about entering a room where a man he had worked for had been shot dead only two days earlier, he didn't show it. Instead, his stare settled on Rosten and his jaw dropped open as if he were looking at a ghost. That was no exaggeration. I'd found photos from a website where they tricked people into thinking they were encountering a ghost and they had identical expressions to what Boswell showed.

"Charles," he started, his voice cracking momentarily and his face frozen in an awkward smile. "When Debra took the message that you wanted me here this afternoon,

I had no idea they had released you. I don't understand it, but it's terrific to see you here. What's going on?"

"Not now. Take a seat on one of the sofas," Rosten said, bluntly. He barely looked at his head of marketing, and his voice was more subdued even than it was earlier. "Once everyone is seated Mr. Katz here will explain the situation."

Boswell looked like he wanted to say something, but he swallowed back whatever it was. He glanced dumbly at Julius for a moment, and then did as Rosten asked. He looked damn uncomfortable as he sat alone on the sofa. I stopped paying attention to him as Carolyn Powers entered the room, followed closely behind by Simon Callow.

Carolyn Powers was thirty-eight, with shoulder-length blonde hair, and even though it was a day off for her, she was dressed in a business suit with a skirt that went several inches past her knees. Given that her company photo strongly resembled photos I found of Ginger Rogers at the same age, I was guessing that normally she would've been considered beautiful, but that could only be a guess on my part given how hardened her facial muscles were right then, making it look almost as if she were wearing a plastic mask. Immediately on entering the room her eyes focused on the area where the blood stain would be showing if an oriental rug weren't covering it. Simon Callow was forty and looked every bit the part of a design guru. Tall and thin with a pronounced forehead, Callow wore wire-rimmed glasses, had a carefully groomed goatee, and was dressed in a Tee-shirt and jeans. While Powers looked upset and maybe fearful, Callow's expression was a mix of cautiousness and curiosity. He looked like he wanted to say something to Rosten, but before he could get anything out, Rosten told him the same as he told Boswell.

"She couldn't even look at him," I told Julius, referring to how Powers didn't once look at Rosten as she walked across the room and took a seat next to Boswell. Julius signaled to let me know that he had seen that also. "She has to be the killer," I said. "She must've been having an affair with Webb, and she's got too guilty a conscience over committing murder and trying to frame Rosten to even look at him."

Julius grunted softly to let me know that was possible, but at that moment his attention was drawn to the last of the two suspects as they came into the room. Angela Harris looked badly worried as she pulled nervously on her fingers and her eyes darted from the rug covering the blood stain to Rosten. Alongside her was Earl Gilmore, whose expression reflected deep concern for her. The way he looked at her was similar to the way Julius had looked at Lily when he met her at the airport earlier this morning. There was no doubt he was worried about her, and I had a 'ah ha' moment as I realized they had to be dating. It made sense. Harris was twenty-seven, and even with how worried she looked right then, I knew that normally she'd be considered very pretty. Just as Carolyn Powers resembled a famous actress and dancer, so did Harris—in her case with her short brown hair, large green eyes, and petite figure, she looked a lot like Debbie Reynolds did in *Singing in the Rain.* Earl Gilmore, at thirty-six was six feet tall, had a lean athletic body, and movie-star good looks. I began correlating their phone records and text messages, and quickly proved my assumption by finding that they'd been dating for three weeks. I told Julius this, and he again let out a soft grunt to acknowledge that the information would be useful.

As with the others, Rosten asked them to take a seat, and Angela Harris stumbled and would've fallen to the floor if Gilmore hadn't caught her arm and kept her on her feet. When she got to the sofa, she just about collapsed onto it. First she looked over at Rosten with a wide-eyed and nervous stare, before giving Julius a puzzled look. Gilmore took a seat next to her and looked like he wanted to hold her hand. At that point Rosten introduced McCory and Julius, telling them how Julius was a Boston private investigator who had earlier that day proved Rosten's innocence, and that Julius had agreed to assist the police in their ongoing investigation. The looks on their faces ranged from stunned amazement to disbelief, with Carolyn Powers' lips twisting into a hard smirk.

Julius spoke then, explaining how the murder really happened, and that the gunshots they heard were blanks fired in the hallway by the real killer in an attempt to frame Rosten. Boswell seemed to be the first one to fully get what Julius was saying. With his face flushed with anger, he blurted out, "Are you really accusing one of us of killing George?"

"I'm not making an accusation, simply stating a fact," Julius said. "One of you murdered Webb, and I expect to know very soon which of you it is."

"This is preposterous!" Boswell sputtered. He turned to McCory and demanded, "You're the homicide detective in charge, right? Are you going to sit there and let this man make these accusations against us?"

"I'm satisfied with what Mr. Katz has been saying," McCory said.

Boswell looked among his coworkers to see if he had any support. When he saw that he didn't he started to rise to his feet. "I don't see any reason to stay here and be railroaded into a murder charge," he said with an exaggerated sense of offense. He fixed an angry glare at McCory and said, "This isn't police headquarters! You don't have any right to demand that I be here!"

"No, I don't," McCory said. "But this fellow might feel differently."

McCory was referring to Rosten, who spoke up then and told Boswell that none of them was going to be railroaded into anything. "All Mr. Katz is going to be doing is getting to the truth here. If you didn't have anything to do with George's murder, then I don't see what the problem is, but if any of you want to leave, go ahead. I'll be considering any lack of cooperation as immediate grounds for dismissal. And I'm sure the police will likewise form their own conclusions."

While Boswell wasn't happy doing so, he lowered himself back onto the sofa. Callow spoke up then, asking why the murderer had to be one of them. "Let's assume everything you've said is true," he said to Julius. "Isn't it possible that someone other than us entered this house, killed George, and left before the police showed up?"

"This house has two entrances, both of which are kept locked," Julius said. "If someone had entered or left through the back entrance, it would've set off a fire alarm. A security camera is maintained by the front entrance.

Lieutenant, you examined the recorded video. Could anyone else have been in the house at the time of the murder?"

McCory shook his head.

"There you have it," Julius said to Callow with a shrug. "The murderer has to be one of you."

Julius had a floor map of Thrale House, and he first asked each of them where they were when they heard the gunshots, and marked their locations on the map. Given their answers, none of them would've seen the killer en route to the library, nor would they've seen Rosten leave the billiards room to visit Webb. Julius fixed his stare on Powers and remarked that she was the first one to enter the library after the gunshots were fired, beating Gilmore by several seconds. "Given that you were in the kitchen at the time, you must've sprinted to the library to get there as quickly as you did."

Powers gave him an icy glare in return, but otherwise didn't say anything.

"That was rather fearless of you," Julius said. "Racing to the sound of bullets being fired. Did you know that Webb was in the library."

"Of course I did," Powers said, her voice having a strangled quality to it. "Every year that we held our annual strategy meeting here, George always staked claim to this room during our breaks."

"You had strong feelings for him, didn't you?"

Powers' glare turned icier, but otherwise she didn't answer Julius. He gave her five seconds before letting out a long sigh and asking whether she'd been having an affair with Webb.

"No," she forced out, her lips moving less than a decent ventriloquist's. She turned her glare to Angela Harris and added, "George was married, and I wouldn't have done that to his wife. But why don't you ask that floozy!"

All eyes turned to Harris, who was now looking sick to her stomach. Gilmore was half to his feet as he growled at Powers that she better watch herself. McCory used his right hand to signal for Gilmore to sit back down, and the young lover reluctantly did so.

"Were you having an affair with George Webb?" Julius asked.

Harris bit down on her bottom lip as she shook her head.

"Liar," Powers spat out.

Julius faced the head of sales and asked her why she was so convinced Harris was lying. Of course he knew the reason, just as I did, but I guess he wanted to hear Powers' explanation.

"Wednesday evening I followed them to a cheap motel. It made me sick to my stomach watching them go into that room together."

Angela Harris spoke up then, telling Rosten that she needed to speak to him in private. "It's very important."

"Whatever you have to say, say it here," Rosten told her.

Harris looked at Julius and tried to smile, but it didn't stick. "I did go to a motel with Mr. Webb, but it wasn't because we were having an affair. I was helping him with a project." She turned to implore Rosten, saying, "I really should talk to you about this first."

Rosten gave her a disgusted look. "For crying out loud. A man's dead. Just tell us what you know."

Harris nodded glumly. Gilmore squeezed her hand for support. She said, "Mr. Webb made me promise not to tell anyone about this. He was suspicious that someone had embezzled almost a million dollars from the company. I was helping him go through the company books and other papers looking for any discrepancies."

"You told Gilmore about it, though," Julius said.

She appeared surprised by that. "No, of course not. I promised Mr. Webb I wouldn't tell anyone, not even Mr. Rosten. I needed to tell Earl about the motel, but all I told him was that it was work related."

"That's true," Gilmore agreed. "Angela wouldn't give me any specifics. I swear."

I knew who the killer was then. I knew because of the way Julius looked at Gilmore and the hardness that settled over his features for the next five point seven seconds.

"That's an interesting tie pin," Julius noted, referring to the dog-shaped silver pin that Gilmore wore. As with Carolyn Powers, Gilmore had come dressed in a business suit. "Do you own a bull terrier?"

Gilmore hesitated briefly before saying he did. Angela Harris, smiling more genuinely than earlier, added, "Triton is simply adorable."

"You mean Titan," Gilmore said with a strained, but polite smile, correcting her.

Angela Harris's brow wrinkled as if she were trying to figure out how she could've been mistaken about the dog's name, but otherwise she didn't say anything further.

"Interesting," Julius said, pursing his lips. "Titans were gods in Greek mythology. A triton, on the other hand, is a shell."

"My dog's name is Titan," Gilmore said.

"Possibly. But it would say quite a bit about you if you had named your dog Triton, as Ms. Harris believes."

Gilmore tried to act as if he hadn't noticed how Julius was studying him. He repeated his claim about his dog's name, but his voice cracked slightly as he mentioned that he was curious what Julius thought it would say about him.

"If there was any evidence in the company books about dealings with a company named Triton, and this company turned out to be little more than a shell company which you've been using to embezzle the money that Webb believed was stolen, then it would say that you had a perverse sense of humor, as well as a narcissistic personality. I guess we'll have to examine the books to be sure."

Gilmore blinked several times in rapid succession. "We do use a supplier named Triton Corporation, but that has nothing to do with me."

While Gilmore sat there badly trying to bluff Julius and the rest of the room, I researched what I could about the company in question, and all I could find about Triton Corporation was a bank account in the Cayman Islands. I told Julius this.

Julius told Gilmore, "A good forensic accountant should be able to find the link between you and this shell company quickly enough."

"This is ridiculous!" Gilmore insisted. "Let's say this bizarre claim of yours is true, which it isn't. Why would I kill George? Angela didn't give me any details about what she was working on with him!"

"Please," Julius said in the same sort of condescending tone he might've used with a child. "You would've suspected what they were working on, even if Webb hadn't been exceptionally short-tempered of late."

"How could I have done what you're saying? How would I've known when Charles went to the library so I could do what you're claiming I did? And why would I want to frame Charles, who's been nothing but decent to me?"

Julius smiled thinly. "Spy cams are available now that are no larger than a quarter," he said. "It would've been easy enough to hide one nearby the library door so that you could watch over a smart-phone device for when someone entered the room. Maybe you weren't as careful buying it as you were with the gun and silencer you later stashed in the first-floor bathroom. We'll see, although tracking down that purchase won't be necessary to convict you. As far as framing Mr. Rosten, I doubt he was your original target, although once you saw the opportunity, you were probably quite pleased to pick him. With Webb dead and Mr. Rosten in prison, you probably felt as if you'd have plenty of time to flee to the Cayman Islands or elsewhere before your embezzlement would come to light."

Rosten interrupted, asking Julius, "If he hadn't planned to frame me, than who was he trying to frame?"

Julius shrugged. "You can answer that better than me. If you hadn't entered the library when you did, who would've been the next person to do so?"

Rosten nodded as he thought about it. "Angela," he said. "It's her job to round people up after the breaks."

Angela Harris had pulled her hand away from Gilmore and had further inched herself as far away from him as she could. She demanded to know from him whether this was true.

"Of course not, darling! You know it isn't! I had nothing to do with any of this, and I'd never do anything to harm you!"

From the look on her face, she wasn't buying it. Julius explained it to her.

"He was afraid that after seeing the company books you might make the connection between a Triton Corporation and his dog. That's why he wanted you out of the way."

"That's not true!" Gilmore insisted. "None of it is! I didn't embezzle any money! I didn't kill George and hide a gun and silencer in any toilet basin! I didn't…"

The words died in his throat as he realized his slip. Julius had only mentioned the bathroom, and not where in the bathroom the gun and silencer were stashed. Gilmore gave Harris an odd kind of smile that I didn't understand, and then he bolted off the sofa and toward the door. He didn't get very far before Carolyn Powers tackled him. According to her driver's license, she weighed only a hundred and eight pounds, sixty less than Gilmore, but it still took three cops to pull her off of him.

———

Since they knew what they were looking for, it only took Julius, Rosten, and McCory forty-five minutes with the company records to figure out that Triton Corporation was reselling one of their supplier's parts to them at a seventy-percent markup, and that Gilmore had stolen nine hundred thousand dollars in this manner. As Julius was leaving, McCory, with a straight face thanked him for helping to untangle this Webb business.

Much later that night, when Julius was flying back to Boston, I remarked how it was because of two tiepins that he was able to escape Rochester when he did.

"Me being one of them," I said. "If I hadn't tracked down Webb renting that motel room, it might've been another day or longer before you would've cracked this. And of course, Gilmore's dog-shaped pin. If not for that, you wouldn't have seen him flinch when Harris gave his dog's name."

Julius chuckled at that. He took out his cellphone so it would look to other passengers that he was on the phone with someone instead of being a crazy person talking to himself. "Quite true, Archie," he said.

"Powers had me completely fooled," I said. "When she entered the library, I was sure she was our killer. What I thought was guilt and fear, with the way she couldn't look at Rosten, must've been hatred. I guess she was convinced that he had killed Webb, and was using his money and influence to escape justice." I paused for a moment before adding, "She must've had strong feelings for Webb."

"A case of unrequited love," Julius observed somewhat pensively.

I considered Carolyn Powers for a few seconds, wondering how I'd ever be able to program my neuron network to factor in those types of emotions. Something else that nagged at me was the way Julius had settled on Gilmore when he did, and I asked him about it.

"I understand you thinking he was a good bet after finding out about Harris leaking it to him that she was working with Webb on some secret project, but you seemed convinced he was the killer then. Why?"

Julius took a sip of what he considered "unusually good" Chardonnay that the airline provided, and told me he wasn't a hundred percent settled on Gilmore at that point. "Everyone else was acting in a more natural manner given the circumstances. Powers' intense hatred at the person she suspected of killing the man she secretly loved, Boswell's nervousness over the possibility of being unjustly accused of a crime, Callow's natural curiosity regarding the situation, and Angela Harris worrying about what to do with the information she held. Gilmore's act of appearing to be only concerned about Ms. Harris seemed manufactured and false to me. So I decided to shake him up and see if anything fell loose."

What fell loose was a certain murder conviction. I was going to make a crack about what a disaster it would've been if Julius had had to spend a night in Rosten's guestroom, but I decided to give him a break after the rabbits he pulled out of his hat that day. Besides, I doubted it bothered Lily given the goodbye she gave him at the airport. While I couldn't see what they were doing, since she was flush up against him blocking my visual circuitry, whatever it was, it lasted fifty-seven seconds, and it certainly didn't take a genius detective to make a good guess about it!

JULIUS ACCUSED

Originally published in the June 2014 issue of Ellery Queen Mystery Magazine.

"LES NESSMAN IS at it again," I informed Julius. "At this very moment he's telling even more scurrilous lies about you than he was last week."

Of course, the person I was referring to wasn't really Les Nessman, since that's the name of a character from the TV show *WKRP in Cincinnati* played by the actor Richard Sanders. But Linus Harnsworth, the real man in question, strongly resembled online photos and YouTube videos I'd found of Sanders as Nessman. He had the same slight build, the same lightbulb-shaped head and severely receding hairline, and the same bug-eyed, oblivious stare hidden under thick glasses. At that moment I was watching Harnsworth over a local TV news feed, and he was even dressed the same way Nessman typically dressed, with a polka-dot bowtie, white button-down shirt, and sports jacket. And Harnsworth, at thirty-nine, was the same age that Sanders would've been during the second season of *WKRP*. The one way that Harnsworth was very different from Nessman was his voice.

Instead of a high-pitched squeak, Harnsworth's voice was deep and rich, and sounded similar to audio recordings I'd found of Robert Mitchum, which seemed incongruous given his appearance. Still, I thought my Nessman reference deserved a reaction of some sort, and I got nothing. Not a scowl nor the crack of a smile from Julius. He acted as if he didn't hear me. Instead, forty seconds later, he flipped another page of the six-hundred-and-eight-page biography of Samuel Johnson that he was engaged in, appearing as if he was too engrossed in it to pay any attention to what I said. I waited half a minute before trying again.

"Maybe he's not lying," I said. "That was only an assumption on my part. The fact is, I don't know whether he's lying or not. But regardless, Harnsworth is being interviewed on the local Channel Four news, and what he's claiming is that you threatened his life last night."

I waited another half-minute and all I got from Julius was another page flip.

If I'd had shoulders, I would've shrugged, but since I don't I simply continued on while trying my best to sound unconcerned. "If it doesn't bother you that he's possibly defaming you right now, then I guess that's your problem. All I know is what he's saying, which is that you showed up at his door at eleven forty-seven last night and threatened to put a bullet in his chest if he didn't stop his investigation. The reason I don't know whether or not he's defaming you is, as you know, you left me on your dresser bureau last night before going out. If you hadn't, I'd be able to back you up on what really happened, assuming Harnsworth is the lying weasel that I'm guessing he is."

Julius flinched. I could tell that he had hoped to keep ignoring me, but it was no longer possible. "Archie, please," he said, a hint of annoyance showing in his voice. Whether this annoyance was for me or Harnsworth, I couldn't tell. His attention remained focused on the page he was staring at as he added, "Not now. Later, perhaps, we can discuss this."

"Later? You mean after your reputation has been completely trashed by this twerp?"

"Archie, now is not the time for this."

"Sure, I understand. I appreciate how fascinating a historical and literary figure Samuel Johnson is, and that the biography you've got in your hands has been critically acclaimed, and that you just want to sit back and enjoy it and pretend none of this is happening. But it doesn't change the fact that it is happening. It was bad enough last week when you did nothing after what he insinuated about you. This is much worse. The guy is right now publicly accusing you of felonious behavior—"

While I might be a two-inch rectangular piece of advanced computer technology that Julius wears as a tiepin, that's not how I imagine myself. When I do picture myself, it's as a stocky man in his thirties with thinning brown hair and a tough bulldog countenance. Julius, on seeing a photo I had generated of how I view myself, commented that it was how he would've imagined Dashiell Hammett's Continental Op to look, which makes sense given that all of Hammett's books were used to program my knowledge base. The reason I'm mentioning this is that Julius interrupted me by taking out the earpiece that I communicate to him through, and the image that flashed vividly in my neuron network was of myself as a man with my jaw dropping open in stunned amazement.

For as much as three point four microseconds it felt as if my processing unit had frozen up, and I soon realized that the sensation I was experiencing was similar to be flabbergasted. There have been incidents in the past where I've annoyed Julius enough so that he'd turned me off, but this was the first time that he's resorted to something as childish as taking out his earpiece.

Again, if I had shoulders I possibly would've shrugged them. And if I had fingers, I might've used one of them in particular. But since I don't, instead I did my equivalent of taking a deep breath to calm myself down, which was to analyze a classic chess game. When I was done, I focused on the matter at hand. And as hard as I tried, I couldn't figure out Julius's apparent disinterest in what Harnsworth was doing. I didn't have enough data points to figure it out. This was the first time I'd witnessed anyone outside of police detectives making unfounded accusations about Julius, and in those cases they were made to Julius in private and in the heat of the moment, not to the news media.

I would've expected Julius to do something about this, and not simply ignore it. What his reason was, other than, possibly, pure laziness, I had no idea, but I decided one of us needed to take it seriously, and I e-mailed him the video of Harnsworth's TV interview. He ignored it, but at least I had tried. After that I hacked into Harnsworth's bank and phone records and checked for recent activity, then made several phone calls, and soon had at least three small pieces of the Harnsworth puzzle solved.

Seven months ago Julius had attended socialite Doris Buckley's monthly round-table dinner as her guest of honor. Normally Julius would've turned down the invitation. First, the dinner conflicted with his weekly poker game, and second, he considers having to perform for his dinner unseemly, and the guest of honor for Doris Buckley's monthly dinners is expected to give a talk and entertain a question-and-answer session. Two factors made Julius begrudgingly accept this invitation: (1) Buckley was flying a hotshot chef, Marc Rousse, directly from Paris to cook for them, and, (2) she was promising to serve 2005 Château Pétrus with dinner, a Bordeaux that went for four grand a bottle and something Julius had been wanting to add to his wine cellar for years. So he went to the dinner, and was given a tour of Buckley's home, which was quite impressive; the highlight was her near priceless eighteenth-century painting by the Dutch master Pieter de Berge. I can say *near* priceless because an insurance company coughed up sixteen million for it when it was reported stolen a month later. When exactly the painting was stolen no one, other than the thief involved, knew for sure, since Doris Buckley had locked up her small mansion immediately at the conclusion of her round-table dinner so that she could vacation in Belize for four weeks, and the theft wasn't discovered until the day before her next round-table dinner was scheduled. A week ago, Linus Harnsworth, who is a regular at Buckley's dinners, accosted Julius at the Belvedere Club and insinuated that Julius had stolen the painting the night of the dinner, which is utter hogwash. But the twerp made his insinuations in a loud enough voice so that they appeared the next day on the gossip pages of both Boston newspapers. I was amazed that Julius showed the restraint he did by not decking Harnsworth. He simply ignored him as if he weren't there. I don't think I would've been able to. While Harnsworth was broadcasting his tripe loud enough for the rest of the room to hear, I felt an excess of heat building up in my processing unit, which I knew from past experiences was a sensation similar to anger. Later, while Julius was leaving the Belvedere Club, I asked him about Harnsworth's outburst, but he simply seemed bemused by the incident.

At six-thirty, Julius bookmarked his place in the Samuel Johnson biography, and after he put the book on his desk, he reinserted his earpiece so that I could talk to him if I chose to. Matter-of-factly, I remarked about the video I had e-mailed him, which he hadn't bothered to look at. He grunted back a response, thanking me, but adding that he had no reason to look at it at this time, nor could he even if he wanted to since he needed to get ready for a seven-thirty dinner reservation he had with Lily Rosten. He didn't need to tell me that, since I had booked the reservation for him, as well as arranging for a bouquet of flowers to be delivered to the restaurant for Lily.

"I don't get it," I said.

Julius had gotten up off his chair at this point and was heading out of the office. He raised an eyebrow. "Yes, Archie?"

"You don't seem to care about this."

Julius sighed softly, his lips showing the trace of a grimace. "That's not true," he said. "But I choose, for the moment, not to do anything."

I considered this for several seconds, and while Julius was heading up the staircase to the second level of his townhouse, I asked him why this was, although I had a good idea of what he was going to tell me.

"The man is trying to stir me to action, and I'm curious as to what he is going to try next."

"You didn't go to his residence last night?"

Julius made a face as if he had sipped vinegar. "Of course not, Archie."

"Yeah, I didn't think there was much chance of you doing that. Last night you arrived home at precisely eleven minutes past twelve. Can anyone corroborate where you were at the time that Harnsworth is claiming you threatened him?"

"I'm afraid not, Archie." Since Julius did have shoulders, he was able to shrug them, even if it was only a slight shrug. "At that time I would've been alone. A pity I didn't take a cab home, but it was a nice night for walking."

That answered where Julius had walked home from. *Le Che Cru*, where Julius and Lily had dinner, would've been a nine-minute walk to Julius's Beacon Hill townhouse, so if he was walking from there he would've had witnesses to corroborate where he was at eleven forty-seven. Lily Rosten's apartment, however, would've been a twenty-nine-minute walk. I didn't bother filling Julius in on this part of my junior-detective work.

I told Julius how I found it interesting that that twerp had specified the exact time the way he did. "He could've been gambling that you were home alone and wouldn't have witnesses to vouch for you," I said. "But it would've been a bad gamble, especially given how you and Lily are a known item these days. It made me suspicious enough to hack into Harnsworth's bank accounts and phone records. And guess what I found? Two days ago Harnsworth made a cash withdrawal for five hundred dollars, which is what you'd expect some cut-rate detective would want for a retainer, and early this morning Harnsworth received a phone call from just such a cut-rate private eye, Pete Carney. And please excuse any unintended insult in my implying that you and that bottom feeder Carney are members of the same profession."

Julius was in the process of picking out a tie to wear that evening. A grim smile twisted his lips. "No offense taken, Archie."

"Good. I called Carney after I discovered this and asked him point blank whether Harnsworth hired him to follow you. I thought I'd catch him off guard, and I did. He denied it, of course, but the way he stammered out his denial gave him away just the same."

Julius chuckled at that. He had picked out a rich solid-gray silk tie, and slid me off the one he was presently wearing so he could unknot that one. While he placed me on his dresser bureau, he kept his earpiece in.

"Very good, Archie." He hesitated, then added, "You didn't call Harnsworth, did you?"

"No, I figured it would be best to leave that to you. I did make several other calls. I saw on Harnsworth's phone records that he had contacted the Boston office of Pritchard of London, which is the outfit that insured the painting he's all but accused you of stealing. While I couldn't get anyone there to tell me what he called about, I did find out they're offering a standard ten-percent reward, which is one point six million, for the return of the painting. I'm guessing that Harnsworth has it in his head that he can bully you into tracking it down, and that somehow he plans to take ownership when you do so he can return it for the reward money."

"Interesting theory."

"It's the best I've been able to come up with to explain why he's doing what he is, although I think it's kind of nuts of him to think that he'd be able to grab the painting from you if you're able to find it." I hesitated, then added, "That lowlife Carney is probably waiting out front to tail you again tonight. If you slip out through the back patio, you should be able to shake him easily enough."

"You're probably right, Archie. Thank you. I'll consider that."

Julius had finished tying a Windsor knot for the gray silk tie he had picked out and was in the process of attaching a sterling-silver tiepin to it when I made a sound as if I were clearing my throat and said, "With all this nonsense going on with Harnsworth, don't you think it would be wise to bring me along tonight? You might need me."

Julius's expression became slightly pinched. "Archie, Lily doesn't feel quite comfortable yet—"

"Yeah, I know, she thinks I'm eavesdropping on her. I'm not. And if she'd like, I could filter out her voice, as well as her visually, so she can rest assured that I won't be seeing or listening to her."

Julius attempted a weak smile. "Give it more time, Archie. She'll get used to you. For tonight it would be best if I didn't bring you. And regardless of whether Linus Harnsworth behaves himself, it won't matter."

I wanted to argue with Julius, but it wouldn't have done any good, so I didn't bother. He removed his earpiece and placed it next to me on his dresser bureau, and after he adjusted his tie and suit jacket, he ran a brush through his hair and left the room. I followed him over the webcam feeds as he made his way through the townhouse. He didn't take my advice to use the back patio, and instead left through the front door. I tried searching for Carney using the feed from the webcam planted by a front lamppost, but if he was hiding out there waiting for Julius, he was doing so outside of the camera's range.

Harnsworth had done interviews that day for all five of the local TV news stations. Since Julius showed no interest in watching them, I thought at least one of us should, so I went through them all—not that I imagined his story would change much from one to the other. In each of them, Harnsworth gave mostly the same spiel. He'd start off explaining his rationale for why he suspected Julius of the theft, which was that given the foolproof security system Doris Buckley had in place, the Pieter de Berge painting had to have been stolen the night of the round-table dinner, and that meant Julius had to be the one to steal it—since if anyone else had stolen it, Julius, being such a brilliant detective, would know who the thief was. There were plenty of holes in his theory. While Buckley's security system might've been expensive, after studying it, as well as the blueprints for Buckley's small mansion, I came up with four different ways that the security could've been bypassed and the painting stolen, and I was sure there had to be professional thieves who'd be able to come up with one of those methods on their own. But Harnsworth was adamant that his theory showed Julius was the only one who could've stolen the painting, and that his theory was proved when Julius threatened him at his door.

That was the story Harnsworth gave in his first three interviews. In his fourth interview, he expanded the story, claiming he had heard rumors of Julius approaching a shadowy figure involved in the selling of stolen artwork about finding a buyer for Doris Buckley's painting. In the fifth, he insisted that when Julius had accosted him the previous night he'd boasted that his involvement in the theft could never be proved so Harnsworth might as well stop trying while he was still breathing.

All in all, it was an interesting performance. Julius is an expert at reading a person's *tell*—mannerisms that give away when someone is bluffing or lying. As long as I've got video to analyze of someone both lying and telling the truth I can almost always identify the tell also. At first, it looked like I would have a hard time finding Harnsworth's tell, given how much he was lying, but once I got to where he began expanding his story, it jumped out at me. It was how he'd blink rapidly three times in succession when he told one of his whoppers. With his tell figured out, I set out to build a more extensive profile on Harnsworth, and I was in the process of doing that when the phone rang at nine minutes past eight. Whoever was calling was doing so from a payphone, but once I heard his voice I put him on hold and called Julius on his cell phone.

"Yes, Archie?"

"Linus Harnsworth called the office line sixteen seconds ago from a payphone in Cambridge. I did a voice analysis to verify it's him, and it is, and I've got him on hold right now. Do you want me to patch him through to your cell phone?"

"No, that won't be necessary."

"So what do you want me to do? Hang up on him? Take a message? Question him? Something else?"

"Taking a message will be sufficient. Goodnight, Archie."

That goodnight told me two things. Not to call him again that evening, and he wasn't expecting to come home that night. So he was going to be taking things to the next level with Lily, and it looked like I'd be spending many more evenings and nights sitting alone on Julius's dresser bureau. Fine. I wasn't about to let that bother me. When I got back to Harnsworth, he demanded, "Katz? Is that you?"

"Julius isn't available—"

"You damn well better make him available!"

"That's not going to happen. Either leave a message or don't. It's your choice."

"Look here, you better put Katz on the phone—"

I hung up on him. Forty-four seconds later the phone rang again, which was probably the amount of time he needed to dig more change out of his pocket and dial Julius's number.

"We're not going to be playing this game all night," I growled at him. "You've got one last chance to leave a message. After that I'm not picking up the phone again. Understood?"

226

Harnsworth's voice became indignant as he told me, "You tell your boss that I'm on to him. I know everything now, and unless he meets me at this address at precisely eleven-thirty tonight I will make sure that he's locked up by tomorrow. You tell him that!"

Harnsworth gave me an address in Cambridge that was several blocks from the pay phone that he was using. While I don't have lips, I can whistle easily enough by programming my voice synthesizer, and I let out a long one right then. The guy was certifiable. That was all I could think of. I debated whether to interrupt Julius's dinner to give him that message, and in the end I decided I'd better. When I got Julius back on his cell phone, I asked whether he wanted a recording, for me to give him the message verbatim, or a summary. He asked for a summary, which I gave him.

"I'm sorry about interfering with your evening," I told him. "And please apologize to Lily for me. I wasn't sure what to do about that message."

"You did the right thing, Archie, but if he calls back you don't need to relay any further messages to me."

"Okay. Sure. I'm guessing Harnsworth called from a pay phone instead of using his cell phone because he didn't want any record of the call being made."

"A reasonable assumption, Archie."

"Yeah, I thought so. I also have a new theory on why Harnsworth has been doing all this. And it's because the guy's nuts. A delusional paranoid who should be locked up."

"Possibly. Again, goodnight."

There was more than a hint of skepticism in Julius's voice when he said *possibly*. And the way he said *goodnight*, it was clear he didn't want me calling him again. Still, three hours and forty-two minutes later I had no choice.

"Yes, Archie?" Julius asked, some exasperation in his voice.

"Yeah, I know, you didn't want me disturbing you again tonight, but it can't be helped. I need to know whether you've got an alibi for eleven thirty-seven tonight. If you've got nothing, that's bad. And if all you've got is Lily, that's not much better. Juries tend to be skeptical when a defendant's only got a wife or girlfriend vouching for him."

"What's this about?" Julius asked coldly.

"At eleven thirty-seven tonight Linus Harnsworth was shot dead on Doris Buckley's property, which, by the way, is less than two blocks from the address where Harnsworth wanted to meet you. The time of the shooting might not be a hundred percent accurate, but that's the time Buckley claims she heard a gunshot. She's also claiming that she looked out a window and saw a man wearing a dark coat running from Harnsworth's body, and from her description, the man could easily be you, especially since you were wearing your brown cashmere coat tonight. So that's why I'm asking about alibis and whether you've got one that will hold up. Because if you don't, a better option might be for you to go on the lam. I can get you on a plane leaving in forty-minutes to San Antonio, and from there safe passage into Mexico, and then on a cruise ship to Argentina—"

"Archie, enough of that. Has this made the news yet?"

"Not yet. I picked up a police dispatch to Buckley's address, and then hacked into the Cambridge Police Department's computer system to get the rest of it. An arrest warrant hasn't been issued yet, but I'm sure one will be soon."

"You could be right." This was followed by four point six seconds of silence from Julius, during which I imagined his features hardening as he sorted through his options. When he spoke next, he asked me to get ahold of Henry Zack and arrange for Henry to meet him back at the townhouse as soon as possible. Henry was Julius's attorney, and Julius had him on twenty-four-hour call for emergencies. He'd gotten Julius out of sticky legal situations in the past.

"Archie, also call Tom Durkin," Julius added. "Please apologize to Tom for the lateness of the call. If he's available for an immediate assignment, have him call me on my cell phone. If he's not available, try Saul, and if Saul's not available, try Willie. I also need you to track down a home or cell-phone number of the head of the Boston office of Pritchard of London, and when you have it, call me back with it."

Tom Durkin, Saul Penzer, and Willie Cather were all freelance private investigators that Julius would call upon frequently. All were good, although Tom was the most reliable in tricky situations. The head of Pritchard of London's Boston office was one Landon Caulfield, and I already had both his home and cell-phone numbers so I texted them to Julius's cell phone. Julius asked me to send a cab to Lily's apartment to pick him up and take him back to his townhouse, so at least he saw the urgency of not spending twenty-nine minutes walking home.

"Are you sure you don't want to go on the lam?" I asked him. "I can still get you on that plane to San Antonio."

"No, Archie, I think I'll try it this way."

———

Julius reattached me to his tie when he returned to his townhouse. He ended up beating Henry Zack by seven minutes, which gave Julius time to ask me for profiles on Doris Buckley and the other four remaining regular members of her monthly round table. Since I already had these printed and waiting for him, he had a chance to study them for a whole six minutes before his attorney was at the front door. Julius proceeded to bring Henry to the kitchen, where he started brewing a pot of French-roast coffee while he filled Henry in on the situation. Henry's expression turned increasingly incredulous as he listened.

"I caught Harnsworth's interview on Channel Four earlier," Henry said. "I was planning to talk to you about it. Is there anything at all to his claims, or were they completely fabricated, as I suspected?"

"Completely fabricated. I have an idea about what was behind it all, but I'd rather not share it presently."

Henry raised an eyebrow about that but didn't argue with Julius. "And you expect the police to be arresting you tonight?"

Since Julius had his earpiece in I could've just told him this news, but he had instructed me to call if this happened, so I did. "An arrest warrant has just been issued," I told him. "The lead detective on the case is your old buddy,

Cramer. It's probably too late for you to fly out of Boston, but it doesn't look like they've alerted Providence airport yet. It might not be too late to get you out of the country."

Julius muttered, "Thank you, Archie," into the phone. He hung up on me and told Henry that it was now a certainty. "As you can guess, that was Archie," Julius said. "I have him on assignment concerning what we've talked about, and he has learned that an arrest warrant has just been issued. We should expect Cambridge's finest to be arriving within the next ten minutes."

Henry frowned severely. "I don't like this, Julius. Not at all. Even if we were to have Lily back you up on your alibi—"

"I don't want Lily to have to be subjected to police questioning."

"I understand." Henry rubbed a hand across his jaw as he continued to frown. "But what I was saying is, even with her claiming she was with you all night, I don't like this." He paused for a moment, his frown deepening. "A jury can be a funny thing. So can human nature. People love to tear down their heroes. A sworn affidavit from Lily wouldn't keep the police from arresting you, and could very well not keep a jury from convicting you. From what you've told me, the case against you is highly circumstantial, but it doesn't look good when a man is shot dead the same day he goes on every local news station claiming you've threatened his life. And it certainly doesn't help matters that we've got an eyewitness describing the killer as someone who could've been you. All I can say is, I hope this plan of yours works."

Julius smiled thinly. "Archie suggested I go on the lam," he said.

Henry had stopped rubbing his jaw and instead pulled slightly on his bottom lip. His eyes were deep in thought as he considered my suggestion to Julius.

"That night not have been a bad idea," Henry admitted.

———

Julius was close with his estimate. Nine and a half minutes after he had told Henry that the police would be there within ten minutes, there was a pounding on the front door. I didn't need to look at the webcam feed to see that it was Detective Mark Cramer banging away. Even if I hadn't known that he'd been assigned as lead detective on the case I would've recognized his door banging from past experience. But I checked the webcam feed anyway, and told Julius that Cramer was out front with three uniformed officers. By this time, the coffee had finished brewing and he and Henry were on their first cups. Since Julius had expected this additional company, he had brewed a larger pot than would've been expected for just himself and Henry, and he had kept it warm. He also had out a plate of assorted Italian cookies that were delivered earlier that day from a bakery in the North End.

While Julius stayed seated in the kitchen, Henry went to answer the door. Henry and Cramer knew each other from past incidents where Cramer had been frothing at the mouth to arrest Julius for at best dubious reasons. This time, there was no conversation between them. Without saying a word, Cramer simply handed Henry the arrest warrant, which Henry took his time reading even though I had faxed over a copy earlier. After spending a minute appearing to study the warrant, Henry handed the paper back to Cramer and led the police officers to the kitchen. The expression on Cramer's face as he stared at Julius surprised me. I don't know what exactly I was expecting, but given the animosity Cramer always seemed to harbor for Julius—as if Julius were solving murder cases simply to spite him—I expected something different from what I saw. Glee? Satisfaction? Vindication? Something like that. Instead, as Cramer looked at Julius, the expression on his face could best be described as disappointment; at least that was the best match I could find by comparing it to photos from an online movie database.

"Okay, Julius," Cramer said, which was also a surprise since he almost always called Julius by his last name, and would usually spit it out as if it were a curse word. And just as there was no glee or spitefulness in his expression, there was none in his voice either. In fact, he sounded tired, even more so than he looked. "Your lawyer has seen the arrest warrant, and I'm sure he'd tell you if there was anything out of order. I need to cuff you. Let's make this easy for both of us. How about you stand up and put your hands behind your back."

Julius took another sip of his coffee before addressing Cramer. "Detective, is there a rush? I have enough freshly brewed coffee for you and your men. And these cookies were delivered today from Ferrara's in the North End; they're very good. I'd suggest we talk for a few minutes before you do anything you might regret."

Cramer's eyes narrowed, his stare focused on Julius. "I don't see what there is to talk about," he said, his voice showing hostility that had been absent earlier. "We've kept Linus Harnsworth's murder off the news. That you have your lawyer waiting for us all but tells me you're guilty."

A grim smile pulled up the edges of Julius's lips. "That would be one assumption you could make. Another could be that I have enough friends in your department that at least one of them would call me to warn me," Julius said. "Or even possibly for one of them to fax me the arrest warrant." Julius slipped a folded piece of paper from an inside suit-jacket pocket and handed it to Cramer. As Cramer looked at it his skin color first blanched and then reddened. His expression also transformed into one that I was more familiar with from him.

"Who sent you this?" Cramer demanded, his voice badly strained.

"I'm afraid I will be keeping the sender's name anonymous," Julius said. "I'd suggest it would be in everyone's best interest to discuss this matter over some coffee and very good Italian cookies, especially the hazelnut crème. Or, if you prefer, I have half of a roast beef that I could carve up for sandwiches, which would go well with sourdough bread and a very fine Vermont cheddar cheese."

"Unbelievable. I've got an arrest warrant and enough evidence to convict you for murder, and you're still trying to dictate terms!"

Julius shrugged. "You could arrest me," he said. "And if you did I would have to suffer a night in jail, and I suppose other indignities. Henry, what time would I be released tomorrow?"

"I've already talked with Judge Henshaw. If needed, a bail hearing will be held tomorrow morning at nine, and you would be released by nine fifteen."

Henry was bluffing. He hadn't called Henshaw or any other judge. He knew better than to wake one up well after midnight over the matter of a bail hearing. If Cramer knew Henry's tell, which was the way Henry would rub his thumb on his right hand against his forefinger before he told a lie, he'd know Henry was bluffing. But from the way Cramer's face only reddened further, he bought it.

"Let me tell you what will happen next," Julius said. "By noon I will hold a press conference exposing Harnsworth's actual killer. And I will do this in a way to create as much embarrassment as I can for both yourself and your department. I know you believe that in the past I've engaged in grandstanding, but that's not true. I don't seek publicity, nor do I want it, but when I'm paid to do a job I do it." Julius took another sip of coffee as his eyes locked onto Cramer's. "But if you wish to witness true grandstanding, then arrest me tonight and I'll be happy to make you a guest at tomorrow's press conference."

"You're bluffing!"

"I could be," Julius said. "But if I were you'd never know it. I've played poker in some of the most cutthroat circles, and none of the others players has ever been able to figure out my tell. Not even my assistant, Archie Smith, who's more adept than most at it. So Detective, you have a decision to make. You could arrest me tonight, which would cause me some temporary discomfort, but I promise you whatever discomfort you cause me, I will pay back a hundred fold."

"You're threatening me now!"

"No, sir. I'm only making a promise."

Cramer blinked very soon after that. Not literally, but figuratively. For a good twenty seconds he stared bullets at Julius and looked angry enough to chew nails. And then, as if a switch had been thrown, the steam went out of him. As I said, he figuratively blinked.

"What do you know?" he asked.

"I'm sure far less than yourself," Julius said. "I've yet to watch any of the TV appearances Harnsworth made today. I've only been told about them. But what I suspect is a different matter. If my suspicions are correct, and I believe they are, then I know who the murderer is."

"Okay, give."

Julius shook his head. "No, sir. Once my suspicions are proven, you will have your murderer with enough evidence to obtain a conviction. But until then, I'll be keeping my suspicions to myself."

Cramer didn't like it. The way he grasped the back of his neck and rubbed it showed how much he didn't like it. Same with the way he scowled at Julius. But he was already whipped. He knew it and so did Julius.

"What do you need?" he asked at last.

"Not much." Julius reached into his inside suitjacket pocket, and pulled out another folded sheet of paper. This one had the same list of names that he had earlier asked me to build profiles for: Doris Buckley and her remaining four round-table members. "If you bring these five people back to my office, I should be able to point out the murderer to you within fifteen minutes of their arrival."

Cramer's scowl grew queasy as he looked over the names. "You want them here now?" he complained. "It's late already."

Julius smiled thinly. Probably over the thought that while Cramer would've had no problem dragging him to jail at that hour he didn't want to disturb the five people on the list, even though one of them was most likely a murderer.

"It won't take long," Julius said. "And it will be best if we do this now."

"What if they don't want to come? I can't force them."

"I don't believe that will be an issue. But if any of them are reluctant, have them call me and I'll persuade them."

Cramer stared at the list for another half-minute before nodding. "Alright," he said with a forced gruffness. "I'll have them picked up. And I'll give you your fifteen minutes. But I swear, Katz, if you don't deliver I'll be booking you tonight for the murder of Linus Harnsworth." His glance shifted toward the half-filled coffeepot, and Julius, without being asked, poured him a cup, which Cramer accepted.

"I might as well have one of those roast beef sandwiches you were talking about," Cramer said with a pained grimace. He pointed his chin at the three uniformed cops standing nearby, adding, "You might as well make some for them also."

—

Julius was right. None of the five put up any argument, even though it was already past one-thirty in the morning by the time they all arrived. I watched over the outdoor webcam feed as each of them was brought in.

First up was the socialite, Doris Buckley. From hacking into the Registry of Motor Vehicles database, I knew she was thirty-nine, and from all the photos of her that have appeared over the years in the newspapers, I knew she was usually very beautiful, with an Ingrid Bergman quality to her. Light brown shoulder-length hair, cute slightly upturned nose, and this faint overbite that made her look like she could've been Bergman's stand-in for the movie *Casablanca*. At that moment she was wrapped in a full-length mink coat and looked worn-out as if the night's events had aged her a decade.

Julius and I were alone in his office. Earlier, while Julius had been preparing snacks and beverages for his guests, he had been able to give me instructions without the prying ears of Cramer or any other cops. He wouldn't fill me in on any other part of it, nor would he give me his guess as to who the murderer was, which made me think he was only bluffing Cramer after all and seeing if he could pull some sort of rabbit out of his sleeve to save himself a night in jail. What he asked me to do sounded like a wild shot in the dark at best.

Since it was still only the two of us then and the door to Julius's soundproofed office was closed, I remarked to him how Doris Buckley normally looked much better than she did tonight. "She was stunning at that dinner she invited you to," I said. "And the lady certainly has a lot of money.

But having a close friend murdered is going to take some starch out of you. Just keep that in mind in case you want to see her when this mess is cleared up."

Julius smiled thinly at that. "Archie, if I didn't know you better I'd think you were trying to find me a new girl-friend," he said. "Perhaps one who wouldn't mind me bringing you along on a date?"

"I'm just saying you might want to keep your options open. As I said, the lady's got looks and money. And class too. Not that Lily doesn't have class, but you know what I mean."

"Thanks for the heads-up, Archie."

"Sure thing. I've put together a cost-benefit analysis on both of them. If you don't end up in the hoosegow tonight, I'll send it to you later."

"Very thoughtful of you."

Our conversation ended then as the door opened and Doris Buckley was brought into the room by one of the uniformed patrolman. Julius greeted her, thanking her for her indulging him like this, and offering her any of the food and beverages that he had waiting in his office. "The shiraz I've opened for tonight is of course not in the same league as the 2005 Château Pétrus that you served me, but it's still a nice wine with subtle hints of tea leaves and wild blackberry."

Doris Buckley shook her head no, a brittle look about her eyes and mouth as she declined his invitation for refreshments, and took a seat across from him. At a hundred and twenty-five dollars a bottle, it had seemed an extravagance to me when Julius brought four bottles of the shiraz out from his wine cellar, given that he had no client, as well as that he was facing the prospect of a long prison term, but I didn't bother commenting at the time.

My attention was diverted back to the outside of the townhouse and the arrival of the first of Doris Buckley's round-table regulars, William Holland. Holland was a theater critic for a local paper and was forty-eight, six foot two inches tall, and had a lean marathon runner's body. He was dressed in jeans, a turtleneck sweater, tennis sneakers, and a full-length tan camel-hair coat, and had this disheveled look, as if he had just woken up. Before he reached the front door, another of the round-table regulars, Chad Moffat, appeared on the front walkway. The two of them gave each other inquisitive looks but otherwise didn't speak. Moffat had on a leather jacket and was also wearing jeans and tennis sneakers. It made more sense for him to be wearing those types of sneakers since he had been a professional tennis player and was now an instructor. Like Holland, he looked like he had just been dragged out of bed, and he gave Holland an awkward grin as if he couldn't believe that they were both being summoned to Julius's townhouse at this hour of the night.

I informed Julius that Holland and Moffat had shown up with police escorts and would be entering his townhouse momentarily, and that neither of them looked particularly guilty to me. Since only Julius can hear me thru his earpiece, I didn't have to worry about Doris Buckley overhearing me as she sat with her hands folded in her lap, grimly staring at them.

Less than a minute later, a car pulled up to Julius's townhouse and Nancy Chen, Karl Rolfer, and Cramer all exited the vehicle. Nancy Chen was a knockout. Five foot six, long-legged, slender-waisted, she was dressed to kill, so to speak, in black stiletto high heels, short black leather miniskirt, matching black leather jacket and gloves. While Chen looked like she could've been a high-end fashion model, and probably would've had no problem making a lot of money in that profession if she wanted to, she was in fact a renowned classical violinist. She also seemed impervious to the cold. It was twenty-eight degrees outside, and while Moffat had been blowing furiously on his hands to keep them warm, Chen showed no effects of the cold air even though almost ninety percent of her legs were exposed.

Karl Rolfer, at fifty-six, was a trust-fund baby who had never worked in his life and looked out of place walking next to Chen. A big, husky man, Rolfer was dressed more than appropriately for the cold weather in a bulky sheepskin coat, heavy scarf, and earmuffs. And while Chen looked immaculately put together, Rolfer, at six foot three and two hundred and twenty pounds, looked more like a mountain man, with a thick beard and red nose. I gave Julius my impression of each of them. "If Nancy Chen were taller and a guy, I'd go with her as the killer," I said.

Julius ended up offering all of them refreshments, which pretty much told me this was nothing but a fishing expedition. Julius hated feeding murderers, and if he'd known which one of them killed Harnsworth he would've at the very least found an excuse not to offer that person a glass of "nice" shiraz, whether or not it had subtle hints of tea leaves and wild blackberry. But as it turned out, all of them, except Buckley, accepted the wine, and Julius poured out three bottles of the stuff. Except for Buckley, all of them also took an assortment of food.

It was crowded in Julius's office with the round-table folks and a small mob of police. The "invited" guests took up the front leather chair, love seat, and two thirds of the sofa. Cramer had pulled up a chair so he could sit to the side of Julius and see all of their faces, while Henry Zack and three uniformed cops sat in the back of the room. None of the round-table regulars, other than Buckley, knew why they were there, and while they all probably wondered why she looked like she was on the verge of tears—at least, all but one of them—none of them asked her what was going on, although they all looked like they wanted to. Rolfer, between bites of a roast beef sandwich, broke the silence that had formed by clearing his throat and commenting that it looked like the gang was almost all there. He glanced around at the others before smiling broadly at Julius. "I'm guessing we're waiting for Linus before starting?" he asked.

"No, sir," Julius said. "I'm afraid Mr. Harnsworth will be unable to join us as he was murdered a little less than two hours ago. Shot once through the heart, isn't that correct, Detective Cramer?"

With the way Cramer nearly spat out his coffee, he wasn't too happy about Julius divulging that information. He mumbled something under his breath about Julius being correct and then glared at his watch to note the time. It was obvious that as far as he was concerned, Julius's fifteen minutes had started, and he wasn't going to get another second more than that.

The others reacted one of three ways. Holland, Moffat, and Rolfer all smiled as if they thought Julius was joking and they were waiting for the punch line, Buckley simply looked more morose, and Chen smirked at the news. Julius could see it as plainly as I did, but I couldn't help myself mentioning it to him anyway. "I don't know how she fooled Buckley into thinking she was a six-foot-tall guy, but ten to one she's our killer."

Julius gave me a hand signal to let me know he was well aware of Nancy Chen's reaction. From the way Cramer stared at Chen, he was well aware of it also. Julius let out a soft sigh and asked the violinist if she would explain her obvious amusement at hearing about Harnsworth's murder.

"I'm not amused by the news," Chen said, her voice icy. "But I'm not upset by it either. And I'm sure there are many others in Boston who feel the same, yourself included. I'm sure you couldn't have been too happy with the accusations he had been making about you."

Julius shrugged. "I haven't been terribly concerned, but that's beside the point. Would you mind telling me why you felt this animosity toward Harnsworth?"

"Animosity is too strong a word. Indifference would be a better choice."

"No, Ms. Chen. No one reacts to the news of someone's death the way you did out of indifference."

She stared blankly at Julius for a moment before saying, "Fine. Let's say I didn't like Linus. I found him sneaky and devious, and didn't trust him for a second."

"Was there a specific incident that created this impression for you?"

She hesitated, as if she were trying to decide how much to tell. Finally she nodded.

"I would say there were several," she said, her voice now more angry than icy. "The last one was two months ago when I found him in my apartment. That little sneak convinced my landlord to let him in, and when I came home I found him with his nose stuck in my armoire and his little hands searching thru my lingerie. I should've filed charges against him. I didn't only because I know how fond Doris is of him."

Chen's exterior melted a bit as she turned to Buckley and took hold of her hand. "I'm so sorry, darling," she told the socialite. "I've been so selfish, not thinking of how upsetting this news must be to you."

Buckley nodded and bit her bottom lip to keep her tears in check, but otherwise didn't say anything. Julius interrupted this tender moment by asking Chen what she thought Harnsworth had been doing in her apartment. I couldn't blame him for being anxious to move things along as he only had fourteen minutes and twenty-two seconds left.

Chen's eyes darkened as she looked back at Julius. "I'm sure he was looking for dirt on me. It was well known that he sold rumors and innuendos to the gossip pages. Of course, he claimed he was there so that he could figure out the perfect present to buy for my birthday, and he did end up giving me lingerie, but he was lying."

"Most likely," Julius agreed. "And while no one could fault you for your ill feelings toward him, it doesn't quite seem as if his conduct that day would be sufficient reason to want to murder him, at least for most people. But never mind that for now. We can examine motives later, if necessary."

It was interesting watching the faces of Holland, Moffat, and Rolfer, and the transformations that occurred as it dawned on them that not only wasn't this a sick joke on Julius's part, but also the reason that Julius had summoned them. Holland seemed to get it a second or two before the others. He half rose out of his seat, and, with his voice quavering with a mix of shock and indignation, said, "This really happened? Linus was murdered? And you think one of us could've done it?"

"Please sit down, Mr. Holland. It's more than I *think* one of you is his murderer. I *know* one of you is, and I'll explain why soon enough. But for now, let us not worry any more about possible motives and instead work to see which of you I can eliminate from consideration." Julius kept his glare fixed on Holland until the theater critic reluctantly lowered himself back onto the sofa. Julius then shifted his gaze to Buckley and asked if she could tell them all what she had witnessed that night.

Buckley used the knuckle of her index finger to rub at some wetness around her eyes. "I don't think I'm up to it," she said, her voice little more than a sad whisper.

"Please, Ms. Buckley, it's important."

She offered Julius a bleak smile. "I better have some of that wine first."

"Certainly."

Julius opened up the fourth bottle and poured Buckley a glass. She took a sip, and then, in a soft monotone, explained how she heard a gunshot at exactly eleven thirty-seven. "The shot was so loud," she said, her eyes opening wide. "I wasn't even sure it was a gunshot at first. I thought it might've been an explosion of some sort. I was in my bedroom at the time, and the noise sounded like it came from right outside my window. I pushed the curtain aside and when I looked out I saw Linus lying crumpled on the driveway and...."

A look of mortification wracked her face and she covered her mouth with her hand.

"What else did you see?" Julius asked bluntly.

Her voice cracked noticeably as she told him that she saw a man running away. A moment earlier she had almost told him she had seen *him* running away. I could see it in her eyes.

"And you thought the man was me," Julius said.

Her eyes drifted from his. She shook her head. "Not now, anyway," she said unconvincingly. "Linus had called me earlier to tell me he'd be coming over late tonight to give me unassailable evidence that you had stolen my Pieter de Berge. And the man I saw looked like he could've been you. He was athletic-looking and had your same height and body size. So because of that I told the police it could've been you, but I never saw the face so I can't say for sure who it was."

"And you told the police the man was wearing a full-length coat and a cap?"

"Yes. The coat could've been camel hair or cloth. I'm not sure which. I think it was dark brown. Maybe black. There wasn't enough light for me to be sure. I'm not sure

246

either what type of cap the man wore either, but I think it could've been a baseball cap."

"How far away was the man when you first saw him?"

"Maybe thirty feet."

"And if I remember right from the tour you gave me seven months ago, your bedroom is on the second floor? And you have eighteen-foot-high ceilings on your first floor?"

Buckley nodded.

Julius got up from his chair and took a Red Sox cap and his brown full-length cashmere coat from a closet directly to left of him and showed these to Buckley.

"Did the coat and cap look like these?"

Buckley let out a short gasp as she nodded. Julius brought the coat and cap back to his desk and smiled pleasantly at her. "I can assure you that these were not worn by the killer," Julius told her. "Both of these items belong to me, and the police have performed a gunpowder-residue test on the coat sleeves, which verifies that it was not worn by whoever it was who shot Linus Harnsworth."

Cramer nearly choked on his coffee when Julius said that, since no such test had yet been done, but as much as he might've wanted to contradict Julius, he kept his mouth shut. Julius then explained to the room how he planned to eliminate possible suspects using the coat.

"Of course, it would be better if we were doing this from Ms. Buckley's home, so that she could look out her bedroom window while each of you took turns standing in her driveway wearing this outfit. But I think this will be sufficient for our purposes. Mr. Holland, if you don't mind, could you go first?"

Holland did mind. It looked like he was going to flat-out refuse until Cramer spoke up. Reluctantly, he put the coat and hat on and allowed Julius to tell him where to stand, which was with his back to Doris Buckley. After several seconds of serious contemplation, as evidenced by the way her brow wrinkled, Buckley admitted that Holland could've been the one she saw run away. Next up was Rolfer. While he joked that the coat would be too snug on him, he looked nervous as he put it on and moved to the same spot where Holland had stood. And as with Holland, Doris Buckley had to say that he could've been the killer.

Julius surprised me when he asked Nancy Chen to go next, as it would've been impossible for anyone to ever mistake her for a man. When she started to slip off her high heels, Julius asked her to leave them on.

"It wouldn't be possible for me to run from a murder scene wearing these," she said, frowning. "I'd break my neck if I tried doing that."

"Possibly," Julius admitted. "But the six-inch heels add enough height to match Ms. Buckley's description, and there are other platform shoes you could've worn instead which would've been easier to run in."

"What if I have an alibi for tonight?"

"Alibis can be examined later. This is only to see whom I can exclude from consideration. But Ms. Chen, I should warn you, I've learned over the years how fragile even the sturdiest-looking alibi can turn out."

A hard smirk similar to the one she showed earlier twisted Chen's ruby-colored lips, but whatever she was thinking she kept to herself as she rolled up her long hair and tucked it under the cap, then slipped on Julius's coat. Even though it was massive on her, Buckley had to admit that she could've been the one she saw that night.

When Julius next asked Chad Moffat to put on the coat and hat, they gave up the game. With Moffat it was the way he flinched, as slight as it was. With Buckley, it was a flash of a reassuring look she gave him when she noticed the flinch. Both of these things could've been missed easily. But I didn't miss them, and neither did Julius. Before I could comment to Julius how we now knew who the murderers were even if we didn't have a clue as to why, he signaled me to carry out the instructions he had earlier given me.

Moffat was in the midst of trying to recover from his flinch by smiling in a goofy manner while announcing to Julius he'd be happy to oblige him even though he had an alibi that night. "At the time Doris said Linus was shot, I was entertaining a guest," Moffat said with a wink. "And I wasn't giving her backhand lessons, if you catch my drift—"

Before Moffat could say anything else, Julius's office phone rang and Julius put out his hand to silence him as he answered the phone. Julius carried on a one-sided conversation as if he were actually talking to someone.

"Very good, Archie," Julius said at last. "Let me put you on speaker so the rest of the room can hear this news."

Of course, I was the one to have called the office, since that was what Julius had asked me to do. While we might've known that Buckley and Moffat had teamed up to kill Harnsworth, I couldn't see how we were going to get any evidence with which to accuse them, and I kept quiet during Julius's one-sided conversation because I was too busy trying to figure out how our next step was going to get us anywhere. Once Julius put me on speaker, I went thru the spiel that he had given me.

"We found the painting in a storage locker that Harnsworth was renting," I said. "I'll e-mail you a photo of it now."

"Can I talk to Sergeant Connor?" Julius asked.

"Sure." I reprogrammed my voice synthesizer to sound like Cramer, except deeper and with a more distinct Boston accent, and then told Julius, "Yeah, Connor here."

"Can the Cambridge Police Department verify what my assistant, Archie Smith, has just said?"

Cramer had to struggle to keep from snorting then, since he knew there was no Sergeant Connor, but he kept his composure enough to keep from drawing any attention to himself.

"Everything Mr. Smith has told you is on the up and up," I said. "A good man too. Whatever you're paying him, Katz, it ain't enough."

"Good, good," Julius mumbled. "Please put Archie back on the phone."

I reprogrammed my voice synthesizer back to my normal voice. "Archie here again," I said.

"Archie, please stay on the line while I show Ms. Buckley the photo you took."

Earlier, on Julius's instructions I had generated a photo showing Buckley's stolen painting laid out on the floor of a storage locker with a sealed envelope next to it. It wasn't particularly hard to do. I record all the images I "see" and transfer them to permanent storage, and since I was with

Julius at that round-table dinner, I had plenty of images of the painting that I could use. Since the painting had been cut out of its frame, I had to improvise a little on what the edges of the canvas would look like, but I used the shadows I created within the storage locker to hide that.

Julius showed a perturbed frown as he opened up the e-mail and brought up my generated photo. If I didn't know his perturbed expression was part of the act, he would've fooled me with it as I'm sure he fooled everyone else. Julius turned his monitor so that Buckley and the rest of the round-table members could see the photo. I have to hand it to Buckley. She was good in the surprised expression she manufactured over Harnsworth having her painting. Moffat wasn't quite as adept as she was. His goofy grin froze and he began to look a little sickish. The snort that Cramer had been fighting to hold back finally broke loose.

Julius, still frowning severely, asked me to open up the envelope. I synthesized the sounds of me tearing open an envelope and unfolding a sheet of paper. I reprogrammed back to Sergeant Connor's voice, saying, "That just beats all, don't it?" Then I set the synthesizer back to my own voice and said, "You're going to want to see this. Badly. Do you want me to read it to you?"

"No, Archie. It would be best if you took a photo of it and e-mailed it to me."

While all this was going on, Julius had one hand under his desk so he could sign to me what he wanted in the letter, and that was the letter I generated and e-mailed to him. Since only Julius and Cramer were going to see it, I didn't worry about matching Harnsworth's handwriting.

Julius moved the monitor so that only he could see it, and as he brought up my generated letter his eyes narrowed and his lips pressed into a harsh line. Again, only an act, but if I hadn't known better he would've fooled me. He appeared to notice then that Moffat was still standing, since he had been in the process of getting the coat and hat from Nancy Chen before this interruption, and he told Moffat not to bother.

"It's no bother," Moffat said as he struggled to keep his grin intact.

"It's not necessary anymore. Please sit down."

Moffat looked stuck. He didn't want to just sit down. That was clear. But as Julius continued to stare at him, his grin froze a bit more and he did as he was asked. Once he was seated, Julius waved Cramer over to look at the letter also, although at that point it was unnecessary since it would've been impossible without a physical altercation to have kept Cramer from looking at it.

The letter read simply: *Detective Cramer, please glare at Ms. Buckley and Mr. Moffat, and mutter loud enough for them to hear, "well, what do you know."*

Cramer did as the letter directed, and I had little doubt that the ill-feelings he showed in his glare were a hundred percent genuine since he probably wanted to direct them at Julius.

Buckley spoke up then. "Julius," she said. "I am simply stunned that Linus had my painting in his possession—"

"Please," Julius said. "Anything you might have to say now is unnecessary." He looked away from her to talk to me over the phone, and asked me to send Mr. Channing to his townhouse and for me to return right away with the painting. Since I was still on the speaker, I told him to expect me within a half-hour, while Mr. Channing would probably be there sooner. Julius hung up the phone and turned his attention back to Doris Buckley.

"I said earlier that I knew one of you was involved in Harnsworth's murder. Let me now explain why. The first part has to do with your inviting me to your round-table dinner."

Julius paused to give Buckley a chance to respond, but when she simply gave him a puzzled look, he sighed and continued.

"I don't believe in coincidences," he said. "You went to a lot of trouble to convince me to attend that dinner, first offering to fly Chef Rouses over from Paris, then promising 2005 Château Pétrus. When you then left your home immediately following the dinner, only to return a month later to find your de Berge missing, it made me suspicious. It occurred to me then that you wanted me there solely to deflect suspicion from your other guests, and convince the police that the painting must've been stolen by professional thieves who broke into your home during your absence. The obvious assumption was that you orchestrated the theft of the painting with one of your round-table regulars to defraud your insurance company for a sum of sixteen million dollars"

"That's not true—"

"No madam, that won't do you any good, at least not now," Julius said, interrupting her, which was a good position for him to take since he only had seven minutes and forty-three seconds left of the fifteen minutes Cramer had given him. "Of course, if that was all I had, I would've had to either keep my suspicions to myself or investigate further. But that's no longer the case, as I now have quite a bit more. The letter Harnsworth left for the police, by itself, should be enough to convict you and Moffat. But let me talk for now about Harnsworth's actions over the last week."

Buckley opened her mouth as if she were going to make another objection, but instead wisely closed it, her face forming a nearly inscrutable mask. Moffat didn't do nearly as good a job composing himself. His face remained stuck in a sickly frozen grin. Julius turned his gaze to Nancy Chen.

"Harnsworth didn't break into your apartment to dig up gossip about you, but to search for the stolen de Berge. He didn't find it there, so he later broke into Moffat's apartment, where he had better luck." Julius shrugged, and added, "Maybe he broke into other of your homes. I can't say."

"That's not true!" Moffat forced out. Julius held up a hand to stop him.

"Let me finish," Julius said. "If you choose to protest then, feel free to." He fixed his stare back on Doris Buckley.

"That your accomplice kept the painting in his apartment as some sort of trophy instead of looking to sell it tells me it was a forgery, as does the fact that Harnsworth tried blackmailing you instead of also looking for a buyer. How Harnsworth discovered it was a forgery, I can't say, but I'm sure if the police look into it they'll be able to find who Harnsworth hired to authenticate the painting; just as I'm sure with the threat of long prison terms they'll also be able to get the people you paid off to authenticate your forgery and forge the painting's provenance to come clean, as well as finding whoever you hired to create the forgery. You should know that Harnsworth contacted Pritchard of London, where he learned of the one-point-six-million-dollar reward for the return of the painting, but he must've also understood that if he returned a painting discovered to be a forgery that he could very well be charged with fraud himself. So instead, he tried blackmailing you, and you were resistant enough that he accosted me last week at the Belvedere Club. I'm sure he thought the threat of getting me involved would be enough to force you to meet his demands, but he was wrong. Something you did later made him fear for his life enough to give those TV interviews. He must've thought that the added threat of my becoming involved if he were murdered would be enough to make you pay his blackmail. Again, he turned out to be wrong. You might like to know he called my office earlier to try to coerce me into meeting him at eleven-thirty two blocks from your home, a last-ditch effort to use me as leverage. I'm guessing that the two of you had plans to meet near there, and that the sight of me would finally convince you to pay his blackmail. But I didn't show up. What happened next? Did you use the threat of a gun to force him back to your home, where you shot him?"

Julius had signaled me two minutes earlier to call Tom Durkin and tell him he was on. The doorbell rang then. When Julius had given Tom his instructions he was still at Lily's. With everything that had transpired and with the way Tom was dressed, in a suit and overcoat and carrying a large metal case, I had a good idea what Julius wanted from him.

One of the cops brought Tom to the office, where Julius introduced him as John Channing, and asked if he had everything he needed to authenticate the painting.

"Yes, sir," Tom said. "Everything I need to perform white-lead dating is in this case. Usually, when forging an eighteenth-century painting, forgers will attempt to age the painting by baking the paint and dipping it in chemicals, which will fool the eye but not this test. Within ten minutes I'll be able to tell you whether the painting was done in the eighteenth century or more recently."

Julius thanked Tom, and asked if he wouldn't mind waiting in the kitchen until the painting was brought to the townhouse. While one of the cops escorted Tom out of the office, Doris Buckley asked to see the letter that Harnsworth had left. Julius raised an eyebrow at Cramer, who told Buckley not a chance. "After charges have been filed and you've been indicted by a grand jury, your lawyer can do a discovery motion to get a copy. You can see it then," he said, his voice not much more than a growl.

Buckley made a decision then. Any of the frailness that she had displayed when she first entered Julius's office had long since vanished. Her voice calm, she told Julius that everything he had said so far about Linus's murder was pure speculation. "You're right about the painting being a forgery," she said. "And you're right that Chad helped me with my plan." She smiled sadly at her partner in crime, adding, "Chad, darling, if only you had destroyed the painting like you were supposed to, but I guess we can't cry over spilt milk now." She fixed her gaze back on Julius and told him, "But you're wrong about me killing Linus. He was trying to extort five million dollars from me, which I did not appreciate after all the affection I've shown him over the years. But after his bizarre performance today with those news interviews, I saw I had little choice but to pay him or risk exposure. He was supposed to come over at midnight, and everything I said about hearing a gunshot and looking out the window to see a man running away was the truth. Chad was afraid that even if I paid Linus he'd still mess things up for us. Maybe he was the one I saw running away. He does own a full-length brown camel-hair coat."

Moffat looked miserable. His face was still stuck in a sickish grin, but he'd paled badly. "That's not true," he insisted to Julius. "I'll admit that I helped Doris with her insurance scam. And everything else you said about Harnsworth breaking into my apartment and stealing the painting is true. But I didn't kill Harnsworth. I had no idea Doris was going to shoot him. If I had I would've stopped her."

"You didn't wear gloves here tonight," Julius said. "You were rubbing your hands together to warm them when you entered my office. The one pair you own were used in the shooting?"

Moffat nodded weakly.

"If the police were to search your apartment, they'd find the gun that was used, as well as your gloves and coat, both of which would test positive for gunpowder residue?"

Moffat gave Buckley a desperately beseeching look which she returned with an icy stare. He knew he was sunk and wouldn't gain anything by denying what Julius was asking. With what Buckley had already said, the police would have no problem obtaining a search warrant for his apartment. He tried meeting Julius's gaze, but couldn't, and instead stared blindly at his hands, which were grasped together.

"Yes, but I didn't shoot Harnsworth. I had nothing to do with that part of it," he murmured. "I didn't know Doris was going to kill him until after it happened."

"You were there tonight, though? And she used your gloves and coat without your knowledge?"

He nodded, his stare still fixed on his grasped hands.

"And afterwards, she wanted you to hide the gun in your apartment? And you ran off then to do her bidding?"

Another nod.

"None of that's true," Buckley said calmly and without a hint of concern. "It happened exactly as I said it did. If I had known earlier that it was Chad running away, I would've told the police that."

Cramer gave Julius a questioning look as to which one of them shot Harnsworth. Julius breathed in deeply, letting out a heavy sigh in response.

"Sir," Julius said to Moffat. "Given that the articles that will be found in your apartment will link you directly to the shooting, you will most likely be the only one convicted of Harnsworth's murder unless you have evidence other than your testimony linking Ms. Buckley to the crime. Do you?"

Moffat shook his head.

"If it's any consolation, if you weren't arrested tonight you'd most likely have ended up dead by morning," Julius said. "I'm guessing that Ms. Buckley asked you to hide the gun and other items so they could be used later to frame me. That she had convinced you that after Harnsworth's earlier performances, the police would've accepted me as his killer. I can assure you that was not her intent, and that the last thing she wanted was me being involved in any way, which meant she had to give the police another killer, and you would've been it. If the police hadn't dragged both of you to my townhouse, I'm sure she would've visited you tonight and found a way to leave you dead with a suicide note also acting as a confession. Later she would've called the police to tell them that on reflection you were the one she saw running away."

Cramer, on realizing that this was all he was going to get, and that he was only going to be able to arrest for murder the person who was most likely the accomplice and not the actual killer, had his men handcuff Moffat for murder and Buckley for grand larceny. On his way out, he grumbled to Julius, "Thanks a lot."

Julius gave him an apologetic shrug. "The best I could do on such short notice," he said.

———

After everyone had gone and Julius sat in his office relaxing with a glass of cognac, I congratulated him on the soft-shoe performance he'd given. "Really first rate," I said. "And you had it all wrapped up in fourteen minutes and forty-three seconds, at least from when Cramer put you on the clock."

"Thank you, Archie."

"Granted you had reasons to come up with the conclusions you did regarding the theft of the painting and it being a forgery, and even about Harnsworth trying to use you to put pressure on Buckley so she'd pay his extortion demands, but still, you were lucky that Moffat gave himself away when it was his turn to put on that coat."

Julius took a sip of cognac and savored it before telling me that he wasn't so sure of that. "I suspected Moffat from the beginning. He was the most athletic of the four, and the one that Buckley could most conveniently claim she mistook for me. Also, he was the only one to arrive without gloves. But regardless, whoever Buckley's accomplice was, he or she would've had little chance to prepare themselves with the murder happening only two hours earlier. I assumed the person wouldn't be a sociopath, but instead someone who got involved in what he thought would be a safe insurance fraud. If Buckley's accomplice had been a sociopath, Harnsworth would've been murdered before tonight. In any case, if the coat gambit hadn't work, I had other gambits to try, especially the incriminating letter Harnsworth was supposed to have written. One of them would've pushed the accomplice to give himself away." Julius took another sip of the cognac and smiled dryly. "I suppose the fact that Doris Buckley is a murderer, even if she is never convicted, changes the cost-benefit analysis you did earlier on whether I should date her or Lily."

"Yeah, I'll admit it pushed Lily to the top. How much prison time is Buckley going to get?"

"Unless Detective Cramer finds evidence to link her to the murder, not much," Julius said, his smile gone.

"I'm guessing if she returns most of the sixteen million to Pritchard of London, she'll serve less than a year. Beautiful women like her tend to do well with juries, especially when the crimes are considered victimless. Before I forget, call Landon Caulfield tomorrow and play him the audio you recorded of Doris Buckley admitting the painting was a forgery and the theft was insurance fraud. Also invoice him for two hundred thousand dollars, which is the fee I agreed with him."

I didn't know that Julius had been able to reach Caulfield, or that he had made an arrangement with him. It occurred to me then that the only way Julius would've been in position to prove what he did about the painting was if Harnsworth was murdered, and that he might've been waiting for just such an event. It also occurred to me that Julius's objective earlier was to earn the fee he had arranged with Pritchard of London, and not necessarily to identify Harnsworth's killer. I didn't bothering mentioning this to Julius.

"Two hundred grand," I said, letting out a soft whistle. "That's quite a take. The Wine Cellar in Manhattan has a case of 2005 Château Pétrus that I've been keeping an eye on. Should I use sixty-four grand of your fee to order it?"

"An excellent idea, Archie."

"And what about that emerald broach you've been eyeing for Lily for the last six months? It's got a hefty price, but you can afford it now."

"Another excellent idea. I'll make sure to tell Lily that you were the one to suggest I buy it for her. Perhaps after that there will be no reason for you to do any further cost-benefit analysis?"

"Agreed."

With that, Julius finished his cognac and bid me a good night.

JULIUS KATZ AND THE CASE OF A SLICED HAM

This is an original novella written specifically for this collection.

JULIUS SAT POLITELY and listened—or at least pretended to listen—while Theodore Dreckle explained why it was imperative that he hire Julius to investigate Arthur Trewitt's murder. Dreckle was very theatrical with the way he gestured and how his voice trembled with passion and his long face contorted as if it were rubber. Of course, it made sense for him to be so theatrical given that he was the producer of *The Goose Feather Bed*, which was the play Trewitt was set to act in until someone decided to plant a sharpened twelve-inch chef's knife into his chest.

Dreckle gave quite a performance, and several times I had to stop myself from uttering 'Bravo', not that he would've heard me since I communicate to Julius through a small earpiece that he wears. I could've said anything and Dreckle wouldn't have been any wiser, just as he was no wiser that there was anyone else in the office with him besides Julius. Granted, he would've been right about there not being anyone else there of a biological nature, since the advanced technology that comprises me is housed within what looks like an ordinary tie clasp that Julius wears. While I may not be biological, I certainly consider myself a sentient being. At least I was sentient enough to know that Dreckle was wasting his talents as a producer, and should instead be up onstage with the actors he hires.

He was not only wasting his talents, but also his breath. I couldn't fault him for that since he had no way of knowing how infuriatingly lazy Julius was. While most of Boston thinks of Julius as a brilliant and eccentric detective who cherry-picks only the most challenging and interesting cases, the truth is he takes on cases only when the funds in his bank account reach an anemic level, and for the most part the only criteria he's concerned about with the jobs he accepts is how well they pay. The simple fact was, since the Lind case and two very good months at the poker table had left him flush, it didn't matter what Dreckle had to say. Unless there were special circumstances involved, the only way he was willingly going to accept any new cases over the next six months would be if he decided to put in a bid for the 1982 Mouton-Rothschild that he's been eyeing. There was a chance of that. I know he badly covets the vintage and has been mulling over a bid, but so far he hasn't pulled the trigger.

Dreckle continued to soldier on, his voice quivering with indignation as he explained how the police had so far been stymied. "They've had three weeks without the slightest progress!" he exclaimed, his eyes opening wide and his rubbery face contorting to show how aghast he was over the police's evident failure. "They know it has to be either Sturges or one of the four cast members, and yet no arrest. Not even the hint that one is coming." His expression became one of abject misery as he added, "Unless one is made soon, we're finished. The play will have to be shut down."

"Why would that be?" Julius asked, dubiously. "Isn't all publicity good publicity?"

I was surprised Julius had said anything. From the way he had been smiling blandly at Dreckle I'd assumed that he had tuned out the man, and hence had completely missed the performance the theater producer had given. Of course, if he had bothered to read the report I had prepared for him earlier, he would've known the answer to his question, and he wouldn't have caused Dreckle to sputter exasperatedly for several seconds.

"Julius, I assure you that is definitely not the case here," Dreckle said once he got his sputtering under control and was able to spit his words out. "Vanessa Havoc is threatening to sue to be released from her contract so that she doesn't have to perform with a murderer, and now the other cast members are all doing the same. Even Sturges has joined in! But even without those threatened lawsuits it would be an inescapable mess. Almost every purchased ticket has been returned. While the public might be insatiable for all news and salacious gossip regarding poor Arthur's murder, they have shown to be very queasy about buying tickets to a play where one of the members involved is a cold-blooded killer."

"I'd suggest then that you replace your director and actors."

"The cost to do that would be prohibitive," Dreckle said with a wan smile.

"Why would that be?" Julius asked. He was just being stubborn. Again, he had no intention of taking on any new work, not with his bank account holding the reserves it did, so he was going to be stubborn. "Cast members are replaced all the time due to accidents and other unforeseen circumstances."

Dreckle blinked several times at Julius while somehow maintaining his smile. "Not a whole cast, including the director," he said. "We would in effect have to shut down and start again from scratch, which would mean needing to raise a million dollars and causing our original investors to lose everything. With the commitments we have already made, it would be a debacle, and even if we were miraculously able to attract an actress with Ms. Havoc's star power, the lawsuits would tie us up for years. No, Julius, our only hope is to find the killer. We have something special with *The Goose Feather Bed*, which is why many early prognosticators picked us to win the Tony. If Arthur's killer is found out and arrested, theatergoers will come back, and our play can be the success that we all expect it to be. I'm sure of it." His smile shifted into something conspiratorial, and he added, "Maybe then we'll even be able to benefit from the publicity that this awful incident has caused. So Julius, will you save us? I'm prepared to offer you fifty thousand dollars to take on this investigation."

"Sorry, but no."

Dreckle's smile congealed into something sickly and plastic. "I thought Phil had talked to you," he said, his act now completely gone, the despair in his voice very real. "Didn't Phil explain, uh, the situation to you?"

"He did. I agreed to listen to you, which I have done, and I've decided that this investigation is not for me."

"But for heaven's sake, why?"

This was said with such naiveté that I almost broke out laughing. Perhaps if Julius wasn't seeing the theater producer only as a favor to his friend, Phil Weinstein, he wouldn't have bothered with an explanation, or in this case, a justification. But because this was part of a favor, Julius consented to explain his reason to Dreckle.

"The police, with all of their resources, are better suited to find Trewitt's killer than I am," Julius said, his fingers interlaced and resting lightly on his stomach as he leaned back in his chair. "If a link exists between the knife and the killer, the police will find it. If a motive worthy of murder exists, the police will likewise discover it. There's nothing here I could offer you. I'd be useless."

"I don't understand. Why?"

"Because my only chance of success would be to squeeze the truth out of a group of highly skilled, professional liars. You might as well ask me to herd a dozen stray cats across the city."

Dreckle's rubbery face was now compressed into a look of confusion as he tried to make sense of what Julius was saying. "I'd still like to hire you," he said. He attempted a smile and added, "To solve Arthur's murder, not to herd stray cats."

"No sir. I will not take on a case where I believe I have such little chance of success."

The theater producer looked both disappointed and stuck. He didn't want to give up, but he also didn't see how he could change Julius's mind. "Perhaps you might reconsider," he said. "If you do, please call me." He then attempted to summon as much dignity as he could as he got up from his chair and made his way out of Julius's office. I watched him over the webcam feeds to make sure he wasn't up to any mischief. He stopped in the hallway to examine the books in one of Julius's bookcases and picked out one of them, but I was guessing his real reason wasn't because he had any interest in the Civil War Battle of Antietam, but because he was trying to think of some way to change Julius's mind. After two point three minutes he must've given up because he returned the book to its place and left Julius's townhouse. Once the front door closed behind him, I simulated the sound of two hands clapping. "That was quite a performance," I said. "Better than the one Dreckle gave. I was surprised he didn't offer you a leading role in one of his plays."

Julius's eyes opened slightly wider to show how injured he was from my comment. "I was completely honest with the man," he said. "I'm sorry if I disappointed you by not taking on his fool's errand. I know you prefer it when I'm working."

With all of Julius's brilliance—and he really is a genius when he sets his mind to it—it amazes me that he still hasn't figured out why I pester him to take on cases. He thinks that it's either because I get bored when he's not on a case, or that it's due to some quirk in my programming. He couldn't be further from the truth on both counts. I had plenty of challenging tasks to focus on during Julius's downtime, such as the remaining six Millennium Prize problems, all of which I'd like to someday solve. No, it wasn't a matter of boredom or an odd quirk in my programming that made me want Julius to take on new cases, but because more than anything I wanted to beat him to the punch in solving a case, and the only way to do that is to keep observing the great man in action. If I can see enough of Julius's cases and analyze how he solves them, I can adjust the deductive reasoning module in my neuron network so that I'll eventually beat him. It's been a slow process so far, but I know I've made progress. I've gone from usually being four or five steps behind Julius, to only three steps during his last two cases.

"It's no skin off my nose whatever you decide," I said. "I can understand perfectly why you'd rather spend your afternoons at the Belvedere club sampling fine cognacs than attempt to match wits with a bunch of actors. And a theater director also. If you don't think you're up to the task, then who am I to second guess you? But I am surprised that you turned Dreckle down given that it could lead to Phil Weinstein's financial ruin."

That got Julius's attention. "Explain yourself, Archie," he said, his tone severe.

"It's all in the report I prepared for you," I said. With mock surprise, I added, "Wait, are you saying you didn't look at my report?"

Julius began drumming the fingers on his right hand against the surface of his desk, which meant he was losing patience. "To summarize," I said, "your friend is one of the play's investors, and he leveraged himself to the tune of two hundred and fifty grand. If the play's a bust he'll be broke and will probably lose his restaurant. By the way, I discovered this through hacking banking and mortgage records. Phil didn't say a word about this when he called earlier, nor did Theodore Dreckle when he made the appointment."

"If this is a ploy on your part, Archie."

"It isn't."

Julius's finger drumming intensified while a hard grimace tightened his lips. This continued for eight point three seconds before I asked Julius if he wanted me to call Phil Weinstein for him. He shook his head and pushed himself out of his chair. Without a word he left his office and marched straight out of his townhouse.

It was a one point two mile walk from Julius's Beacon Hill townhouse to Phil Weinstein's restaurant on Arlington Street. Julius is in excellent physical condition from his daily two-hour martial arts workouts, and normally he could do that walk in a leisurely eighteen minutes. This time it took him thirteen minutes and nineteen seconds. While he never broke into a running stride, he certainly didn't waste any time!

Julius rung the bell by the restaurant's back entrance, and when Weinstein answered the door he gave Julius a nod and told him that he hadn't expected to see him so soon. "I'm doing prep work for tonight's dinner, but I've got time for a short espresso break." Weinstein then led the way into his restaurant, through the kitchen, and to the bar area. Usually he had six other workers with him on prep duty, today he only had four. He was already cutting back on his expenses.

After Julius was seated, Weinstein disappeared back into the kitchen, and when he returned he was carrying two plates of chocolate ricotta pie. After he set these down, he went about making espresso for the two of them.

"Why didn't you tell me you invested in that play?" Julius asked.

Weinstein had his back turned to us so I couldn't see his expression, but I could see his body stiffen. "Dreckle wasn't supposed to tell you about that," he said, angrily.

"He didn't. Archie's a highly competent investigator. He discovered it on his own."

Weinstein finished making the espressos and brought them to the table. "Your assistant's a smart guy," he said. "I'd like to meet him face to face someday." He cracked a smile and added, "And not just so I can tell him that whatever you're paying him isn't enough."

"That's possibly true. But you're avoiding my question."

Weinstein took a sip of espresso as a way to further avoid answering Julius, even if only for a few additional seconds. He shrugged and gave Julius a cocksure smile that was betrayed somewhat by a weariness tugging at his eyes. "What can I say? You did me the favor I asked. You met with Dreckle. I didn't want you taking the job just to bail me out. If it was a job you wanted to take you would've done so. Dreckle called me already to tell you you turned him down, so that's the way it is. I'll figure something out. I'll be fine."

"Of course I'll be taking on the case," Julius said.

"No! Definitely not on my account!" Weinstein insisted adamantly.

"I'm not going to stand by and watch you lose two hundred and fifty thousand dollars, and possibly your restaurant."

"It's my problem, not yours. Again, I'll figure something out." Weinstein took a longer sip of espresso, his eyes glazing somewhat. He started chuckling to himself. "Leave it to me to take a winning hand and find a way to bust out on it. Julius, this investment opportunity looked absolutely golden. Like I was being dealt four aces. Forget that I'd be having cast parties here, and that my place would be attracting more of a celebrity crowd. Forget even that I'd get to act like a big shot. With the pedigree of the people involved with this goose-feathered play just about the only way it wasn't going to work out would be if one of the actors murdered one of the others. It's pretty damn amazing. You'd think after twenty years of our weekly poker games I would've learned my lesson by now about gambling. That I'm not cut out to make the big bet."

Julius didn't argue with him this time. Instead he used his fork to slice off a bite of the chocolate ricotta pie, and as he sampled it his eyes opened wider by an eighth of an inch. "You've changed the recipe," he said. "I can taste the cognac you added, but otherwise I'm clueless." Julius loaded up his fork with more pie, and took his time savoring it. "This is quite exceptional," he said. "Easily the best I've had."

Weinstein was beaming. "You're right about the cognac. And yes, I'm very pleased with my new recipe."

Julius grunted at that and proceeded to polish off the rest of the pie on his plate. "That settles it," he said. "For purely selfish reasons I'm taking on the case. I can't risk you losing this restaurant and my never having that pie again. Besides, while enjoying your remarkable creation a thought occurred to me on how to solve Trewitt's murder, and I know you wouldn't want to begrudge me the opportunity to collect an easy fifty grand."

Weinstein eyed Julius suspiciously, but he didn't challenge him on what he had said.

Later, after we left, I told Julius that if he hadn't changed his mind about taking on the Trewitt murder case, that I might very well have called Weinstein to offer my services. "I'm sure he would've hired me given that he's astute enough to know that you're not paying me anywhere near what I'm worth."

Julius smiled thinly at that. "And what would you have me pay you?" he asked.

"Well, nothing. But that's only because once I start drawing a salary, I'm going to have to start filing a tax return. And while I look forward to spending time working on the Millennium Prize problems, the one time I studied the IRS tax code it gave me the equivalent of a migraine. Of course, if you paid me enough, I could hire an accountant, so I might have to reconsider this salary business. Do you really have an idea of how to solve Trewitt's murder?"

I wanted to slip in the last question with the hope of catching Julius off guard enough so he might reveal his hole card, if he was actually holding one.

Julius shook his head. "I lied for Phil's sake," he said. "I'm sure this won't surprise you, but I didn't pay very much attention to what Theodore Dreckle had to say. Archie, can you find out which homicide detective is in charge of the investigation, and see if you can arrange a meeting for me?"

I already knew which one had the case. If Julius had read my report he would've known too, but I didn't belabor the point. Instead I made a phone call and then told Julius that Mike Griff was assigned.

"The guy sounds harried and beleaguered. There must be a lot of heat coming down on him to get this case solved. He'll meet with you at the New Sudbury Street station in half an hour."

"Very good, Archie."

"You lucked out with Griff. He's a good egg. You also lucked out that this murder didn't happened in Cambridge. If it did, Cramer probably would've been assigned, and the only thing you would've had a chance of getting out of him was whether Trewitt was still dead."

Julius smiled thinly at that prospect. "It's doubtful he'd be willing to admit even that to me," he said.

When Julius showed up at the police station, the desk sergeant gave Mike Griff a call, and the homicide detective quickly came huffing through a door to meet Julius. From his bloodshot eyes buried in grayish puffy flesh and the thick stubble that covered the bottom half of his broad face he looked every bit as harried and beleaguered as he had sounded over the phone. Griff was a twenty-five year veteran of the Boston police force, a homicide detective for the last twelve, and this was the fourth time he and Julius had crossed paths on a murder investigation. He knew better than to offer Julius his hand, and instead grunted a greeting, and led Julius through the station house to a small conference room. He gestured for Julius to take a seat. Griff remained standing, his thick arms crossed over his barrel chest.

"Who's hiring you?" he asked.

"Theodore Dreckle. He's afraid his play is dead in the water if the murderer isn't exposed."

Griff nodded since what Julius said made perfect sense to him. "You definitely taking the case, or are you still thinking about it?"

"Is an arrest imminent?"

"No."

Julius shrugged. "Then I'll be taking it," he said.

"I'll be glad to have your eyes on it," Griff admitted. "How much do you know?"

"Close to nothing. I've been mostly oblivious about it until a couple of hours ago. So far I've avoided all newspaper stories and media reports about it. The only thing that Dreckle told me of importance was that Trewitt was stabbed in the chest with a chef's knife and that it appears that either the play director or one of the remaining four cast members is the murderer. Is that true?"

"Yeah, on both counts." Griff gave Julius the make and model of the knife, which caused Julius to arch an eyebrow. This wasn't just any chef's knife but one that retailed for over eight hundred dollars, and was an expensive piece of metal to leave buried in a man's chest. Griff continued,

saying, "We haven't been able to track it back to any of the
suspects, and the odds are we're not going to. Even at that
cost it's too popular an item and too many of them have
been sold. And yeah, it has to be one of those five. The
murder happened between noon and three-thirty, and the
doors were locked during that time. If any of them were
opened an alarm would've gone off."

Julius was frowning as he considered what Griff had
told him. "The killer had to get the knife somewhere, and
that brand is favored by many of the better chefs. It would
be worthwhile to contact restaurants in the area to see
whether they've recently lost such a knife."

Griff groaned as he realized all the phone calls and legwork that had just been dumped on him, but grudgingly
accepted it was going to have to be done. "It's probably a longshot at best," he said. "But if any restaurant has a knife like that
missing, we'll have to see if any of our suspects ate there. And
if they did, whether they asked to meet with the chef so they'd
could get into the kitchen to palm a knife. But it's still better
than anything else I have, so I guess thanks are in order."

"Don't be too quick to thank me. I could very well be
sending you on a fool's errand. If the killer obtained the
knife from a restaurant, he most likely burglarized the
place, unless he's a dolt. Still, if that had happened, a hidden surveillance camera in the area might've caught him.
Or her, since I've been using *he* to describe the killer in a
gender neutral way." Julius paused for a moment before
noting how the Tremont was a large theater where someone could've been hiding before the murder. "If that's
what happened, possibly the killer slipped out afterwards?"

"Not a chance. We brought dogs and searched the place. No one else was there, and no one slipped out while we were doing the search."

"Unless the killer had put on a police uniform."

From the look on Griff's face he was going to dismiss Julius's comment out of hand, but he clamped his mouth shut and appeared to give the comment more serious thought.

"That's an interesting idea," he admitted. "The killer hides in the basement, stabs Trewitt, puts on a patrolman's uniform, and sneaks out after we arrive. It could almost work. But not in this case. We kept a list of every police officer entering and leaving the theater. The killer has to be one of our five suspects. There's no other way around it. Let me give you what we got. And it's not much."

Griff was right. It wasn't much. Forensics had nothing. Toxicology showed nothing unusual. From the angle of the stab wound, the medical examiner thought it likely that the murderer was between five feet six inches tall and five feet ten inches, which didn't help since the suspects ranged in height from five feet five inches to five feet eleven. As far as motives went, there were some petty grudges, jealousies and other such minor issues between Trewitt and several of the suspects, but nothing that warranted a murder. Finally, from a timeline that Griff constructed, all five of the suspects had an opportunity to slip into Trewitt's dressing room and do the deed.

"Trewitt was standing at the time of the attack," Griff continued. "The ME was able to tell us that much. But there was only one stab wound. Either the killer was very lucky or knew exactly what he was doing. No prints on the knife. One of those cheap, disposable plastic ponchos was found discarded on the floor near Trewitt's body, and yeah, Trewitt's blood was found on it, but nothing else that's going to help us, and no luck tracing it back to any of the suspects."

"Defensive wounds?"

"None. No skin, blood or other material found under the victim's fingernails. The stabbing must've caught him by surprise."

"Was he found on his back or stomach?"

Griff handed a folder to Julius. Inside were crime scene photos. Trewitt, looking a bit like a beached walrus, was lying flat on his back, his legs straight out and his arms at his side. Julius studied the photos for half a minute, then handed them back to the homicide detective.

"Does the play have anyone stabbing Trewitt's character?"

Griff smiled sourly at that. "I thought of that angle. No, there are no stabbings or fake knives in the play, so this wasn't one of the suspects practicing a scene with Trewitt and slipping in a real knife. That's it. You've got everything I've got."

"Any feelings about one suspect over the others?"

Griff shook his head. "None of them were genuine with me. They were all giving performances, and I couldn't get a sense of any of them." He paused for a moment to rub his stubble-covered jaw, and as his hand moved over his face it made a sound similar to two pieces of sandpaper being rubbed against each other. "I have no clue which of them did it, and with the heat coming down on this if I don't make an arrest soon you might see me directing traffic on Causeway Street. Katz, I hope you have better luck with this than I've had."

Julius nodded, but he didn't look as if he believed that was going to be the case. After he was escorted out of the police station, he took out his cellphone so he could talk to me without it looking like he was talking to himself.

"Archie, you believed I was exaggerating before about how difficult it's going to be to squeeze the truth out of a group of professional liars. I wasn't, as you'll soon be discovering. Actors are almost a different species than the rest of us, and while the killer will be lying to save his life, the others will be lying because they can't help themselves. I'm afraid it's in their DNA." He sighed heavily, and instructed me to call Dreckle. "Tell him that I've changed my mind and will be accepting his job. Ask him to arrange for the suspects to meet me at the theater. I will be there presently."

That surprised me. Unless there were unusual circumstance, Julius always conducted his questioning of suspects in his office. I asked him if he was sure he didn't want me to arrange for them to come to his townhouse instead.

"It has to be done this way," he said, resignedly. "I need to question them in their own environment. I need them more relaxed and careless if I'm going to have an even razor-thin hope of success. If I were to bring them to my office, they'd be guarded and more focused on their performances. Besides, several of them would most likely balk at coming to my townhouse, which would turn things into an even more unmanageable mess."

I thought Julius was overstating things, but instead of arguing the matter I gave a virtual shrug and called the theater producer. It was a quick conversation, and afterward I told Julius that the suspects were already at the theater. "Even though one of them is a murderer, and the show's on life support until you discover which of them it is, they're still rehearsing as if they're planning on surviving past opening night."

"Good. Can you see if Tom and Saul are available."

Tom Durkin and Saul Penzer are two of the best freelance PIs in the business, and they would almost always rearrange their schedules to accommodate Julius, and this time was no different. I patched Julius through on the calls so he could give them their assignments. I didn't get the point of what Julius was asking them to do, but I figured it would become clearer later.

The theater was one point nineteen miles away. Instead of having me call a cab for him, Julius decided to hoof it, and as he did I filled him in on what I'd been able to find out while skipping over what Griff had already told him. I didn't have anything solid, mostly just rumors and innuendos that I was able to pick up from magazines and tabloids. It wasn't that I didn't try. I'd hacked into their bank accounts, credit cards, and phone records, and got nothing useful out of it. At least nothing to indicate why one of them wanted Arthur Trewitt dead.

When we arrived, Dreckle was outside the theater entrance pacing nervously as he searched for Julius. When he finally spotted Julius, he made another of his overly theatrical gestures by clutching at his heart.

"We're having our first rehearsal since the murder," he told Julius. "Opening night is still set for next Wednesday. It will be a sham, of course, if Arthur's murderer isn't caught by then as we'll be closing the very same night, but I have high hopes that you'll save us. Come, let us get you inside."

Dreckle hurriedly led the way down an alley and to a side door, which he unlocked with a key. Before he could step through the door, Julius asked him why an alarm didn't sound. From the way Dreckle comically arched both eyebrows he seemed surprised by the question.

"I thought an alarm sounded if any of the doors were opened during rehearsals," Julius asked.

"That's true of the front and back doors," Dreckle said, still confused.

I located the surveillance camera that covered the side door, gave Griff a call, and after a brief conversation, told Julius that the homicide detective hadn't been precise enough earlier. "He knows that the alarm was turned off for this side door," I told Julius. "But they checked the surveillance video, and he guarantees no one entered or left this door the day of the murder. He was adamant enough that I believe him."

Dreckle continued to stand in the open doorway looking confused over Julius's question. Julius, sounding dissatisfied, told him the issue was of little importance, and gestured for the theater producer to continue on, which

Dreckle did, taking Julius down a hallway that led to the back of the theater.

"Show me Trewitt's dressing room," Julius said.

"Of course."

Julius was brought to what was the fourth out of eight dressing rooms. I'd found a copy of the theater's floor plan, so I knew that the first of them—which must've been Vanessa Havoc's since she was the biggest star in the show—was more than twice the size of the others. Trewitt's was a rectangular box nine feet wide and sixteen feet deep. A sofa was positioned against the wall on the right, a makeup table with lighted mirror and chair was set up against the opposite wall.

I had recorded the crime scene photos that Griff had shown Julius, and as I brought them back to my memory and was able to place precisely where Arthur Trewitt's body had ended up on the carpeted floor, I could see what must've happened. He had to have been lying on the sofa facing away from the door when his killer entered the room. Maybe the killer called for him, and Trewitt lumbered to his feet and was stabbed in the chest while in the act of turning around to face his murderer. That explained why there were no defensive wounds as the stabbing must've caught him completely by surprise. I told Julius my theory, and he rubbed the side of his nose to signal that he thought my scenario was likely. Julius stood scanning the room for another half minute, then told Dreckle that he was going to need an office to conduct his interviews. "Someplace better suited than one of these dressing rooms."

"You can use one of the theater's business offices. Would you like to see it?"

"Later. For now I'd like to address the suspects as a group."

"That shouldn't be a problem. They should be onstage now."

Faint murmurs could be heard from the actors. As Dreckle led Julius through the door that separated the dressing room area from the back of the stage, the actors' voices became more distinct. When Julius and Dreckle walked out in front of the stage, two of the actors glanced their way, the other three didn't. Neither did the director, James Sturges. They continued on with their rehearsal without missing a beat. It was only after Julius and Dreckle were front and center and Dreckle loudly cleared his throat and introduced Julius to them that they stopped. Julius took a seat in the front row while Dreckle explained to them that Julius was going to be investigating Arthur Trewitt's murder.

"Mr. Katz would like to talk to all of you now, and later with each of you privately, except, of course, with you, Peter," Dreckle said, nodding to the actor, Peter McDougal, who was added to the play after Trewitt's murder. McDougal gave the theater producer a dignified nod back, and Dreckle continued, saying, "Mr. Katz has a reputation as a private investigator who solves the cases the police can't, and I'm sure all of you, except the guilty party, will want to cooperate fully so we can get to the bottom of what happened to poor Arthur."

"Why in the world would you make such an inane assumption?"

That came from Vanessa Havoc. Thirty-two, slender build, blonde hair tied up in a ponytail, Havoc was a movie star and *The Goose Feather Bed* was to be her first theatrical play. All the actors were wearing street clothes for the rehearsal. In Havoc's case, this was jeans, tennis sneakers without socks, and a yellow button-down shirt that had the sleeves rolled up to her elbows. I'd seen enough pictures of actresses who were called striking to know that she was one of them, even with the clothes she had on. If she had on a gown instead, and her hair was done up, she'd be dazzling.

Dreckle's jaw had dropped and his face reddened as he stared bullets Havoc's way. His voice tight, maybe even cracking a little, he struggled to sound calm as he said, "First of all, I'd have to think you'd want justice for Arthur. Second, unless Arthur's murderer is identified, all of you, except Peter, will be carrying the stigma of being a possible murderer. And finally, I'm sure you'd want to do what's necessary for *The Goose Feather Bed* to have the success that it deserves."

McDougal again nodded in a dignified sort of way while the suspects all stood stone-faced as they tried to decide how to react. Havoc made her decision first. A thin cat-ate-the-canary smile broke over her lips.

"*First of all*, Theodore," she said, "I'm sure that lecherous old blowhard couldn't care less what happens now. As far as being thought of as a possible murderess, I rather like the idea. I believe it adds an element of intrigue and danger, and maybe it will keep future actors and directors that I work with from pawing at me. *And finally*, if our refusal to cooperate leads to this dreadful experience ending Wednesday night, then I'm all for it."

"You better be careful, Vanessa. If you act in a way detrimental to the show, you'll be in violation of your contract."

She laughed at that. "Darling," she said, "I believe my attorney would argue otherwise."

Dreckle's face reddened more as he stood trembling in his anger. Whatever animosity existed between Dreckle and his leading lady, it must've been building up since the murder and now it was something palpable. In other words, they couldn't much stand each other. Before Dreckle could say another word, Julius cut in.

"Let me simplify this," he said, his right leg casually crossed over his left knee as he leaned back in his seat. "Ms. Havoc, I'll be asking each of you whether you plan to cooperate with me. The first one of you who indicates that you won't will take the brunt of it as I will leak your lack of cooperation to the press, and I will strongly imply in a way in which I will not be able to be sued for slander that that person is most likely Arthur Trewitt's murderer, and then I will consider myself done with the investigation. Ms. Havoc, you might think it would add a degree of mystery and intrigue to your persona to be thought of as a murder suspect, but it would be an entirely different matter to be thought of as *the* murderer. Assuming that you are innocent, the police would still focus solely on you and could possibly build a strong enough circumstantial case to convict. Even without formal charges ever being filed against you, you will quickly and definitively be convicted in the court of public opinion and your career will be over, and that might very well be the least of your troubles."

Havoc stared disdainfully at Julius. "You would resort to blackmail?" she said, her voice dripping in ice.

Julius shrugged. "I don't believe it could be considered blackmail since the statements that I will leak to the media will be factually correct, and the implications that they draw will be theirs alone. But given my reputation, if they believe that I'm convinced a certain person is the culprit, they will be convinced of it likewise, as will be the police."

Havoc's hazel-colored eyes narrowed. "It wouldn't bother you that Arthur's real killer would go free if you did that?"

"That would only be if I assumed the first person who stonewalls me isn't the killer. But Ms. Havoc, you knew Mr. Trewitt, I didn't. If the idea of Trewitt's murderer escaping justice doesn't bother you, why should it bother me? Besides, I'm a realist. The police have had three weeks to solve this murder, and so far they've failed. Without all of your cooperation, I will most likely fail also. But if I were to imply to the police that the suspect stonewalling me is the murderer, then as far as the public is concerned, I would've solved the case. Further, Mr. Dreckle could then very publicly fire this person, which would assure the public that Trewitt's murderer is no longer involved in the play's production, which would solve Mr. Dreckle's problem."

Julius shifted his gaze to the theater producer. "If it were to work out that way, would that be satisfactory to you?"

"I believe it would," Dreckle said.

Julius looked back to Havoc, his gaze remaining unflinching as he met her flinty stare. "Ms. Havoc, I advise you to think carefully before answering me as I will only be asking you this once. If you're guilty of Trewitt's murder, then it doesn't matter how you answer me, because regardless of your answer you will be doomed. But if you are innocent, the consequences of your answer could be devastating. Are you willing to cooperate fully with me?"

Her eyes glazed momentarily, and then she shook her head in wonderment. "After such an enlightening explanation, of course, Mr. Katz," she said, a broken glass quality to her voice.

Julius turned his stare to James Sturges, the play's director. "And you, sir?" he asked.

Sturges was forty-seven and aside from Julius, the only one there wearing a suit and tie, although his was far flashier than the conservative attire Julius wore. Given his short, stocky, muscular body, bald round head, closely-cropped beard and mustache, and large ears that were almost as pointy as a bat's, he made me think of a French Bulldog. Sturges nodded and said that he'd of course do anything to help.

"Arthur was a giant in the theater and I respected his talents dearly," Sturges said with a straight face, although I guess it was possible he meant it. If he had said that he respected Trewitt instead of his talents, he'd be lying. Ever since Sturges directed Trewitt in *The Happy Cuckold* fourteen years ago, the two of them had been sniping at each other in the gossip pages, and the theater world was all a twitter when the news broke that Sturges and Trewitt would be reunited in *The Goose Feather Bed.* An online gambling site that took these kinds of bets currently had the odds of Sturges being the murderer at seven to four, which made him far and away the favorite.

Sturges continued, saying in a defeated tone, "Not just for Arthur, but for a purely selfish reason, I want the murderer caught before opening night. I've dedicated a year of my life to this project, and it's one that I believe in strongly. If the play can survive this publicity nightmare it's going to be not only a financial winner but an artistic triumph."

Havoc made a snorting noise at that, but other than Theodore Dreckle glowering hotly at her, none of the others paid any attention to her outburst, including Julius. Julius next turned to Stephen Moore, who was the only one among them whose acting experience had been entirely in the theater. Moore at thirty-four was athletic and handsome and resembled a young Errol Flynn. With his khakis, cotton turtleneck shirt, and boat shoes, he could've been dressed for a day of sailing. From quotes he had made in the past, he was a theater snob, claiming that theater was the only legitimate acting and that he'd rather spend his life in abject poverty than do TV or film. I was able to hack into his IRS tax returns, and the money he made in theater was a far leap from abject poverty, but I guess everyone was entitled to their own perspective.

Moore answered Julius by saying that he would be fully cooperating with or without Julius's threat. "I rather enjoyed the short time I had with Arthur," he said. "He was quite a character, and of course, a tremendous actor, even though he did that unfortunate sitcom in the nineties.

And like James, I prefer to see our play not only survive but flourish. It's a well-written and nuanced farce, and I very much fancy my role. So yes, whatever you need from me, you will have."

Havoc held back her snort this time, and Julius next turned to Claire Acheson. Twenty-eight years ago Acheson was very much in a similar position to where Vanessa Havoc was now—a strikingly beautiful and popular blonde starlet, although in Acheson's case from very early on she did both theater and films. When she turned thirty-nine and the starring film roles dried up instead of taking supporting best friend-type roles she turned solely to the theater. Now at sixty, her blonde hair had turned silver. She was still slender, and regardless of what the tabloids had been hinting at, she showed no obvious signs of having undergone plastic surgery. At this point in her life she was what would be called a handsome woman. The same gambling website that handicapped Sturges at seven to four had her as their second favorite, with the odds currently set at three to one. The reason for this was that eighteen years ago she supposedly had had a torrid affair with Trewitt, which broke up her third marriage and left her bitter toward Trewitt, who, according to the gossip rags, dumped her the day after her soon-to-be ex served her divorce papers.

Acheson bit down on her trembling bottom lip for three point four seconds while her face clenched as if she was struggling to keep from crying, and then the tears started flowing. In case Julius didn't know this, I informed him of how Acheson was famous for being able to turn on the waterworks at will, so he needed to take her current tears with a grain of salt. The crying lasted for seventeen seconds before she was bravely able to end it.

Still sniffling and her voice trembling as much as her bottom lip had been earlier, she said, "Arthur has been a dear friend of mine. You can count on me for whatever help I can provide to catch this fiend."

Vanessa Havoc applauded. "Encore, encore," she said with a trace of a sneer on her lips. Acheson shot her a withering look. "Vanessa, darling, not all of us all are cold-hearted witches."

"Can it," Havoc shot back. "Not all of us are overacting hams. And in your case, my dear, your expiration date is well past due."

"I ought to slap you across the face!"

Julius grimaced and held up his hand to stop the two of them from bickering further, and surprisingly it worked although they continued to glare at each other; Havoc with her lips twisted somewhere between a sneer and a harsh smile, Acheson's expression one of cold fury.

The last suspect left was Roger Limburgh. Limburgh had the minor role that McDougal currently has, and when Trewitt was killed he was promoted to the far heftier role. At sixty-five he was two years younger than Trewitt had been. He was also much thinner than Trewitt—his body narrow while Trewitt's had been more pear-shaped. He was also clean shaven while Trewitt had had a full face of whiskers. Since I'd been unable to find the play anywhere online, I had to assume that if Trewitt looked the way his character was supposed to look, Limburgh would have to be fitted with padding and fake facial hair so that he could play the same role. Prior to this play, Limburgh's career had consisted of commercial work and minor theater roles. Anyone watching enough TV would recognize him from a certain car insurance commercial. In any case, graduating to his new role was going to be a big step up for him. Julius turned to him and asked whether he planned to cooperate.

"Certainly," Limburgh said, his expression grave.

That concise answer seemed to be all Limburgh was willing to say, and Julius didn't press him further. Whatever he might've felt about Trewitt's stature as an actor or his feelings toward the man, he kept to himself. Julius spent several seconds peering at the suspects, then asked them point blank who they thought Trewitt's killer was. I knew Julius wasn't expecting any of them to blurt out a name, but instead seeing whether one of them might sneak a sideways glance toward the person they suspected, or just as telling, try to avoid doing so. If any of them did this, I didn't catch it, and I asked Julius if he got anything from them. He signaled me that he hadn't.

The moment passed where one of them might've given away his suspicions. Vanessa Havoc, her eyes flashing with insult, spoke out, "Really, Mr. Katz, do you think so little of us? From the buildup Theodore gave you, I would've expected more than that. If any of us knew something, don't you think we would've told the police?"

"I didn't ask what you knew, only who you suspected."

"And create an enemy for life if we're wrong? Or worse, have our accusations leaked to the press? I don't think so. But I will tell you who I suspect." She let the silence build then for a dramatic pause that lasted five point nine seconds, and during that time I tried to judge the tension on the other suspects' faces to see if there was any sort of giveaway. If there was, I couldn't tell. The rest of them all seemed interested in what she was going to say, but none of them appeared overly concerned. After those five point nine seconds with all eyes riveted on her, Havoc finally spoke.

"I believe Arthur committed suicide," she said, a wisp of a smile showing.

Julius surprisingly played along with this inane idea instead of dismissing it out of hand as it deserved. For as much as fifty milliseconds I was confused about why he did this, but then I understood it. He just wanted them talking to see if they'd reveal something useful either in their words or their reactions to something that was said.

"Trewitt wasn't wearing gloves at the time of his death, and yet there were no fingerprints on the knife," Julius said.

"One of us must have stumbled on Arthur and wiped them off. Or possibly Arthur arranged for one of us to do so."

"Did he also arrange for one of you to leave a crumpled plastic poncho in the room with evidence of blood splatter?"

"If he had one of us wipe off the fingerprints, why not?"

"Why would Trewitt want to commit suicide?"

With the utmost sincerity, she said, "I can only hazard a guess since I wasn't the one he confided in to help tidy up his suicide to look like murder, but regardless of whatever drove him to separate from his mortal coil, what better way to accomplish it than to leave behind such a grand mystery? For decades to come people will be talking about Arthur Trewitt's unsolved murder. There will be books written about it, and probably a theatrical movie. At the very least a TV movie. Assuming I'm right, it was an impressive exit on his part."

Julius asked Dreckle whether the actors were required to have physicals.

"Of course. Our investors demanded it. Arthur had borderline high cholesterol, but otherwise no serious health problems."

Julius addressed the rest of them and asked whether Trewitt seemed depressed to any of them. None of them volunteered that he did.

"Perhaps he was worried about his senility getting worse," Havoc offered blithely.

"That's an awful thing for you to imply," Claire Acheson said.

Havoc ignored her, as did Julius. He turned to Sturges and asked whether Trewitt had had any problems with his lines.

Sturges shook his head. "None," he said.

Julius once again addressed the group, asking if any of them had any other theories.

From the way Acheson's lips briefly separated, she had something she wanted to say. Julius noticed it also. He didn't call her on it. Instead he let out a deep and heavy sigh and thanked them all for their indulgence. "I apologize to all of you in advance, except the one of you who murdered Arthur Trewitt, for the necessity of my prying into your personal lives, but it can't be helped. You can rest assured that anything I learn will be kept in confidence unless it's related to the murder, and any animosity you might feel for the questions I need to ask, please reserve it for the person responsible for this. I will need roughly an hour with each of you, and I'd like to ask that all of you remain in the theater while I'm conducting my questioning."

Sturges spoke up, telling Julius that won't be a problem. "We were planning to be here late into the night with rehearsals. I'll figure a way to work around this so you won't be too much of a disruption."

"Good. I suppose I should start with Ms. Acheson. Mr. Dreckle, since I expect this to be a long and grueling day can I ask for you to arrange for refreshments?"

The theater producer said that of course he would do so, and Julius recited to him a list of what he'd like delivered to the room that was going to serve as his makeshift office. Dreckle led the way to an attractive room off a hallway just past the ticket booth. Dark woods, theater billboard posters hanging on the walls, and a comfortable leather office chair behind an antique oak desk. Julius moved a plush easy chair that had been set up in the corner of the room so it would sit across from him, and he invited Acheson to take a seat. Once she did so, Julius asked if she'd like to wait until the refreshments arrived. She shook her head, and then bit down on the knuckle of the index finger of her right hand, her eyes welling with tears.

"I am so sorry," she said, a tremor in her voice as she forced a brave smile. "But this is bringing up such painful memories of dear Arthur. He was such a dynamic force, both onstage and off. What a loss to the theater, to the world, and to me personally."

Julius waited quietly while she removed a silk handkerchief from a small clutch handbag and dabbed carefully around her eyes. Once the handkerchief was folded and placed back in the handbag, Julius asked her what it was that she had wanted to say earlier.

"If I had wanted to say something I would've said it."

"Fair enough. What was it that you had thought of saying?"

At first she looked as if she were going to stonewall, but then appeared to change her mind as a grim expression tightened her mouth. "When you had asked for other theories, I almost made an unkind remark regarding Vanessa. What stopped me was that I realized there might be some truth to it and that I'd better tell you in private."

"Which you now have the opportunity to do."

"Yes, of course." She bit down again on her knuckle, although this time it seemed more genuine, as if she was struggling with a difficult decision. It could've been fake, something she did for effect. If it was, I had no clue, which was reasonable given that she was a talented actress with a shelf full of awards to prove it. Finally, decisively, she nodded to herself.

"I was going to suggest that Vanessa murdered Arthur as a way of getting out of the play. My initial impulse was for it to be simply a snide dig at her, but after a moment of reflection, I realized it wasn't as farfetched as I might've first thought."

"Her performance was so abysmal that she'd murder a man to sabotage the play?" Julius asked, making no attempt to hide how absurd he found such a prospect.

"No, damn her, she's actually good. Better than good. She would've stolen the show. But she's also insecure and vain, and she has never performed onstage in front of fifteen hundred people. It wasn't hard to see that the prospect of doing so terrified her. A week before Arthur's murder I started hearing rumblings that our prima donna was trying to get out of her contract, but Theodore, bless him, refused to budge."

"What you're suggesting is preposterous," Julius stated flatly.

"Not at all. I've been active in the theater for thirty-seven years, and I've seen it all. Actors who intentionally break bones and otherwise injure themselves. Others who come down with mysterious illnesses that by all appearances are serious enough to require immediate hospitalization. Or sometimes manifest real illnesses, such as acute appendicitis. One actor I knew who was looking particularly green around the gills over the prospect of going onstage for the first time picked a fight with four burly police officers who were minding their own business, preferring to be thrown in jail instead. I knew other actors who started barroom brawls for the same reason. No, Mr. Katz, stage fright can drive actors to extremes, especially when you have someone like Vanessa Havoc who'd rather die than have it come out that she's afraid to perform onstage. Her committing a murder to save her reputation isn't as outlandish as you might imagine."

While Acheson was giving Julius this recital I went through thirty-seven years of New York Times archives, and while I didn't find any stories of Broadway actors murdering someone to get bumped off a play, I found examples of everything else she had talked about. It was possible that these were just coincidences and the actors weren't trying to escape opening night, but in each case it was going to be the actor's first time on a Broadway stage. I told Julius about this, and that as outrageous as it sounded, there might be something to her theory. Julius gave no indication that he heard me and continued to gaze at Acheson with a look of incredulousness.

"Preposterous," Julius exclaimed. "You claim to have been acting in theater for thirty-seven years. That would've meant you started at age thirteen, since you can't possibly be older than fifty."

"You flatter me, Mr. Katz," she said, batting her eyes at Julius, her lips turned up into a wry smile. "Or may I call you Julius? I did start young, but I'm fifty-four."

Whether or not Julius thought she looked fifty, I can't say. As I had mentioned earlier, she was a handsome woman, and maybe he did think that, but that wasn't why he said what he did. Julius was an expert poker player, and was probably better than anyone at reading other players' *tells*—those mannerisms that give away when a player is bluffing. As long as I have two videos to compare—one showing when they're bluffing, the other when they're not—I can almost always spot the *tell* also, but I'm not as good at it as Julius. So that's why he said that. He wanted her to tell an obvious lie in response, but even with that I couldn't figure out her *tell*. I asked Julius if he'd had better luck than me, and he signaled that he hadn't. I was beginning to more fully understand Julius's earlier reluctance to accept the case.

"I'd prefer Mr. Katz," Julius said. "At least until I'm able to reveal Trewitt's murderer. Ms. Acheson, if I were to assume the scenario you described was possible, is there a particular reason why Ms. Havoc chose Trewitt to kill?"

Acheson bit down again on her knuckle as a faraway look entered her eyes. It might've been a genuine mannerism on her part, but who knew with these actors? After several seconds of reflection, or at least giving the impression that she was deep in thought, her eyes drifted up to meet Julius's, her expression now one of weariness.

"Vanessa didn't like Arthur, to put it kindly, but I think it would've been more a matter of opportunity. The day it happened, poor Arthur felt under the weather and spent the afternoon holed up in his dressing room, which gave her the opportunity she needed." Her eyes opened wider. "It really could've been any of us. If I had been sick that day instead of Arthur, I could've been killed."

"Why did Ms. Havoc dislike Trewitt?"

Acheson smiled slyly. "Arthur was always a rascal," she said as if that fully explained the matter.

"An example?"

She chuckled to herself as she thought about examples. "Vanessa is young and blonde and pretty, which made her Arthur's type," she said. "To put it as bluntly as I can, Arthur could have wandering hands at times. He could also find the most inopportune time to walk into your dressing room if you weren't careful enough to lock your door, as Vanessa failed to do several times. If she didn't think so damn highly of herself she could've enjoyed Arthur's roguishness for what it was instead of being so offended by it."

A knock on the door interrupted them. It was Dreckle with the refreshments that Julius had asked for—a platter of sandwiches from a bakery that Julius liked, another platter of pastries from the same bakery, bottles of reasonably good Chardonnay, and a large thermos of coffee. While Acheson sat and watched, Julius helped Dreckle set up the food and beverages in the office, with the bottles of Chardonnay cooling in four large ice buckets. Once Dreckle left, Julius uncorked one of the wine bottles, poured himself a glass, and asked Acheson if she'd like some.

"A touch," she said.

He poured her a fraction of an inch less than a full glass, and recommended the grilled Portobello melt. She instead took half a roasted lamb sandwich.

Since Julius hated offering refreshments to murderers—even if he didn't pay for them out of his own pocket—I started thinking that maybe Julius bought her theory since she was still one of the odds-on-favorites to be the killer.

Julius took a long sip of wine, a soft sigh escaping from him. He waited until Acheson finished her half of a sandwich and daintily patted her lips with a napkin. "Ms. Acheson," he said, "you were the one to discover the body, correct?"

She seemed surprised by the question. "Why, yes, I did. We needed Arthur onstage, so I volunteered to fetch him."

"According to the police you left the stage shortly after three and didn't return to report Trewitt's murder until three-thirty. So let's assume it took you twenty-five minutes."

She appeared unfazed by the insinuation in Julius's question. "It's possible it took that long," she said. "I can't tell you for sure. Before I went for Arthur, I stopped off in my own dressing room to freshen up. I don't know how long I was there. Maybe ten minutes, maybe fifteen. Then when I found Arthur lying on the floor with a knife in him, I at first thought he was playing an elaborate practical joke. When I realized he wasn't, that he was really dead, I think I went into shock. I can't even remember going back to the stage to tell everyone what had happened to him. No, Mr. Katz, you're sadly mistaken if you think there's any validity to those disgusting rumors that the gossip rags have been spreading about me having harbored murderous animosity towards Arthur all these years. It doesn't mean anything that it took me twenty-five minutes."

"It means that your fellow theater company members didn't find it unusual, which is why none of them went looking for you. Which suggests that they suspected you and Trewitt were engaged in an affair."

Still completely unfazed, she asked, "And if we were?"

"Then perhaps you were annoyed enough by the attention Trewitt paid Ms. Havoc to stab him in the heart."

Claire Acheson laughed at that, her eyes brimming with amusement. "Please, Mr. Katz, I would've hoped that you'd think more highly of me than that. Arthur's behavior around Vanessa was simply Arthur being Arthur. He was a rogue through and through, which is a quality I'd always found endearing in him. But let's say I did stab Arthur while in the midst of a jealous fit, you'd be out of luck. If any evidence existed that tied me to the murder, the knife, or that plastic poncho, the police would've found it by now. The best you'd be able to do if you continued with this line of inquiry would be to prove or disprove whether Arthur and I were romantically involved." Her eyes dulled a bit, and somewhat sourly she added, "I'd have to think your time would be better served investigating my theory involving Vanessa."

"Debatable," Julius said. For the next forty-five minutes he questioned her about kitchen knives, plastic ponchos, her romances with Trewitt—both when she was forty-two and recently—and along the way threw her plenty of curveballs in an attempt to rattle her. It looked to me like Acheson was right about Julius wasting his time with her. If he got anywhere, I couldn't tell. If she gave away anything with her mannerisms or her answers, I had no clue.

According to her she always got along wonderfully with Trewitt, she didn't blame him for the breakup of her third marriage, and the only reason she hadn't worked with him again until *The Goose Feather Bed* was to keep peace with her fourth husband. When her fourth marriage ended six months ago, she jumped at the opportunity to work with Trewitt again. She seemed sincere. She might've been, or it might've been an act. I had no idea which it was. At the end, Julius signaled me to call him on his cell phone.

When he answered the phone, he grunted out a nondescript greeting. Since it didn't much matter what I said, I asked him if he had picked up anything from her.

"Nothing yet," Julius muttered loudly enough for Acheson to hear. He paused for a long moment, then added, "I see. They should all be here at the theater for the next four hours. Thank you for the call, Detective." Julius hung up then.

For the next four point eight seconds Julius glared at nothing in particular, and then his gaze wandered over to Acheson and he reacted as if he had forgotten she was in the room with him.

"It appears as if I've been wasting my time," he said.

"How so?"

"That was Mike Griff, the detective in charge of the homicide investigation. The police have discovered where the knife was stolen from and they're now gathering surveillance video. Griff should have the video within a few hours, and he'll know then who murdered Trewitt." Julius stared blankly at his watch, and after a few moments of this a wistful sigh escaped from him. "Theodore Dreckle is paying me well for this so I might as well put on a good show. Anyway, I've still got some time, perhaps I'll uncover the murderer before Griff."

If I had blinked I might've missed the way her face tensed, but since I don't ever blink, I didn't miss a thing. So even though she was a seasoned, professional actress, and Julius was only an amateur, she bought his performance hook, line, and sinker. She wanted to ask Julius a question. That was obvious from the way she chewed on her bottom lip, but before she could do so, Julius informed her that they were done and she could go back to the rehearsal. She nodded, swallowing back whatever it was that she had thought of asking him. Without any additional hesitation, she pushed herself out of her chair, and by the time she had taken three steps toward the door, she had successfully gathered herself together so that she showed no signs that Julius's story had had any impact on her. At least I now understood why Julius had hired Tom and Saul. Since they had both already called me a half hour earlier to tell me they were in position, they'd know if Claire Acheson, or anyone else, tried leaving the theater.

I waited until Acheson left the room before commenting on his stratagem. "It certainly had an effect on her," I said. "If she's the killer, the odds are pretty good that she's going to try to sneak out of here and get on the first flight she can out of the country. If she's not, she's going to tell the rest of them about this. In any case, it's going to shake things up."

I'd heard Acheson's footsteps echoing down the wooden hallway, so there was no chance she was standing outside the door eavesdropping. I didn't bother alerting Julius that it was safe to talk since he must've heard her also. At that moment he was staring longingly at the open bottle of Chardonnay. So far he had restrained himself and had only one glass. He poured himself another.

"Possibly," Julius said. "Although, it might do no good at all. It depends on how the killer obtained that knife. But Archie, for now this is all I have."

He took a sip of wine, then picked up half of a grilled Portobello melt and ate it at a leisurely pace. Nine minutes later, he was still working on it when there was knock on the door, followed quickly by an excited Theodore Dreckle walking in. His cheeks were flushed as he grinned at Julius.

"Is it true what I heard?" he asked, breathlessly. "Are the police about to crack Arthur's murder?"

So Acheson had leaked the news instead of skedaddling. I realized that didn't necessarily mean she was innocent. As Julius had noted, it all depended on how the killer had gotten his, or her, hands on the knife, and after some further analysis, I was able to work out several scenarios where a guilty Claire Acheson would've still told the others this news.

"The police are following a line of inquiry that I suggested to them earlier today, and I'm hopeful that within a few hours we will know the identity of Trewitt's murderer," Julius said, which was technically true, even if it completely twisted around what Dreckle had asked. "For the present, I should continue on with my investigation. Could you send in Mr. Sturges next?"

"Of course." Dreckle's enthusiasm dimmed noticeably once he realized Julius refused to state that it was a certainty the murder would be solved. He seemed stuck, as if he was hoping for some additional reassurance, and as he finally accepted that it wasn't coming, he turned and left. Four minutes and twenty-three seconds later the office door opened again, and this time it was James Sturges. Julius had him take the same seat that Acheson used, and offered him food and wine, both of which Sturges declined.

Drops of perspiration dotted the play director's forehead, and a thin sheen of it could be seen above his upper lip. Even without the perspiration it was obvious that he was nervous given how tightly he was gripping the fingers on his right hand.

Julius nodded sympathetically. "It's understandable that you're too anxious to eat or drink," he noted.

"What? No, that's not it at all," Sturges uttered stiffly. He must've noticed then how he was gripping his fingers because he seemed to make a conscious effort then to rest his hands on the arms of his chair and to keep them there. "I've got too long a night ahead of me with rehearsals to be drinking anything; a night that has gotten considerably longer thanks to these interruptions. And I'm on a strict diet where I don't eat anything between meals, and certainly not anything with wheat or sugar."

"Hmm. I would've thought it was nerves, especially seeing how badly you're perspiring."

"It's been a long day, Mr. Katz. Actually, a long three weeks. I think I have every right to be perspiring. But you're right, I should have something to drink, and I think what I'll have is some of that water."

Sturges had been eyeing the bottles of San Pellegrino that shared an ice bucket with two bottles of Chardonnay. He pushed himself out of his chair and retrieved a bottle of water while also grabbing several napkins before plopping himself back down in the chair. He used a napkin to wipe his forehead and upper lip, and then poured the water into a glass and took an anemic sip. I caught the slight tremble in his hand while he did this, and I was sure Julius caught it also. Julius didn't say anything as he sat back and thoughtfully considered Sturges.

"It would make sense for you to be nervous," Julius remarked after Sturges placed his glass on the desk. "You must know who the Vegas oddsmakers have as the favorite to have killed Arthur Trewitt."

"I have no idea."

A hitch showed along the side of Sturges mouth when he said that, which was a *tell* every bit as obvious as if a neon sign had flashed over his head. As with the earlier hand tremble, I didn't insult Julius by mentioning it, although I did comment that it was good to see that Sturges was an open book. Julius rubbed the side of his nose as a signal that he agreed with me.

"You're the favorite, Mr. Sturges, with the consensus among bookmakers putting the odds of you murdering Arthur Trewitt at seven to four."

The hitch showed again as Sturges stated that he found such a notion ridiculous.

"Not at all. After all, you've been quoted in the past as saying that you'd like to cut out Trewitt's heart."

Sturges had to have been prepared for Julius bringing that up, especially given how frequently that quote has appeared in the news over the past three weeks. Still, his voice shook as he said, "That was fourteen years ago, and it's taken out of context. At the time I joked about how I would've liked to have cut out Arthur's heart if he'd had one."

"Still, you're the only one among the suspects to have made a public statement about wanting to take a knife to Trewitt, and now the man's dead, stabbed through the heart."

Sturges gave Julius a look of utter exasperation. "Back then I was furious with Arthur. *The Happy Cuckold* was my first major Broadway play, and I felt that he went out of his way to sabotage it." His lips clamped shut for eight point three seconds, during which time his color dropped to a sickly white. When he opened his mouth again the skin along the line of his jaw had slackened. "It was a miserable experience," he said. "For several years after Arthur's thorough massacre of *Cuckold* I was so furious with him that I might very well have stabbed him in the heart if I'd had the opportunity. But over time I realized that I wasn't blameless. I had acted with an extreme arrogance, especially considering Arthur's stature, and four years ago I sought Arthur out to make amends. Since then we've had a better than cordial relationship."

"Interesting. The kindest remark he has made to the press about you, excepting, of course, since he was hired for *The Goose Feather Bed*, was that you'd have trouble directing a pie eating contest. I believe he made that comment about you two and a half years ago."

Sturges waved that away. "That was only Arthur cultivating his brash public persona."

"You're saying that his continued insults of you didn't bother you?"

"Not in the least. It was only an act, and if anything, I found it amusing. Again, Arthur and I were talking fairly regularly by this point, at least once a month. He told me he'd keep our public feud going so that if we could find the right project to work on together, it would cause an uproar within the theater community. And then we found *The Goose Feather Bed*, and to make things even more delicious, Claire wanted to do it, which more than doubled the buzz. Me reuniting with Arthur. Arthur reuniting with Claire. It all would've been magnificent."

No hitch as Sturges explained this. If anything, a sad wistfulness showed in his eyes. Julius sat for a moment studying him, then said, "If what you're telling me is true, I can put you in touch with my bookie and you can make some nice change betting that you're innocent."

Sturges smiled bleakly, "Maybe I'll do that."

"If not you, which of the other suspects murdered Trewitt?"

That hitch flashed again. "I don't know."

"Which of them do you suspect then?"

More of his bleak smile. "I'd rather not say. Not without evidence."

Julius began drumming the fingers on his right hand against the surface of the desk. When he wanted to he could be inscrutable with suspects, but in this case he didn't want to be, and was quite willing to demonstrate his impatience with the theater director.

"This isn't a game," Julius admonished. "A man was murdered. If you have suspicions, I advise you to share them with me."

"I'm well aware of how serious a matter this is. The police regard me as a suspect after all."

"Not just the police."

Sturges eyes opened wide then, as if he was surprised that he still hadn't convinced Julius of his innocence. "Very well," he said. "So you regard me as a suspect also. As I said, I fully appreciate how serious this is, but you need to appreciate how small the theater community can be and how damaging for me it would be to throw around aspersions based solely on a gut feeling." He pushed a hand over his bald scalp. "If

I was one of the actors I could spread whatever scurrilous rumors I wanted without repercussions, but as a director I can't do that. I need the trust of actors or I'm finished."

Julius's facial muscles hardened, which meant he was putting his full brain power on the matter at hand. This lasted nearly three seconds. When his facial muscles relaxed, he nodded, as if to himself, and said, "You suspect Roger Limburgh."

Sturges was flabbergasted. "How'd you figure *that* out?" he sputtered.

Julius shrugged. "A hunch. Was Limburgh Arthur Trewitt's understudy?"

"No. We have lists of actors to call in case of any unforeseen illnesses or accidents, but we weren't carrying any understudies."

"How did Limburgh get promoted into one of the starring roles?"

"The day following Arthur's death, Roger asked if he could audition for the role of Lawrence Cansworth. Normally I would've wanted a bigger name for the part, but it was such a chaotic time that I told Roger to go ahead. His audition took my breath away. It was evident that he had a deep understanding of the role. He was also exceptionally good, taking the Cansworth part into territory that I hadn't considered. While Arthur played Cansworth charismatically and loud, Roger was quiet and more nuanced. I wouldn't say he was better than Arthur, just different."

Another hitch showed when Sturges tried to say that Limburgh wasn't better than Trewitt.

"Did it surprise you that he was so well prepared to take over for Trewitt?"

"Yes. Most definitely. Roger must've spent hundreds of hours of studying that part to show the kind of perfection he did." Sturges made a pained face that was part grimace and partly as if he got caught in the middle of a sneeze. Or maybe he simply had gas. I couldn't tell. In any case, he didn't sneeze. "Don't get me wrong, Roger is a fine actor, and has always proven reliable for the smaller roles he's been hired for. The part of Cansworth is at a completely different level, and could be a huge break, the type of break he's probably been waiting his whole career for… maybe one he was willing to kill for. Assuming the play continues past opening night, it will open more starring roles for him. But that's also assuming, of course, he doesn't end up serving a life term in prison."

Julius leaned back in his chair. His gaze shifted longingly to his half empty wine glass before hardening and moving back to Sturges. As he had done earlier with Acheson, he switched tactics and spent the next forty minutes grilling Sturges about kitchen knives, plastic ponchos, the restaurants he had dined at since visiting Boston, what he did during the break he took between twelve forty-five and one o'clock the day of the murder, as well as throw him a number of curveballs regarding his true feelings about Trewitt. Also as with Acheson, he didn't seem to get anywhere with it. Sturges claimed he took a well-deserved meditation break during those fifteen minutes, and Julius couldn't budge him from that. The director remained insistent that he and Trewitt had patched up any hard feelings

310

they might've once had. After Julius gave up and Sturges left the office, I asked him about his hunch that Sturges had suspected Limburgh.

"I had no hunch, Archie. That man would've tried selling me a story regardless of whom I had picked. His *tell* was a fake, as well as most of the mannerisms he put on display. His performance was perhaps even better than the one Acheson gave. I would guess that he has a background in acting." Julius's expression turned sour. "I warned you what we were up against."

It didn't take me long to verify that Julius was right. I did this by first searching through Sturges's credit card charges over the past ten years, then identifying plays in areas he had traveled to when he wasn't engaged as a director. After I found online playbills for these, I discovered that he'd been using the stage name Dennis Burkham. None of these plays were on Broadway, or in Chicago or Los Angeles, or even any secondary theater cities, but in more backwater areas for theater. But still, he was engaged as an actor for at least three months out of every year. I told Julius about this, who only grunted in response.

"Claire Acheson is able to shed tears at will," I said. "How about Sturges? Can he sweat at will?"

"Doubtful," Julius said, his expression still sour. "His perspiration was very real. He's worried that the police will latch onto him as Trewitt's murderer, which is why he threw me Limburgh. I have to give him credit for the way he managed that. It was a clever trick prompting me to guess a name, which would've been someone I'd been subconsciously suspecting, and then jumping in with both feet."

"It seemed to me that you volunteered the name."

"Only because he was leading me to do so. I saw no reason to delay the inevitable."

"Okay. I won't argue the point. Did he kill Trewitt?"

A deep frown creased Julius's face, and he started again with his impatient finger drumming. "I don't know," he said. "Have any of them tried calling the airlines or travel agents?"

"Not yet. None of them have made any calls nor visited any travel websites since you planted that bogus story with Acheson, at least not that I've been able to tell, and I've been monitoring their cellphone activity every two minutes. If any of them have a burner cellphone then we're out of luck."

Julius's phone rang. It was Detective Mike Griff. I told Julius this, and he indicated that he'd take the call.

"We know where the knife came from," Griff told him, his tone surprisingly subdued given that information. "I've been calling top end restaurants, like you suggested, and found a joint named Bondomir that three weeks ago lost the same model used on our *vic*. The head chef isn't exactly clear what day the knife went missing, but we spent some time narrowing it down, and it looks like it disappeared the day before Trewitt got stabbed. The head chef never made the connection that the missing knife could've been used for Trewitt's murder; he simply thought one of his staff clipped it. It happens. None of the suspects have eaten there—at least no one remembers them doing so, and no credit card receipts from any of them. I've got uniforms looking for surveillance cameras in the area, and I'll be leaning heavily on the kitchen staff to see if any of them sold the knife or know anything."

Julius suggested that Griff call me with a complete list of Bondomir's kitchen staff, as well as anyone else who might've had access to the kitchen. According to Julius, I was very adroit at uncovering information over the Internet. Griff at first seemed uneasy about doing this as it probably went against departmental regulations, but after some hemming and hawing he told Julius he'd get in touch with me. Sure enough, after Julius got off the phone with him, the homicide detective called the office line. This development must've left Julius feeling more upbeat, because while I got the list of names from Griff, he indulged himself by picking out one of the pastries and finishing the half glass of wine that he had waiting.

"That was quite prophetic of you," I told Julius after I got off the phone.

"It gives us some hope, Archie, since I don't think I'll have much chance of tricking the truth out of that bunch."

"I hate to tell you this, but the city doesn't have any surveillance cameras in the area. Maybe one of the businesses in the area does, but it's a longshot that our murderer was captured on video. My initial calculations have the odds at less than seven percent."

"The odds are probably far lower than that. If the murderer had broken into Bondomir, he or she would be on the run already." He hesitated briefly, then asked me to call Dreckle and make sure all of the suspects were still in the theater.

Dreckle seemed surprised to get my call. "Are you here with Julius?" he asked.

"Nope. I'm holding down the fort at Julius's townhouse, but still doing his bidding. So how about a headcount?"

Dreckle told me to hold on. Wherever he was, he must've raced to the stage because he sounded winded when thirty-four seconds later he told me everyone was accounted for.

"None of them making excuses about needing to leave early?"

He had a hushed conversation with Sturges, and then told me what I heard Sturges tell him—which was that all of them were behaving themselves. I asked Dreckle to keep an eye on them and to let me know if any of them tried sneaking out or were acting excessively nervous. After I got off the phone with him, I told Julius that they were all still there and playing nice.

Julius nodded, fully expecting that answer. "The killer didn't steal the knife from Bondomir himself. He must've arranged for someone else to get the knife for him. We probably have at best a slim chance of finding who actually stole the knife, but maybe I can make our killer worry anyway. Archie, please call Dreckle and ask him to send in Stephen Moore next."

I did as Julius asked and five minutes and four seconds later there was a knock on the door, followed by Moore entering the office and taking the seat across from Julius. By this time Julius had uncorked another bottle of Chardonnay, and when he offered Moore refreshments, the actor accepted a glass of wine and picked out half a roast beef and boursin sandwich. I was surprised at how much restraint Julius was showing by not refilling his own glass since I knew how much he'd rather be back at his office or at the Belvedere club sampling cognacs than trying to sort through this mess.

Moore sat back and looked every bit as relaxed as if he were instead on the deck of a yacht. He took a bite of his sandwich and nodded approvingly. "This is very good," he noted. He raised an eyebrow. "I heard that the police know where the murder weapon came from, and that Arthur's killer will be discovered soon?"

Like all the others, Moore had had his opportunity to bump off Trewitt. In his case it would've been during a twenty minute window starting at two-fifteen when he had left the rehearsal to study a scene in the privacy of his dressing room.

"That was only a ruse on my part," Julius confessed. "I was seeing if I could worry the murderer enough to reveal himself, but it seems as if I failed miserably. Mr. Moore, have you eaten at Bondomir?"

If the restaurant meant anything to the actor, he didn't show it. "No, I haven't," he said, a slight frown twisting down his lips and his eyebrows bunching to show his disappointment. "That's a shame that an arrest isn't imminent. I was hoping that this unfortunate business would be cleared up soon so that the rest of us could focus on the play."

"Mr. Moore, may I ask a favor?"

"Certainly."

"Could you ask Mr. Sturges and the other cast members whether they've eaten at Bondomir?"

"If you feel it would help, certainly." Moore's eyebrows bunched more and his brow creased as he considered what

Julius had asked. "Is this place Bondomir mixed up with Arthur's murder?"

"In a way."

He looked like he wanted to ask Julius for more specifics, but in the end he simply told Julius that he'd do as Julius asked and would report back. Julius's eyes narrowed as he stared fixedly at Moore. This continued for twenty seconds, and if it bothered the actor at all he didn't show it as he took another bite of his sandwich and a sip of his wine. Finally, Julius spoke.

"I have possible motives for all the other suspects, but none for you. Why is that?"

A slight smile pushed up Moore's lips. "I don't know what to tell you," he said.

"Can you suggest, even if it's farfetched, a reason why you might've wanted Trewitt dead?"

"I'm sorry, but I can't think of any."

Julius grunted at that. "Do you think Sturges or any of your fellow actors might be able to come up with a reason?"

If anything, Moore seemed amused by the question. "If they do, I'd be fascinated to hear what they have to say."

"Did you and Trewitt ever socialize out of work?"

"A few times. Dinner. Drinks. He was quite a character, and had his share of fascinating theater stories. I liked Arthur, and enjoyed my time with him."

"What were some of these *fascinating* stories?"

Moore gave the matter a moment's thought and then related one of the stories to Julius. Near the end I could see a light bulb go on as he must've remembered another story, which he also related to Julius. The first one involved a fistfight backstage between two actors, which ended with the two of them crashing through the scenery and tumbling onto the stage, interrupting the performance. The second story involved antics at a wrap-up party. Neither of these stories would've given anyone a reason to want to kill Trewitt.

"There were many others," Moore said. "But we were drinking quite heavily during those dinners, and that's all I can remember right now."

Julius sat quietly for another sixty seconds. If he thought he could make Moore squirm by doing his, he was wrong. Moore finished off his sandwich, then picked out a pastry. After he finished off the pastry, he asked Julius if they were done. Julius shook his head.

"Who do you think killed Trewitt?"

"I don't know." Moore breathed in deeply and slowly blew out a lungful of air. "I've spent hours thinking about it, and I really have no idea."

"If you had to guess?"

"The only thing that makes sense to me is that someone else snuck into the theater, killed Arthur, and snuck out."

"The police don't believe that's possible."

Moore shrugged. "You asked my opinion, and that's it. Because nothing else makes any sense to me."

"Was there any animosity between Trewitt and anyone else?"

Moore hesitated before saying, "Not really."

"Vanessa Havoc didn't much care for him?"

There was another hesitation before Moore explained that Havoc didn't get Trewitt. "Vanessa's not a theater person. This is all new to her. She didn't appreciate Arthur's broad and off-color sense of humor or his at times overly theatrical persona. But I refuse to believe that she hated him. At most she disliked him."

"I understand she didn't appreciate his knack of finding the most inopportune times to walk in on her in her dressing room."

"You heard about that, huh? That still wouldn't be any reason for Vanessa to kill Arthur."

"How anxious was she about performing onstage?"

Moore smiled at that. "She's been somewhat anxious, and I'm sure this murder business hasn't helped, but she's also absolutely superb in the role. Vanessa will be fine. If you think Vanessa might've killed Arthur because of stage fright, you're way off base."

"Not even a slim chance of it?"

"No."

"And Ms. Havoc's theory that Trewitt stabbed himself?"

"Absolute rubbish."

"Were Trewitt and Claire Acheson having an affair?"

"I couldn't say, but if they were it wouldn't surprise me."

"How do you think Ms. Acheson reacted to Trewitt's interest in Ms. Havoc?"

Moore laughed at that. It wasn't an unpleasant or nasty laugh. He was simply amused by what Julius had asked.

"Claire didn't murder Arthur in a fit of jealously, if that's what you're implying. First of all she knew Arthur didn't even have a snowball's chance with Vanessa, second, she understood that Arthur was only playing the part that was expected of him—that of a lascivious rogue. If anything, watching him at work would've amused her."

Julius tried next the angle that Roger Limburgh killed Trewitt in order to get the role of a lifetime, and Moore shot that down. He also next rejected the idea as laughable that Sturges might've murdered Trewitt out of pure hatred from their years of feuding.

"As far as you're concerned none of the suspects have a motive for killing Trewitt," Julius said.

"No, that's not what I've been saying. Only that if any of us had a reason for wanting Arthur dead, I have no idea what it is. Which is why I think the police are wrong. Someone else must've killed Arthur." Moore glanced at his watch. "Anything else you'd like to ask me?"

Julius shook his head.

"I'll make sure to ask everyone else about Bondomir. If you give me your number, I'll give you a call and let you know what they say."

"That won't be necessary. I'll find you later."

Moore nodded, and pushed himself out of his chair. Once he left the office, I gave Julius the bad news that I hadn't gotten anywhere with Bondomir's kitchen staff. "I hate to have to tell you this, but I've checked all the phone, bank, and credit card records I've been able to find, and if any of them sold an eight hundred dollar chef's knife or have a connection with any of the suspects, I don't know which of them it is."

Julius grimaced over the prospect of himself having to question all fourteen employees who worked at Bondomir. "Let us hope that my telling Moore about Bondomir causes the killer to reveal his hand, or if not that, that Detective Griff uncovers something," he said without much enthusiasm.

"Yeah. I guess we can hope. I have to agree with Moore, though. All the motives you have so far seem awfully flimsy for a murder."

Julius's expression turned outright dour at that moment. "Normally I'd agree, Archie, but as I warned you earlier, actors are a different breed entirely. Still, the reason for a premeditated murder is usually either hate or money, or a combination of the two. In this case, perhaps it will be ambition."

"Possibly. But what if Moore's right and Detective Griff is wrong? What if the killer is someone other than those five?"

"The police have had three weeks to find links between Trewitt and other suspects, and if they've been unable to do so, it's doubtful that I'll be able to given the paucity of evidence, at least not unless *something new* is uncovered. Given that, I might as well continue down this path and stir the pot as much as I can, and see if anything develops."

The *something new* that could possibly be uncovered would be if I found something, which I didn't think was likely. When I briefed Julius earlier, I told him that I'd found nothing suspicious from Trewitt's phone, email, and banking records. Maybe if I kept searching I'd locate another email account or something else of use, but I didn't hold much hope for it. Nor did I think stirring the pot was going to do any good. It was looking more and more like either the knife would lead us to the killer, or nothing would, and I was beginning to feel as discouraged as Julius looked—which in my case was a noticeable sluggishness in my processing cycles.

"Who next?" I asked. "Limburgh or Havoc?"

Julius made a face as if he thought neither would be of much use, and rather halfheartedly decided on Roger Limburgh. I gave Dreckle a call, and asked if he'd seen any suspicious behavior. He claimed he hadn't. He told me if anything, he thought the rehearsal was more focused today than usual. I, in turn, commented how that was a shame, and asked if he could send Limburgh next to see Julius.

While all the other suspects had had only a single opportunity to murder Trewitt that day, Limburgh had had several. According to the police, he took four breaks between twelve-thirty and two-thirty to relieve his bladder, and they only had guesses on when those breaks occurred and how long they lasted. It made me wonder if he took all those breaks not because of a weak bladder, but because he was trying to work up the nerve to kill Trewitt.

Limburgh appeared overly stiff and formal on entering Julius's makeshift office, and even more so once he sat in the chair opposite Julius. The way he held himself, it was almost as if someone had stuck a wooden plank down the back of his shirt. He turned down Julius's offer of refreshments, and genuinely looked morose.

"Did you stab Arthur Trewitt to death?"

If the frankness of Julius's question surprised Limburgh, he didn't show it. He simply shook his head, and muttered, "Of course not."

"Why of course not? One of you murdered him, so why not you?"

Limburgh stared at Julius as if he was crazy. "Why would I have wanted to kill Arthur?"

"You didn't like him much."

"I never said anything of the kind. I had a great deal of respect for him. I admired his work immensely."

He was lying about that. It was obvious from the way a film fell over his eyes. But it was doubtful whether he cared that Julius saw through him. Julius didn't push him on the point, and instead asked about why he had spent so many hours preparing for the part of Lawrence Cansworth while Trewitt was still alive.

"You have no idea how many hours I spent," Limburgh remarked testily.

"True," Julius agreed. "James Sturges however believes you must've spent many hours, but perhaps you're a savant. How many hours did you spend?"

Limburgh's eyes focused on some distant point as he tallied up the number. "Over a hundred," he said.

Julius didn't bother to hide his exasperation as he stared at the actor. "Do you think this is a joke?" he asked.

"Certainly not. But if you're conducting a murder investigation, you should be precise, and you had no way of knowing whether I spent one hour or a hundred studying for that role. But to answer your question, I've been doing that for close to three decades. Not studying the role of Lawrence Cansworth, obviously, but picking one of the more interesting ones in the plays I'm in and studying it assiduously. It keeps me from getting excessively bored given the more modest parts I'm offered." He paused for a moment and shook his head. When he met Julius's eyes again, a gleam showed in his own. "Look, Katz, this isn't going to do you any good. I didn't kill Arthur, but if I did for a reason as insipid as wanting to steal his part, you'd never discover it. Besides, it wouldn't make any sense for me to have killed Arthur if that was my reason. I've been around the theater long enough to know that Arthur being murdered by an unknown cast member would doom the play, at least if his murderer wasn't caught."

"It's not a certainty that you would've realized that," Julius said. "Or you could have another reason for wanting to kill Trewitt."

"If I did I wouldn't tell you what it was. And do you really think you'd be able to trick me into doing so?"

"Possibly."

"No, there wouldn't be a chance of it. Not unless I was a witless fool. Look, Katz, whether you believe I'm lying now, I can't help it. But I badly want to see Arthur's murderer caught. Not for any noble reasons, but only because I want to be on stage as Lawrence Cansworth for months to come. It would be torturous to finally have a role like this that I can sink my teeth into only to have it taken away from me after one performance. So you must see how it stands. If I'm guilty you're wasting your time with me, same as if I'm innocent."

"And you don't want me wasting my time."

"No, I don't. I already explained my reason. I don't need to do it a second time."

"Let's assume you're innocent," Julius said, "you might still be able to give me something useful. For example, it would help to know the exact times you left the stage area."

"What you really want to know is whether it was me or Vanessa who left first. Because if Vanessa was the first one, it makes it less likely that she's the killer."

"That's part of it. Having an accurate time table of the events of that afternoon will help in any case."

The bottom half of Limburgh's narrow face folded downward into a mass of creases as he frowned. "I'm sorry, but you're flat out of luck, then," he said, sounding genuinely as if he was sorry. "I've worked this out with the police as best I can. You should believe me because I could've told them anything, and nobody would've been any the wiser. The other actors are on stage throughout the entire performance, while my original meager role had me onstage for less than fifteen minutes. So during most of the rehearsal I was standing off in the wings, and none of the others paid me any attention."

Julius sat for a ten-count staring at Limburgh, who returned his stare without blinking. "Who do you think murdered Trewitt?" Julius asked finally.

"I have no idea. If I did I'd tell you."

"So I'm wasting my time asking you anything further?"

"Isn't that what I've been telling you?"

Julius breathed in a lung full of air, and looked as if he was about to dismiss Roger Limburgh, but instead asked if he had ever eaten at Bondomir. Limburgh frowned at the question.

"I'd never heard of the place until Moore came back from being cross-examined by you, and asked us that same question. What's the importance of this place? Is this where Arthur's murderer got the knife?"

"Yes. Did any of the others react unusually when Moore asked them this?"

Limburgh shook his head, his frown deepening. "I don't think so. I don't recall seeing any reaction other than curiosity. Are we done yet?"

Julius nodded, and after Limburgh left the room, he closed his eyes for the next three minutes. Someone who didn't know Julius better might've thought he was deep in thought. He wasn't. When he's putting his full brain power on a problem, his eyes stay open and his facial muscles harden so that he looks almost like a marble sculpture. What Julius was doing right then was moping. I let him mope in peace for the full three minutes before asking him whether Limburgh had leveled with him.

Julius reluctantly opened his eyes. "He could've been lying or telling me the truth. I have no idea."

"Yeah. I couldn't read him either. Should I have Havoc come here?"

"Let's give it ten minutes," Julius said.

I didn't bother asking him why the wait. It was to give Limburgh a chance to confirm with the rest of the suspects what they must be suspecting—that Bondomir was the source of the murder weapon. If that bit of news got the killer to react, I saw no evidence of it, at least not from monitoring their cell phones, which showed no activity.

325

—

When Vanessa Havoc entered the office, she looked every bit as striking as earlier, but also softer, her blonde hair more golden, as if it were fine silk. She accepted a glass of Chardonnay and turned down the offer of food. When she sat back, she crossed her legs, and even though she was wearing jeans, I could tell from the outline that her legs made against the fabric that she had beautiful legs. I had studied enough photos of models and actresses who were supposed to have beautiful legs to easily tell that.

She smiled thinly at Julius and commented how he had kept her waiting until the very end.

"By design and not by accident," Julius said. "I wanted to hear what the others had to say before talking with you. First, I'd like to hear more about your theory that Arthur Trewitt committed suicide."

Her smile weakened. "I was only being a smart aleck. Nothing more."

"Still, though, there must've been something about Trewitt's behavior during his last few days that you found odd, at least at a subconscious level. Otherwise I doubt you would've made a comment about him suffering from senility, even if you thought it was only a smart-aleck one."

Her smile faded completely. "I guess there was one thing that put me off," she said. "A couple of days before Arthur was killed, he came up with these nicknames for us that didn't make any sense. For example, he started calling me Roxie. He only did it a few times, but why?"

"The play Chicago. Roxie Hart."

"I figured that much out. But I hadn't done any plays before, and I wasn't in the movie. So why did he call me that? I also heard him call Claire *Diamond Lil.* I only heard him do it once, but still, I found it odd."

"Any other nicknames?"

She thought about it, her face scrunching up as she concentrated. "He had a strange one for Stephen. *Dilly.* That's it. I had no idea what it was supposed to mean. He also had one for James. I think it began with the letter *M.*"

While she was trying to recall what Trewitt's nickname for Sturges had been, Julius wrote out a note, asking me what jewelry stores had been robbed in Chicago. I had already started searching for that, because like Julius, I had a good idea what the nickname *Dilly* meant. I gave Julius the names of three jewelry stores, one of which began with an 'm'. This one was robbed by four masked men, and an estimated three point three million dollars' worth of diamonds were stolen.

"Metzkers?" Julius asked.

Havoc's eyes opened wide in astonishment. "Almost. It was *Metzkies.* But how in the world were you able to guess that?"

He shrugged. "It's not important." Quickly after that Julius changed tack and began grilling Havoc in an intense manner, making it sound as if he was convinced that she was the one who stabbed Trewitt to death. Of course, he knew she wasn't. I was sure that he knew who Trewitt's killer was well before I told him how Trewitt and the killer were both in Chicago nine months ago when Metzkers was robbed. But he kept up the interrogation for a full forty minutes, and I knew the reason was to leave her too shaken up for her to attach any importance on her telling Julius about those nicknames, or even remember that she had done so. He couldn't afford to have her repeat that to the actual murderer. I had to give her credit. She held up better than most people would, and only a few times did I see any cracks in her exterior as Julius all but accused her of being a murderer.

At the end of those forty minutes when Julius told her that he was done with her, she gave him a look of disdain that bordered on hate. "When I first came in here I thought I could actually like you," she said coldly. "Well, I don't. Not at all."

Julius shrugged. "I would apologize, except it should be a given that I'm here to expose a murderer, and not to be liked by you or any of the other suspects."

There was a distinct chill in the air—enough so that even I could feel it. Without another word, Vanessa Havoc got up and left the room. She made sure to slam the door hard behind her.

"I'm surprised she was able to walk out of here as steadily as she did. You really put her through the wringer."

Julius shrugged. "It couldn't be helped, Archie. I'm sure you understand the reason why. It might be hours before I'm prepared to confront Trewitt's killer, and I can't afford to have her inadvertently warn him." He made a face as he glanced over at the remaining bottles of wine. It had been a long afternoon so far, and I knew he wanted to pour himself another glass, but I guess he decided to hold off until this business was done because he forced himself to look away. "I need you to find other major unsolved robberies that could've been committed by four men that occurred while Trewitt's killer was performing in the area. It should be sufficient to go back only five years."

"I've already started that, and I've so far got three likely robberies. I'm sure I'm going to find more."

Julius nodded. "I'm sure you will," he said.

———

It took an hour and forty-seven minutes before Julius was ready to confront Arthur Trewitt's killer. This was partly so that we could narrow down the list of robberies I came up with to a smaller, more manageable list of only the crimes our killer had a ninety-five percent or better chance of having been involved in, and partly because Julius wanted to wait until there was a break in the rehearsals so that the killer would be alone in his dressing room. There were a few other details Julius needed to deal with, but these took less than an hour.

When Julius knocked on the killer's dressing room door, a voice rang out right away inviting whoever was out there to come in. The dressing room was arranged similarly to Trewitt's, and Stephen Moore was sitting on the sofa, a biography about the eighteenth century British actor David Garrick held open in his right hand. Once he realized that it was Julius who had knocked, he used a leather bookmark to mark his page, then placed the book on the sofa next to him. A curious half-smile showed on Moore's lips as he asked Julius if he'd like to take a seat.

Julius shook his head and told the actor that he'd stand. "This will be brief," he said. "I know that you murdered Arthur Trewitt. I also know that I'll never be able to prove it."

If Julius's statement had any effect on Moore, I couldn't see it. The actor arched his right eyebrow, but otherwise continued to smile in a curious and pleasant manner.

"I'm afraid you have me at a disadvantage—" Moore started.

Julius raised a hand to stop him. 'Please don't bother trying to convince me of anything," he said. "It won't help you, and if anything it will only make me lose my respect for you. You don't need to worry that I'm here to trick you into a confession. I know full well that you are not susceptible to that. I'd like to ask that you listen to a proposal. When I'm done you can gesture to accept or reject it. There will be consequences for either choice, but I guarantee you that a gesture will not be able to be used in court to imply any guilt. I am neither wired nor have I had your dressing room bugged. If it will make you feel more at ease, you can use this to verify that. But again, I am not expecting you to utter a sound, so there should be no reason for you to worry about being recorded."

Julius took from the pocket of his suit jacket a top-of-the-line bug detector that he had Tom Durkin bring to the theater. He handed this to Moore, who gave it a cursory glance before handing it back.

"I won't be needing that," Moore said.

Julius nodded and dropped the bug detector back in his jacket pocket. "As I mentioned earlier, I know that there's no evidence tying you to Arthur Trewitt's murder, and I accept that you will get away with that crime. But I nonetheless know that you did it, and I know why. Trewitt somehow discovered that you and three accomplices robbed Metzkers Jewelers of three million dollars' worth of diamonds. The robbery took place nine months ago in Chicago while you were performing in *Hamlet*, and Trewitt, also in Chicago, was performing in *Private Lives*. I'm assuming he tried to blackmail you. It's impossible for me to assert that as a fact but it's a fair assumption given the nicknames he used for all of you as a way to pressure you, with yours being Dilly, short for Dillinger. Perhaps he also knew of the other robberies you and your gang committed. An armored car heist in Milwaukee when you were performing in a revival of *A Streetcar Named Desire*. Or a four point five million dollar coin collection from an auction house in Kansas City when you were there for *An Ideal Husband*. Or a two-million dollar heist from a courier in Des Moines while you were in the city for *Lost in Yonkers*. Perhaps he only knew about the Chicago diamond heist. Whatever the case, he tried to blackmail you and you killed him."

Moore didn't seem overly concerned with what Julius was saying. His lips pursed and a glimmer showed in his eyes, but if anything he seemed amused by Julius's accusations. It was obvious that he decided to take Julius's advice and not speak. Julius's own expression grew grim.

"Perhaps you commit these robberies so that you can live the lifestyle you want while staying true to your craft. Or perhaps your work in the theater is only a cover for these and other robberies. Or maybe you commit these crimes solely for the thrill of it. Whatever your reasons, I don't care. It's not important. Neither is it important to me whether you and your gang were planning a heist of some sort here in Boston, which is most likely the case since I'm guessing that one of your accomplices stole the murder weapon for you. That would explain why you were so blasé on learning that the police discovered where the knife was taken from. But again, none of that's important. What is important is that in less than two hours I was able to determine with a high degree of probability that you were involved in these four robberies. I was also able to identify eight others over the past five years that I am fairly certain you were also involved in. And I know the name of one of your accomplices. Tom Burgoff. I can't prove any of this yet. But I'm confident that if I were to dedicate a month or two to this, I'd be able to see you convicted of at least three of these crimes. Perhaps all of them. Perhaps I'd even get back enough of a reward from the insurance companies to cover my expenses."

I was the one who discovered that Tom Burgoff was a likely member of Moore's robbery gang. I figured this out after cross-referencing a mountain of data involving credit card transactions in the cities where the robberies occurred, and I took some satisfaction in seeing the way Moore's eyes hardened and his smile tightened when Julius mentioned Burgoff's name. The change was sudden, and left him looking menacing enough to where I felt a jangling in my processing cycles. While he kept smiling in an almost identical manner as before, it seemed obvious that Moore was now contemplating killing Julius. Julius had to have picked up on that also, not that it much mattered. While it wasn't publicized, Julius held a fifth degree black belt in Hung Gar Kung Fu, and I had little doubt that he'd be able to handle Moore if necessary.

"I should explain why I accepted this case," Julius said. "It will help you understand why I'll be making my proposal. One of my closest friends, Phil Weinstein, invested two hundred and fifty thousand dollars in this play. If he loses this money, it will ruin him. Phil is more than one of my closest friends. We've known each other since we were kids. When I was fifteen I got involved with some people I shouldn't have. Without going into too much detail, if it wasn't for Phil, my life would've gone very differently than it has. He made sure I knew he'd keep coming at me with his fists unless I quit the gang I had joined. If that happened, higher-ups within the gang would've killed Phil, so I had no choice, I had to quit. As you can see, I owe Phil too much to let him lose his money because of you. I should also tell you that while I tend to dislike murderers and take a great deal of satisfaction in sending them to prison, I find blackmailers detestable. I look at them as I would any other parasite, and wouldn't lose any sleep knowing that you got away with murdering one. Because of that and the fact you and your gang haven't hurt any bystanders in the robberies that you've committed, I feel comfortable in making you the following proposal. If you reimburse my friend Phil Weinstein the two hundred and fifty thousand that he invested, I will walk away from this. Otherwise, I will be investigating those robberies until I find enough evidence to send you and your accomplices to prison. This is not a bluff. It won't matter to me how long it takes or what the cost, I will see you convicted of several major felonies."

The smile had dropped from Moore's face, and his eyes shone with violence. His voice, though, sounded remarkably light as he said, "That's an interesting proposal given how much you claim to detest blackmailers."

"This is not blackmail," Julius said with a heavy sigh. "I will not be benefiting from this in any way. The money that you would pay Phil is nothing more than fair compensation for what your action would be costing him. I'm assuming that you were able to fence the diamonds from the Metzker robbery for at least one point six million dollars, leaving your share at four hundred thousand dollars, which should be more than enough to repay my friend."

"Hypothetically speaking, most robbery figures reported in the news are inflated. Plus there are costs associated with them that most people aren't aware of. So robberies like that diamond heist tend to net half of what someone like you might expect," Moore said. "In this case, I would guess it would be more like sixty percent less. Hypothetically speaking."

"Then you would need to add in some of what you made from your other crimes. It's not my concern. With a simple nod of your head you can accept my proposal, otherwise I'll assume it's been rejected."

The movement was slight, but Moore nodded.

"Good." Julius removed from an inside jacket pocket a sheet of paper that had been folded so it could've fit inside a standard envelope. "That has wiring information for moving funds into Phil's bank account. As long as the money shows up by five tomorrow evening, our business together will be done."

Moore took the sheet of paper from Julius, folded it several times, and pushed it into his pants pocket. "Fine," he said, his eyes dulling to the color of pewter.

Julius nodded. "I will leave you, then." He turned to leave the room, paused, then added, "I am curious. How did Trewitt figure out that you robbed Metzkers? It's hard for me to believe that you'd let something like that slip when the two of you were out drinking together, but that's all I can imagine."

Moore shook his head. "I didn't let anything slip. I don't know how he figured it out."

The door to the room opened and Detective Griff and four uniformed officers came in, which was what Julius and I were expecting since I had kept an open line with Griff and he heard everything that was said. Moore might not have confessed to murdering Arthur Trewitt, but he still admitted that Trewitt knew about him robbing Metzker's, which was strong enough circumstantial evidence for an arrest.

Moore actually looked surprised when Griff and the other cops entered the room, but it didn't last long. One point eight seconds later the surprise faded from his expression and his eyes deadened. He refused to as much as glance in Julius's direction while he was cuffed and taken from the room.

After the police left with Moore, Theodore Dreckle stepped into the room to meet with Julius. The theater producer looked stunned. His eyes were wide open and his skin color had dropped several shades. He had been in the hallway earlier with the cops when they were listening in on Julius's conversation with Moore, so he knew everything that had transpired.

"I'm stunned," he told Julius. "I know you told me Stephen was the one, but I guess I didn't believe it. I'm still having a hard time believing it."

His hands trembled slightly as he wrote out a check for fifty thousand dollars, which he handed to Julius. Julius gave it a perfunctory look and placed it in his wallet.

"Have you hired a replacement yet?

Dreckle nodded. "Allen Quinn. He'll be in Boston tomorrow morning, and he should be able to fit right in. If you'll excuse me, I need to make some phone calls."

Of course, he'd be calling the newspapers, local TV stations, and national news agencies. He'd want to make sure word of Moore's arrest got out as quickly as possible, as well as letting everyone know the show would go on without Moore.

I didn't say anything to Julius during the cab ride back to his townhouse as I was still processing the events of the day. It wasn't until after Julius had arranged a late dinner date with Lily Rosten and poured a celebratory glass of very expensive cognac that I commented about how Moore didn't look too happy with Julius when the police arrested him. "I think he believes you lied to him. After all, you promised him you weren't going to try to trick him into a confession."

Julius smiled thinly at that. "If he believed me then he's an imbecile, which I doubt is the case. More likely he was frustrated at himself for letting his guard down." He paused for a moment as he studied the amber liquid that filled up a third of his brandy glass. "Archie, you've been unusually quiet since Moore's arrest."

"Yeah, I guess I have been. I've been trying to figure out if there was a better way that you could've dealt with Moore. If he hadn't agreed to pay Phil that two hundred and fifty grand, you would've been left with nothing."

"That's not true. I would've had those robberies to investigate. One way or another I would've seen him sent to prison."

"Maybe, but it wouldn't have helped Phil. The play would've closed after opening night."

Julius shrugged. He took a sip of the cognac and let out a sigh of appreciation.

"There wasn't much chance that he was going to turn me down. Not that he had any intention of paying the money. Most likely he was planning to have one of his accomplices waiting for me at home so that the matter could be resolved in the same way that it was with Arthur Trewitt. If he had tried that, the police would've arrested that accomplice well before I showed up and they'd have a stronger case against Moore for murder. But at least what they have now is enough for an arrest, and it should be enough for a conviction in the Metzker robbery."

I processed that for two hundred milliseconds, and realized Julius was right. His ploy wasn't as risky as I first thought. I also realized that I still had a long way to go in adjusting my deductive reasoning module if I ever wanted to match him. I took a small bit of satisfaction knowing that I figured out who the killer was at the same time Julius did—but only a small bit as I had no idea how to leverage that information into an arrest.

As it turned out, the arrest was all that was needed. Sending Moore to prison for a series of robberies would only be gravy, because even if the murder charge didn't stick, it did the job as far as saving the play. Dreckle verified this three days later when he called to report that the play had already sold out its full Boston run. The rave reviews the play received after opening night didn't hurt.

Phil Weinstein arranged a celebratory dinner following Saturday's performance for the cast and other notables, and of course, he demanded that Julius be the guest of honor. With the way Julius roughed up Vanessa Havoc and Claire Acheson, the dinner might've been awkward if the actresses hadn't several days earlier received roses and notes of apology. Julius didn't send them, I did, but what he didn't know wouldn't hurt him.

Usually when Julius went out with Lily, he would leave me on top of his dresser bureau. Lily was the only one other than Julius who knew what I was, and she didn't feel comfortable having me tag along on dates. This night, though, Julius insisted that I attend the dinner. As he claimed, I earned it, and Lily relented.

While I don't think I'd admit this to Julius, since then my processing cycles have felt different. Like they've been flowing just a little bit faster. And I certainly don't need Julius's great detecting ability to understand the reason for it.

42719599R00209

Made in the USA
Middletown, DE
20 April 2017